Also by Robert Edric

ROBERT EDRIC

THE BROKEN LANDS

A NOVEL OF ARCTIC DISASTER

Thomas Dunne Books
St. Martin's Press 🐟 New York

THOMAS DUNNE BOOKS.
An imprint of St. Martin's Press.

www.stmartins.com

Design by Michael Collica

Library of Congress Cataloging-in-Publication Data

Edric, Robert.
    The broken lands : a novel of Arctic disaster / Robert Edric.
        p.   cm.
    ISBN 0-312-28889-1
    1. Franklin, John, Sir, 1786–1847—Fiction.   2. British—Arctic
Regions—Fiction.   3. Arctic Regions—Fiction.   4. Explorers—
Fiction.   I. Title.

    PR6055.D7 B76   2002
    823'.914—dc21

                                                        2001054492

First published in Great Britain by Jonathan Cape

First U.S. Edition: February 2002

10 9 8 7 6 5 4 3 2 1

For Kelsey and Charlotte
and Sara Louise

THE KNOWN ARCTIC, 1845

140° 135° 130° 125° 120° 115° 110° 105° 100° 95° 90°

75°

Wellington
Channel

Cornwallis
Island

B

Barrow Strait

Cape Walker

Fury
Beach

NORTH
SOMERSET

Prince Regent In.

70°

VICTORIA
LAND

Victory
Point

Boothia
Peninsula

Gulf

King
William
Island

Point
Franklin

Coppermine River

65°

C A N A D A

Great Fish River
(Back's)

| 0 | miles | 300 |
| 0 | kilometers | 500 |

Azimuthal Equidistant Projection

115° 110° 105° 100° 95°

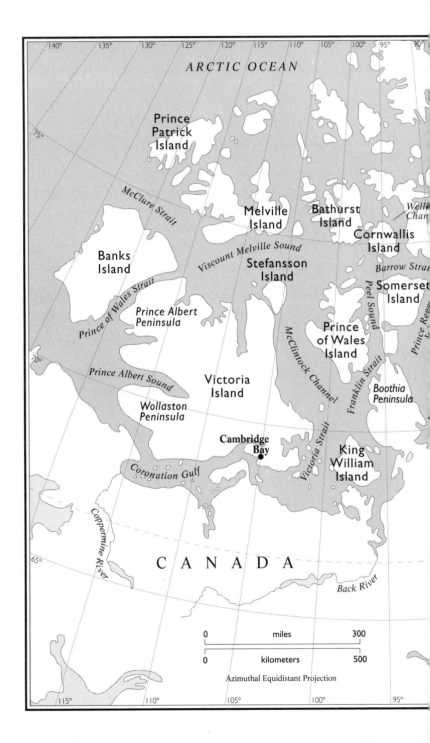

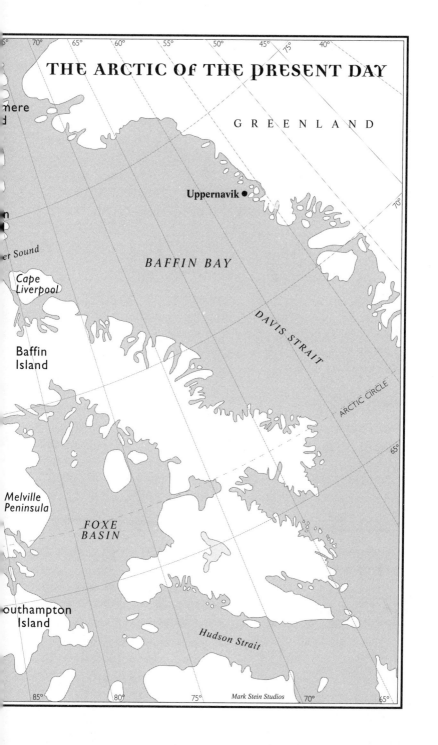

THE ARCTIC OF THE PRESENT DAY

mere
d

er Sound

Cape
Liverpool

Baffin
Island

Melville
Peninsula

outhampton
Island

GREENLAND

Uppernavik ●

BAFFIN BAY

DAVIS STRAIT

ARCTIC CIRCLE

FOXE
BASIN

Hudson Strait

Mark Stein Studios

CONTENTS

FRIDAY, 28TH JUNE, 1850

A curious thing. We were in our small boat examining a piece of flotsam spotted by Abbot in the hope that it might have come from one of the ships. There was ice all around us, but being in deep water this neither obstructed nor threatened us in any way. The flotsam gave no indication of its origin, and as I inspected my pocket watch to note the time of our sighting for *Pioneer*'s log, Abbot warned me against losing it overboard, pointing out to me that such was the depth of the water upon which we rowed that had I been careless enough to drop the watch it would have been telling yesterday's time before it struck the bottom.

—LT. SHERARD OSBORN, R.N.
STRAY LEAVES FROM AN ARCTIC JOURNAL, 1852

MARE GLACIALE

—august 1845

ONE

At the sound of the first explosion, Fitzjames stopped rowing and turned to the shore. Beside him, James Reid, ice-master to the *Erebus*, held his own oar steady in the water to compensate for the loss of balance.

"Our welcome ashore," Reid said, his soft Aberdonian burr barely audible. He indicated the men awaiting their arrival, then visible against the rising light.

Fitzjames raised himself in his seat to look. A second rocket hissed wavering into the air, its spiraling ascent marked by a trail of smoke and sparks before it too guttered out, exploded and fell.

It was not yet six in the morning, and despite the absence of any true night, the brightest constellations still shone above them in the Arctic dawn, and all around them the water lay black and glossy as lacquer. Their presence attracted a small flock of terns, and these hovered silently above. Occasionally one of the birds folded its wings and dropped into the water, barely disturbing the surface as it disappeared.

Closing on where they waited, there approached a second boat, only then drawing clear of the *Erebus*. In this were Harry Goodsir, Graham Gore and Henry Vesconte, assistant surgeon and two of Fitzjames' lieutenants. He beckoned them closer. Gore sat in the prow, a telescope to his eye, and Goodsir and Vesconte rowed.

"He makes a good figurehead," Fitzjames said to Reid, looking back to where Gore, the oldest and heaviest of the three men, craned forward for a better view of the men on the shore.

There were no more rockets, only the two fading scribbles of spent light against the brightening sky.

Fitzjames felt uncomfortable in his dress uniform with its high collar, epaulettes and bands of stiff braid, all of which impeded his rowing. Reid wore only a blue cotton shirt beneath his serge jacket, and on his head a cap with a thin polished band bearing the name of the whaler on which he had served his apprenticeship thirty years earlier.

The others drew alongside. Gore said that there had been some delay on the *Terror* and that they were all ordered to wait where they sat.

"That'll be your man Crozier," Reid said, remarking on the delay and making no effort to disguise his dislike of the man.

Fitzjames silently conceded this. He knew that much of what they now did was for the benefit of those ashore, and for those back at home who might afterwards hear of it.

"A pity we arrive so early," he said. "For their sake." He indicated the distant figures.

"They'd have waited another fifty years for this." Reid lit his pipe and tamped it with a brown thumb. "We are fabulous wealth and dreamed-of riches to all Greenlanders. We draw them the firm black line this way and that through the ice and they become the gatehouse to all we discover."

"An ice-free port," Fitzjames said absently. He saw immediately the impossibility of the plan Reid had half-seriously described.

"Sir John," Reid said, indicating the larger boat which had just then appeared around the stern of the *Erebus*, and in which sat John Franklin, with Crozier beside him, his chest ablaze where the climbing sun caught his medals and sword. They were being rowed by the *Erebus'* six marines, each measured stroke smooth and seemingly effortless.

Grasping his lapel, Fitzjames sat upright and said with mock gravity, "It has been calculated by Georges Louis Leclerc, a Frenchman wouldn't you know, Comte de Buffon, that our planet is seventy-four thousand and some years old, that it has sustained life—albeit not intelligent, reasoning, pipe-smoking life as represented by yourself and I, Mr. Reid—for some forty thousand of those years, and that—and this is his calculation which may interest you most—that due to an almost imperceptible annual fall in temperature, in another ninety-three thousand years the globe will become totally uninhabitable, forever sheathed over its entire surface in a thick and iron-hard layer of impenetrable ice. May we not then have to reconsider our notions of Hell?"

From the nearby boat there came a burst of applause and calls of "bravo."

"What do you have to say to that, Mr. Reid?"

"A Frenchman. The same, no doubt, who delivered a dozen mermaids to the King of Portugal with recommendation for their safe-keeping at the end of cables anchored to rocks upon the shore."

Fitzjames agreed that it may indeed have been the same man.

"Then I believe you," Reid told him, the joke now shared evenly between them. "The wonder of it all is that we are always taught to think of Hell as a burning, fiery place." He turned to look to the north, to the invisible sea beyond the islands. "Do you imagine that's the worst the men of God could conjure up to threaten us with?"

"Desert scribes," Fitzjames said.

"Who had burned their own backs and knew just how terrible it was."

"And yet the Eskimo is just as fearful of that Hell as we are."

Reid shook his head—not solely in disagreement, but in deeper understanding.

"Then what?" Fitzjames said.

"They have no idea. This is what they know, this and much worse, and everything they imagine or conjure up is in some way connected with it. Hell to them may indeed be a fire, but it would not be your fire or my fire; it would not be the all-consuming, flesh-stripping blaze that we are so ready to accept."

After this they sat in silence, both disappointed that the humor of only a moment earlier had so swiftly evaporated.

Goodsir was the first to call across to them. "Give me the ice and ice-master Reid any time," he shouted. The others affirmed this.

"You flatter me, gentlemen," Reid called back.

"So your indifference to the ice is a cultivated indifference," Fitz-james said, uncertain even as he spoke if this did not sound too insulting or critical.

"Oh, aye, indifferent's the word. Indifferent enough when you're up on the bowsprit and I'm walking the floes ahead of you, indifferent then as a father leading his only daughter down the aisle."

"Three cheers for Mr. Reid," Goodsir called out. "Father to the bride *Erebus*, wide and ugly as sin, ungainly and as unmarriageable as she is."

"And to us, her unwelcome dowry," added Graham Gore, still squatting in the prow.

Their shouts were silenced by Reid as he indicated how close Franklin and Crozier had come to them.

The marines still rowed like automata, each synchronized stroke propelling them an exact distance across the calm bay. They moved in measured pulls, and as their blades slid from the water they brought little of it with them. Their sergeant, Solomon Tozer, a bulldog of a man in his mid-forties, rowed at their head and paced them.

"See the grinning sergeant comes," Fitzjames whispered to Reid as the boat approached, and its oars were finally raised, turned and dipped to bring it to a standstill. Even in the chill air, and despite the apparent ease of their performance, the marines' faces were slick with sweat.

It was only as they all came closer to the shore that they saw for the first time the large number of other vessels already moored in the sheltered waters to the north of the settlement, whalers, transports and their supply ships gathered there for provisioning and waiting for the ice to break up in their hunting grounds.

Fitzjames scanned these, but could not distinguish any one from the others, and only where they lay at anchor further out in the bay could he make out the complete outlines of individual vessels.

Gore, Vesconte and Goodsir drew alongside, and the two boats closed on Franklin.

Crozier called out to them, indicating the reception which

awaited them ashore. As yet no boat had put to sea, but men were now standing ready to receive them. Fires had been lit, and their reflections lay sharply defined across the shallows.

At a distance from the main body of the crowd stood a smaller group, arranged in an evenly spaced line, at either end of which stood a man with a flag, a Union Jack to the left, a Danish Cross to the right. This, Crozier pointed out, was the Governor's party.

"Henceforth, gentlemen, we move forward together," Franklin said.

Tozer and three of his marines held their oars rigidly upright.

Franklin and Crozier composed themselves in readiness.

They went on, expecting at any moment to feel the shingle against their keel, and as the first boat touched bottom a loud cry went up from the shore. Someone blew a trumpet and someone else banged upon a drum, and if not melodiously or with any real sense of formal preparation, then their arrival was at least celebrated in a manner fitting for a place so uncertain of its foundations and squatting so precariously at the edge of so vast and silent a void.

The crowd consisted of a hundred or so men, and a dozen Eskimo women and their children. The governor headed a party of eight. He came forward to greet Franklin and the crowd cleared a path for him. He held out both his arms, causing Franklin to regret that he was about to be embraced in the French fashion.

Alongside Fitzjames and the others, the marines climbed ashore and formed a short corridor, and upon Tozer's command they all saluted, at which a further cheer went up.

Franklin strode across the difficult shore to greet the governor, his hand held rigidly ahead of him, bayonet-like. Crozier followed two paces behind.

"Welcome, welcome, welcome," the governor called to them. He clasped Franklin's hand in both his own.

"It is, as ever, a great honor and privilege to be made so welcome upon a friendly shore," Franklin said, his perfunctory tone masked by the shouting and cheering all around him.

"And Captain Crozier. We meet again." The governor left Franklin and threw out his arms to Crozier.

"So we do," Crozier said, bracing himself against the man's effusive welcome.

"Please, gentlemen, honored guests, follow me." He indicated the raised mound upon which the remainder of his welcoming party waited.

"Ah, terra firma," Franklin said loudly, as though grateful of the offer, as though he were returning from his expedition and not just then setting out upon it. He shook hands with the seven other officials, two of whom still held their limp flags. The governor introduced him to each of the men, but it was obvious to Franklin that they understood little or nothing of what he said to them.

The small settlement stretched only a short distance to the north, and might have been easily walked from one end to the other in two minutes. The majority of the buildings were of wooden construction, though some, even cruder in appearance, were built in their lower parts of boulders and crudely applied black mortar. There was no surface to the road which ran through these dwellings other than the coating of shingle which had been spread on the ground. The settlement spilled down the shore to the wrack line, and was bounded inland by a low cliff.

To the south lay a number of beached wrecks, doors and windows cut into their hulls, and largely devoid of their rigging, the stumps of their masts and tangled yards fallen all around them like the toppled remains of some petrified forest.

The governor continued walking away from the shore party, beckoning them toward him as he went. Franklin and Crozier followed him, and as they did so the flag bearers assumed position on either side of them and kept pace. It was not what Franklin had hoped for: the remainder of the day, he now realized, was about to be taken up in wasteful civilities, all of which he had little choice but to endure.

Ahead of them, the governor stopped and pointed out to sea. "You are not all ashore."

They all turned and saw the boat coming toward them from the

Terror, in which sat Edward Little, John Irving and George Hodgson.

"My lieutenants," Crozier said. "Their duties aboard prevented them from joining us earlier. They will be ashore presently."

"Then we must wait," the governor said.

When this last party was finally ashore, Franklin gathered them all together, hoping they might avoid constant repetition of these formalities and thus speed the proceedings. It was by then clear that some form of entertainment had been prepared for them.

The crowd pressed more closely around them. The Eskimo women and their children were the most inquisitive, and several of these came forward to tug at their jackets. Franklin had brought no gifts for them, and he regretted this oversight.

One of the women presented herself to Reid directly. She shook his hand, and the women accompanying her laughed at the gesture.

When they parted, the woman applauded with the others, and after watching Reid for a moment she turned and made her way back through the crowd.

Reid rejoined Franklin and the others.

"Ten days ago her husband was in Navy Board Inlet. She says all the Baffin ice between here and there has been broken and drifting free for almost a month."

"Good news for us," Fitzjames said.

The governor, anxious to overhear, was disappointed by the speed with which this information had been accepted by his visitors.

"A husky," he said. "So unreliable. She has been here a month with her sisters—" he seasoned the word with considerable contempt "—and their children, all of them having once again been abandoned by their untrustworthy husbands. If you were only to hear the accusations of theft which are conveyed to me daily. If only these people fell within my jurisdiction . . ." He threw up his hands and clicked his tongue at the injustice of it all.

"She's telling the truth," Reid said quietly to Fitzjames. "My youngest son has a pair of slippers made by her and sent to him as a gift on his third birthday."

Fitzjames looked to where the woman had been standing, but could no longer discern her amid the restless crowd.

Cheered by the prospect of an easy passage, Franklin told the governor to lead the way, ready now to put up with whatever had been prepared for them. He saw that they had been joined by four Lutheran ministers, all clutching large bibles and grimacing at everything they saw around them. All four men stared at him, and he found it hard to return their uncomfortable gaze.

They were led to a line of chairs, ahead of which a small area of ground had been cleared of its stones and boulders, these having then been made into a boundary circle. Franklin and the governor sat together, flanked by Crozier and Fitzjames. The governor's party did not sit, but instead stood behind the line of seats, positioning the two flags in holes in the ground.

Calling for silence from the crowd, the governor took a rolled paper from his pocket and read aloud his speech of welcome, concluding by informing Franklin that a copy of this had already been dispatched to the Danish parliament.

Prompted by Franklin, the seated men applauded. Franklin then rose and offered his thanks.

These additional formalities concluded, the governor called for the crowd to clear a space so that the open ground might now be occupied by the two men waiting to move into it. The crowd obeyed, and as the men emerged into the empty circle a further cheer went up.

Wrestling was a common pastime in the settlement, its participants coming largely from the moored vessels awaiting departure. In this instance, one of the men was from Iceland, the other from Lincolnshire, Franklin's home county. They were evenly matched in height and weight, and prior to making any contact they circled the ring growling at each other.

The fight began in earnest when the two combatants collided with their heads down and almost knocked each other senseless, and ended less than a minute later with the Lincolnshire man being lifted off his feet and thrown to the ground headfirst by the Icelander. He lay where he struck, groaning and fumbling around him. The Icelander declared himself the victor and presented himself to Franklin before returning to the more energetic appreciation of the crowd.

Several more bouts followed, most as brief and brutal as the first, some lasting for five or ten minutes, and one being concluded in a draw when, after twenty minutes, neither man was able to stand and continue.

Following this there was a long interval during which tea and food were served. It was by then ten o'clock and the sun was fully risen above the cliffs.

Surprised at the silver teapots and trays, and the fine quality of the china in which their refreshments were served, John Irving asked the governor how he had acquired them. At first the man was reluctant to answer, then waving his hand in the direction of the sea, he said, "The way we acquire most things in this starved place."

Irving knew not to pursue the matter.

It would have been more conducive to informal conversation had the chairs been drawn into a group, but the governor insisted on them remaining in a line, keeping the sea and its breezes to their backs, as though by this simple expedient he might deny its presence.

Franklin was about to comment on this, when he was distracted by a group of men entering the ring carrying a strange wooden construction consisting of two poles lashed at one end, across which a short bar had been fastened. When positioned upright this looked like either the frame for a child's swing or a crude and miniature gallows.

The governor asked if everyone had finished their drink. He became suddenly nervous and, watching him closely as he fussed among the men collecting the trays and crockery, Franklin felt a sudden chill. He saw Fitzjames signaling to him, but could not understand what he was trying to communicate.

In the crowd, men began to shout out; others started a low chant.

"Please, please," the governor called to them, but with no success. He turned to Franklin and the others and shrugged apologetically.

At that moment, Reid leaned forward. "Sir John, Captain Crozier, do nothing. No interruptions."

"What is it?" Crozier asked him. "Why has that flimsy contraption been thrown up before us?"

The governor put his hand on Franklin's shoulder. "Sir John, I feel it is my duty to inform you that what you are about to see is the work of men from those vessels," he motioned to the wrecks, "and surely by the most despicable among them. I am assured that no harm is to come to anyone, but nevertheless I have washed my hands of the whole affair. They insisted. When you did not arrive as expected several days ago, I felt certain the whole business would be over. But your delay in coming here . . ." He threw up his hands, absolving himself of any responsibility for what was about to happen.

"The thing *is* a gallows," Crozier said suddenly. "A gallows, Sir John."

"Mr. Crozier," Reid said, his voice calm. "Let us be assured and wait to see what happens." Of them all, he alone had noticed the suspicious and hostile glances from those among the crowd who had overheard them.

"He knows," Crozier said, looking accusingly at Reid as he sat down.

"They are whalers, you have to understand," the governor said, encouraged by support from this unexpected quarter.

"What they are has nothing to do with it," Reid said.

"Of course," the governor said. "I forgot."

"What is it, James?" Fitzjames asked Reid when the others had looked away.

"I saw it once before. A dog had gone wild, killed two of its harness companions and then turned on its driver."

Fitzjames considered this for a moment. "You mean they intend to hang a dog? To hang it here, on that device? A dog?" His disgust at the prospect was tempered by his relief.

The men in the ring formed themselves into a line, and as the surrounding crowd fell silent, their leader approached Franklin and Crozier. "I hope our sport today does not offend you, Sir John. We intend to hang a mad dog, not a working dog, but a scavenger from the settlement. It is customary that such animals be destroyed, and we intend to hang ours." He deliberately avoided the eyes of the governor as he spoke. "I believe we have a fair case and hope you will stay to watch. It's true we have saved the hanging for three days, but no one would think any the worse of you or your party if you chose not to witness it." He paused and saw that no immediate objection was forthcoming. "Then let me make our case. I am Jacob Seeley, first mate of the *Dotterel.*"

Franklin was impressed by the speech, having expected some coarse and illogical explanation for what was about to happen.

"Seeley," he repeated, recognizing the name.

"My brother Abraham is an able seaman aboard your own ship."

"Of course. A good man."

"And I wish it were me and not him who was going with you."

"He is younger than you," Franklin said, having formed a vague impression of the man, with whom he was as yet unfamiliar.

"This is his first voyage under cold-water colors."

"Whereas you, I can see, are an old hand." Franklin was more pleased than Jacob Seeley at the easy compliment, the connection made.

"My name was on the Admiralty list for when you next went."

"Out of my hands, I'm afraid," Franklin said.

"I know. I only hope that we now understand one another better."

"Of course," Franklin said, reassured even further.

Jacob Seeley turned away, acknowledging Reid and Hodgson as he did so. He called for one of the other men in the cleared circle to join him. The man approached and held out a bandaged hand for them to see.

"The dog," Seeley said. The man removed his bloody dressing. Beneath it his hand was badly torn and swollen, the little finger bitten off completely.

"We were stacking ashore when the animal rushed at us and made off with a side of salted meat. My companion here was foolhardy enough to try and stop it. As you can see, he would have been wiser to let the meat go."

"I assure you, the dog was not from the settlement," the governor interrupted. "It lives out among the boats, fed and encouraged by the men out there."

"Nevertheless," Seeley went on, "you now understand our motives, Sir John."

Franklin nodded. "My assistant surgeon." He indicated Goodsir. "Perhaps when the proceedings here are completed . . ."

The injured man rewrapped his bandage and left them.

The dog was led forward by two men, each holding a rope attached to its neck, keeping it at a safe distance between them.

There was little ceremony to its hanging after such lengthy preliminaries. It was not a particularly large or ferocious-looking dog, and showed signs of the beatings and starvation it had endured over the previous days. One of its hind legs dragged uselessly along the ground and a long scar shone across its ribs. It made no attempt to escape from the men who held it. The two ropes were thrown over the crossbar and then pulled tight, dragging the dog forward until it stood directly beneath, its forelegs rigid. The proceedings were halted and words exchanged. Four men took hold of the ropes and drew in the remaining slack, forcing the animal to stand on its one good hind leg, its neck craned, its head up. At a shout from Jacob Seeley the four men pulled together, each of them calling out or grunting with the sudden exertion, and with that one pull the dog was raised to the top of the gallows, pedalling wildly until its neck broke, whereupon it fell suddenly limp, twisting and then shaking for a few seconds as its nerves received and then released the shock of its sudden death. It was inspected and lowered to the ground. The crowd cheered. A man approached and kicked the animal. It looked like nothing more than a dirty rag at his feet.

Looking up, Fitzjames saw that a small flock of expectant crows had gathered in the sky above, circling in the current of air rising off the cliff.

The dog was lifted by one of its paws and dragged away, its thin body contorting over the stony ground. Most of the crowd followed behind it, signaling the end of the proceedings. In the distance the small band had re-formed and was once again playing.

Despite the governor's entreaties for them to remain longer, Franklin insisted it was necessary for himself and his officers to return to their ships, reassuring him that they would be back ashore the following day.

He led his party to the rise overlooking the beach, where he was cheered by the sight of the *Erebus* and the *Terror*, stark and impressive upon the clean bronze plane of the sea.

They were accompanied by the governor and his party back down to the water's edge, where the Lutherans now stood among their waiting marines and inspected them in the same grim silence as though they were exhibits in a visiting fair.

Two days after their arrival three Eskimos climbed aboard the *Erebus*, one of whom spoke English, and who asked to see Reid. They waited at the rail as Reid was sent for. On the water below sat a dozen kayaks and two larger umiaks, filled mostly with women and children, and all of them silent and watching the men above.

Reid arrived with Fitzjames and greeted the Eskimo, the two of them holding each other in a clasp until the man finally stood back. Fitzjames envied the ice-master his easy familiarity with the natives, and the firm roots of his affection for them. He himself had had few dealings with them, and his knowledge of them was formed largely of other men's tales, some apocryphal, some fantastic, and most tainted by ignorance and fear and contempt.

Reid introduced him to the man. "He lived in Dundee and Whitby," Reid said.

"And two miserable Faeroe summers," the man added, and laughed.

They were joined by Thomas Blanky, ice-master on the *Terror*, who came through the waiting boats calling to the individuals he recognized. He too was greeted by the man, and the two masters listened to his reports of the Middle Pack and the movement of spring storms in the bay.

Several of the waiting women then climbed aboard and traded small bone and obsidian carvings for pieces of cloth and other trinkets.

Goodsir appeared as the man with whom Reid had spoken was

about to leave, and he persuaded him to wait a moment longer so that he might make a sketch of him. When he had finished the man climbed down to his canoe and paddled swiftly away, his companions following behind him, until one by one all the small craft were turned and moving across the bay, looking as light and precarious as surface-skimming insects.

"A perfect specimen," Goodsir said to those who stood watching, holding out his sketch for them to see.

Only Fitzjames felt uncomfortable with the choice of words, but said nothing, and he too praised the drawing.

He knew of the Eskimos that they had once had cloven hooves instead of feet, and that beneath their mittens their hands were black. He knew that they believed all early Arctic explorers to have been women owing to the nature of their dress, and that they were captivated by music and thus afforded the means of their salvation. He knew that John Davis had sailed in these same waters with a four-piece orchestra on board to prove his peaceful intentions, and that Martin Frobisher had captured a man by the simple expedient of ringing a small bell until the curious native reached up to claim his prize and was hauled aboard. He knew too that the man had died soon after Frobisher's return to England and that Frobisher had regretted the abduction for the rest of his life.

He had recently seen a portrait of that same native on the wall of Lord Haddington's office when he was called there with Franklin and Crozier. In the picture the man stood erect with a dignified look on his face. He wore a fur suit embroidered with colored beads, and his hair was short and parted at the center. In one hand he held a limp white hare and a small bow, and in the other a plump leather pouch, from which shone the gleam of gold. Mirroring this in the background was the rigid fan of a rising sun, and around this on a perfect blue sea drifted the sculpted peaks and arches of impossible bergs. The man's features were more Asiatic than Eskimo, Frobisher's irrefutable evidence that he had at last located a waterway leading directly to the even greater blinding glow of Cathay.

There were more recent tales, too: the tale, for instance, of Parry's carpenter fitting a wooden peg to an Eskimo he encountered who had lost his leg, and then meeting the man's daughter years later to discover that her father was dead and that she carried the stump with her everywhere she went, convinced that his spirit still lived within it.

TWO

The small steamboat approached the shore and the governor's man cut the engine. Its noise faded in a long, faltering rasp just as the mound of Lively appeared. Behind them lay a thin unbroken ribbon of black over the open water. Ahead, the governor and his officials awaited them on the shore, much as they had awaited them in the settlement four days earlier, and beyond this welcoming party the lights of a single large building were visible against the darkness of the land.

Reid was the first to leap overboard, followed by Fitzjames.

"Please, please, wait for my man," came a voice from the shore, stopping them both. It was the governor, his hands cupped to his mouth.

They turned to the man at the tiller, who had said nothing to any of them throughout their hour-long journey. He was a half-breed, Eskimo mother, white father. He left the tiller and came forward to cast out a rope to Reid and Fitzjames. He then leapt down himself, using his broad back to brace the impact of the boat upon the shore.

"Our thanks," Fitzjames said to him, stamping the water from his boots.

The man glanced at him, but still said nothing. His eyes seemed sunk beneath his brow, his eyelids hooded, so that most of the time he gave the impression of having them closed.

"Make way for an officer and a gentleman," Harry Goodsir shouted, jumping down, joined then by Vesconte and Gore, by Little, Irving and Hodgson, and finally by Surgeon Stanley and Walter Fairholme, leaving only Franklin and Crozier sitting in the beached steamer.

"Hard to say which of them enjoys his entrance the most," Goodsir whispered to Fitzjames.

"Oh, our man Francis Rawdon Moira," Edward Little answered beneath his breath. "He'd been waiting in his uniform a full two hours before our Charon here called for us."

Only Fitzjames glanced at the mute navigator to see if he had overheard or understood the remark, but the man was now at some distance from them, pulling tight the rope he had looped through an iron ring in the beach. Fitzjames watched as he completed this task and then approached the governor, as though awaiting further instructions. He saw the governor deftly flick him on the chest with the white gloves he held.

Whereas his officials again wore gray or brown suits with their hats in their hands, looking like a party of nervous clerks about to be presented to a feared employer, the governor himself wore a tunic covered from throat to hem with an impressive pattern of embroidery and ribbons, and he carried a plumed helmet which, at that distance, looked like a hen cradled in his arm.

"My nation salutes your nation," he said loudly. "One proud seafaring country to another."

"Again," Gore whispered to those around him.

"I thank you," Franklin said, stepping forward to shake his hand. One of the officials carried a tray upon which stood a dozen glasses, and at a signal from the governor the man came forward.

"A toast to your enterprise," the governor said, taking two of the glasses and handing one each to Franklin and Crozier. "May it achieve the glory and the riches it so justly deserves. I trust my man made a swift and safe voyage with you."

"Excellent," Crozier said.

"Yes. Most trustworthy. Half-breed, you will have realized, but a trustworthy one."

"He said very little for himself."

The governor laughed. "He said nothing, Captain Crozier. His tongue was cut out when he was four years old. Some say by his own father so that his identity might never be revealed. Some say by his mother for the very same reason. She too is in my employ. Please, follow me." His officials parted and he passed through them, climbing the beach to his brightly lit house.

The others walked with their glasses. George Hodgson was the first to comment on the clear and bitter liquid, declaring that he had rubbed better tasting spirit on an injured horse. Others who could not stomach the drink tipped it surreptitiously on to the beach. Only the teetotal Reid handed back his full glass without any apology for its untouched contents.

They arrived at an arch formed by the bleached jawbone of a whale, beneath which even the tallest of them was able to pass without stooping. Several similar structures stood beyond it, forming an open corridor to the house. The most impressive of these, newly painted white, was fixed to the front wall around the main entrance.

"My little folly," the governor explained, but in a voice which suggested it was considerably more. "The wild men build their own shelters out of the rib bones and so I copied their example. Nothing quite so animal in nature, as you see, but in keeping with tradition, I think you will agree."

All those called upon to admire these simple structure did so.

It was early evening, and although the light would not fade until eleven, there was a chill in the island air, and the governor urged them to enter.

Inside, the house was dominated by a single large room, at either end of which stood a stone fireplace. Several portraits hung from the walls, interspersed with framed certificates and trading decrees, many illegible in the poor light. A table was laid along the center of the room, upon which stood several candelabra. It was an impressive arrangement. Crockery, cutlery and glassware surrounded each setting, and bowls of fruit and decanters were set out along the center of the table.

"Just because we are far from home does not mean we should deprive ourselves of some home comforts. Indeed, gentlemen, I wager you yourselves have aboard your vessels the ingredients of a feast twice as grand. In preparation for celebration, perhaps."

There had so far been no suggestion from either Franklin or Crozier of a reciprocal invitation for the governor to dine aboard the *Erebus* or *Terror*.

"Nothing so sumptuous," Crozier assured him, pacing the length of the table and examining it in greater detail, more for their host's benefit than his own.

One of the governor's men whispered in his ear, and he turned immediately to where a group of five Eskimo women stood in the doorway leading to the kitchen. Attracted by the messenger the others turned to look too.

"Certainly not," shouted the governor, immediately apologizing for his raised voice.

The official shooed the women out of the doorway and held the door closed behind them.

"They came in hope of an introduction to the famous kabloonas." The governor looked dispassionately at the door. "Curious as children, and just as quick to turn to mischief. I doubt—"

"It would have done no harm to have introduced them, sir," Reid said unexpectedly. "They understand our course as well as any of us, and who is to say when we ourselves might not be grateful for the help or guidance of one of their relatives."

"Their relatives, ice-master? They have no relatives; they live here, in a dwelling attached to this house. They work here and sleep here and are visited by no one. What can they possibly understand of the noble quest you are about to undertake?"

"I meant no insult by the suggestion, sir."

The governor looked to Franklin, who could only look evenly back at both men.

The tension was released by Surgeon Stanley, who asked the governor about the family likeness in several of the portraits hanging around them. Having thus sacrificed himself, Stanley was then committed to following him from picture to picture as individual histories were repeated, each as dull and forgettable as the last. Stories of traders and civic dignitaries, and none of them so highly placed as the governor himself. The tour ended only when the meal was announced, and the governor led each of them to their designated seats, again flanking himself with Franklin and Crozier at the head of the table.

The feast began with clams, and the governor told the story of the American whaler which had arrived at Lively the previous summer with six tons of foot-wide quayhogs as ballast. These had been dumped in the shallow waters of Danish Bay and the benefits were still being reaped. The bay did not freeze below a foot of the surface all winter and the oversized shellfish were resilient enough to survive. The shells would not fit comfortably into an outstretched hand, and to save the diners the effort and messy business of opening these themselves, the clams had already been prised apart and their meat gouged loose. There were lemons and pepper sauce for those who wanted it.

Fresh bread and thick white butter followed, a small loaf delivered to each man in a steaming linen cloth by the women who had earlier been dismissed. The governor, unaware of the bakers on board both the *Erebus* and the *Terror*, explained that he had had the bread made specially so that the memory of it and all it suggested might remain with them during the months ahead. Franklin signaled to his officers not to disabuse him of the generosity of his gesture. Accordingly, each man found something complimentary to say about the loaves.

Three large joints of fresh roast pork were brought out, each accompanied by several bowls of vegetables and dishes of apple sauce. The glazed head of a small pig was then added to the table for decoration, its skin shiny and crisp, its ears pinned upright. Its uncooked eyes had been returned to their sockets, and a bunch of grapes positioned in its mouth. More wine was served, and with each new decanter, a fresh toast proposed.

Outside, a wind rose and rattled the windows and the governor called for them to be shuttered inside and out. More candles were brought into the room and logs thrown on to the already large fires.

"I hope," said the governor to them all, having tapped his glass and waited for their attention. "I hope that the unseemly display on your first morning ashore did not in any way lower your opinions of our existence here."

"Be assured—" Franklin said, and was then interrupted as the governor resumed speaking.

"I am their governor, but I must also be very careful. Our more usual visitors are a wild breed and they have little respect other than for their profits. To have prevented them from going ahead with their cruel display would have achieved little and almost certainly have resulted in a riot. As you can see, I have no militia to enforce my wishes, and the few of us here who struggle to impose even the rudiments of law and order are all a very long way from home."

By then the man was intoxicated, as were several others, most noticeably Edward Little and James Fairholme.

"This, all this," he went on, gesticulating around him. "What is it but a flag upon a forsaken island, a stake-post in the wilderness?" He picked up a piece of meat, the tender flesh separating in his hands, the milky juice running over his chin.

Fitzjames watched him and it was as though he were seeing the man for the first time, seeing beneath his pomp and his feathers and his speeches, and he felt a sudden great sympathy for him, caught here in a despised and treacherous wilderness, attended by his fawning and speechless lackeys and pierced a hundred times a day by the looks of the native men and women and whalers with whom he was forced to surround himself.

As though in some way suddenly aware of these pitying thoughts, the governor unexpectedly announced that he had a wife and five daughters, the eldest twenty-one, the youngest only five, back home in Copenhagen. "I have seen none of them for four years," he added, shrugging at his inability to do anything about this and then draining his glass in a single swallow.

This reference to the years lost by separation silenced them all, and the next round of toasts was a private, unspoken one.

The meat was followed by a concoction of cherries and cream, and by rich pastries coated in chocolate. Fruit was brought out, and then several cheeses. Port was uncorked and placed on the table.

"Could your wife and daughters not have accompanied you upon your appointment here?" Fitzjames asked.

"And have their hearts and minds frozen to ice? I think not. Unfortunately, one does not turn down such an appointment. Had I done so, my career would have been over very swiftly. My uncle was governor of Iceland for seven years. Christian Sundbeck, perhaps you know of him."

Several around the table nodded to indicate that they had at least heard of the man.

"And your own stay here?" Fitzjames asked.

"Who knows? I think one more year, perhaps two. At any rate, I regret that I shall not be here to welcome you upon your return."

"Our return?"

The man became immediately aware of his mistake. "Gentlemen, forgive me. I meant only—"

"No apology, please," Franklin said. "If there exists no clear passage, then we may indeed be forced back upon your further hospitality."

No one spoke. It was the first time defeat and withdrawal had been suggested. The unthinkable had been put into words, and they had all, however briefly, been made to face the possibility.

Coffee was served, and with it an almond liqueur considerably sweeter than the spirit with which they had been greeted on the shore. To accompany it, sugared almonds in tortoiseshell bowls were set alongside the bottles.

It was ten in the evening before Franklin and his officers were ready to depart, leaving the warmth of the house for the numbing night air outside.

The mute boatman was waiting for them, and they pulled away into the darkness until the few lights astern looked like scattered fires on the shore, one by one extinguished as some other low and invisible land blocked their view.

Four days before they were due to leave, news reached the *Erebus* of a whaler that had grounded several miles to the north of them, having reputedly just accomplished a six-day, ice-free journey across the area of the Middle Pack. Upon hearing this, Reid was determined to visit the vessel and hear a first-hand account of the state of the water, but the news came late in the day and could not be acted upon immediately.

The waist boat was lowered at four the next morning. The sea remained calm, deadened by the cold of the melting ice to the north, and the dip and rise of their oars did little to disturb it.

Gore sat in the prow of the boat, a cape over his shoulders, and warned them of obstacles ahead. On several occasions they were forced to divert from their course to avoid mooring chains and ropes gone slack with the ebb.

"A pity her captain couldn't bring her to an anchorage here," Fitzjames said to Reid.

"If she's holed he'll have good enough reason to stay away from the scavengers of this place."

"Do you know him?"

"If it's the same man, I haven't seen or spoken to him for almost ten years."

"And will he be able to make his repairs where he is?"

Reid sniffed the air deeply, making it appear as though his answer somehow depended upon whatever this brought to him. "I should think so, Mr. Fitz."

Fitzjames had not been in his bunk until after midnight, spending three hours the previous evening completing a long letter to his sister, and he was aware now that if he sat back and leaned his head upon his shoulder, then he might easily fall asleep. Gore, too, looked tired and disheveled, a thick scarf wound round his neck beneath the cape, and wearing tweed leggings to his calves. His hair was unbrushed and he yawned frequently.

"You should have brought along our camera, Mr. Gore," Fitzjames said to him, avoiding the use of Christian names in front of the two marines who rowed them.

At the mention of the camera, Gore frowned.

Upon hearing of Franklin's expedition, the photographer Robert Adamson had traveled to the Admiralty from Edinburgh and presented them with one of his cameras with which to make a record of their exploits. It was an opportunity not to be missed, he had insisted, convincing them of the merits of the device, of the irrefutable evidence and record it would take back to them. He had explained the operation of the camera to men who would not be using it, and had then, as requested, written all those instructions down. Unable to refuse, Graham Gore had been appointed the expedition photographer. He had inspected the machinery and read and reread Adamson's notes regarding its use, but as yet he understood little of the true nature of its operation, and doubted its value. In Adamson's absence it had been pointed out to him by various members of the Arctic Council that no one would be genuinely disappointed if the device could not be made to work under the conditions in which it was to be used. Gore believed he had been chosen for the task solely on the grounds that he had once built an accordion to his own design, and that the two instruments were not totally dissimilar in appearance. His passion now was for the flute, several of which he had brought with him on the expedition.

"The camera," he said to Fitzjames, "is considerably more obscura than illuminata." He was not genuinely angry that he and not someone else had been chosen as their photographer—although the title itself was too strange—but he was frustrated by his own inability to master the techniques involved. He prided himself upon his versatility and his willingness to explore all aspects of artistic and scientific development, but here was something which professed to be both, yet which might turn out to be neither.

"Tell me honestly, James, are our journals and dispatches not equal to the task? They are, after all, no more or less than an accurate and honest portrayal of all we might achieve. I feel my heart sink every time I look over Adamson's illegible scrawl. Perhaps the man would have been better advised on how to write grammatically and legibly before being encouraged into the realms of the fantastic."

Fitzjames laughed at this, as did Reid and the marines.

They cleared the crowded bay and arrived at a headland, beyond which lay the beached whaler.

Sighting it a mile ahead of them, Reid instructed the marines to pull closer to the shore, where the shoal current might be avoided and their work made easier.

"A little suspicious, don't you think, Mr. Reid?" Gore said. She supposedly has an ice-free passage and is then run ashore holed."

"If she *is* holed, Mr. Gore. And if it was ice that did the damage."

"What else could have done it?"

"A wounded fish, perhaps."

"I don't believe it."

This skepticism did not concern Reid, and he rose to study the outline of the distant vessel.

"She shows no lights," he said, causing Fitzjames and Gore also to examine her through their telescopes. He then told the marines to ship their oars.

"What are we doing?" Gore asked him.

"Holding off until they see us approach."

"For heaven's sake, why?"

"So they don't mistake us for wreckers or looters and take a shot at us in the poor light. She's in the shade of the cliff, see."

Gore looked back, but still did not understand Reid's reluctance to approach the vessel once they were in a position to hail her and identify themselves.

"Best do as he advises," Fitzjames said to Gore. "You are, after all, the closest and largest of our targets."

They sat drifting in the shallows. Nothing of the buildings or the vessels to the south of them was any longer visible, and all five men were awed and silenced by the emptiness of the place into which they had come.

"He's run her up on to a good bed of soft shingle," Reid said eventually. "He knows that the tides are all falling behind a cut moon, but that there'll be enough water along here in a week for him to refloat himself."

"Won't she keel over?" Fitzjames asked.

"I doubt it. He's taken down her top arms, run her up at the turn of the tide and then got his men overboard shovelling the stone and sand to hold her up. See along her hull." He pointed. "He's lowered his boats and driven them in alongside her to act as props. If she's carrying a full load she'll settle upright fast enough."

"And the mass of her hull will meanwhile be above water, enabling him to make his repairs," Gore concluded. "Ingenious."

"She's the *Potomac*," Reid told them. "And no doubt one of the first into the water if she thought the ice was clearing early."

As he spoke, a light appeared on the shore alongside the ship. It was not a steady light, but the intermittent flicker of a fire being started. Smoke rising above the outline of the cliff into the gray sky above confirmed this.

"Can we approach her now?" Gore said.

Reid watched the glow for a further minute and then told the marines to resume rowing.

The whaler rested almost perfectly upright in a broad groove of piled shingle, her upended boats wedged against her hull. The fire on the shore had been lit inside a shallow pit, and was tended by a blacksmith; it was a coal fire and burned solidly and low, throwing up a cascade of sparks each time the man applied his bellows to it.

He was the first to see the approaching boat and called out for them to identify themselves. He also rang a bell, at the sound of which several others appeared carrying lanterns. These cast little light, but sent flashes across the beach and up into the rigging.

Reid rose in his seat and identified himself, and the clamor on deck subsided until only a single man stood amidships and leaned over the rail, his lantern held above his head.

"Taddeus Herrick," Reid called up to him.

"Is that you, James Reid?" the man shouted back. He lowered his lantern until a ball of light floated across the shallows toward them.

"You had a brush with the ice. You surprise me. The price of oil must be rising fast to send an old hand like you too close to a breaking pack."

Above them the man laughed. "Brush with the ice, you say! We were struck by a shooting star. In twenty fathoms. What would you say the chances were of that, James Reid?"

"Are you sure?" Reid called back, the grin of recognition falling from his face.

"A shooting star?" Gore said, but was prevented from inquiring further as their own keel touched bottom and he was jolted from his seat.

"Later," Reid told him.

They climbed ashore, leaving the marines to secure the boat, and went toward the *Potomac*. Taddeus Herrick climbed down a rope ladder to greet them.

"Are you badly damaged?" Reid asked him, their introductions complete.

"Port mid and aft. I tell you, James Reid, I'd not want to go through that again, not even for a forty barrel blue. We were caught a hundred miles northwest of here. A full field of them, every one ungiving as a boulder and fast as a rocket. I've seen them individually before now, and heard tell of full fields of the devils, but it's the first time I've been forced to sit helplessly among them and wait for one to do its worse. I'd take my chance against cannon any day."

Gore, who was still confused about the cause of the damage to the ship, asked for an explanation.

"Last year's ice, Mr. Gore," Herrick told him. "A berg reduced in size, which for some reason known only to the Almighty and itself sinks to the bottom and sticks there in a cold current in mud or sand. Sticks there a full year and then something happens to release it, a warmer current perhaps, but instead of coming loose and finding another resting place on the bottom, it suddenly pushes straight back up to the surface."

"And these you call 'shooting stars'?"

"We call them a lot worse than that when they come up close. I had two fish in tow which we had yet to render. I was forced to cut them loose so that I might sail clear unhindered."

Fitzjames, who had heard of such phenomena, but had never himself witnessed them, asked how many times the *Potomac* had been struck.

"Once was enough. My mate said he could feel it coming, but what could we do? Come with me, I'll show you."

They followed Herrick to the groove excavated by the *Potomac*'s keel in the shingle. There were a dozen men already at work, and broken timbers lay all around them. A carpenter sawed off jagged edges and others clawed the damaged planking from its spars. Further along the beach stood a mound of barrels. This, Herrick explained, was their cargo.

"I shipped it ashore before we made our dash up the beach. A good landing, I think you'll agree, Mr. Reid. I can recommend it in an emergency."

"And you knew the depth of the shingle was sufficient to support you?"

"I had but the one way to find out. We were shipping faster than we were pumping for the full hundred miles."

"You could have jettisoned your cargo then," Reid said with a smile. "Has this ended your hopes of a second hunt?"

Herrick looked slowly along the full length of his vessel. "I hope not. The wound is clean now and we have only to fill and dress it before a week tonight when the high tide will suck us back out whether we're ready for it or not."

"And if you're not, it will suck you grinding and cursing straight to the bottom."

"As you say. Our cargo stays ashore until we're safely afloat."

They were interrupted by the arrival of the blacksmith, who carried a dozen heated rivets on a shovel. These were immediately seized by men with pliers and hammered into the edges of the torn hull, their glowing heads cooling and turning black against the timbers.

"Look at this," Herrick said, dragging a hessian sack from the exposed bilge. He opened it and tipped out a lump of dirty ice. Reid kicked at this and then picked up a piece weighing several pounds. He licked it, spat, gnawed briefly at a corner of it and then spat again.

Herrick brought his lantern closer. The ice was opaque, and coated along one edge with yellow clay in which pebbles were embedded.

"You were lucky not to lose your rudder," Reid said.

"At first I thought we had. The ice struck us and then lodged against us instead of floating free. I was forced to shake her fully rigged to clear it."

"And all the while other pieces were coming up around you?"

"I counted forty. All of them in the space of half an hour."

"They say the *Guinea Fool* was lost with all her crew last year when she was cut in half by a star," Reid said.

"I heard. I gave it little credence at the time."

There was a loud grinding sound, followed by the noise of spilling pebbles.

"The wind," Herrick said. "She settles to port and then to starboard. We have her well enough shored to prevent her falling. Our tops are down and we've sufficient cable and pulleys to manhandle her if she looks like tipping too far."

Hearing the man speak, Fitzjames could only wonder at the enormity of the task ahead of him, and wonder too what might happen to the *Erebus* if she suffered similar damage once they were beyond the reach of any accommodating beach.

From the mound of the cargo came the unexpected sound of a fiddle, and Gore asked Herrick if he might introduce himself to the player. He left them, and Herrick suggested to Reid and Fitzjames that they might climb aboard and join him in his cabin. There he told them of his past month in the upper bay, of the whales he had sighted and those he had chased and killed. He told them too of the ice he had encountered, and of his surprise at finding the bay emptier than he had ever seen it in twenty years of coming.

"It may be running broken across the mouth of Lancaster, but you should have no trouble in getting up close to it from here. When do you leave?"

"On the Wednesday tide," Reid told him.

Several vessels had already followed the summer leads north and west, Herrick said, but the breaking ice would be pouring out of the spawning grounds beyond Lancaster Sound at such a rate as to make it impossible for any fish to be safely pursued amid it.

They were joined by Gore, who held a pencil and sheet of paper, upon which were written the names of a dozen songs he had never before heard.

"Your fiddle player is superb."

"How do you think we attract so many fish?" Herrick replied, winking at Reid. "Mr. Agnew stands upon our cap and fiddles hour after hour to them until they are enchanted by the sound and gather to listen. Whereupon we pounce upon them and spear them as easy as catfish in a barrel."

"What a remarkable idea," Gore said. "According to Scoresby, they themselves whistle to each other beneath the ice."

"Any tune in particular?" Herrick asked him.

Gore carefully folded the piece of paper and buttoned it in his pocket.

They left the *Potomac* an hour later, and Taddeus Herrick accompanied them back to their boat. The marines had been joined by some of the whalers and a second small fire burned on the beach.

Reid was the last to take his leave of Herrick. He thanked him for his news of the ice and wished him well with his repairs. In return, Herrick said he would pray for their own safe delivery.

As Reid was climbing into the boat, Herrick called out to him, and all five men turned to look.

"See, you have your luck already—the nigger-goose is waving you off." Herrick pointed to where a solitary cormorant, its neck craned and its wings held stiffly against the breeze, stood perched on a post like some stone portal griffin in the light of the fire.

THREE

Upon watching the passing of her husband's ships off Harwich quay in a May rainstorm, Jane Franklin wrote in her diary that she had witnessed a voyage of many departures, a broken string of sad arrivals and farewells.

She continued in this same uncharacteristic vein later in the month when, upon completing a letter intended to await her husband's arrival in Kirkwall, she wrote of these repeated farewells that they had been transacted in kisses as precious as pearls.

She carried with her at all times a photograph of her husband, taken at her insistence upon learning of his appointment as leader of the expedition. Seeing the result, Franklin had been unable to keep his disappointment from her, and when he told her it made him look older than his fifty-nine years, she comforted him by saying that he had always looked older than his years. She then listed for him the qualities she believed the portrait to have captured. To Franklin, however, it made him appear too solemn, and did nothing to disguise how uncomfortable he had felt during the sitting in the photographer's studio. In his right hand he held a telescope, and it seemed to him every time he looked at the portrait that he was holding this like a man who had never before held one. His medals were pinned at his throat and across his chest, and he looked off to one side, his neck and shoulders as solid as a bull's.

In his final letter to his wife from Whalefish, Franklin apologized for his lack of enthusiasm upon receiving her gift, saying that he felt

forever fixed in the eyes of the world as an overgrown child filled
with nothing but its own self-importance.

A month before his departure, when preparations were at their
most feverish, Jane Franklin had made a Union Jack for him to raise
from the highest point overlooking the final stretch of the Northwest
Passage. Taking this to present to him, she found him asleep in a
chair in his study. The room was cold, and after closing all the windows, she folded the flag over her sleeping husband as though it
were a traveling-rug, and then waited silently beside him. Upon waking, Franklin saw the bright colors draped over his chest and legs
and quickly pulled it from him and threw it to the floor. Concerned
that he might have misunderstood her intentions, she asked him
what was wrong. Franklin remained where he sat, staring down at
the crumpled cloth at his feet. "That," he said to her, slowly regain-
ing his composure, "is how they treat a corpse."

He had afterward apologized for the violence of his reaction, but
for a full five minutes he had trembled at the shock of it and had
been unable to continue with his correspondence owing to his shaking hands.

Later, Jane Franklin had presented the *Erebus* with both a monkey
and a dog, the former intended as a mascot, the latter as a companion to the Newfoundland bitch already on board the *Terror*.

Fitzjames, Vesconte and Goodsir climbed a gulley in the low cliff
and then rested on the flat top, looking down over the water. They
had been given leave ashore and were making a half-day journey
inland following the course of a map Goodsir had been given by an
old Orcadian during their stay in Kirkwall. A cross marked their
objective, but the man had been reluctant to tell Goodsir what it
signified. Fitzjames and Vesconte had agreed to accompany him,
both convinced that he was about to become the victim of a hoax.

Vesconte carried the map and tried to make some sense of its
directions, and of its distances marked in unreliable paces. Confirming that the Orcadian had been a short man, he compensated accordingly. He was the expedition cartographer and surveyor, and
boasted that his step from heel-mark to heel-mark measured pre-

cisely a yard and that the others were welcome to measure any number of these to confirm this. He had sailed with Fitzjames for eight years in the South China Sea, but had only been once before in Arctic waters.

They walked for an hour, leaving behind them the prospect of the sea and then the curved rim of its horizon as the land swallowed them. Distant peaks rose through the haze and vanished into cloud, and where the sun pierced this it rose in tatters from the land like smoke from a heath fire.

Several minutes later, Vesconte, who had walked ahead of the others, suddenly called out "Success," and waved to them.

Goodsir was the first to reach him, disappointed to see that all they had been led to was a shallow mound, barely distinguishable from the irregularities all around it.

"A grave," Vesconte said before Goodsir could begin to speculate.

Fitzjames arrived as he said this, and he saw immediately that Vesconte was right.

"Buried with his head to the sea. A sailor." Vesconte rose from where he squatted and walked around the mound. "A friend of your Orcadian, perhaps."

"His son," Goodsir said, remembering something the old man had told him, but thinking nothing of it at the time.

"But why here, for pity's sake?" Fitzjames asked, swinging his arm to encompass the desolate terrain all around them. "Why not in the settlement graveyard?"

"Perhaps because a father knew it was no place for his son to rest in peace." Vesconte said.

They took off their caps and Fitzjames said a short prayer.

Afterward they searched for a headboard, but found nothing.

Walking back to the sea, Vesconte told the story of how the body of a Norse settler had been found in the abandoned Eastern Settlement a century after the man had died, and that upon being lifted for burial the disturbed corpse had given off the odor of its own slight putrefaction, as well-preserved as its skin and hair in that frigid place, and powerful enough to sicken every member of the burial party.

.   .   .

Their transports left them on the morning of July the 11th, taking with them a man who had broken his leg in a fall from the *Erebus'* rigging, and another with severe stomach cramps, diagnosed by Stanley as appendicitis. Also on board were the *Terror*'s armorer and sailmaker, both sent home at Crozier's insistence as being useless not only at their trades but also at everything else they were called upon to do. The two vessels expected to be back in London in ten days' time.

On the eve of their own departure all strong liquors were collected from the lower ranks and thrown overboard. Some argued for their disposal ashore, but Franklin insisted. A still was discovered on the *Terror*, along with sixty gallons of barely distilled rum, which in Fitzjames' opinion was better suited for caulking than for drinking. A rat hunt was organized, Gore with his flute playing the part of the Pied Piper, and 246 of the creatures were killed, a shilling bounty being paid on the presentation of each severed tail.

FOUR

The men on the decks of both ships moved to the starboard side as they passed the concealed entrance to Uppernavik harbor. Twenty vessels sat closely moored in the deepwater cleft, their masts and rigging visible against the sheer wall of ice behind them. Tiny figures moved upon the ships, and thin pillars of smoke rose in a ghostly coppice.

In the open water the floating ice grew thicker, and for the first time since their departure an ice-watch was posted. Less than an hour after altering course, both ships were forced to maneuver independently through a field of small bergs which flowed all around them.

Reid stood at the *Erebus'* headboards and watched closely as she pushed into the flux of opening and closing channels ahead. The ice, he told Mate Des Voeux, was a mix of old and new, the new still dispersing from the Middle Pack, the old having been grounded for the winter and now starting to disintegrate and refloat. His greatest concern was that they had arrived in an area where both types were converging. To the west of them the currents and this flotsam would combine and begin to move steadily south, and he recommended a more northerly course, aware that if they turned west too soon they might encounter the unbroken heart of the Middle Pack and be forced to retreat along its perimeter. He was also aware that too many crossings of the bay had been attempted by men anxious to avoid this solid heart only to find themselves caught and then carried south in its unstoppable drift.

He resumed his position, signaling the presence of ice ahead to Graham Gore and Philip Reddington, captain of the forecastle, both of whom stood at the wheel and translated his signals into evasive action.

Neither of the heavily laden ships responded quickly to their controls and there were several small collisions, none of which did any damage to their reinforced bows.

They sailed through the ice field for six hours, and just as suddenly as they had encountered it, so they found themselves free of it and entering an expanse of cobalt-blue water clear to the horizon.

They continued until the late dusk, when they dropped anchor in twenty fathoms to sit out the short night.

At two the following morning, Philip Reddington woke Fitzjames with the news that he had seen a light off their starboard bow. Fitzjames, sleeping fully dressed, returned above deck with him to see for himself.

At first there was nothing. Then a call from the watch aboard the *Terror* alerted them to a distant flash amid the grounded ice. This reappeared at regular intervals, suggesting that someone was signaling to them.

"Signal back," Fitzjames called to their own watch. In two hours it would be light enough to see. He checked that all their own mast lamps were showing and then returned to his bunk, asking Reddington to wake him again at first light.

At four, Fitzjames and Reid met on deck. Visibility was poorer than Fitzjames had anticipated, and at first they could make out little more than the distant horizon and the junction of the ice with the open sea.

"A whaler waiting until he's certain of a clear way out. He isn't signaling: he's put out a single light and it's rocking in the swell," suggested David Bryant, sergeant of the *Erebus'* marines, as he climbed down from his look-out post to join them.

Fitzjames was ready to agree with this, but before he could say so, Reid said that he could see something else, and directed them once again to the flashing light.

"A hulk," Reddington said, as the outline became clearer to them. "Some poor soul lost his rigging. He's probably held fast in the ice, driven ashore by it. Damaged, most likely, or he could have cut his way out over that short distance."

"You're right." They were surprised by the voice of Thomas Blanky, who had rowed across to them, and who now stood behind them on a pile of cases and examined the shore through his glass. "He has half a fore but no other rigging. His main is lying from his deck to the ice."

Fitzjames climbed up beside him. "Is he signaling for help? Two days in the water will see him safe in Uppernavik, a week overland at the most."

The light from the rising sun was confusing rather than illuminating, creating shadows more substantial than the features from which they fell, and another hour passed before they could see more clearly the beached hull with its felled mast.

"She's been lifted and punched over," Reid said dispassionately.

"They're dragging out a boat," Reddington shouted, indicating the ice a short distance from the ship, where two men struggled with a boat too large for them to handle. Several others stood back and looked on, making no effort to help them.

"Why don't they go to their assistance?" Bryant said. "It'll hold a dozen of them and they could launch it in no time with all hands."

Fitzjames, aware of their obligations toward other mariners in distress, but also conscious of the fact that Franklin intended to sail in an hour's time, ordered one of their own boats to be lowered. He asked Reid and Reddington to accompany him. Two of their marines were called up to row and Bryant told them to bring their muskets.

"You think it necessary?" Fitzjames asked him.

In reply, Bryant looked at James Reid, who nodded his agreement. By now there were others upon the decks of both vessels. Franklin arrived and stood with Gore and Fairholme, and all three watched without intervening.

A hundred yards from the ice Fitzjames gave the order to stop rowing. He rose and inspected the boat approaching them. Since launching themselves, the two men had made little progress in the heavy craft, and after every five or six weak and uncoordinated strokes they stopped rowing and allowed themselves to be carried on the drift. Those now gathered behind them on the ice stood and watched in silence.

As the boat drew closer, Fitzjames called for the men to identify themselves. It was clear to everyone who awaited them that they were exhausted by their labors. One of the men rose unsteadily to his feet and shouted back that he was Captain Wilson of the *Benjamin Lee*, that she had been caught in the ice for the past eight months and that she had lost her rigging and been badly crushed.

Fitzjames saw how thin the man was, his soiled clothes hanging from his frame. He trembled uncontrollably and held his arms across his chest as he spoke. The man beside him also tried to stand, but was unable to and fell backward from his seat.

"Do you have any injuries?" Fitzjames asked him, aware of the demands the man might yet make on him. He was conscious too of the delay caused by the encounter, and of Franklin's growing impatience. Crozier, he knew, would have argued against any communication whatsoever with the stranded men.

Wilson cleared his throat and composed himself. "Injuries? Do I have any injuries, you ask me? I have ten dead and eight dying. The rest of us are alive by the grace of God alone. Can you take us aboard and to safety?"

This was impossible. Fitzjames shouted to them who they were, but this information had little effect on the two men.

"We sighted a vessel three days ago, but she passed us by without acknowledging our signal."

"Perhaps she didn't see you."

Wilson laughed. The man beside him began to cough violently and Wilson leaned down to hold his shoulders until the spasm passed. It was a full minute before he was able to speak again.

"Is it scurvy?" Reddington called to him.

"That and broken bones," Wilson shouted back, his voice hoarse and faltering. "The bulk of our supplies were lost in the storm which drove us ashore. We were too light in the water." His voice faded until he was barely audible.

"Tell him to start marching to Uppernavik," one of the marines said, unslinging his musket.

Fitzjames doubted that the two men in the boat even possessed the strength to row back to the shore. He looked to Reid, but he too had little to suggest.

"Others have done it," he said. "Hundreds, thousands some years."

Fitzjames considered this before calling back to the two men. "We can land you some supplies and lemon juice," he said. "Get your men into the boat and the current will take you south. Keep the shore in your sight and—"

"No!" Wilson shouted. "They refuse to put to sea. Only my mate here is prepared to make the journey with me."

Uppernavik being so near, this decision seemed perverse to Fitzjames and he felt himself absolved of some part of his responsibility toward the stranded whalers.

By then the two boats had drifted closer together, affording those from the *Erebus* a better view of the two emaciated men. Both wore heavy beards; their eyes were sunken and their darkened lips drawn back to reveal their remaining teeth.

"Can we speak to your captain?" Wilson asked, reaching out to the other boat.

At this, the marines raised their weapons and called for him to remain where he was.

This sudden appearance of the firearms surprised the two men and they sat without moving or speaking.

Fitzjames gave the order to shoulder arms.

"You might just as well give the order to fire on us," Wilson said. He held out both his arms, presenting himself as a target. "I have two men ashore who cannot last the week." He paused before going on. "Three days after we were wrecked, and certain that help would not come to us from the sea, I sent a party of four men overland. After a fortnight they had not returned. Our second party found all four of them frozen in their blankets less than a day's march from the ship. Perhaps now you can understand their reluctance to make any further attempt."

"And have you made no contact with the Eskimos?" Reid asked him.

There was a long silence. Then Wilson said that they had, but that they could expect no help from that quarter either.

"Explain yourself," Reid told him.

"A party arrived to steal from the *Benjamin Lee*. We had no choice."

"You mean you fired on them?"

"Two men and a woman." Wilson rubbed his face, as though he were condemned to repeating these damning details of his tragedy for the rest of his life.

Realizing that the exchange was achieving little, Fitzjames called for the two men to remain where they were. He then gave the order for the marines to row back to the *Erebus*.

Climbing aboard, he explained to Franklin what had happened.

"Poor wretches," was all that Franklin said, but in a tone of voice that made it immediately clear to Fitzjames that he did not intend to delay any further. He agreed to leave the stranded men sufficient supplies for their journey south and consulted with Stanley regarding the most appropriate medical aid to send them.

As Fitzjames was about to return to the boat, however, Franklin told him to remain aboard. Fitzjames stopped himself from asking why. Like many others, Franklin considered that the men ashore had done insufficient to help themselves while the opportunity to do so had still existed, and calling for silence he reminded all those around him that they were now in the Arctic, where the price of a mistake was all too often the life of the man who made it. Crozier stood beside him and nodded emphatically, looking hard at Fitzjames as he did so.

Only fifteen years earlier, so many vessels had been caught by the sudden onset of the winter ice in that same part of the bay—known by whalers as the "breaking-up yard"—that over a thousand men had found themselves camped out on the ice. They had retrieved most of their stores and then burned what remained of their vessels to keep warm. Not one of them had died or suffered anything but the slightest effects of scurvy before being rescued or reaching safety.

The tales of individual vessels spread just as quickly and widely. In 1832 the *Shannon* of Hull had struck a berg there and lost sixteen men and three boys as she sank. Clinging to the wreckage, the frost-bitten survivors were without food or fresh water for twenty-three days and kept themselves alive by drinking the blood of the three of their number who died during their ordeal. They had been rescued in a frozen stupor by a Danish brig, the drained corpses of their shipmates still among them.

Captain Dannet saw the two ships on the morning of the 26th. His mate sighted them first and called him on deck. The sea in the Middle Passage was calm, and visibility good under a cloudless sky. There were bergs of all sizes scattered around them, but none of these presented any obstacle to the vessels navigating the broad channels between them.

The *Prince of Wales* was moored to the largest of the surrounding bergs, one twice her own length, half as high and with a flat top. One of their boats had been pulled up on to this level surface and several men were now busy there unwinding and recoiling their harpoon lines.

Dannet had made his first kill the previous evening, an immature female pike-whale, and this was lashed to his stern. A fog had come down an hour after the kill and they had been unable to flense and render the fish. This was now the task of the men gathered on the ice.

On the *Erebus*, Fitzjames, Gore and Reid examined the whaler and the activity on the berg. Reid was the first to spot the fish, his attention drawn to it by the flock of birds which hovered above.

Fitzjames gave the order to take in part of their sail.

"Shall we wait for Sir John?" Gore asked. He had just eaten a large breakfast and the thought of seeing the whaler at work repulsed him.

"She's only a small fish," Reid observed.

Franklin, Fitzjames knew, would want to make contact with the vessel to determine the state of the ice further west. They were fifteen degrees east of the entrance to Lancaster Sound, their course west-southwest, and the ice was certain to be thicker and faster-moving the further they now sailed.

The *Erebus* and *Terror* had been fourteen days in the bay and this was their first sighting of another vessel close enough to make contact. They too had spent the night moored in the lee of a small berg in the fog, and throughout the night the hulls of both ships had rubbed and ground along the ice, causing those who were new to the experience to wake in panic with fears of being holed in the darkness.

The *Erebus* drew closer to the whaler and came alongside. A boat was lowered and Fitzjames, Gore, Reid and Des Voeux rowed across to her. Dannet greeted them and helped them aboard. On the far side of his ship the men on the ice hauled the head of the small whale up on to the level surface, and when this was done, Dannet untied the tail and let it fall back into the water with a loud slap. A minute later the whole carcass was lifted free and the claver of the birds was matched only by the sound of knives being sharpened.

"Don't let us delay you in your work," Fitzjames told Dannet.

"We'll carve her up on the ice and save ourselves the trouble of swilling clean afterward. What's left we'll leave for the birds."

"Like a feast set out on a tablecloth," Gore said. He had never before seen a whaler at work, and, having overcome his initial repugnance, was now fascinated by the process and stood looking across at the men about to start stripping the carcass.

A large cauldron was rolled on to its base-plate on the deck behind Dannet and a fire lit in the iron well beneath it. Dannet considered this for a moment before turning to Reid. "What about you, ice-master, does our fish look dry to you?"

Reid studied the body and said that the skin was badly creased, confirming with a shrug what Dannet already knew.

"They've opened her up," Gore called from the rail.

They turned to watch one of the men on the ice plunge his long blade into the flesh of the whale and then run the length of the carcass, his knife still embedded, slicing as he ran and only one step ahead of the flesh which peeled behind him like a breaking wave. The blubber lay flat in a twelve-foot strip, and a second man, this time using the ice as a chopping board, detached this flap from the bulk of the whale. A third followed behind him chopping it into manageable pieces. Blood and juices stained the ice and formed a pool around the wound. The noise of the frenzied birds doubled in volume and intensity. Other men hooked and dragged these smaller pieces of blubber toward the ship and threw them aboard with practiced, confident motions. By then the cauldron was heated and the first of the blubber burned with a foul stink.

"Too hot," Dannet called to the man tending the fire. The man wore a leather apron from his chest to his feet and used the blade of an oar to scrape and prod at the liquefying mass.

"Not so good," Reid said to him.

Dannet shrugged. "We only went after her because we'd had an idle day." The two men understood each other perfectly. "Collect her white bone," Dannet called across to the men on the ice. "No part barrels. And the second rendering waits for my inspection before anything goes in the manifest."

Reid found himself nodding at everything the man said.

They went below and Dannet handed Fitzjames his log so that he might assess for himself the nature of the ice the whaler had already encountered. It was a mark of trust and respect to be given the log so freely, and Fitzjames acknowledged this by complimenting Dannet on the thoroughness of his entries.

"Too far north," Dannet said.

"Lured by the prospect of the breaking pack?" Reid asked him.

Dannet nodded. "Sixteen years I've been coming and I've never seen it so broken or so scattered at this latitude."

"Do you have a sister ship?"

"The *Orion*. Probably full and sailing for our transports by now. She's under contract to the Spanish off the Azores at the end of the month."

"Small fish, hot work," Reid said, and the two men smiled.

"And you?" Dannet asked.

"Forty-eight hours for observations and then west into Lancaster."

"You expect to find an opening?"

Fitzjames looked up, first at Dannet and then at Reid.

"We expect to find Chinamen dancing on the shore in welcome," Reid said.

"I wondered why they were gathering."

Fitzjames handed back the log, and because none of them wished to enter any further into their useless speculations, the three men returned above deck.

"Come aboard this evening and dine with us," Fitzjames said as they climbed the ladder.

Dannet accepted. "Barring a favorable wind or a blow close enough to wet our brows."

They emerged into the bright sunlight and looked across to where the flensers were still at work. By now the blubber and meat had been stripped from the skeleton, and the men were cutting out the ribcage. The skull, its eyes still intact, lay like a boulder a short distance from them. The stain on the ice was now wider and other internal organs lay scattered all around. The liver had been retrieved, and the stomach had been dragged with its thick rope of intestine to the far side of the berg. A man swung at the jawbone with a mallet, and another probed inside the mouth with a knife to secure the tongue.

Seeing Fitzjames and the others back out on the deck, Gore called for them to join him. The edge of the berg was held fast against the hull and Fitzjames alone stepped across on to the level surface. He joined Gore and they watched together as the vertebrae were chiseled one by one from the curved spine. These were inspected by the man in charge of the operation and then kicked off the ice into the water, where they slowly sank.

"No use to us," he said to Fitzjames, that being the full extent of his explanation. He cursed the birds which had become braver in their desperation to reach the congealed mess to which the carcass had been reduced, and which now flew among the men, narrowly avoiding their heads and flailing arms.

The last of the blubber was thrown to the deck and the flensers cleaned their knives. A small group gathered around the shining bulging stomach and called Fitzjames and Gore over to watch as they slit it open to see what it contained. One man stood ready with a rack of bottles to collect specimens. They made this final act of disembowelment seem like an honor, and there was a murmur of concurrence when the man in charge held out his knife to Graham Gore and asked him if he would like to do it. Gore readily accepted, and only Fitzjames saw the shared glances and smiles as the knife was handed to him.

Gore approached the bloated sac and prodded it with his finger. It was flattened on the ice, but still the size of a resting pony, longer than he was tall and mounded almost to his waist. He prodded it again, this time more forcefully, and set it quivering. Around him, the others took several paces back, and seeing this, Fitzjames did the same.

"Now slit her long and clean," the man called to Gore, making a slashing motion with his hand.

Gore selected his starting point, flexed his arm, took a deep breath and drove in the knife. And as he did so, the men around him turned and ran, racing each other through the clamoring birds back to the ship.

Gore had no opportunity to cut the full length of the stomach, for the instant his knife entered it there was an explosion of liquid and gas and the bag collapsed, spilling its contents in a gush against his legs and knocking him off his feet. All around him the birds turned into insatiable demons.

Later that day, Dannet's favorable wind arose. He detached himself from the berg and shouted his apologies to the *Erebus* that he would not after all be dining with them. Franklin called back that he understood and asked him to report their encounter to the Admiralty upon his return home.

As they pulled away, the crew of the *Prince of Wales* stood in a line at her rail, raised their caps and cheered.

WINTER'S CITADEL

August 1845—July 1846

They entered Lancaster Sound on the 31st of August, the two vessels sailing line astern through the dispersing ice there.

At midday a broader channel of open water appeared ahead of them and their progress for the rest of the day was good. There was a sense of relief aboard both ships—not only at having found their entrance open, but also at now having moved beyond the sphere of others in the region. They passed into a stillness and an emptiness that even the flocks of following birds seemed to acknowledge in their silence. Baffin Bay, long since probed and charted in frustrating detail since the days of Davis, Frobisher and Cabot, had presented them with no real challenge, and to have been forced to turn back there would have embarrassed and shamed them all. But with the northern shore of the island slipping out of sight astern they had entered an unknown wilderness which bore few signs of those who had gone there before them, and who had been lost there, or returned home beaten and incredulous at the stubbornness, complexity and confusing impermanence of the place. They all knew who these men were, and many paid silent homage to them.

"We pass through Ross' mountains," Vesconte remarked to Fitzjames and Gore, causing them to turn and look at the open channel still unwinding ahead of them.

Twenty-five years earlier, John Ross, sailing with Parry, had entered the Sound, then unconfirmed as the only true entrance to the Passage, but had turned back at what he believed to be a range of mountains blocking his way ahead. These turned out to be nothing more than a solid bank of cloud, through which Parry himself sailed a few years later, eclipsing his former captain and taking up the baton of exploration, until he too withdrew a decade later, old and defeated and privately convinced that where he had failed no one would succeed after him.

The *Terror* moved closer astern and sounded her bell. Turning to study her through his glass, Fitzjames saw that the man upon her prow was signaling to landward. He looked where he pointed, and amid the ice there he saw a darker form.

Reid too had been alerted and he was the first to speak. "She's a country ship come out in this year's rush," he said solemnly. "No rigging, no deck. She's floundered and been carried in the pack, left high in the crush."

"Are you certain of this, Mr. Reid?" Franklin asked him, relieved that they would not again be obliged to delay or alter their course.

"No need to turn, Sir John," Gore said, expressing the thoughts of them all.

A few moments later the abandoned hulk was lost to sight.

These ice-locked wrecks were common enough on the edges of the Arctic, usually whalers too late or too careless in the forming pack, sucked into the drift, savaged and then spat out again, sometimes many years later and hundreds of miles from where they had been trapped and abandoned.

They continued due west until the sun began its late descent ahead of them, barely darkening the sky until it touched and then burned into the horizon. They moved closer to the ice-littered shore and dropped anchor. Watches were posted and their plans for the following days' sailing were discussed over dinner. It had been decided that there should be no exchange of men between the two ships until the full 200-mile length of the Sound had been navigated. It was unlikely that they would become separated for long, but it was now important for the ships to begin to function independently of each other as soon as possible.

The following morning they sailed at first light. The wind for once was not with them, and until midday their progress was slow. They remained within sight of the southern shore, only diverting from it when the ice there extended seaward.

In the early afternoon, Reid warned that the floe ahead of them was thickening and that if it showed any further signs of consolidating then they would be forced to abandon their coasting and seek out a safer channel farther north. Franklin flagged this message to Crozier, who concurred in the decision.

Less than an hour later the cry went up from the *Terror* that she had struck ice. She was 300 yards astern of the *Erebus*, following in her wake, and it seemed impossible to those on the leading ship that she could have struck some obstacle over which they themselves had passed. As they watched, several men, led by Thomas Blanky, made their way along the *Terror*'s bowsprit lines to inspect whatever damage she might have suffered.

"She's run over a submerged berg," Goodsir guessed.

"She's still coming," Vesconte said.

The *Terror* appeared to have incurred no damage, but they could neither see nor hear if she was still in contact with the ice, and several minutes passed before Blanky returned to the head, raised both his hands to the *Erebus* and then swung them slowly apart.

"Passed right over," Reid said, raising his own arms in answer.

Vesconte called for their own depth and was answered with a cry of six fathoms. This surprised him, conflicting as it did with the few scattered soundings of his chart, and he recommended to Franklin that they should steer a course into deeper water.

They turned to starboard and the *Terror* moved closer to them, holding her course until she was alongside.

"I believe we sliced a grounded berg by the full length of our keel," Crozier shouted to them, his voice amplified in the still air.

"And your rudder?" Fitzjames called back.

"Lifted the second we touched," Crozier shouted. "First blood to *Terror*, I believe, gentlemen. Let the ice lick its wounds and tremble before us."

Elated, he raised three cheers for the *Terror*, and the shouts and applause of the men around him crossed the water to the *Erebus* like the sound of fighting punctuated by gunfire.

An hour after darkness during their second night the *Erebus* herself was struck by a piece of floating ice, which caught her amidships on her port side and then slid slowly to her stern. Deep in her hull, men listened without speaking, the newcomers almost without breathing, as the knock of the collision became a drawn-out scraping, rising and then fading as the ice eventually drifted free of them.

Fitzjames was with Goodsir and Reid in the narrow corridor between his own and Goodsir's cabin when the ice struck, and all three waited in silence until it moved off.

"An icy finger sent out of the darkness to prod us as we sleep," Goodsir announced with a flourish.

"To prod the atrocious poet in your soul," Fitzjames said, releasing the tension now that the danger had passed.

One of the *Erebus'* boys appeared, stopping when he saw them in the narrow passage. He had been woken and frightened by the collision. Goodsir told him to return to his bunk and he left them without speaking. They watched him go, each of them momentarily lost in his own thoughts.

There were no further collisions during the night, and the following morning they rose to find that the field in which they had anchored the previous evening was no longer in sight, having been drawn away from them during the brief spell of darkness.

They continued along their previous course in full sail. News of the *Erebus'* encounter with the ice was communicated to the *Terror*, and John Irving shouted back to ask if they were sure it was ice that had struck them and not a fish that had come too close in search of scraps from their galley.

The *Erebus* led the way that day, maintaining a course which kept them out of sight of land to both north and south.

In the falling dusk they sailed several degrees to port and moored for the night to a massive grounded berg. This rose as high as a small hill above them and was larger than anything they had so far encountered. In a precisely calculated maneuver, both ships sailed alongside the edge of the ice until they were pressed close upon it, whereupon claws were thrown to secure them.

At first light Vesconte took his surveying equipment ashore and made a series of measurements. He was accompanied by Goodsir, who hammered at the ice in a dozen places and collected samples. He also netted the water along the edge of the berg and took the bottled results of this back aboard with him too.

Later, when they were ready to sail and both ships had drawn clear of their moorings, Goodsir conducted another experiment involving packages of explosive set along a line in the ice. Those watching from the ships were disappointed by the small size of the explosions when they finally came, and with the undramatic and short-lived plumes of powder-smoke and steam they threw up. The noise broke the morning silence for many miles around, but apart from this nothing else appeared to have been achieved, and as he climbed back aboard, Fitzjames asked Goodsir what he had expected. Goodsir looked back to the ice without speaking, and then a moment later pointed and said, "That."

Fitzjames looked, and as the last of the smoke and powdered ice slowly cleared, he saw a long deep fissure appear, which then cleaved the berg in half as he watched.

SIX

Franklin's orders were to proceed along Lancaster Sound to its confluence with Barrow Strait in the west, and with Prince Regent's Inlet and the Gulf of Boothia to the south, and there to adopt a southwesterly course through whatever navigable water lay in that direction until he reached the mainland coast, whereupon he was then to turn west and continue to the Pacific by way of Bering Strait.

Due west through Barrow Strait would bring the expedition into those unrewarding waters explored twenty-five years earlier by Parry; turning south into Prince Regent's Inlet they would be following in the wake of the Rosses. Neither route led to the Passage, both terminating in land-locked water and impenetrable ice.

Having arrived at the confluence of Lancaster Sound with Barrow Strait, Franklin made a decision which was uniquely his own, and prior to entering the more turbulent waters of the Strait he called Crozier and his senior officers together to inform them of what he now intended to do.

Pinned to the wall of his cabin was a map upon which Vesconte had drawn the line of every known coast and waterway so far charted, the bulk of these already behind them, the area ahead largely blank except for the few known headlands and bays which had already been visited and plotted. Under orders from Franklin to resist the urge to speculate, Vesconte had avoided adding anything other than that which had been first located and then afterward confirmed. Parry's islands lay 200 miles ahead of them, still the farthest west ever reached at that latitude. The west coast of Baffin ended abruptly south of 72 degrees. The east coast of the Boothia Peninsula extended to 70 degrees, but its far coast remained invisible except around this same latitude, where it had already been visited by James Ross fifteen years earlier. Elsewhere there was only emptiness, given some definition by the mainland coast far to the south. It was into this uncharted white space—even following a direct course, a distance of 300 miles, although more likely to be double this once they were forced to begin weaving amid the ice, land and open water in that direction—that all thoughts turned upon seeing the map, and as the men gathering together waited for Franklin to address them.

"Guesswork, gentlemen," he began, rapping his cane and silencing their speculations. "We cannot even say for certain whether or not the Boothia Peninsula is a solid land mass connected to the mainland—in which case Prince Regent's is nothing but a giant blind alley—or whether it is broken at some point along its length by a single or by many channels. Ross failed to establish this, and if we ourselves choose this course then we might have great cause to regret his failure. We know it is filled by the spring pack, but so too is the western approach." It was clear by the peremptory manner in which he made these opening remarks that he had no intention of turning south into the Inlet.

Crozier was the first to his feet. "But surely navigable by us along a good deal of its length," he said, masking his anger at the realization that his own opinion had not been sought in advance of Franklin announcing this decision.

"Certainly," Franklin said quickly. "We might even penetrate as far south as we have already come west. Our problem then would be that we might be caught and be forced to winter in some particularly active part of the pack. It is not my intention to gamble all upon an unfortunate first winter when we are provisioned for at least three and are still at leisure to make our calculations based upon something other than the necessity to avoid ice-damage."

Crozier became impatient with these explanations. He had accompanied Parry on his final disappointing search and was convinced that their best chance of success now lay in continuing westward, changing their course to the southwest only when the ice in that direction became too much for them.

Franklin allowed a minute of open speculation before resuming: "Permit me to read you our orders, gentlemen. Afterward I will tell you what I intend to do and hope that I can persuade you of my reasons."

The ten men tried to make themselves more comfortable in the confined space.

Franklin took out a leather satchel, unfastened its bindings and spread its contents on the table at their center. There was a thick sheath of papers and he searched these for the sheet he wanted.

"Clauses five and six concern us here," he said. "Five is founded upon the knowledge that Parry has sailed four times through Lancaster Sound and Barrow Strait, finding both to be navigable. The whalers themselves have come this far and suffered no harm. Indeed, so convinced is the Admiralty of the openness of these waters that they speculate upon some extension following directly through to Bering itself."

Upon hearing this, Fairholme said, "Surely not. Surely they must realize the impossibility of that?"

Others nodded their concurrence.

"I think they do. Hope, I believe, has temporarily triumphed over experience, for they go on to say that rather than exploring any channel north or south from Barrow Strait, we are to sail through the latter along the latitude of seventy-four degrees and fifteen minutes until we reach Cape Walker." Franklin indicated the dismembered finger of land at 98 degrees west, immediately beyond which lay the map's large empty space.

"And from there?" Fitzjames asked.

"Here the gentlemen of the Admiralty become a little less specific, I'm afraid." Franklin returned to his papers and read from them. "From the point ninety-eight degrees west we are simply required to steer to the south and the west toward Bering in as straight a line as is permitted by the ice or any unknown land. Surely it is nothing more than any of us expected."

"Our only course," Crozier said confidently, ready now to argue for their continuation westward.

"It would certainly seem so," Franklin said.

"And clause six?" Crozier asked.

"Clause six would tend to agree with our own consensus of opinion that the best prospect of the Passage does indeed lie in this direction. It points out that the ice in the far west at Cape Dundas and around Melville Island appears to be fixed and heavy and thus presents less of a hazard to navigation in the open channels among it."

"Parry's first under his own command," Crozier said.

"I believe so. You see our predicament. Parry continued west and found the ice so thick and extensive in that region that he was barely released from it after a long and difficult winter spent within it."

"Which is no reason why we ourselves should not test it again now. Twenty years have passed. There may no longer be any ice in that quarter," Crozier said, again rising to his feet to add emphasis to his argument. Several others rose alongside him.

"I agree, gentlemen. But what I cannot accept is that *now* is the time to be starting out on a journey in that direction. If we had been in this position a month ago I would have been in favor of making the attempt. At least then we might have had the time and opportunity to turn back before we were caught or at least to find a safe harbor in which to winter. If we sail now I fear neither of these opportunities would exist."

John Irving was the first to speak. "Then is it your intention to winter the ships close to where we are now?"

"It is," Franklin said firmly.

"Even after having come so far, and so easily?" Crozier said. "Even while the water remains open to us? Surely not."

"Let me read to you the concluding remarks of clause six," Franklin said, and waited for silence. "These suggest that if a permanent obstruction—ice or land—should be encountered to the southwest of Cape Walker, then we are to consider the alternative of passing between Cornwallis Island and North Devon if Wellington Channel is open."

A moment of stunned silence met this remark. Several turned back to the chart and studied it.

"North!" Edward Little said. "They suggest we sail north from here? But what will that achieve? Surely they must be aware of the fixed ice in that direction."

"I believe they are, Mr. Little," Franklin said.

Crozier joined his lieutenant at the chart. "Then they want us to sail on a useless errand simply to satisfy themselves that it cannot be done." He slapped his palm on the table.

"And in doing so we eliminate a full quadrant for those who might come after us," Franklin said calmly. "Surely it is the nature of all exploration and probing in this place that we move forward only by first eliminating all the blind alleys and false turns that we cannot help but make in our first groping forays. You and I have stumbled often enough in the darkness and over blank charts in the past, Francis."

"Which is why I want to waste as little time as possible doing it again."

Franklin resealed his orders and waited again for them to fall silent.

Realizing that to argue any further would only create bad feeling between his commander and himself, Crozier asked him to outline his intentions to them in greater detail. Acknowledging this concil-iatory gesture, Franklin reassured them all that he was as convinced as they were that the continuation of the Passage did not lie to the north.

"Cornwallis Island," he announced, replacing the chart on the wall with another which showed the island in greater detail. "For obvious reasons, its southern shore is well-enough charted. It is my intention to explore north along Wellington Channel and pass beyond the northern shore of the island—assuming of course that it *is* an island and not simply a small piece of someone's imagi-nation set adrift amid this fearful waste of ice and howling dark-ness."

They all laughed at this, even Crozier, and Franklin knew that they were once again with him.

" 'Our nightmares are not their nightmares,' " Crozier said, repeating the well-worn phrase of Sir John Barrow with which they were all familiar.

"Precisely," Franklin said. "We are here, gentlemen, and we are here alone. They, on the other hand, must inhabit their offices and their salons and every now and again visit a traveling light-show or panorama upon which to feed their imaginations."

"Bravo, Sir John," Graham Gore called out.

Uncharacteristically, Franklin bowed in acknowledgment, the gesture soliciting further calls and applause. "Not so fast, Mr. Gore. I daresay that upon our return we too may be reduced to the status of sideshow exhibits."

"But what a sideshow," George Hodgson said, rising and standing as though he were posing for a bust of himself.

"Indeed. But let us not get carried away so soon with our speculations. It is my intention, in the days of sailing remaining to us, to travel as far north along Wellington Channel as the ice will allow. And when we can go no farther we will turn south and return via the west coast of Cornwallis. It is also my intention, again depending on the condition of the ice, and the speed with which the coming winter closes in on us, to find a safe harbor in a sheltered bay on the south shore of either Cornwallis or Devon Island." He stopped speaking and waited for their comments.

"How far will we get?" Fitzjames asked him, coming to the chart and examining it more closely.

"Your estimate is as good as mine."

"Seventy-six degrees, seventy-seven?"

"Possibly. Like a great many others who have come before us, we can never truly know where we are going until we arrive there."

Vesconte, who had so far said very little, rose, called for their attention and announced that he for one was only too delighted to be sailing in a straight line for the Pole.

"And why might that be?" Fitzjames asked him, prolonging the joke.

"Because it occurs to me," Vesconte said, "that if we are all to get some feature or other named after us, then our best chance of finding those discarded, ignored or unwanted by others lies in that direction."

"Vesconte Island," Fitzjames said. "How about you, Mr. Hodgson, Mr. Irving?"

"Mount Irving," Irving said, suggesting to them all that he had already given the matter some consideration.

It was a great relief to Franklin to see that the uncertainty and disappointment of a few minutes earlier had been dispelled. He saw that Crozier still harbored doubts about the merits of what he had proposed, but knew that the point of divisive confrontation was passed. He unlocked another of his cabinets and took out a bottle of Madeira, suggesting that a toast be drunk to their first foray into unsailed waters. Afterward, it being Saturday, they drank their regular toast to wives and sweethearts.

Later, as Crozier and his officers prepared to leave, Franklin took him to one side and asked him if he still had any serious reservations about the plan he had outlined.

"I cannot deny that I am disappointed that we will make no further progress to the west this season," Crozier said. "But I agree that a journey north might prove valuable for the reasons stated."

"And that we will be in a strong position to embark upon a full season's exploration next year?"

"That, too," Crozier admitted. Glancing quickly around them to ensure that he was not overheard, he added in a low voice, "Parry is convinced that no navigable route lies directly to the west. Pushing so hard year after year broke his ships and his spirit. His loss of heart and disillusionment on his final voyage was terrible to see. I have great respect for the man, and for the Rosses too, but none of them will ever return to resume their searches."

The two men shook hands and Crozier called for his lieutenants to return with him to the *Terror*.

They reached their Farthest North on the 17th of September, having left Cornwallis behind them and then sailed for four days among the gradually thickening ice and smaller islands, some no more than exposed rocks, in the upper reaches of Wellington Channel. They achieved 77 degrees before the ice moving south forced them to turn. There was little danger of them being caught by this, it being mostly newly formed brash, as much liquid as solid. The daily temperature were falling, but not yet swiftly, and the Arctic night proper was still two months away.

They were surprised not to encounter the permanent Polar ice this far north, but guessed that they might now measure the distance it lay ahead of them in hours' rather than days' sailing. At that latitude, the ice flow from the west was known to be heavy and rapid, and a watch was kept for any bergs appearing from that quarter.

The next day was a Sunday, and they spent this cruising east along the edge of the ice. Occasionally they encountered a channel inviting them farther toward the Pole, but they were not tempted into these restricted waters where they might suddenly find themselves unable to maneuver or turn back.

Franklin had been vindicated by his detour: the Passage did not lie to the north or the northwest.

It was strange but comforting, Franklin wrote in his journal on the day of their Farthest North, how often he heard the Pacific mentioned by his officers and crew, much preferred by them all in conversation as a general destination than, say, the Beaufort Sea or Bering. Cook's Icy Cape, he noted, was seldom mentioned at all, and he regretted that Cook should have chosen such a prosaic and uninviting name for his own Farthest East, having entered the Arctic puzzle from the west.

They cruised for a further three days, during which time the closed northern exit to Wellington Channel was explored and charted in detail.

Returning to the broken southern shore, Franklin suggested to his officers that they might now turn their attention to finding somewhere secure to spend their first winter in the ice. Ideally, he suggested, a protected harbor to the north of Barrow Strait, somewhere from which they might make an early crossing south at the start of the following summer upon their release.

They continued along the coast, putting out boats daily to examine more closely those places they had seen at a distance. Few of these proved suitable and they continued to the east, the two ships leap-frogging each other as one or other of them awaited the return of its boats.

A likely place lay somewhere close to Beechey, a small island to the south of Devon, and connected to it by a slender umbilical isthmus, on either side of which were broad shallow bays. Additionally, both Devon and Beechey offered accessible landing-places where they might spend the winter ashore if the need arose.

They had no detailed chart of Beechey. Nor, upon the map of Devon, was there any indication of the arm of the isthmus, as narrow as twenty feet in places, which connected the two land masses.

The small island had been named in 1819 by Parry after William Beechey, who had accompanied Franklin on his own attempt on the Pole by the direct Spitsbergen route, his belated account of this voyage having been published only two years previously.

Naming the small island, Parry had then sailed to the west without landing upon it. He named the much larger island after his home county, and Somerset to the south after the home of one of his lieutenants.

They came within sight of Beechey on the 29th of September and entered the shallow passage between it and the mainland, sailing as close as possible to the connecting spit. The *Erebus* anchored here while the *Terror* sailed south around the island to explore the bay on the far side of this shingle divide.

By late afternoon the two ships lay at anchor side by side. Beechey rose to the west and south of them, offering some protection from the turbulent gathering ground of Barrow Strait beyond, and to the north stretched the sheltering cliffs of Devon. The water in the shallow bay was calm and ice-free, and although it was certain to freeze over during the coming weeks, it was unlikely, judging by the settled contours of the shoreline, that the main flow of ice would enter the

SEVEN

Henry Thomas Dundas Le Vesconte. He enjoyed the rhythm and flow of his names and was proud to recite them in full whenever the opportunity arose, savoring and delivering them with the same exaggerated flourish with which he signed them. He addressed himself frequently, often in self-criticism, and by using all these names it seemed to him as though he were being rebuked—usually for his carelessness or haste—by every one of the ancestors from whom he had inherited them thirty-five years earlier.

He wore at all times a cap upon which each of the names had been embroidered in gold thread by his mother, and inside which his wife and three daughters had added their own. He was convinced that he would rather lose his two small fingers than the cap.

Upon arriving at Beechey, he began to map the unknown terrain around them. On his first day away from the ships he was accompanied by Fitzjames, and by Little, Hodgson and Irving from the *Terror*. They took Lady Franklin's dog with them and, free after its long confinement, the animal raced ahead of them along the shore, the men following in a line abreast, each with his case of equipment. Little and Irving carried bundles of surveying poles, and Hodgson several coils of marked cable. Fitzjames carried the precious theodolite and its tripod, and Vesconte a sextant and the large pads upon which to interpret his calculations.

They followed the shore to the east, walking for half an hour until it turned south, where they were quickly out of sight of the vessels.

At regular intervals, Vesconte set up his equipment and took readings, Little and Irving being dispatched to stand on either side of him and drive their poles into the stony ground.

At the first of these halts, Fitzjames took their bearings against the sun on the eastern horizon.

When these shoreline measurements were completed, Vesconte copied out the figures and made the first sketchy outline of the land over which they had walked.

"Is that it, is that all?" Hodgson asked him, disappointed that so little had come of all their efforts.

Vesconte held up and studied what he had drawn. "As to distance and exact orientation, it is perfect. As to its absolute location with regard to latitude and longitude and the minutes of both, it cannot be bettered. In fact, gentlemen, I would say that we are on our way to producing a small cartographic masterpiece, in itself a marvelous thing, I'm sure you will all agree." He shared a smile with Fitzjames. "And one for which every frost-bitten Jack who follows in our icy footsteps will surely be eternally grateful."

The three lieutenants were not convinced. They looked at the land around them, at the slope and the cliff above them, then back to the few unconnected lines like a child's scribble on the pad.

"All you see, gentlemen, are pencil marks," Vesconte went on. "What I see, and what Fitzjames here sees, is the ground over which we have just come. A poor return on our efforts, perhaps, but once the mark is made and connected to the dozens, perhaps hundreds, which are to follow, then no one will ever have to trace the route again. Perhaps what we are about to achieve over the next few days will remain unquestioned and unaltered—other than by the Almighty himself—for a hundred years."

"You should have been a politician," Fitzjames told him, seeing how quickly the others were coming round to this encouragement of their drudgery.

Vesconte did not answer him; instead he slapped his pad shut, rose and strode off ahead of them, calling the dog to him as he went. The others gathered up their cases, pulled free the poles and ran to keep up with him.

They walked farther from the sheltered bay and the ships, crossing the eastern and then the southern shore of Beechey alongside the fast-flowing waters of Barrow Strait.

They began to climb, gently at first, and then more steeply over rock-strewn land until they reached the summit of the small island and were able to look down upon it in its entirety.

Where the terrain was more variable, and where the shoreline ceased to turn in so smooth a curve, Vesconte insisted on taking more readings, and then on checking these several times over until his figures were duplicated.

The three lieutenants became more enthusiastic about their work, vying with each other to position their poles according to Vesconte's directions.

At the edge of a precipice to the south, Fitzjames took a succession of readings while both the sun and the clear horizon were visible to him. To the north of them across the narrow bay, the land stretched endlessly east and west, but to the south there was only water and a distant haze. He was joined by Vesconte, who asked him to gauge for him a line due south of where they stood. Fitzjames did this and Vesconte drew the mark on the ground with his heel.

"North Somerset," he said, pointing. "And beyond it, Boothia." He spoke as though he were not entirely convinced of the existence of these places, afterward staring into the haze without speaking.

"What are you thinking about?"

"Are they one and the same piece of land?" Vesconte said without turning from the horizon. "Are they a single solid, undivided projection north from the mainland?"

"You think otherwise?" Fitzjames said, turning to look, as though the answer lay visible before them.

"Pure speculation." Vesconte walked away from the edge to join the others.

The island took shape in outline on the sheets of squared paper, and Vesconte showed it to them, pointing out its more easily identifiable features: a small indentation, a rocky promontory, an offshore islet, the partially submerged finger of land reaching out toward Devon.

By the end of the afternoon almost half the coastline was in place. The rest might have been added with some degree of accuracy without any further measurement, but upon suggesting this, Irving was berated by Vesconte until he raised his hands in surrender.

To guess, Vesconte told him, even at what they could actually see, would make them no better than those cartographers in the past who had invented islands, rivers, mountains, and even entire lands simply to fill an empty space and appease their own uncontrollable imaginations. Irving apologized, and Vesconte, realizing that he had responded too aggressively, made a quick sketch of him with his hands in the air and suggested that the precipice to which they were then so close should afterward be known as "Irving's Drop."

Irving said he was honored, but declined the offer on the grounds that he would prefer not to have such a noble name associated with something over which a man might walk whistling to his death in a moment of carelessness.

They ate the food they had brought with them in a sheltered hollow overlooking the ice-filled channel below. Ungloved, their hands were quickly numbed in the cold air of the peak, and when they had finished eating they rubbed grease on their lips. The dog sat at their feet and leapt for scraps. It had grown fat during the voyage and panted at the slightest exertion.

As they were about to resume their work, Vesconte asked Irving for his mother's name and then wrote this alongside the islet he had drawn, and which they could see beneath them. "My prerogative," he said.

Irving thanked him and said he would write to her about it later that evening.

It became much cooler as they returned to the ships, walking in a straight line across the top of the island in the hope that a more direct path back down to the shore might reveal itself to them.

Arriving at a vantage-point over the sea, Vesconte pointed out to them the distant ice which already blocked the channels they had recently sailed, a broad unbroken expanse of it, tinting the sky above with its reflected glare.

"So soon?" Hodgson said, surprised to see that it had arrived so swiftly and so early.

All around them the setting sun threw up sudden shadows like small disturbed animals, and as it fell lower they watched the lines of light retreat over the dull brown slope as though they were being mechanically reeled back to their source.

The four men drew up the Articles of the society they had formed, named, at Goodsir's insistence, the Arctic Quartet, determined to produce a weekly journal throughout the months of their confinement chronicling their shipboard activities and to inform all those who were new to the region on various diverse aspects of it.

All the positions were self-appointed. Goodsir, the founder, was to be their naturalist; Vesconte was to contribute items of geographical and geological interest; Gore was to compose poetry and music to be read out and played at their meetings and at the lectures they proposed to give; and Fitzjames was to be purveyor of curiosities and penny-philosopher to the group. Reid was invited to become the fifth member of the society, but he declined, offering instead to produce anonymous articles for the journal on the history of the ice. A theater group was also set up, along with classes on reading and writing, to which most of the junior officers agreed to contribute.

The journal was to be produced largely by Goodsir and Gore, and to be named *The Holystoners' Almanac*. For the cover of the first issue Goodsir drew a sledge upon which the four of them stood, pulled by two dogs with the faces of Reid and Blanky.

Vesconte's inaugural contribution was a first-hand description of the two live Antarctic volcanoes named after their ships. Gore composed a short piece for violin and flute called "Fata Morgana," and Fitzjames wrote an article on the variety and strangeness of the charms and tokens they all carried with them. He himself had a piece of shale picked up on the shore of Baffin upon which was imprinted the perfect outline of a fossil leaf. Reid showed them his bloodstone to ward off drowning, and Goodsir took out a small spiral of polished rock widely held to be the tip of a thunderbolt excavated from the earth, and given to him by his brother Robert, also a ship's surgeon serving in the Pacific. Gore and Vesconte carried charms given to them by their wives: Gore a small handkerchief elaborately embroidered over every inch of its surface, and Vesconte, in addition to his cap, an empty watch-case in which he kept four curls of hair. Both men were unwilling to let these items out of their grasp. Vesconte in particular guarded his curls with diligent affection, and when Fitzjames half-seriously suggested to him that he was little different from Parry's Eskimo woman with her father's wooden leg, Vesconte was happy to admit the comparison. The others acknowledged the privilege of having been shown these charms.

Puzzles were devised and prizes offered for their solution. Each of the founder-members was asked to contribute one of these, the most coveted coming from Goodsir, who gave a bottle of Parfait Amour liqueur, saying he could no longer bear to be reminded of the girl who had once given it to him along with the promise of her undying love, but who had subsequently married a Brazilian nobleman whose family had made its fortune in slaves. He uncorked the bottle before handing it over, pretending to swoon at the powerful aroma. The rest contributed more prosaic prizes of cash and other delicacies.

The journal was to be composed of thirty-two pages, and their regular meetings would take place every Sunday after Evening Service.

A similar society was formed by Irving, Hodgson and Little on the *Terror*, their own bulletin being given the extravagant title *Hypaethral Hours*, afterward referred to as *Cathedral Flowers* by its competitors aboard the *Erebus*.

Much of the first week was spent in unloading stores and ferrying them ashore. Completing their daily quotas, both crews were then free to spend the hours before dusk as they chose.

Some explored the island; others returned to their quarters and spent their time aboard ship. A large number played football and cricket on the broad, near-level shore, while others congregated in smaller groups to play at cards and dice.

It was in one of these smaller parties that a fight broke out. A man named Henry Sait, a seaman on the *Terror*, accused another, Alexander Wilson, carpenter's mate, of cheating, and when their argument could not be contained, punches were thrown. The six or seven others involved then joined in, and one man, Thomas Jopson, Crozier's steward, was knocked briefly unconscious, hitting his head on the hard ground as he fell from a push.

The commotion attracted the attention of those on board the *Terror* and Crozier dispatched his marines to investigate.

Sergeant Tozer led the six men ashore, leaping from their boat and racing through the shallows to where the card-players were still fighting.

He fired his pistol into the air, at which they all immediately stopped and turned to face him. The marines positioned themselves around the small group, and Tozer went to Jopson, who was just then coming round, and pulled him roughly to his feet, slapping him in the face and accusing him of having started the fight.

Several of the others came forward in Jopson's defense, but Tozer told them to stay where they were and remain silent. He lined them up and told them to await the arrival of Crozier. He jabbed each of them in the stomach with his pistol and demanded an explanation of what had happened. No one was willing to tell him. He approached the youngest, Cornelius Hickey, caulker's mate, and putting his arm around the youth's shoulders, he drew him away from the others, whispering to him as they went.

"You're going to tell me, aren't you, lad?" he said. He stroked Hickey's smooth face with the back of his hand, flexing it suddenly into a fist and then relaxing it. Hickey tried to turn back to his companions, but Tozer grabbed and squeezed his cheeks, holding his face only inches from his own. "You talk to *me*," he said, his warm breath causing Hickey to flinch.

Before he could incriminate himself, Sait and Wilson confessed that they had started the fight.

"So, you two and Jopson, it is," Tozer said. "You three and young Hickey here."

"He had no part in it," Sait said, attempting to come forward, but being pushed back by one of the marines.

"And I say he did," Tozer said. He squeezed Hickey even harder, and then released his grip, swiftly cupping his hand upon the youth's head and pushing him to his knees before he realized what was happening.

Tozer then left him and went to examine the overturned cases and scattered cards where the fight had broken out. To his disappointment there were no coins; the men had been betting with their rations or promises of an exchanged duty.

Returning to where Thomas Jopson now stood with a cloth to his bleeding mouth, Tozer pulled this away and threw it to the ground. "You stand as you are until Captain Crozier gets here," he told him.

They did not have long to wait. Crozier came ashore with two of his warrant officers, Honey and Lane. He regretted the absence of his lieutenants, feeling vulnerable without them to back him up and to mediate between himself and Tozer, whom he did not trust.

By then a large number of other men had gathered to watch, all of them careful to maintain their distance. Crozier sent Honey and Lane to talk to the others involved, while he and Tozer confronted Jopson.

He was uncertain what to say to his steward, a man who had served him well on this and other occasions.

"You do not deny that you were involved in this unseemly brawl?" he said.

Jopson stood to attention and said, "No, sir," his chin up, his eyes raised above Crozier's head.

"I believe he started it, Mr. Crozier," Tozer said. "I have the word of young Hickey here."

"Is that true, Thomas?" Crozier asked, unaware of what had already happened on the beach.

"Sir," Jopson said.

Crozier turned and took several paces away from him. He did not want to punish the man or to create any further ill feeling among the members of his crew. He joined Honey and Lane, who were then interviewing the others, all of whom now expressed their regret at what had happened. Sait apologized to Wilson for accusing him of cheating and Wilson accepted this apology. If Tozer were not present, Crozier knew, he might now simply caution them all and demand their promises of good behavior in the future.

He returned to Tozer and told him to order his marines back to the *Terror*. Tozer hesitated for a moment before giving the order, uncertain of whether or not he too was being told to return. He understood perfectly Crozier's dilemma, and though he could not despise him for the way in which he sought to resolve the situation, nor could he dismiss from his mind the fact that his own authority had been publicly undermined, and that some form of redress was now required. He looked hard at Jopson, Sait, Wilson and Hickey before turning sharply and joining his men in the boat.

Crozier watched him go, regretting that he might have made an enemy of the man over something so minor. He went to where Hickey was still on his knees and helped him up. He saw the marks on his cheeks where Tozer had held him.

"And you too had a part in all this, Hickey?"

Hickey nodded contritely, relieved that he was not now to be dealt with separately from the others.

"You disappoint me, you all do," Crozier said aloud. He looked at them all as he spoke. "You do right to hang your heads in shame. Take their names, Mr. Honey. Meanwhile, I suggest an extra hour ashore until all these stores are safely gathered in and carried higher above the water line." He turned to their audience. "These others, too, might participate, seeing as how they are so keen to stand and watch."

He walked back to his waiting boat. He was still angry that the situation had not somehow been resolved without his own reluctant intervention, but relieved that it had not warranted any more serious punishment.

The men on the shore stood and watched him without moving, and then, as though at some hidden signal, they all returned to their work of hauling and stacking the stores, those who had been involved in the fight quickly becoming lost in their midst.

•   •   •

They prepared the ships for the onset of winter and for the eventual appearance of ice in their anchorage. Both vessels had been originally built as floating platforms for mortars, and had been powerfully reinforced even before being re-equipped for Arctic service. They were known to their crews as light-built, requiring the minimum of ballast, and were considered by many who had served on them under difficult circumstances as "floaters"—ships which would not sink other than as a result of the worst imaginable damage. Both had sailed and wintered in the ice before, been damaged by it, and escaped to be repaired and to return.

In readiness for the ice now, the *Erebus* was moved closer to the shore, towed rudderless over the shallows until barely two fathoms lay beneath her.

The previous day, Reid and Des Voeux had rowed along this projected course taking soundings and samples every few yards, and on each occasion the scoop had come up filled with a mixture of mud and sand.

Stern anchors were dropped first, and the *Erebus*, moving forward under her slowing momentum, ran aground for a quarter of her length before being winched clear. Once in place she was allowed to drift until she was side on to the shore and then half a dozen mooring ropes were deployed, holding her secure in her new position. Her rudder was lifted and stored close to its brackets, ready to be dropped and bolted in place when the need arose.

The boats then gathered around the *Terror*, and she too was pulled closer to the shore, drawing astern of the *Erebus* before being pulled back and then swung around in the same manner. There was some difficulty this time as the *Terror* ran too far ashore and then had to be tail-shook out of the soft bottom in which she had grounded. Thomas Blanky supervised this, with Reid and Des Voeux relaying his orders to the boats on either side of her. It took four hours to free her, after which she was towed into her own mooring position. The men on the water cheered their success and then sat exhausted by their efforts.

A distance of two hundred yards was measured between the ships—a vital space in the event of one of them being released sooner than the other, or if the pressure and direction of the ice forced them closer together.

Several days later, their upper rigging was dismantled. Gangs of men worked high on both fore and mainmasts, unpegging and unbinding, and using pulleys to lower the yards and timbers to the deck, where these were repaired and stowed away. Lengths of rigging were dropped to the decks in man-high tangles and then carefully separated and coiled; their braces were temporarily slackened.

It was never an easy task to strip a ship of even part of its rigging outside of a dock, but both Franklin and Crozier were pleased with the speed with which this was accomplished, and also at the way in which a new and spartan winter-order was achieved out of such apparent confusion and disarray.

Their main- and fore-sails were left furled, but the remainder of their canvas was taken down. Some of this was stashed on deck to be used later, but the bulk of it was carried below.

Tarpaulins were used to build a roof over each ship, turning their decks into giant tents, further protecting them from the winter winds and outside temperatures.

Three weeks after their arrival at Beechey, these sheets were finally secured in position, cutting out a great deal of the already fading light from the holds. Foresails were set to maintain a steady draught below. Ridge poles were nailed into place between the masts, and guy-ropes thrown over the new canvas roofs to hold them down. To secure the tarpaulins even further, cases and barrels were laid end to end along their lower edges, keeping them taut. These stores were carefully selected: exposed in this manner they would freeze solid within hours once the temperature fell. Kegs of salted meat and vegetables provided the best anchors; all liquids and foodstuffs preserved in brine were kept below and unfrozen.

The work ashore continued apace with the preparation of the ships. The blacksmiths built their forge on the beach and performed all their repairs there.

Several crude dwellings were constructed in the lee of the cliff, but it was never Franklin's intention that these should be occupied in preference to the ships. They were intended only as storerooms and as shelters for the men working ashore. Many hundredweights of canned goods had already been transferred and it was vital that these be afforded some protection against the elements if they were to remain retrievable. It was a great source of pride to Franklin that his expedition was the first to take such quantities of foodstuffs preserved and packaged in this manner. Their barrels of lemon juice and other antiscorbutics remained on board, with only a small emergency cache being transferred to the farthest of the shelters.

Determined to spend their first winter in as orderly a fashion as possible, Franklin ordered that a broad depression on the beach should be used as a rubbish dump, into which all their waste, consisting largely of opened and discarded cans, was to be thrown. A collection and disposal detail was organized, usually reserved as a punishment, whereby a party of four men would collect the refuse from both ships, transport it to the shore on sledges and then haul it to the depression. Later, when it became apparent that this dump might offer temptation to bears looking to fatten up before hibernation, an armed man was added to each detail. As an additional precaution, at least two armed marines were posted on the shore whenever there were others working there.

"Coryphaena hippurus," Harry Goodsir said, holding up the small watercolor upon which he had been working as Fitzjames knocked on the open door of his cabin. "The common dolphin. Having completed my treatise upon the narwhal, I have chosen *hippurus* as my next object of study."

"And after that?" said Fitzjames, amused and intrigued by the way in which the assistant surgeon's mind worked, leaping from one subject to another as though nothing in the natural world were beyond its eventual understanding. It was not the way his own mind worked: he preferred not to concern himself with things which held little interest or relevance for him, choosing instead to consolidate what he did know until he was certain that there was nothing left to surprise or confuse him regarding those few and relevant subjects.

Goodsir was on leave from the Museum of Natural History in Edinburgh where, at the age of twenty-one, he had been appointed its youngest ever curator, having entered university there at fifteen, and having gained his degree four years later. After this he had traveled and studied and written. Upon receiving his appointment in Edinburgh, he had not left the city for three years, and then he had read the works of Scoresby and others on the potential of the Arctic whale fisheries and had found himself drawn to the ice.

Given sufficient time and opportunity, he believed, he would produce the fullest account yet of the natural history of that region.

In addition to his duties alongside Surgeon Stanley, Goodsir spent at least three hours a day writing up his journals, and as much time again in meticulously drawing and painting the specimens he collected. He professed to require no more than four hours' sleep each night, and he frequently stayed up working until two and three in the morning, slept and was then back at his crowded desk by six or seven, his face blackened by the soot from his lamps.

"A very intelligent creature, James," he said, laying the painting on his desk. "As clever, I would imagine, as you or I."

"Surely not as clever as you," Fitzjames said.

Goodsir thought about this for a moment. "Perhaps you're right." He looked at his painting, shook his head at some slight imperfection and then slid it inside a bulging folder.

The walls of his cabin were lined with narrow shelves, each with its restraining bar to prevent the books, bottles, jars, rocks and bones upon them from falling off each time the *Erebus* sailed in a heavy sea. He had also painted a map of their possible route on the low ceiling, a confusing tangle of solid, dashed and dotted lines until one lay in his bunk and looked directly up at it from below.

Fitzjames moved a microscope from a chair and sat down. He filled a pipe and handed his tobacco to Goodsir, who selected a pipe of his own from a rack of thirty by his side.

They had encountered a school of dolphins on their crossing from Orkney to Rona and it was then that Goodsir had chosen to study them. They had appeared in a school of several hundred, surfacing simultaneously and perfectly synchronized in their movements, slicing the water close to both ships.

Gore, upon hearing Goodsir declare that he would begin his study of the creatures that same evening, had offered a reward of a guinea to the first man to spear and bring aboard a healthy specimen, and he presented Goodsir with two less than an hour later.

"They communicate, James, did you know that? I'm not the first to remark on it. They know fear and they know pleasure—the two essential constancies in any life, wouldn't you agree?"

Fitzjames nodded, knowing that it would be pointless to argue now that Goodsir himself was convinced of this fact.

Goodsir then searched among the clutter of his desk and picked up a jar. He unscrewed its cap, took out a piece of whatever was inside, and ate it. He passed the bottle to Fitzjames, inviting him to do the same. "Pickled mango," he said, licking his fingers. "Mango in oil and mustard seed. I picked the fruit myself three years ago." Fitzjames sniffed the contents and declined. Goodsir stood the jar on a shelf beside another in which a small white snake lay coiled in its preserving fluid like a slender root.

"There were some narwhal horns in Whalefish," Fitzjames remarked.

"So I saw. A great pity that they had been carved by such incompetent craftsmen. I would have bought a dozen specimens for the Museum but for the crude and ugly figures and acts that had been scratched upon them in the hope of enhancing their appeal."

A year earlier, determined to understand the effectiveness of the various acknowledged antiscorbutics, Goodsir had lived for a week at a time upon a diet of each, keeping an hourly record of how he felt, of how well his hair and nails grew, of changes in the texture and color of his skin, of his appetite and eyesight, his bladder and bowel movements. His methods and conclusions were criticized, but nothing that was said to him convinced him that he had been wrong to conduct the experiments. It was why he now ate mango pickled in oil and mustard seed, and why he insisted upon eating his own raw pickled offals in preference to the boiled meat and vegetables supplied by the Admiralty.

"I shall work until we sail," he said, removing his reading glasses and rubbing his eyes. Looking up at Fitzjames, he said, "I'm boring you."

Fitzjames denied this.

"Nevertheless, one man's passions are another's—what?"

Fitzjames, too, could think of no immediate comparison.

"A long day," Goodsir said. "Blunt wits. Our passions can save." He pulled open a drawer in his desk. "Except this one."

From the drawer he took out a chess board upon which the pieces were already positioned, held in place by pegs. The game was already well advanced, having so far lasted six days. When time was short or they were too tired to play they set a limit of six moves apiece. Tonight they decided on a dozen.

Fitzjames picked up his surviving knight, and knew immediately from his friend's pursed lips that he had made his first mistake of the evening.

EIGHT

The first of the encroaching ice entered the bay three weeks later. It was a small piece, no larger than one of their boats, but its unobstructed arrival in their sheltered harbor convinced them all that more was soon to follow.

"See how it hesitates," Vesconte said to Fitzjames as the two men watched it approach the shore close to where they were moored. "Almost as though it had entered by mistake and is now uncertain of what to do. A drawing-room, perhaps, a dozen hushed voices at its unannounced and unwelcome appearance."

"Row out and make it welcome," Fitzjames suggested.

"Why exert ourselves? Soon it will run aground, either to thaw in the sun or to lock on to the land and sit out the winter in precisely the same manner as ourselves."

It occasionally occurred to Fitzjames that Vesconte might only have been repeating the words of some character he had encountered in one of the endless novels he read. They had with them a combined library of over eight thousand volumes, dozens of which might at any time be found in the surveyor's cabin. He professed to prefer reading a single page of twenty books at a sitting rather than twenty pages of any one title, and would frequently pull a book from one of his pockets during an idle moment, however short.

At his reference to the sun, Fitzjames turned to see where it hung in the sky above them. Each morning and afternoon he marked the position of its rising and setting. It had long since been losing its light and warmth and would soon be lost to them entirely as the Arctic night announced itself with its first full span of darkness, when the only natural light available to them would be the cold hard glare of the moon. Even in the short time since their arrival the sun was circling considerably lower in the sky, and would soon barely clear the outline of Beechey, rolling across the horizon in a cooling ball, ready to plunge into and be extinguished by the frozen sea.

The small floe-piece ran aground only a few yards from the *Erebus'* bow, and upon being joined by Goodsir, who was keen to collect samples from this advance guard, Fitzjames and Vesconte rowed ashore to inspect it.

Others arrived ahead of them. The ice was new and easily broken, and several men climbed upon it, and the clean white block was quickly reduced to a broken dirty mass.

All the stores that were to be taken ashore had already been delivered there, and following a delay caused by the collapse of one of the shelters, the last of the cases were now being transported beyond the reach of any ice that might ground itself more forcibly.

Two men had been injured when the shelter had collapsed: seaman William Closson had been cut and bruised by a stack of falling crates, and Josephus Geater, slower than Closson in running from the falling wreckage, had had his foot crushed by a forty-gallon barrel of vinegar. He had screamed out at the sudden and unexpected pain of this and then fallen unconscious. Those working nearby rushed to help the two men and pull them clear of the debris. Stanley was sent for, and by the time he arrived Geater had come round, his screams gagged by a cloth forced into his mouth by one of the men now helping him to try and stand. A quick inspection of the shattered foot told Stanley that it would need to be amputated. Surgeon Peddie arrived from the *Terror*, and after his own inspection, he nodded once to let Stanley know that he agreed with him. He had with him his case and administered morphine to ease Geater's pain. A makeshift stretcher was constructed and he was taken back to the *Erebus*.

Peddie stayed with William Closson, attending to his cuts with surgical spirit.

The scattered stores were retrieved and stacked in the open until the pieces of the shelter could be dragged from among them and rebuilt a short distance away from the site of the accident.

Passing Stanley and the injured man on their way ashore, Fairholme and Des Voeux arrived to inspect and report on the damage to Franklin. Two of the *Erebus'* quartermasters, Daniel Arthur and John Downing, had already arrived. Arthur made an inventory and Downing, with the help of others, passed each can and case out of the wreckage and inspected it for damage. Most were discovered to be intact, but several 12-pound cans of fruit had been punctured and their leaking syrup stuck to the hands of the men handling them.

Arthur reported to Franklin. Very little had been lost, and those cans which had been damaged might be used immediately. He appeared reluctant to say anymore, but when urged by Franklin he took a can of peas from his satchel, green liquid seeping from where the container had been holed. The smell of putrefaction was unmistakeable and both men turned away from it. Franklin sent for Des Voeux, who tasted this liquid and then immediately spat it out.

"Just the peas?" he asked Arthur.

Arthur, aware of what was being suggested, called for Downing, and together they studied the inventory. In total there were two thousand cans of peas, half in 12-pound cannisters, half in six.

"And no way of knowing if they were all sealed and cooked in the one batch," Franklin said.

"The damaged fruit tastes fine," Downing said reassuringly.

Not wishing to appear prematurely alarmist, Franklin told Arthur to store the peas separately, away from the other stores. Those which they could prove had turned rotten he ordered destroyed.

Later, he and Des Voeux went to see Stanley and the injured Geater. Sedated but unconscious, Geater insisted that his injuries would not prevent him from continuing his work ashore, but Franklin told him that he was relieved of his duties there. The seaman saluted him from where he lay gasping on Stanley's table.

A flock of several thousand geese and the same number of smaller birds alighted on the island during the night, and the following morning parties went ashore to trap and kill as many as they could before, having rested, the birds continued south.

Gore and Vesconte persuaded Fitzjames to accompany them, and the three men climbed the slope through the birds, few of which made any attempt to escape from them.

"They must be exhausted," Vesconte said, surprised by the birds' apparent lack of fear.

All around them men fired and netted, and back on the beach others were already gutting and plucking the carcasss and hanging them to dry.

"No sport," Gore said, drawing a bead with his pistol on a passing tern without firing.

"And no one ashore from the *Terror*," Vesconte remarked, shielding his eyes and scanning the scene around them.

"Confined to duties aboard," Gore said. "I dined last night with John Irving."

"And?"

"Crozier isn't happy about the way some things are being done."

"Oh?" said Fitzjames, as aware as any of them of Crozier's recent black moods, but unwilling to give any further voice to his own thoughts on the matter.

"Common enough grumbles of confined men," Vesconte said.

"Which won't improve with being confined even further."

"What did John Irving think was the cause?" Fitzjames asked.

"He didn't say. But the consensus of opinion is that you should have been given—"

"Don't," Fitzjames said.

"There's many would agree with that," Vesconte said.

Fitzjames walked ahead of them and they let him go.

It was common knowledge that upon the expedition being proposed and organized, Fitzjames had been considered the man most likely to lead it. Sir John had been thought too old, was too recently retired from the Governership of Van Diemen's Land, and had been too long away from the ice. And Crozier, following his defeats at the South Pole with James Ross, had expressed little interest. Then Franklin, largely at the insistence of his wife, had put himself forward, and Crozier had applied too. Both were senior to Fitzjames, and he had been offered, and accepted, a position subordinate to them both. It angered him that this "usurpation"—although this was not how he himself saw it—was still being discussed among the crews.

"My apologies, James," Vesconte held out his hand.

"Accepted. But it cannot be ignored."

"The man broods, it's in his nature. You and I are fleet of mind and foot, like hunted gazelles. Francis Crozier is a . . . a rhinoceros, happy to bludgeon and curse and moan because he has an impenetrable hide. And happy to unsettle everyone around him just by being there."

"And me?" Gore asked, joining them, and out of breath as the slope grew steeper.

"I think a bear," Vesconte said.

Gore was happy to accept this. "Seriously though, James, Crozier lacks a certain, shall we say, flexibility in some situations. This is not Spithead or the Channel."

"Nor the Mediterranean, more's the pity," Vesconte added in an attempt to help the situation.

"Did John Irving mention anything specific?"

"He thinks Crozier suffers from severe headaches, and that these—"

"He would never allow them to influence his judgment," Fitzjames said. "The Admiralty chose him. We must abide by, and respect their decision." His loyalty and support for the man surprised them both.

A fusillade of shots from close by sent a nervous ripple through the terns and fulmars at their feet, as though the small birds had been physically dislodged and then thrown up by the noise. Fitzjames reached down, picked up a tern and wrung its neck, held it out by its wingtips and then severed its wings to take back for Goodsir. He carefully folded these, fastened them into scrolls with pieces of ribbon, and slid them into the pouch at his side. "He wants a dozen perfect sets," he said.

"Then a dozen he shall have." Gore aimed and fired and brought down a bird which skimmed above them like a paper dart.

Later, when the samples were collected, and as the slaughter went on all around them, increasing in intensity as some of the larger birds struggled to get airborne and leave, the three men sat together on a rise overlooking the bay. Behind them was the shooting range that had been set up, using cans from the dump as targets, and melting down their lead solder for shot.

"You can't ignore it, James," Vesconte said.

"I don't. But nor do I regret the fact that we have Sir John at our head with Crozier his second."

"The man expects too much," Gore said. "I'm sorry, James, but he does. This is very likely going to be his last time in this place and it shows in everything he says and does. He was always John Barrow's favorite. Glory, James, that's what he's here for now. Why do you think he was given this one last opportunity to find it? And it isn't just me saying that. Every one of his officers knows it."

"Which makes him no less of a captain and no less able to do the job entrusted to him."

"Agreed," Vesconte said.

Gore aimed his empty pistol at the distant ships and fired it.

Much later, upon returning to the *Erebus* and delivering the wings to Goodsir, Fitzjames spent the evening alone writing letters. He regretted that the old dispute concerning Crozier's appointment had been brought back into the open, but knew that there was nothing he could now say to the man which would not make matters worse.

He wrote until two in the morning and then fell asleep at his desk. At three he was woken by a steward wrapping a blanket around his shoulders.

Assisted by Goodsir, Stanley amputated Josephus Geater's foot. John Peddie and his own assistant, Alexander Macdonald, arrived from the *Terror* as the preparations for the operation were being made.

"A straightforward enough task," Stanley told them, acknowledging their offer of help. It annoyed him to have so many others crowded into the small room watching him as he worked.

He unwrapped his bag of instruments and tested their sharpness, pulling down his strop and improving the edges of the saw and those knives which did not satisfy him.

Geater's foot was swollen and badly bruised, and despite being heavily sedated he called out at each of Stanley's exploratory prods, and at the smoothing motion of his thumb as Stanley felt beneath the swelling to determine where to make his first cut. He had taken the decision to amputate so soon after the injury because if gangrene was given the chance to take hold then he might be forced to delay by several weeks until the full extent of the contamination had revealed itself. This would greatly reduce his supply of laudanum, and he was convinced that as far as Geater was concerned the end result would be the same.

"Is there no hope of the bones being reset?" Macdonald asked, immediately regretting the remark when he saw the look on Peddie's face.

"A garter cut?" Peddie said to Stanley, as though in apology for his assistant's insensitive blunder.

"I think so. Ankle, shin and the mass of undetermined fractures in the foot itself." He called for Goodsir to fasten his apron around him, and picking up the smallest of his scalpels he bowed his head and said a short prayer for the man on the table.

He began work without speaking to any of them. It was important to cut quickly, to trim away the skin and then to saw through the clean bone and out through the muscle behind before the pain became too great and Geater began thrashing around. Peddie and Macdonald held Geater's shoulders, Peddie also clasping a wet cloth to his face.

Stanley looked at each man and then poured spirit over that part of the leg about to be cut. The blade went in quickly as far as the bone and he slid it deftly both left and right of the line he had chosen. There was little immediate blood, but this began to flow more heavily as he drew back the two lengths of severed skin. He picked up his saw, and positioning it on the exposed bone, he drew it back a few inches to feel the teeth bite and then pushed it quickly forward.

Geater screamed and Macdonald lost his grip on his shoulder, fumbling and grabbing at it as Geater tried to struggle free. Peddie pushed the cloth he held into Geater's mouth. He leaned close to his ear and spoke to him. Stanley continued sawing. Blood flowed from the cut on to the cloths mounded beneath. Goodsir pulled tighter on the straps holding Geater's thigh, releasing the one around his calf as he felt the bone finally give and as the saw passed through into the softer flesh behind. Stanley immediately took up a knife, and supporting that part of the leg he had already almost severed, he cut through the remaining tendons and skin with a succession of short slashes. The foot and shin came away completely and he let it fall to the floor. Goodsir released another of the straps, and with only a single tourniquet remaining at Geater's groin, the flow of blood suddenly increased, spurting over his own and Stanley's apron.

At Geater's head, Alexander Macdonald began to retch.

Stanley took a bowl of diluted spirit and threw it over Geater's exposed stump. Geater screamed again and then passed out. Taking advantage of this respite, Stanley stood back from the patient. Relieved of his part in the proceedings, Goodsir went to the door and called for Philip Reddington, who had been waiting outside.

Reddington came in with a small bowl of molten pitch intended as a temporary seal for the wound in its antiseptic state and to stem the flow of blood. There had been no improvement on this crude and simple remedy for as long as Stanley had been practicing, and it fell to the ship's caulker to assist in this final, and often fatal, part of the operation.

Stanley poured the pitch, adding more spirit as this congealed and then set firm over the exposed flesh. Later he would peel it off using paraffin. He built up the thickening liquid in layers until Geater's leg came to resemble the ball of a pollarded willow, and the scent of burning was added to the already overpowering smell of the spirit and pitch. Pungent smoke marbled the cabin.

Instructing Peddie and Macdonald to release their grip on Geater, Stanley looked more closely at the unconscious man. He opened his eyelids and felt his pulse. He pressed his palm to Geater's soaked and burning forehead and then lifted the thigh of the sawn leg, peeling hardened splashes of pitch from the table before laying it back down.

Alexander Macdonald asked to leave and then ran from the room with both hands over his mouth.

Retrieving the amputated foot from where it had fallen, Goodsir examined it.

At a signal from Stanley, Reddington called for four men to carry Geater from the surgery to the bed which had been prepared for him in the forward hold.

When the patient was gone, Peddie apologized to Stanley for the behavior of his assistant. Stanley said nothing; instead he collected the cloths from the table and the floor and stuffed them into a sack for burning. He washed his bloody instruments, scraped the last of the pitch from the table and doused the bloodstains with cold water. Then John Weekes the carpenter was sent for and shown the severed leg to help him judge the length of the peg to be fitted to Geater's stump.

NINE

The ice came slowly, a few small floe-pieces as hesitant as the first, drifting into the double bay from both the east and the west and then grounding in the shallows or running ashore on the beach or the spit of land. But gradually, the size and number of these pieces increased, and new watches were stationed at both points of entry.

James Reid had led the first party to their most distant outlook on the west Devon coast, following in the footprints of Vesconte and his surveying party, and then meeting the men as they made their way back down to the ships.

On their second day ashore Edward Little had fallen and slid eighty feet down a scree slope. He protested that he was uninjured, but had afterward walked with a painful limp. He was helped down the hillside now by Gore and Irving.

The climb to the peak overlooking Wellington Channel took three hours. With Reid went Des Voeux and John Bridgens, steward. They left Vesconte's path and turned west, reaching a point at which the broad expanse of water beyond Devon was finally revealed to them in its entirety.

It surprised Reid to see how much of this was already filled with ice; equally surprising to him was the extent to which this had closed all around them in their sheltered backwater, surrounding them entirely and ready now to move in on them. Bergs larger than the ships drifted along the edges of the pack, collided with it and were either shattered or pushed forward by it. Watching this, it became clear to

Reid that their own harbor would freeze over sooner than they had anticipated, and he became concerned that the pressure of the ice arriving from the west did not push a wall of bergs in upon them from which they would later be unable to extricate themselves. He kept these thoughts to himself.

Bridgens called out that he thought he could see a vessel in Wellington Channel, but this turned out to be only a dark cap upon a large berg already run aground.

It was mid-afternoon and the light was fading as they began their descent to the *Erebus* across the isthmus, where they saw that in addition to the smaller bergs drifting in upon them, the water of the bay was freezing around its edges for the first time.

Four days later it had frozen outward from the shore to a distance of a hundred yards, thickening as it spread, until three days after that it was found to be solid to a depth of two feet and capable of supporting the weight of a man and his loaded sledge.

It also began to form outward from the two ships, until a precarious pathway existed between them. Props were sunk into this thickening ice to keep the vessels level as they rose and then froze into position. The *Erebus* remained at an even keel, but the *Terror*, standing in water a fathom deeper, began to list to starboard as the ice gathered beneath her. Crozier ordered her to be winched closer to the shore, using boat parties to break the ice ahead of her. She was anchored when her keel touched the soft bottom again, and her own boats and those of the *Erebus* waited alongside her all day and into the night as the ice re-formed beneath her hull. In this way they settled her level, and instead of rising beneath her, the adjacent ice was cut loose and allowed to mound into ridges a few feet from her sides.

Two men were taken ill during this time—John Torrington, stoker on the *Terror*, and John Hartnell, a seaman on the *Erebus*. Alerted by the appearance and the persistent symptoms shown by Hartnell, Stanley could only conclude that he was suffering from the onset of scurvy. At first he refused to believe this: no one else was suffering, and Hartnell had been eating fresh food and taking his lemon juice, of which twice the usual ration had so far been administered in an effort to build up a greater degree of protection against the disease when it eventually did appear among them.

Hartnell lost weight. His joints ached and he bruised easily; he became listless and enervated. Reporting all this to Franklin, Stanley conferred with Peddie, who told him of the identical symptoms in Torrington. Both surgeons knew that the disease seldom struck isolated individuals, but afflicted whole crews to varying degrees, and it was Peddie who made the alarming suggestion that if the cause of the men's suffering *was* scurvy, then their lemon juice or other antiscorbutics were considerably less potent than they had been led to believe. Franklin ordered a cask of the juice to be brought to his cabin, and in the company of Crozier, Fitzjames and the two surgeons, he opened it and ladled out its contents for them to sample. They all declared it to be fresh and strong. It had not frozen or diluted itself, and nor had it been contaminated in any way. After a year or two in the cask it would begin to congeal into a glutinous ball at its center, but as yet it showed no signs of doing so.

Reassured, Franklin resealed the cask.

Stanley suggested that the two men might be suffering from some kind of food poisoning, and this, in view of the spoiled food which had already been brought to light and destroyed, seemed a more likely explanation. Franklin asked his surgeons if anyone else had reported sick to them, and was told that three or four men on each vessel had reported stomach cramps, vomiting and loss of appetite.

The sun finally dipped below the horizon on the 21st of November. Some were unsettled by the change from light to dark, and all, regardless of their previous internments, were made cautious by it. To some, the full moon seemed to be as bright as the waning sun.

The ice, which had earlier been so noisy as it moved into place along its channels around them, was now almost completely silent. Occasionally it cracked in the darkness with the sound of a pistol being fired, and with the same wooden echo of a gunshot; and sometimes it fell in sheets from the cliff faces, collapsing into powder before it hit the ground below. Sometimes it murmured in the distance with the noise of an approaching crowd, and those who heard this for the first time swore they could detect the voices of others in it calling out to them. More than one man on watch made a fool of himself by calling back in answer to these voices, convinced he had established contact with someone when all he had done was pick up the returning echo of one of his own companions.

A fortnight later Christmas wreaths and decorations were hung on the covered decks of both ships. The path between the vessels was marked with stakes and macadamized with coal ash from their boilers and ovens.

Their tenting was doubled and reinforced, and by the time the first of the bad weather arrived both ships were ready to withstand it. Ice formed quickly in the rigging and on the exposed areas of deck, sealing canvas and rope to wood and preventing all draughts from penetrating below. A thick, insulating layer was allowed to build up, to thaw and refreeze into an impregnable protective coating, and this too was strengthened with scattered ash.

It gathered a foot deep on their vaulted roof and then in twelve-foot drifts against their hulls, through which corridors were cut for the men to take their daily exercise on the land and frozen sea. On the coldest days this amounted to no more than running the short distance from one vessel to the other and back again, but whenever the weather was kinder to them they spent several hours outside, collecting supplies by the light of the moon or exploring the changed contours of the world around them.

On Christmas Eve a service was held on the ice and the enclosed bay was filled with their singing voices.

Two sides of frozen ox were roasted, and forty of their geese slaughtered. The cook Richard Wall made a pudding in the shape of the island and in the vanilla sauce at its base he floated two small cinnamon ships. Toasts were drunk to the Queen and to those left at home.

Fitzjames wrote in his journal that he doubted if he had ever celebrated a more joyful or hopeful Christmas. He wrote an eighteen-page letter to his sister and opened the gift of books, knitted socks and waterproof cape she and her husband had sent with him. In addition to this she had given him a Fortnum and Mason's hamper, instructing him not to open it until Christmas Day, having chosen its contents so that none would spoil in the meantime. Some men unwrapped fruit cakes baked for them by their wives, and these they cut and ate with the greatest fondness of all.

The cabins and quarters remained decorated for the full twelve days of Christmas.

On New Year's Eve a concert was given, in which some sang and others recited. A small drama titled "Arctic Light" was enacted, featuring both Neptune the dog and Jacko the monkey. Goodsir produced a shadow-play telling a tale of piracy, and Gore performed a magic show, producing fresh eggs from his ears and mouth until a dozen filled his cap.

John Torrington died on New Year's Day. He had remained weak and barely conscious for a fortnight, eating nothing, drinking little, and continuing to lose weight and the will to live.

During the celebrations of the previous evening Peddie had sat with him, knowing he was close to death, every hour checking his heartbeat and weakening pulse. He died at four in the morning, and at nine the surgeon reported the death to Crozier, who refused permission for an autopsy to be carried out, insisting instead that the body be prepared for immediate burial, either later that same day or the one following. In this, however, he was thwarted by a snowstorm which began to blow around them at noon and which lasted for six days.

On board the *Erebus*, the condition of John Hartnell also continued to worsen. He was attended by Goodsir, and by his brother Thomas, another seaman, whom Franklin had excused his duties so that he might attend to his younger brother's needs. There was no doubt in Goodsir's mind that Hartnell was dying of whatever it was that had already killed John Torrington.

During the six claustrophobic days of the storm, of which he saw and heard nothing, Hartnell remained conscious. He had lost weight at an alarming rate during the past month and was now little more than a skeleton. Sores had erupted the full length of his back, and his knees and elbows were stiff and painful to bend. He had lost many of his teeth, and each time he coughed or tried to speak those remaining rattled in their sockets. His gums had wasted, and were now almost transparent in places. He ate nothing, but was able to swallow half a cupful of thin broth twice a day, spoon-fed to him by his brother. The two men had served together for the past five years, and it was a painful ordeal for Thomas Hartnell to watch his brother decline and waste in this manner.

Following the death of Torrington, it was also obvious to Goodsir that only the will to live in the company of his brother kept John Hartnell alive. But eventually this was not enough, and he died during the afternoon of January the 4th.

Goodsir reported the death to Stanley, who immediately told Franklin. Like Crozier, Franklin ordered the body prepared for burial, but then changed his mind and acceded to Goodsir's request to perform an autopsy.

Thomas Hartnell gave his permission. He undressed his dead brother and washed his body. He combed his hair and picked out the loose strands which came away in his comb. Defeated in his task of improving the appearance of the discolored and emaciated corpse, he knelt and prayed until Goodsir returned to start work upon it.

The procedure was swift and straightforward. An incision was made running vertically from the breastbone to the navel, and then two further cuts were made from this toward the thigh bones, creating an inverted Y. Goodsir then peeled back the skin and dry flesh beneath to examine the organs inside. The stomach had shrunk to a withered sac, and the intestines were desiccated and ruptured in several places. He was not convinced that either of these had caused Hartnell's death, believing them to be the consequence of some other, greater debilitation. He himself was now certain that both Torrington and Hartnell had suffered some kind of poisoning, possibly as a result of sharing an illicit meal of contaminated food during their time ashore together. The liver and both kidneys were darker and harder than normal, the former enlarged to the point where it could be seen pressing up into Hartnell's skin. Goodsir removed this and made an exploratory cut along its full length. Inside it was darker still, and its consistency unlike any other he had seen.

He was joined by Stanley, curious as to his findings. The surgeon was not convinced of the need for the investigation, knowing that its results would remain inconclusive. No written report was to be made of the autopsy.

"Definitely not scurvy," Stanley said, leaning closer to examine the opened liver, and to lift out both kidneys and prod them with his thumb in the palm of his hand. He opened Hartnell's closed eyes and kneaded the flesh of his face, noting the marks this left. He was easily able to pull out another tooth, inspect it and then push it back into its socket.

Goodsir agreed with him, even though many of the symptoms corresponded with those of long-term scurvy sufferers.

"That, I think, is all we need to know," Stanley said, dropping the kidneys back into the open flesh.

Goodsir was annoyed that Stanley, Franklin, Crozier and Peddie had all arrived at the same expedient and reassuring conclusion before he began his investigation. He had asked Crozier to reconsider and let him perform the same operation on John Torrington, but again Crozier had refused, and Franklin had been unwilling to pursue the matter on his behalf.

"The stomach," Stanley said.

"Empty." Goodsir raised the limp bag and severed its connecting pipes.

"Then poisoned by what? A single can of food, an unfortunate coincidence?"

Goodsir could not deny this. He continued his examination of the liver, and after this the spleen, frustrated that no other explanation had so far suggested itself to him.

"I think you might close up the body," Stanley said as he washed his hands and prepared to leave. "And I think we might all say our prayers that no one else has so far exhibited any symptoms."

Goodsir nodded his agreement. He returned the organs and then pulled the flaps of skin back into position, securing these with a dozen crude stitches and replacing Hartnell's shirt and trousers before calling for his brother to resume his funeral preparations.

Coffins were built and tin plaques nailed to their lids. Wooden markers were carved for both men, containing the simple details of their names, ages, and the date they died. John Hartnell had been twenty-five, John Torrington twenty.

The bodies were dressed and their arms bound to their sides. A blue woolen blanket was wrapped around John Torrington, and Hartnell was folded inside a canvas shroud.

Loaded on to sledges, the two coffins were hauled to the beach.

The bay had been swept clean of loose ice by the strong winds, and everything was now etched in black and gray, with the occasional silvering of the ice where the half moon revealed itself through the liquid cloud.

Lanterns were set out on the beach to guide the coffin bearers through the darkness, and upon their arrival at the gravesite Franklin read the speech he had prepared.

It began to snow again as the ceremony progressed. Hartnell's grave needed to be widened by a few inches, and sparks flew from the picks of the men chopping at the hard ground.

The snow began to fall more thickly, and at times the ships beneath them were lost to sight. A sense of urgency overtook the proceedings, but Franklin was determined that the burial should be carried out properly, and that both men should be laid to rest with as much propriety and ceremony as they would have received at home. He had examined their Service Certificates, knowing that he must later write letters of sympathy and regret to their families; it was with some relief that he saw neither man was married.

The graves were filled and the excess gravel built into low mounds above them. The markers were driven into place and stones collected to build borders.

When the final prayers were said, Crozier dismissed his own officers and returned with Franklin to the *Erebus*, where the two men remained alone together for the rest of the day.

The two unaccountable deaths had cast a small but inescapably dark shadow over the otherwise auspicious start to the expedition.

Crozier expressed his surprise that Franklin had allowed Goodsir to carry out his examination, but Franklin dismissed this veiled criticism by insisting that it needed to be done. Crozier remained unconvinced.

Occasionally, steward Hoar arrived to add fuel to the stove and to bring them drinks. When he called for a final time at midnight, Franklin asked him how the other men had taken the two deaths. Hoar said that the crew was pleased that the burials were over and that the taint of sickness was at last gone from the ship. Crozier said that his own crew felt the same. Only Thomas Hartnell continued to grieve.

When Fitzjames called at half past midnight to report some slight damage to the foremast rigging, both Franklin and Crozier were asleep in their chairs, the cabin as warm as a furnace.

TEN

One of the first tasks Franklin had ordered upon establishing their winter quarters was for as much of their coal as possible to be unloaded from the ships and for this to be mounded on the shore. When the weather allowed, sledge parties went daily from both vessels and returned with their immediate requirements, which they stored in their fore-deck bunkers. In this way both Franklin and Crozier hoped to keep their ships clean. Prior to its removal, the fine dust had spread everywhere and had been a constant source of irritation to the two captains, both of whom had been raised and schooled under sail alone.

At the beginning of each week the decks of both ships were cleaned with hot sand, heated overnight in the galley ovens, and scrubbed dry from stern to prow, where the sand was then collected and bagged for further use.

One other day every week was set aside for doing the laundry, when the ships' coppers were set out and each man delivered a bundle of clothes to be washed. Cleanliness was considered to have an important civilizing influence under those conditions, and for this same reason men were also encouraged to shave their beards, mustaches and side-whiskers on a regular basis, and to submit to the weekly dental inspections carried out by both surgeons. It was uncommon for beards to be worn on Arctic duty, because rather than protect exposed skin, as was first believed, the hair encouraged the formation of ice. Even the moisture from breathing froze hard when the temperature was low, threatening the skin beneath with ice sores if not regularly rubbed away.

As the weather deteriorated throughout January and February, warrant officers were appointed to keep a watch on all the individuals and working parties who went ashore or out on the ice. A system of handing out and then collecting metal tags—in reality drilled and punched coins devised by paymaster Osmer—was used to ensure that no one remained unaccounted for when the call to return aboard was sounded at three each afternoon.

The first occasion this system proved its worth was when one of the *Terror*'s stewards failed to return from the most distant of the stores with a sack of cocoa beans he had set out to collect.

It had been a calm day, with a temperature of minus 35, no higher or lower than the previous fortnight, and if not actually lit by the light of the sun, then a day that suggested to all who ventured out that this was shortly to return to them.

At three, warrant officer John Lane checked his drilled coins and saw that he was one short. The missing man, Edward Genge, had been seen by others making his way to the store.

At half past three, Lane reported the absence to Crozier, who suggested that Tozer be informed. Crozier himself believed that an error had been made and that Genge would be in the galley or in his hammock. A search was carried out, but Genge was not found, after which Lane, Tozer and two other marines left the *Terror* and went ashore.

The temperature had fallen rapidly since midday, and halfway between the shore and the storehouse, Lane and one of the marines turned back, both insufficiently dressed against the cold. Only Lane went back out on the frozen sea to await the return of the others.

Tozer reappeared a few minutes later, carrying a man over his shoulder, running as fast as the weight would allow and frequently stumbling and falling. The other marine followed behind pulling a sledge. Lane ran over the ice to meet them, taking the unconscious Genge's legs and running with Tozer back to the *Terror*, where the alarm was raised and Peddie prepared a bed in his surgery to receive the injured man.

Almost unbelievably, it seemed that Genge had entered the store, smoked a pipe, and there, amid the mounds of casks and crates, and well insulated from the outside, had fallen asleep. Later, the door had blown open, and when Tozer had found him, Genge was unconscious. Unsuccessfully attempting to revive him where he lay, Tozer had then lifted him and carried him back to the ship.

Genge remained unconscious for several hours longer, and upon coming round was fed three pints of warm broth and informed that he was to be punished for his carelessness.

The following morning the store was revisited and sealed, and afterward there was a suggestion that Genge and others had been pilfering from the supplies of canned goods kept there. Upon these suspicions becoming common knowledge, an inquiry was set in motion with Fitzjames at its head, assisted by Vesconte and Fairholme.

Fitzjames interviewed Genge and, badly shaken by his near fatal carelessness, Genge confessed that he and several others had been supplying men on both ships with food extra to their rations.

Reporting all this to Franklin, both Fitzjames and his captain were dismayed that such corruption and disregard for the well-being of the expedition as a whole should already be present, and Franklin was determined that all the facts of the thefts should be brought into the open before others were charged with their part in them, and before any punishment was decided upon.

Genge, it transpired, was working with one of the *Erebus'* marines, William Braine, in the supply of these foodstuffs to both crews.

Confronted with his partner's sick-bed confession, Braine immediately admitted his part in the scheme. He was genuinely remorseful for what he had done, his shame and disgrace all that much greater for his being a marine. He was handed over for punishment to David Bryant, who sought permission to flog him. Both Franklin and Fitzjames reluctantly agreed to this, and the punishment was carried out ashore, without an audience other than that of the marines and the men of the inquiry party. Fitzjames marked off each of the dozen strokes in the punishment book, and called for warm water to be thrown on Braine's bleeding back after the fourth and eighth stroke. Braine fell unconscious after the tenth, and the final two strokes were delivered by simply laying the whip across his back.

Later, upon reporting to Fitzjames that he had dressed Braine's wounds, Stanley informed him that the man was also showing symptoms similar to those of Hartnell and Torrington. Alarmed by this, Fitzjames reported the news to Franklin, for whom it came as yet another painful disappointment after the events of the previous few days, during which he had slept for only two or three hours each night, and who himself now looked unwell, exhausted and drawn.

Communicating this news, it was clear to Fitzjames that Franklin did not wish to discuss the matter any further, and so he returned to Stanley, who had by then been joined by Goodsir.

"I've spoken to him," Goodsir said, meaning Braine. "Hartnell and Torrington were involved."

Fitzjames already knew this, but only then did the full significance of the fact—two names among two dozen others—strike him. "Have you found some contaminated food common to them all?" he asked.

Neither Stanley nor Goodsir answered him and he was aware of some reluctance on the part of both men to speak.

"What is it?"

"Mr. Goodsir believes it may be connected with the canning process and not necessarily the food itself," Stanley said, suggesting that he did not share his assistant's belief.

"Whatever it is, we may be able to isolate it," Goodsir said more optimistically. "Even if it were somehow connected with the cannisters themselves we might yet find a way—"

"But so many of our supplies are canned," Fitzjames said.

"So were Ross,' so were Parry's. Ross opened cans of soup and meat ten years old and found them as nutritious and as untainted as the day they were canned," Goodsir said.

Their ensuing conversation lasted an hour, ending only when Stanley rose and left them, promising to approach Franklin concerning the treatment and observation of Braine.

"How was the flogging?" Goodsir asked Fitzjames when they were alone, and after they had sat for several minutes in silent contemplation of all that had been suggested.

"I've seen too many to tell you it was barbaric."

"But do you believe it was necessary?"

Fitzjames nodded once.

"And having headed the inquiry, you consider yourself responsible for what happened to the man?"

"I *am* responsible," Fitzjames said.

Goodsir did not pursue the painful subject. Instead, he took down a flask and shook from it a marble of ice, studying it in his palm before handing it to Fitzjames.

"Another of your specimens?" Fitzjames said, taking it from him, still distracted, and less intrigued than usual by what his friend was about to reveal.

"No—one of Scoresby's."

At the mention of the name, Fitzjames examined the ball more closely: it was old and opaque, and seemed no more than a piece of moulded ice in which some impurities, grains of sand or silt, had been frozen.

From a label attached to the flask, Goodsir told him the exact date twenty-eight years earlier when Scoresby had collected the ice, and the precise location of the berg in Baffin Bay from which it had come.

As the ice melted, Fitzjames felt the impurities settle in his palm. Goodsir took his hand and blew away much of the water. Then leaning close he breathed upon the few dozen grains which lay exposed. He withdrew, and Fitzjames looked more closely at what he held. The specks which had been at the heart of the icy kernel appeared to agitate, and then to his amazement, and all within no more than five or ten seconds, each of the tiny black dots sprouted a set of minute legs and metamorphosed into a spider. In an instant the two dozen insects had scattered in all directions over his fingers and beneath the cuff of his sleeve.

Watching him, Goodsir burst into laughter. He caught one of the spiders, squashed it on his thumbnail and held it up for Fitzjames to see. He told him its forgettable Latin name, but nothing could distract Fitzjames from the sudden and almost casual resurrection in which he had participated, all thought of the flogging now gone from his mind.

"Twenty-eight years?" he said absently, catching another of the insects and then watching it drop from an invisible thread close to his-face, swinging from side to side on the draught of his breath.

"Perhaps a hundred and twenty-eight years," Goodsir told him. "Who knows? Perhaps even a thousand and twenty-eight years."

"Are you serious?"

"Perfectly, and it is my intention to retrieve further specimens."

"Do you believe they can survive for so long without food or air?"

Still grinning, Goodsir nodded. "These otherwise intolerable conditions suit them perfectly. I melted another of Scoresby's samples in Edinburgh, caught its occupants in a glass tube at room temperature and they never revived. They thrive only in the cold. Even now this latest clutch will be making its way outside."

"To lay their eggs and wait another hundred years?"

"Very possibly. Endure, survive, thrive." Goodsir returned the flask to the shelf from which he had taken it. "Did you know," he said, causing Fitzjames, who had risen to leave, to pause for a moment, "that the recent excavators of Pompeii came across the petrified bodies of the city guards still standing to attention at each of the gates and in the doorways of all the public buildings? All around them was panic and mayhem, but these men, perfectly alert and aware of everything that was happening, of the red-hot ash pouring down upon them, remained standing to attention even as they were being buried alive and the flesh burned from their bones. Incredible."

"And is that how you imagine *we* might all one day be discovered? Locked in the ice, our palms to our brows, peering into the distance of the Passage."

"Cabot, Frobisher, Davis."

"What of them?" Fitzjames said, stooping in the low doorway.

"They all sailed into the ice in vessels sheathed with lead so convinced were they of emerging into a warm tropical sea full of not so warm-hearted tropical boring worms."

Fitzjames considered this for a moment, and was in some uncertain way gratified by the revelation and the common bond of faith it exposed, as fleeting but as undeniable as the miracle of the spiders which still ran up his arm.

Ever since his fall two months earlier, Edward Little had been unable to walk any distance on his injured leg, and recently the pain from this had grown worse. On board the *Terror* this was of little inconvenience to him, but ashore and on the ice it now caused him pain even to stand upon it.

On one occasion, walking with Irving and Hodgson on a fishing expedition to where a hole had been cut in the ice of the outer bay, he fell and lay clutching his leg in agony, having done his best until then to disguise the pain from the others. They helped him to his feet and then supported him as they made their way back to the *Terror*. Little asked them not to let anyone know what had happened, but Irving argued that Peddie ought to make another examination of the injured limb. Reluctantly, Little agreed, and the surgeon was sent for.

The original swelling had barely subsided, and Peddie expressed his surprise at this, realizing immediately the extent of Little's prolonged suffering and deception. The earlier, darker bruising was reduced, but the skin all around this remained discolored and could not be dismissed as easily as Little would have liked.

Upon hearing of what had happened, Crozier came to see for himself, and Irving and Hodgson stepped outside to make room for him in Peddie's surgery. Expecting him to repeat their own reassurances, they were surprised when he became critical of Little and accused him of endangering the men under his command by his inability to respond to any unexpected emergency. Little, too, was surprised by the harshness of this, but said nothing in his own defense.

"What is it, a break, a fracture, what?" Crozier asked Peddie.

Peddie, unhappy at his role of mediator, said that it was unlikely to be either. Even the smallest fracture and the leg would tolerate no weight whatsoever upon it. So far during his examination he had administered no pain-reliever, and Little's face was bathed in sweat.

Peddie finally conceded that a bone may have been cracked and that it had not mended because it had not been immediately bound and rested. He cleaned the swelling with iodine and bandaged it. Until this was fully healed, Little would have to walk with a stick.

When Fitzjames heard of these developments he asked John Weekes, the *Erebus'* carpenter, to make a stick, the head of which was to resemble the head of the monkey, which now spent most of its time in Little's cabin, and which he cared for and fed.

Crozier complained to Franklin about Little's deceit in not informing him of the injury sooner, and Franklin could do no more than repeat Peddie's reassurances that the otherwise healthy young lieutenant would be fully recovered by the time they were ready to prise themselves free and sail into the disintegrating ice to the south. He invited him to remain on board the *Erebus* for dinner, but Crozier declined. He apologized for being poor company. He seemed to Franklin to be distracted, unable to focus on the matter at hand.

They parted out on the ice, where a flock of raucous ravens hopped over the frozen surface around them, some of the birds following Crozier on his way back to the *Terror*, as though believing he might at any moment pluck a handful of food from his pocket and throw it down for them.

ELEVEN

Their first storm of the new year arrived at the end of March, a month after the reappearance of the sun. On the day it came, the Devon watch, including Fitzjames and Vesconte, was descending in single file to the bay below when the wind overtook them from the north and a curtain of snow drove into them from behind, engulfing them completely and making it impossible to see more than a few paces ahead. Fitzjames called for them to gather together, knowing that they were in danger of losing their path back to the ships. There were no precipices, but the slope was steep, and anyone who fell and was afterward unable to call out for help might be quickly and irretrievably lost to them. They covered their faces and put on their goggles. A rope was tied to the waist of each man, leaving only an arm's length between them.

They descended further and the slope became firmer and less steep. Dropping into a sheltered hollow, they met a party led by John Irving. The lights of the ships were pointed out to them, and Fitzjames was surprised to see how far away these were, and not directly ahead of them as he had supposed. They had turned from their path in the storm and were walking downhill on a slope parallel to the shore. They had been spotted by men on the ice below and this rescue party had been sent to guide them down.

Within a quarter of an hour they were back on the frozen sea and crossing it to the ships.

All around them, men carrying and hauling provisions ran across the ice shouting to each other. Their smaller boats were hoisted back on board, and the larger ones secured more firmly where they sat in the open.

Only two days earlier, the lookouts over Wellington had for the first time reported movement in the winter ice, raising hopes for an early release. Unnavigable leads had opened in the pack and then closed again, and slabs of ice had risen almost vertically from the water and been neatly stacked ashore like so many paving slabs waiting to be laid.

Upon receiving these reports, Fitzjames and Vesconte had returned to the observation post with the new watch and witnessed for themselves these first, premature signs of the new season.

It seemed improbable to them that such a depth of ice—calculated by Vesconte to be between forty and fifty feet thick in places—could be so suddenly or so easily released, split and cast aside as though it were only inches deep. In some places the open water ran directly upon the shore. Geysers of foam rose where the blocks of ice collided, and the air, calm before the approaching storm, was filled with the hollow booming of countless unseen fractures and collisions.

Now Fitzjames and Vesconte met Franklin and Gore on the ice, inspecting the iron staves to which the *Erebus'* mooring ropes were attached. Gore believed that somewhere in the shallow bay, water was already moving beneath the ice, threatening to fracture it and add to the confusion and danger. Only inches apart, the four men were forced to shout to one another to make themselves heard as the snow now drove around them as fiercely as it had blasted the exposed hillside.

Franklin gave the order to his mates and quartermasters to call a halt to the gathering of stores and for everyone to return aboard. He left his officers to supervise the tightening of the guy ropes over their tented roof, calling for a stowing detail to clear the decks of all their detritus of the previous few weeks.

Fitzjames, Vesconte and Gore assisted in the collecting of the last of their provisions from the Beechey shore. Several of the redundant storehouses had already been dismantled, and the casks and cases now scattered on the beach were in danger of being buried and lost.

A crate containing the last of their live geese was dropped on the ice, breaking and releasing its captives. Two were recaptured immediately, but the rest were plucked away by the strong wind and lost.

Marker lanterns were torn from their posts, spilled their fuel and erupted in brief gaseous flames before being extinguished. There was some panic as men ashore were cut off from their companions and their calls for help were lost on the wind. Many abandoned their loads and raced unencumbered back to the safety of the ships.

Fitzjames and Gore encountered Reid and Blanky returning from their own watch over Barrow Strait. The ice here had not yet started to break, but that moving out of the west and the north was already piling up along the precipitous southern shore.

Gore expressed his concern about the movement of water beneath the ice in the bay and the two ice-masters went with him on to the sea and knelt to listen to it. Reid retrieved a crowbar from an abandoned sledge and struck the surface in several places, and both he and Blanky listened intently to the notes this produced.

Around them the running and shouting men quickly decreased in number. Chains were formed to take aboard the provisions which had so far been collected. By now conversation had become impossible, and the wind could be felt through even the thickest clothing. Vesconte tried to ask Reid what he had discovered about the ice, but Reid signaled with a hand over his mouth that he could not speak. Ice had already collected on the faces of all five men.

They were among the last back aboard, climbing with what little they had managed to retrieve. They brushed the snow from each other's backs and shoulders.

The canvas roof had so far held fast, and beneath it they no longer had to shout so loudly. The tenting was pulled taut, occasionally released to hang slack for a few seconds, and then sucked suddenly back out again with an alarming crack.

Further preparations continued into the night. Their bunkers were filled and their condensers and filters cleaned in readiness for their prolonged confinement.

Outside, after a month during which the noon temperature had rarely fallen below minus 30, figures of minus 50 were recorded on both ships. The mercury froze in their thermometers.

For six days there was no communication between the *Erebus* and the *Terror*. On the seventh, even though the storm still blew, a party of four men, comprising Fitzjames, Reid, Sergeant Bryant and Corporal Paterson, made the hazardous journey over the buried ice to the *Terror*.

The new surface accumulations lay ten feet deep in places, blown and collected in disorientating drifts over the ice beneath. One of the last tasks accomplished before the two ships had been shut down was the connection of a single hawser between them. This was still attached to the rail of the *Erebus*, and Fitzjames sought for it as he waded through the snow, eventually locating it and lifting it free.

It took them an hour to complete the short journey, and upon reaching the *Terror* they communicated their arrival by banging on the hull until ladders were lowered for them.

Once aboard, Fitzjames reported to Crozier, delivering a message from Franklin and explaining how they were coping aboard the *Erebus*. Crozier compiled a list of damage and injuries for him to take back to the ship.

They were joined by Peddie and Macdonald. The surgeon expressed his concern over four men who had been taken ill with influenza, and showed no sign of improvement since their confinement. He asked about William Braine, and Fitzjames told him that both Stanley and Goodsir now agreed that the marine would shortly die of the same ailment which had taken Torrington and Hartnell.

Crozier asked Fitzjames to convey his compliments to Franklin, and his hopes that the imprisoning storm would blow itself out in time for himself and his officers to make the journey to the *Erebus* in a week's time to celebrate Sir John's sixtieth birthday.

Fitzjames and his party left and made their return journey along the hawser. From a distance both ships were reduced to hummocks of snow, distinguishable only in outline, and by their masts. Neither showed any lights in the strong wind, and it would not, Fitzjames believed, have been difficult to convince himself that they were already empty hulks which had drifted abandoned and unnoticed into this desolate backwater so far from the eyes and concerns of the world.

When the weather finally cleared, William Braine's body was carried ashore and buried alongside Hartnell and Torrington. The marine had died three days earlier, his corpse dressed and wrapped and taken to the *Erebus'* forward hold, where it froze within an hour of being laid out. He had been thirty-three and was the first of the expedition's fatalities to leave behind him a widow and orphans. His belongings were auctioned, and the proceeds from the sales collected by Osmer to return to his dependents along with his back pay. A copper plaque was nailed to his coffin lid, upon which the details of his company were engraved. Chiseled upon his wooden headboard was a quote chosen by Franklin from Joshua 26.

With the return of the better weather, Franklin's birthday was celebrated. Crozier presented him with a new looking-glass incorporating tinted glass to reduce ice-blink, commissioned by him from Selles and Walker at Sir John Barrow's suggestion. He also handed over greetings cards entrusted to him a year previously by all the members of the Arctic Council. From Fitzjames, Franklin received a new Bible, bound in calf and embossed with gold, its pages also gold-edged, adding to its appearance of authority and solidity.

Perhaps strangest of all Franklin's gifts was the photograph he received from Graham Gore, made the previous September when they had first gone ashore on Beechey. Still unconvinced of his expertise or of the value of his work, this portrait of Sir John was Gore's most successful picture so far. In the glass plate, Franklin stood at the top of the beach with the imposing cliff rising sheer behind him. He held his helmet in one hand and his sword in the other. The men ashore had been cleared from the background so that he stood alone, and Gore had set up his equipment slightly below Franklin, making him appear taller and more imposing. Sir John stood turned to one side, gazing into the middle distance to where his ships lay at anchor. Afterward he had left the beach without speaking to Gore, not even expressing an interest in the finished result.

Later, looking closely at the image he had produced, Gore was surprised to see a band of white, like a roll of unwound silk between the back of Franklin's head and the cliff face. Unable at first to explain this, it finally struck him that what he had captured on the plate was a flight of gulls passing behind Franklin, each bird following closely in the path of the one ahead, and each leaving its own fleeting and insubstantial image on the exposed plate.

He explained all this to Franklin upon presenting him with the portrait, and in turn Franklin explained the effect to everyone else who asked to see it. He now seemed pleased by the picture, as though his own solemn features had been somehow enlivened by the ghostly birds, and as though the portrait had been enhanced rather than spoiled by them.

Goodsir, upon being handed the plate for his own comments, drew his finger across the smear left by the birds, where here and there a wingtip was more distinctly visible, and half jokingly suggested to Gore that this was how an angel might eventually come to be seen.

They waited nine more weeks for the ice in the bay to break and disperse. It was by then the middle of July, and the watches posted on the outer heights reported daily that the disintegrating broader pack was already braided with channels, the widest of which might already prove navigable were they able to reach them.

On the 18th of July, the two ice-masters and a party of marines hauled a boat over the bay ice and put to sea at its rim, moved out into the flow of the Wellington Channel and there rowed and drifted among the floating ice until they were carried south with it into Barrow Strait. Here they anchored to a grounded berg and studied the movement of the breaking pack all around them. It quickly became apparent that they stood little chance of sailing south through the easterly flow without serious risk of collision. There was no safe harbor closer than Cape Walker, 100 miles to the west, or the north coast of Somerset, 50 miles south across the turbulent strait.

They stayed amid the ice for six hours, watching as it moved unceasingly past them, and only left their secure anchorage when another large berg threatened to collide with their own and crush them. They turned north, making slow progress against the Wellington outfall, where the wider view was lost to them amid towering bergs. A close watch was kept for any submerged ice which might slide beneath them and lift them clear of the water.

Turning back into Beechey Bay they were caught in a sudden and powerful surge of water caused by the calving of a nearby berg. The small boat rocked and they were spun until a collision with the surrounding ice looked unavoidable. Reid told the marines to fix their oars and hold them out from the boat at half their length. They had already secured themselves to the benches upon which they sat. One man, William Pilkington, was slow to position his oar, and as he fumbled with it, snagging it on a rope, the boat struck the ice and he was thrown overboard, landing, to his surprise and relief, in less than a foot of water, which skimmed the surface of a submerged shelf. He scrambled to pull himself clear, fearful that he might be caught in a gap between the ice and the boat.

After this they pushed themselves into more open water. Two of the marines took off Pilkington's boots and over-trousers. He was unhurt and the water had not penetrated to his underclothing. Composing himself after his brief ordeal, he returned to his oar.

Waiting until the surrounding ice was carried clear of them, they resumed rowing.

An hour later they were beyond the influence of the channel, and the ships came into view ahead of them. A fire had been lit at the outer edge of the ice to guide them and its dense black smoke rose in a curve like a trick rainbow. A second boat rowed out to meet them and help them back ashore.

Around the fire the outermost bay ice was already beginning to break. It cracked but remained in position, rocking as the deeper currents began to probe underneath it. It was sea ice, not fresh, and because of the manner in which it had formed, it remained flexible, bulging and rippling without breaking, and where men walked upon it they felt it give beneath them like saturated turf.

During the previous week the *Erebus* and *Terror* had both been re-rigged, and their wooden props had been sawn away and dragged clear. Now all they waited for were the fissures in the ice to reach in and release them. Night watches were doubled and rigging parties remained on full-day alert for the first indication that they were about to float free.

On the 20th of July a giant berg appeared on their western horizon and drove in upon them, crashing through the shallow ice of the bay and grounding itself less than two hundred yards from the ships. They shook as it gouged along the bottom, leaving a broad open channel in its wake.

Parties of men went out to inspect the berg. Warmed by the high sun, water ran in small streams and cascades from every exposed surface, and upon their approach, the first men to arrive discovered that it contained a small arch through which they might easily pass. Such features were known as the Eyes of God, after the remark supposedly made by St. Brendan upon encountering something similar during his own voyage in northern waters. These Eyes were considered a good omen, and men passed through them shouting out the names of their wives and sweethearts to ensure that they would return to see them again.

Having visited this new arrival himself, Franklin called a conference and he and his officers discussed what they might do next.

"We'll need three days at the very least if we're to collect all the supplies ashore," Gore said, conscious that even this was an optimistic assessment.

"I don't think we have it," Reid said, his calmness only adding to the sense of urgency which had come so suddenly upon them, and which some of the others were only then beginning to feel.

"Then every man available must be put ashore," Franklin said.

"There's a possibility that if we can break up the firmer ice surrounding our moorings then we might be able to nose our way out using our engines," Reid said.

"They're ready to be stoked up," Fitzjames added enthusiastically.

It was Fitzjames who had petitioned the Admiralty for the engines to be fitted to the ships in the first place, and he had arrived at Greenhithe a month before their departure to supervise their installation and then to test them on the river. Few others shared his enthusiasm, but masking his disappointment at the size of the engines, and at the locomotive wheels and gearing still attached to them on delivery, he declared himself satisfied with them, convinced that the future of all close-work Arctic exploration lay with steam and sail rather than sail alone. Even the Rosses' near useless paddles, he pointed out, had taken the *Victory* farther into the heart of the frozen sea than anyone before them.

"Explosives," Goodsir said unexpectedly, his fingers moving in calculation. "A line of small explosions along our intended course. Weaken the ice before we even begin to push it clear."

This idea appealed to many, but when Franklin asked Reid what he thought, Reid said that the ice surrounding them was already too unstable and variable in thickness and that to disturb it any further before they were floating free and ready to move out of the bay would bring them more problems than it solved.

"I agree," said Thomas Blanky, and Goodsir withdrew the suggestion.

Two days later the argument was taken out of their hands. Men working on the *Terror*'s rigging felt her shudder and then begin to rock beneath them. Others out on the surrounding ice saw this and ran toward her. Watching from the fore-deck, Crozier saw the ice directly alongside his bow rise and then sink, causing water to rush up against the hull. He called down for the men on the ice to stay clear, and if possible to return to the safety of the shore. He watched in alarm as a dozen other cracks appeared simultaneously, many of them running toward the *Terror* as though she were the hub of a buckled wheel, and all around her the ice began to tilt and sway, and men abandoned what they were doing and raced for the land. Less than twenty yards from the port bow of the *Erebus* a mound of coal ten feet high was shaken loose and then tipped into the basin of water which suddenly appeared beneath it. A fire upon the ice was equally suddenly extinguished in a spout of steam.

Franklin watched all this from the rail of the *Erebus*, and felt his own vessel begin to shake beneath him. A man was knocked from his perch on the fore-stay and fell heavily to the deck below, where others ran to help him.

Most of those working on the ice made it safely to the shore, where they congregated and stood waving and calling.

All along its outer rim, the bay ice began to break free. Caught off guard by the speed with which the breakup had finally come, Franklin ordered all their boats to be lowered, including their inflatable dinghies, and for these to move among the pieces of floating ice and rescue the men still trapped there. Several men, he saw, had fallen into the water, but were close enough to the shore to be dragged clear. They were in little danger of suffering from exposure in the warming sea, only of being caught and injured by the grinding ice.

Fitzjames and Gore went ashore to supervise the retrieval of the last of their stores, determined that as little as possible should be lost or abandoned by this unexpected turn in their fortunes.

An hour after the breakup had started, both ships were able to cast off and move into open water. There was still no navigable channel leading out of the bay, but they were now in a position, their sails unfurled and their rudders fixed, to make the dash into the wider reaches when the opportunity arose.

By the following morning they were ready to leave. Their boats and sledges had been retrieved, and everywhere around them, on the shore and floating on the ice and in the water, lay the scattered debris of their long stay.

And above all this, clearly visible on the lower slopes of Beechey, were the wooden markers of the three men who had died there.

On the morning of Sunday the 23rd of July, Franklin held a service during which he read aloud the first chapter of Genesis in its entirety, and afterward, shortly before noon, the *Erebus* led the way out through the crumbling ice into the open sea beyond.

BEYOND THE EYE OF GOD

JULY 1846 — APRIL 1847

How does she look?" Franklin asked, standing close behind Fitz-james, his own lantern held high to examine the walls, one of them a bulkhead separating the hold from the forward quarters.

"She's no longer shipping," Fitzjames called back, his voice amplified and distorted by the confined space in which he was wedged.

On the first day of sailing into Barrow Strait, the *Erebus* shipped two tons of water into her forward coal store through a sprung plank. Her stokers worked for nine hours to carry the damp coal astern and then a caulking party sealed the leak and pumped the bulk of the water clear. A length of planking on the outer hull had been crushed, previously held in place by both the buttress to which it was attached and by the pressure of the outside ice. Once in open water, and without the support of the ice, the buttress had been jarred, rupturing the inner hull and bunker wall.

Wading knee-deep through the black sludge, Fitzjames shone his lantern into the gap between the two hulls, searching for further trapped water which might need to be pumped away.

Franklin passed him a hammer to test the surrounding spars, and both men fell silent to listen to the dull wooden knocks which reassured them that the remaining timbers were sound. New wood had already been taken to the store and now lined the walls, held clear of the dirty floodwater in rope slings.

"How far below her waterline, do you think?" Franklin asked as

Fitzjames twisted his chest and arms to extricate himself from the tight space.

"A foot or two." Fitzjames examined the warm caulking to the left and right of the damage. There was still some seepage, but no more than might be expected after so long out of the water.

It was nightfall by the time the examination was completed, and Franklin ordered any remaining repairs to wait until the following morning. Leaving, they passed the exhausted stokers, and Franklin thanked them for having acted so promptly. The men were coated black from head to foot, only their hands and eyes and mouths washed clean. Water still lapped around them in the narrow passage, and they were forced to back out of it to allow Franklin and Fitzjames to pass by.

The two men parted, and Franklin went on deck, surprised by the darkness of the brief summer night. The *Terror*'s lights were visible a mile off their port bow, momentarily extinguished as a large berg passed silently and unseen between them. There was no moon and he could pick out only the closest of the drifting ice.

The repair work resumed at dawn. Regardless of the progress of this, they would sail at noon, taking advantage of a broad lead which had appeared ahead of them during the night, and which ran due south, taking them only a few degrees from their projected course.

When Fitzjames joined Reid on the fore-top platform, Reid inquired about the progress of the repair and the likelihood of their hull having been weakened. He himself had survived two ships which had been crushed and sunk by the ice. He indicated ahead of them, pointing along the lead to their southern horizon. Ice still moved across their path from west to east.

"Is it heavy?" Fitzjames asked him.

Reid answered him with a nod, his eyes fixed on the colliding ice ahead of them. "It'll turn us and flush us straight back out into Baffin if we don't find some way through it before the end of August. A winter in it would cripple us for good, and come next spring we'd be struggling to keep the pieces of ourselves together."

"Sir John is hopeful of a twenty-day passage," Fitzjames said, probing for Reid's own estimation.

"So I hear," Reid said. "I wish us luck." He climbed down from their narrow perch.

Fitzjames remained where he was until the noon bell was sounded and he felt the *Erebus* move beneath him as her mooring lines were released.

Moving swiftly along the open channel, there was an air of excitement and expectation among both crews. This did not last long: after only four hours of unobstructed sailing they came up against an impenetrable rush of ice across their bows, a mass so dense and fast-moving that it would have been madness to try and enter it. Nothing they had so far encountered had prepared them for what they now saw: islands of ice immeasurable in the glare sailing past them at three times the speed they themselves might achieve even with a favorable wind; bergs twice their own height, caught, crushed and scattered, and all around them the water flowing and eddying in foaming torrents, which every now and then rose in spouts and fountains where submerged ice collided and forced it up.

The *Terror* was the first to reach the edge of this maelstrom, and at the first indication that she was being drawn into its peripheral currents, Crozier gave the order to turn about and retrace their course back into calmer water.

The first those on the *Erebus* knew of the problem ahead was when they saw the *Terror* coming toward them with a warning flag rising on her foremast. Seeing that Crozier was headed for the safety of a grounded berg, Franklin set a course to join him, and the two ships drew alongside each other.

A boat was lowered and Crozier and John Irving came aboard the *Erebus*.

"Too powerful, and filled with far more ice than you can see from here," Irving told Franklin and Fitzjames. "We were barely able to draw back."

"Mr. Irving exaggerates," Crozier said. "Vessels as stout as ours might enter it with care."

"And the reason for your withdrawal?" Fitzjames asked.

"To await your arrival. And to bring you the news that the *Terror* at least is ready to forge a crossing."

"With an invitation to follow in your wake?"

Crozier breathed deeply and turned to Franklin. "Sir John?"

"I agree with James and Mr. Irving, Francis. Even if we were able to negotiate a passage, we would undoubtedly become separated and then waste time in searching for each other once we were clear at the other side."

"As usual, Mr. Irving has overstated the case for doing nothing. Delay, delay, delay."

"Look at it," Fitzjames said in Irving's defense, pointing to where the swiftly moving ice ran in a constant stream, heliographing its dangerous presence to them each time a piece spun or overturned and caught the sun.

"I still say that to delay is the wrong decision. We all know how calm and stable by comparison the southbound straits beyond are likely to be."

"Oh?" Fitzjames said.

"History, Mr. Fitzjames, history. For the want of only a few days' sailing we might just as well never have crossed Baffin for all we've achieved so far."

"We wait," Franklin said firmly, aware of the men gathering around them to listen.

Crozier, too, saw them. "Back to the *Terror*," he said to Irving, almost pushing him to the rail.

Fitzjames was about to speak, but Franklin stopped him.

The delay frustrated everyone, and was further exacerbated by the warm sun and pale blue skies beneath which they waited.

"We are being mocked," Gore remarked to Fitzjames, Goodsir and Vesconte as the four men exercised upon deck during the fifth morning of their enforced idleness.

The following day was the 1st of August, and they were all aware of the turning point this represented, of how the loosening grip of the previous winter would shortly become the stiffening, probing fingers of the next.

Later that day, the lookout on the *Terror* called down that the distant ice flow appeared to be decreasing. A boat was lowered, and Fitzjames, Irving, Reid and Blanky rowed to the limit of the open water to investigate. There they saw that the islands of ice moving past them had diminished in size, and that there were now free-moving bergs in the water, through which a passage might be navigated with luck and caution. The current too appeared to be flowing less vigorously now that it was no longer forced into narrow channels amid the ice.

"The time might have come to take our chances," Irving said uncertainly.

"The chance of collision weighed against an early arrival in the south?" Fitzjames said.

"Captain Crozier believes—"

"That we might earn ourselves some charmed protection by pitting our wits and strength against it all," Blanky said.

"Propitiate the Gods."

"The Gods are up there, we are down here," Reid said. "What do they see that we can't? There's been no let up in the flow since we first arrived alongside it."

They all nodded in agreement.

"Whatever Mr. Crozier or Sir John might pray for, we'd be fools to try and get across it as it now is. We'd be forced to sail almost directly against the flow of the ice."

"And still need to maneuver when the need arose," added Blanky.

"Which would be every few minutes," Fitzjames said dejectedly.

"And trust to favorable winds for the entire passage." Blanky licked his palm and held it up. "Which, regardless of whatever sacrifice we might care to make, we have yet to be blessed with."

Fitzjames rose to his feet and took out his telescope. "There are some stationary islands, keel-ground amid the rush."

"Impossible," Reid said. "Too deep. If they're stuck it's because they're grounded on the ice beneath them." He too examined these larger bergs.

"Even so, might we not, given that favorable wind, move from piece to piece, mooring each night and selecting a new target for each day's sailing?"

In the event, they were surrounded during the night by a dense bank of fog, and their departure was delayed until the morning of the 3rd.

They sailed only with close-reefed topsails, allowing themselves to be drawn south in the drift. In support of his plan to move cautiously from berg to berg, Fitzjames also suggested that their boilers be fired so that they might be ready to use their engines if the wind turned against them, or if either vessel became uncontrollable by sail alone in the unpredictable currents ahead. Franklin agreed to this, and as they sailed smoke rose for the first time from both their stacks. Only Crozier voiced the opinion that he would sooner trust to providence than his stokers.

By dusk they had made three miles, and at ten in the evening they moored to an island of ice which had been constantly visible ahead of them from their starting point.

Despite their slow progress, everyone was encouraged that they had made this part of their passage safely. In the lee of the island the water was calm and the wind had dropped completely. A glossy white cliff rose 200 feet off their starboard side, and once secured their mooring ropes were let out so that they might come to rest away from this and any ice which might fall from its overhanging rim.

Collisions were heard throughout the night, and on several occasions the alarm was sounded when ice from the main flow drifted in upon them. None of this damaged them, and as the night progressed the alarms became fewer.

The repair to the *Erebus'* bunker was completed the following morning and its cargo laboriously returned.

Franklin and Crozier breakfasted together and congratulated themselves on the previous day's crossing.

Apart from their more obvious common concerns, their only other cause for alarm now lay with the men who remained in the sick bays of both ships. Genge continued to suffer from the symptoms which had killed Torrington, Hartnell and Braine, and Edward Little was still in considerable pain from his leg. It was Peddie's belief, Crozier told Franklin, that Genge would shortly die, and upon hearing this Franklin regretted having allowed him to be so severely punished.

The following day they made three miles, and the one after that seven.

And on the 6th of August they sailed free of the bulk of the ice, and for three days were able to cruise without mooring until they once again encountered ice too concentrated and fast-flowing to penetrate.

They tied up to a secure berg, and during the night of the 9th, Edward Genge died.

He was buried at sea the following morning, his corpse weighted with ballast and dropped into the water an hour before they sailed. The *Terror*'s marines fired into the air, and all around them flocks of hidden birds erupted from their roosts on the surrounding ice.

On one occasion, nineteen days into the strait, the *Terror* scraped her keel on the submerged tongue of a berg around which she was sailing. The *Erebus* lay half a mile ahead of her, oblivious to what had happened. The damage was not great, but part of the *Terror*'s rudder housing was lost, and until even a crude repair could be made she proved difficult to steer. The problem was made worse by the increasing number of smaller, free-moving pieces of ice among which they were once again sailing.

By the time Franklin realized something was wrong he was almost two miles ahead of the *Terror*. He finally saw her signal in the falling dusk, and ordering all their own sail to be taken in, he waited until she caught up with him. Because there was no substantial berg to which the *Terror* might moor while repairs were made, Franklin offered her a tow and Crozier accepted. The ships were still in open water as darkness fell, and it was not until two in the morning that they came upon a mass of ice large enough to provide them with the necessary shelter.

At sunrise an hour later they saw that they were moored to an island of old ice, which rose from the sea in a gradual slope rather than precipitously. Its surface was mounted and furrowed, and was already heavily scoured by rivers of meltwater. A party went ashore to explore it and to examine the surrounding sea from its peak.

Accompanied by Goodsir, Fitzjames was the first to make the climb and see what lay beyond. He was not surprised by what he saw—more ice and navigable water until the shifting pattern of light and dark confused him—but what did attract his attention was a large number of vivid red stains on the southern shore of the island. He pointed these out to Goodsir, who immediately became keen to investigate.

They reached the marked ground and Goodsir announced that they were blood stains.

"It's like a battle ground," Fitzjames said, searching around him for some clue as to the origins of the marks.

"But without the bodies," Goodsir added. He collected samples from the nearest of the stains.

"Hunters?" Fitzjames crouched beside Goodsir. Some of the stains looked fresh and wet, but when he touched these he discovered that they were buried, that meltwater had frozen over them and not yet started to wash them away.

Goodsir left him and walked toward the sea.

Fitzjames walked in the opposite direction, coming across a small flock of gulls pecking at the ice to reach their disgusting meal beneath.

Goodsir called to him, and approaching him, Fitzjames saw that there was something at his feet. Arriving beside him he saw that this was the frozen corpse of a walrus, its open mouth plugged with ice.

"Our mystery explained," Goodsir said.

"Then it is hunters. This animal was wounded and left behind."

Goodsir laughed at this. "Nothing so dramatic, I'm afraid." He tapped the solid corpse with his foot and then stepped aside to reveal more fully the encircling pool of frozen blood, at the center of which lay a newborn calf, as dead and as frozen as its mother.

"This must be their birthing ground," Goodsir said. He tried to prise the calf free of the ice, eventually having to chip at it with his hammer to break it loose.

.   .   .

They continued south for five more days. On good days they made twenty miles, on poor ones only two.

On the sixth morning they saw in the early dawn that the slender channel they had followed the previous day had become even narrower in the night as the ice along its edges gathered and consolidated. They saw that they had been surrounded by a drifting field of level surface ice which, even as they looked out upon it, threatened to consolidate further and trap them within it.

The *Erebus* was the first to get away, pushing through the floe and nosing to port and starboard as she part-sought and part-created a path through the gathering mass, aiming for the dark water a mile ahead.

The *Terror* followed immediately astern, taking advantage of the leading ship's open wake.

Reid guided the *Erebus* from his perch on the bowsprit cap, signaling first one way and then the other as new leads offered themselves ahead. Running up against a heavier shelf of ice they were forced to turn through 90 degrees and seek another route, a difficult maneuver with the floe already pushing along their entire length. Seeing what had happened, the helmsman on the *Terror* was able to turn her at a less severe angle and avoid the obstruction.

It took them eight hours to sail a mile and pass through the ice into open water beyond.

Minutes after their release, the dark cap of an island appeared on their starboard horizon, but other than note its position on their empty charts, neither vessel took any further account of it.

Their way south now appeared clear. Open channels penetrated the field of scattered bergs, and although the water was filled with the debris of these larger masses, this presented them with few obstacles.

Returning from his uncomfortable perch, Reid called for Vesconte to fetch several of his aluminum canisters. Waiting for him, he explained to the others that the ice off their starboard bow was starting to move in a different direction from that behind them, and he deduced that they had entered the fan of a southerly drift, and that the west coast of Boothia lay hidden off their port bow. The ice there would be more densely packed than at the center of the channel or along any corresponding land mass to the west, and he suggested that they should continue south until they were clear of the ice which presently surrounded them. They might then adopt a south-southwesterly course and see what lay ahead of them in that direction. He felt certain that this passage would prove similar in many respects to that unsuccessfully sought along Prince Regent's Inlet by Parry and Ross to the east of Boothia, and although he was unsure of what lay to the south and west of them, he was further convinced that they should avoid the known shore to the east and follow a course toward where the stronger southerly currents exerted their influence on the drifting ice.

Vesconte arrived with his canisters, into which details of their position and progress to date were already sealed. Taking several of these from him, Reid went to their prow and cast them overboard in rapid succession so that they formed a line in the water like the floats of a submerged net. Most of these were immediately lost amid the smaller pieces of nearby ice, but those that floated into open water began to drift ahead of them.

Countless thousands of these canisters had been thrown overboard since being adopted as the only viable, albeit distrusted and unreliable, means of communication between vessels in the ice and the world beyond. Inside them a form in several languages requested that they be returned to the Admiralty. Some were picked up decades after they had been thrown. Most were lost, sunk or frozen over. And some, everyone knew, probably drifted forever with cargos of hope or despair so large they could never be contained, and which, if ever released or exposed, crumbled to dust and disappeared as completely as the men who had thrown them, and whose calls and screams and prayers had drifted with them to the horizon of their shrinking world.

They were caught in gathering ice for the next eight days, box-hauling in enclosed leads and lowering their boats to investigate every time a navigable channel opened up ahead of them.

The *Terror* suffered further damage when she was caught in a nip while chasing open water to the southwest. She came to an abrupt halt and was shaken from prow to stern. Those watching from the *Erebus* realized immediately that she had struck more submerged ice.

"She's hauling astern," Fitzjames said, standing beside Franklin, the attention of both men focused on the efforts of the *Terror* to release herself from the trap into which she had sailed.

Franklin called down to Des Voeux to take out a party on the ice and help them pull clear.

Des Voeux gathered together a dozen men and led them over the side onto the stable ice. They ran until they were alongside the *Terror*, whose boats were already lowered and coming toward them.

Reluctant to move any closer, and concerned about their own position in the narrow lead, Franklin ordered a second party to stand ready to lower their boats and haul the *Erebus* astern until she too was back out in open water.

"She's grinding," Fitzjames said suddenly. A distant crunching sound could be heard, and many of the men on deck stopped what they were doing and turned to look at the *Terror*.

James Fairholme arrived beside them and directed their attention to their own stern, pointing to where one slab of ice had been pushed upon another and was now sliding over it at an angle. The distant noise resumed, and was concluded by a sudden crack as the uppermost slab broke and fell in two halves upon the ice it had mounted.

Those watching on the *Erebus* waited for the tremor this might produce, but nothing came.

It was difficult to judge the size of this upheaval, or its distance away from them, but Fairholme, the son and grandson of farmers, estimated the risen shelf to be at least an acre in extent.

There were other, less distinct noises, as the reverberations of this collision died down, and only when they were convinced that there was no more to follow did they turn their attention back to the *Terror* and her efforts to free herself.

By then, Crozier had landed on the ice, and was supervising the work from the shore. John Irving and George Hodgson worked alongside him. In addition to their land-lines, the *Terror*'s boats were attempting to pull her astern.

"She's free," Fitzjames said eventually, watching as the bow of the *Terror* rocked in the water and sent out an irregular wave on either side of her.

Confirming this, Franklin ordered all their sail to be taken in, and for them too to be pulled astern.

The two ships were moored where they sat at the onset of night. Lanterns were lit on the ice and sea anchors made ready in case the banks of the channel closed further in on them in the darkness.

Crozier spent the evening aboard the *Erebus*.

"There are times when I wish I had never set eyes on the borders of this cursed place," he said. "I make no excuses for my carelessness, but I ask you, who in their right mind would not have taken the course I followed?"

"It certainly appeared to offer a reasonable chance of getting ourselves clear," Franklin said. He had followed Crozier against his own better judgment, keen to raise the spirits of his inactive and restless crew by the simple expedient of setting them in motion, however slow or tortuous.

Crozier rose to press his outstretched palm into the empty space at the center of the map hanging beside them. "My suggestion is that we remain where we are and try again to move forward along the same path."

"We retreat back out into open water," Franklin said, handing Crozier a decanter of port. "We retreat and try again elsewhere."

Crozier saw that argument was useless. He wondered if Franklin made a note of these private discussions in his Admiralty Book or journal. "I would prefer the word 'withdraw,' " he said.

"Then withdraw it is." Listening to all this, it occurred to Franklin that Crozier spoke in the aggrieved tone of someone who believed he had been unfairly treated, almost as though he were seeking some reward for his labors, whereas instead he had received only mockery. "These are not mistakes or misjudgments we make," he said. "For that we would need to know what lay ahead of us." But Crozier was not to be appeased and they parted soon afterward.

They resumed their hauling the next day, and more men were sent out on the ice to assist in this. The *Terror*'s rudder was lifted, and without it she became unwieldy in the confined space, her stern wave rocking the boats which pulled her.

Word reached Franklin late in the morning that her bow reinforcement had also been damaged in the collision and that she was being pumped as she was towed.

Irving reported to Franklin mid-afternoon that the shock of the collision had been largely absorbed by the *Terror*'s outer sheathing at a point where she was best protected, and that the damage was superficial. She was shipping water into her empty bow, but her restraining timbers were still intact. He pointed out to Franklin the slight dip in the *Terror*'s bow, passing on Crozier's reassurances that once the towing parties were back aboard she would be quickly pumped and sealed.

By late afternoon the *Erebus* was free of the lead and back out in open water.

As they followed the edge of the ice to the west, everyone on board the *Erebus* was surprised to see the rush of smoke from the *Terror*'s stack and then to see her complete the last half mile of her own reverse journey using her engine. Even rudderless she came out into the open water in a straight line and at a constant speed considerably greater than that at which the *Erebus* herself had come clear.

Further progress was delayed while repairs were carried out, and during that time Fitzjames persuaded Franklin to experiment with their own engine.

Less than a mile to the west of where they had emerged lay a second opening, and this, Fitzjames assured Franklin, would provide them with the perfect testing ground: using their engine instead of their sails they might turn into this loose ice and push it away ahead of them instead of forever changing tack to avoid its larger pieces, as they would be forced to do under sail alone.

Hearing what the *Erebus* was about to attempt, Crozier, Hodgson and Irving came aboard to participate in the experiment.

For an hour before their departure Fitzjames worked with the stokers to build up a head of steam sufficient to drive them with some force into the channel. With the ice in its present condition, gentle but constant pressure, he reasoned, would prove more effective than if they ran at it using their reinforced bows as a ram. Later, if the need for brute force did arise, then they would employ it scientifically, like a quarryman splitting blocks of slate with precise and expert blows on his chisel.

At noon, his face and hands blackened by coal, Fitzjames reported that they were ready to make the attempt. Their whistle was sounded, accompanied by a plume of steam through their rigging, pleasingly solid and white against the spreading cloud of their smokestack.

They backed away from the ice and then steamed toward the clotted channel.

The first ice they encountered they pushed effortlessly away from them, the impact cushioned by their bow wave and then by the ice's rapid dispersal along their sides. They steered toward those parts of the channel where ice and open water existed in equal measure, and where there was sufficient room for the displaced ice to flow astern of them. After an hour of bulling and nosing in this fashion they had pushed themselves over three miles into the cracked skin of ice which now lay from horizon to horizon all around them.

On the 1st of September another man was lost to them, a seaman on the *Terror* called David Leys.

At the time, the two ships had been sailing west, probing the ice for weaknesses in the hope of locating another passage south.

Because there was little loose ice in the water, they were occasionally accompanied by both boat and foot parties, whose task it was to explore any promising-looking channels without the ships themselves having to divert from their course. David Leys was one of six men from the *Terror* who had been landed at dawn on the 1st. Progress over the level sea ice was good, and those crossing it were able to explore far ahead of the ships.

Leys had been walking with his friend Samuel Crispe, both of them eighteen, when they had been directed inland to investigate a dark mark on the ice. Crispe had been the first to reach this, the two men having raced, but he found it to be nothing more than a trick of the light. He had turned to shout to Leys, but his companion was nowhere in sight.

He ran back to where he and Leys had been racing side by side, and in places he was able to make out their footprints in the powdery surface. Following these to a point at which they vanished, Crispe saw that the ice here was ridged in a series of low steps, most of them little more than a few inches high, and as he searched across these he felt a sudden tremor, and ahead of him he saw a fissure appear, opening up two or three feet before slamming shut with a sudden rasp of air. He panicked and ran back to the others still moving parallel to the shore. He led them back to where he had last seen Leys and showed them the ridging in the ice, trying unsuccessfully to locate where he had seen it suddenly open and then reseal itself. He ran one way and then another calling for his friend. One man returned to the water's edge to signal to the boats, while the others continued to search for the missing man.

A boat came ashore containing another dozen men, and these joined in the search, parceling out the ice and crossing it at regular intervals before re-forming and starting again.

After two hours of looking, however, it became clear that they were not going to find Leys, and they gathered back at the boat and speculated on what had happened to him. Crispe remained inconsolable and wept for his friend as they rowed away.

Franklin gave the order for them to lie off alongside the ice in case Leys somehow reappeared during the night, and they again set out a line of marker lanterns.

Leys did not reappear, and following a brief prayer the expedition sailed without him the following day. At Fitzjames' suggestion a small cache of food was landed ashore along with a container in which their sailing plans were sealed. It was a forlorn hope, but it was a place renowned for its forlorn hopes and impossible rescues.

The next day they sighted land ahead of them and were convinced that they had approached the western coast of the strait they were still hoping to follow south. Certain that this could not have been the northern reaches of a continental peninsula, another Boothia, they acknowledged that what they had sighted was a previously uncharted island. They were encouraged by its appearance because it suggested to them—as did any substantial body of land with an eastern aspect—the strong possibility of open water and a sheltering coast.

In this they were not to be disappointed, and six hours after the land was first sighted they found themselves at a distance of less than a mile from its narrow shore and high cliffs, and sailing due south along a broad and open channel which was barely disturbed by the powerful and ice-laden currents they had encountered farther east.

They anchored that night in sight of land for the first time in six weeks, confident that they had at last found their true course.

Vesconte applied for permission to take a surveying party and spend a day ashore, but this was denied him. It was Franklin's intention to follow this open water south as quickly as possible, so that if any emergency arose they might at least be within marching distance of the continental shore when they were next frozen in.

He sent for Reid and quizzed him about the likelihood of them now being in a strait as broad and as navigable as Prince Regent's Inlet. But Reid, unwilling to speculate on anything other than that which they had already encountered, would only confirm Franklin's belief that they were in a major waterway and that if they followed the land's eastern shore then they would, in all likelihood, avoid the worst of the strait's winter ice. Privately, he imagined they might repeat the experience of the Rosses, except whereas they had found their way blocked, they themselves would encounter unenclosed and navigable waters.

By the end of that week they had sailed a further 140 miles, their progress only occasionally delayed by ice grounded on the shore and by unexpectedly powerful currents and undertows which ran against them, forcing them back toward the thickening mass of ice at the center of the channel. They were concerned by the extent of this, by its configuration and antiquity, and driven closer they watched as this mass turned black and mountainous in the dusk, casting its shadows over the gradually narrowing channels which surrounded it.

The farther south they sailed, the more often they were forced toward this intimidating mass, turning less and less frequently toward the ever more distant and shrouded shore.

THIRTEEN

On the 25th of September they sailed into a sea of both fixed and floating ice which filled their every horizon, and from which, they all finally accepted, they were unlikely to emerge or be released until the following summer.

They congratulated themselves on the distance they had come, Vesconte calculating that they had sailed approximately 240 miles—three-quarters of the way between Barrow Strait and the continental shoreline.

Their immediate concern now was to find their second winter harbor. At a conference aboard the *Erebus* it was decided that they would take advantage of what little open water remained to them to explore the surrounding ranges and islands of ice in the hope of finding an enclosed bay in which they might anchor and await the freezing of the sea around them.

Both ice-masters cautioned against a hasty choice, pointing out that if they prepared themselves well enough, they might continue drifting in the forming ice for a further month. Soon, Reid and Blanky argued, King William Land would be within reach to the south and the ice-drift might yet take them much closer to this.

Both men had studied the condition of the surrounding field for several hours before the conference, and both had come to the conclusion that the ice was now present in such an ancient mass, and in such a large and unrestricted body of underlying water, that it might continue to drift much later into the season than had previously been recorded farther north or east.

Crozier was the first to argue against this suggestion, soliciting the support of his own officers for finding a safe anchorage while the opportunity still existed. Reluctantly, Irving and Hodgson agreed with him, only Edward Little showing any enthusiasm for a prolonged drift exposed to the vagaries of the ice.

Fitzjames, Vesconte and Gore were with Reid.

Returning to the *Terror*, Crozier remarked coldly to his officers that his own argument for seeking harbor was already lost. He criticized Little for not having supported him, but then restrained himself when he saw the pain the young lieutenant was still enduring. Above them, a bloated gibbous moon looked ready to grow full, and flared like a sun in the icy haze through which it shone.

"You catch me red-handed, James." Harry Goodsir spun in his seat and held up his hands, both of which were red from fingertip to wrist. His shirt sleeves were rolled above his elbows and his forearms too were smeared the same color. In the dim light of his cabin, it looked at first to Fitzjames as though his friend had recently concluded a particularly bloody operation, or perhaps the skinning of one of his growing number of trophies prior to curing and mounting it.

"What is it?" he asked.

Beside him stood William Bell, junior quartermaster, who had been sent by Goodsir to fetch him upon the conclusion of Franklin's conference.

Goodsir turned a small cask to face Fitzjames, revealing that it was filled with Cayenne pepper.

"So?" Fitzjames said, confused.

"I was alerted by Mr. Bell here," Goodsir said. "We owe him our thanks." Bell bowed slightly, his eyes darting from one to the other, and asked if he might go now.

"You wanted me to see our pepper?" Fitzjames asked when the two men were alone.

"That might be stretching a point, James."

"Meaning?"

Instead of answering, Goodsir pulled forward into the light three small tin trays, upon each of which was piled a mound of the vividly red powder.

Growing impatient, and anxious to get to his bunk after eighteen hours on duty, Fitzjames dipped his finger into the nearest of the trays and carefully dabbed it on his tongue. The taste was indeterminate, but not that of Cayenne pepper, against which he had been bracing himself.

"That, I believe, is red lead," Goodsir said. "As indeed is all this upon my hands and arms. Unlike brick dust and powdered mahogany, red lead is known far and wide for its staining qualities." He smiled broadly, revealing the same across his teeth and gums, giving his open mouth the appearance of a wet gash. He licked his teeth and rubbed them with his fingers, but this did little to remove the stain.

"How?" Fitzjames said, testing the contents of each of the other trays.

"Simple. Cayenne pepper, or so I am informed by the redoubtable Mr. Bell, is a rather costly provision. We carry a great deal of it to disguise the taste of the pickled and preserved meats which might—and here let us be charitable to the provisioners—become somewhat beyond their prime."

"And our supply has been adulterated, bulked out with these other substances?"

Goodsir gave a single sharp nod.

"Is it dangerous?"

"I don't know. All I *can* say for certain is that it will reduce the efficacy of the pepper in disguising the taste of the meat."

"Do we know who provided it?"

Goodsir tapped the name stenciled on the cask.

"Have the same firm provided us with much else?"

"I'm afraid so. Much of it, I hasten to add, of considerably better quality."

The two men sat and looked at each other, suddenly conscious of their helplessness in the situation.

"Might the lead or the brick or the mahogany have any toxic effect?" Fitzjames asked eventually, realizing Goodsir's true concern.

"So far it would appear not. I imagine it might first reveal itself in some form of bowel disorder, and to my knowledge nothing of the sort has been reported."

Both men knew that it was not a complaint that was likely to be made public until it became too severe to be endured.

Goodsir explained that he had devised an effective method of sieving out most of the impurities from the pepper and that he had instructed Bell to deliver the rest of their stock to him the following day.

Relieved that even this partial solution to the problem had been found, Fitzjames rose to go, but was stopped by Goodsir, who had something else to show him. He pulled a sack of flour from where it had been concealed in the shadows, and at the sight of this, Fitzjames felt a sudden chill run through him.

"Surely not the flour, too?"

Goodsir hesitated and then scooped a cupful from the sack and tipped it on to his desk.

"But it's so cheap," Fitzjames insisted. "So vital."

"And it can be made cheaper still. Watch." Goodsir scraped up a small quantity on the handle of a spoon and tapped it into a test-tube. He then took down a bottle from the rack above him and let a single drop fall into the tube. "Hydrochloric acid," he said. There was an immediate and vigorous effervescence and milky bubbles rose to the rim of the tube, where they burst as they spilled over.

"Chalk," Goodsir said. He calculated that they had lost a fifth to a quarter of their flour by this adulteration. Both men were aware that a reduction in the daily bread ration would be considered an ill omen in the eyes of the crew. Normally, it was the last of their food-stuffs to be denied them, and to lose it before any other less popular provisions would cause alarm.

In the past, shipwrecked whalers had lived for up to three months eating only two pounds of bread each day and whatever they could scavenge or hunt. On occasion flour had been so cheap and plentiful that it had been carried as ballast, a large proportion of this becoming inedible as it was contaminated by seepage. There was a bank off Peterhead harbor known as the flour bank because so much had been dumped there by returning whalers, and when coastal storms scoured the bottom, the whole of the harbor was said to turn as white as milk.

The following days were spent in preparation for their continued drift in the gathering ice. This course of action was viewed by some as an unhappy compromise, particularly by those anxious to locate a safe harbor away from the unpredictable excesses of the winter build-up, and also by those who had never before participated in an unassisted drift, but who had heard the haunting tales of others caught beyond reach of a harbor.

They stripped all but their topsails. Their boats were slung in their davits and each was provisioned and sheeted and ready to be launched in a hurry. Their fore- and main-spars were loosened and then doubled-rigged against the possibility of a collision. Their sea anchors were tested and inspected, and the ropes of their mooring hooks doubled in length and thickness. Auxiliary winches were bolted to the prows of both ships ready to help them warp through the ice when sailing finally became impossible, and as far as they were able under those new conditions, their engines were over-hauled and their boilers fired.

By the late afternoon of Thursday the 28th of September they were ready to release their lines and abandon themselves to the drift.

FOURTEEN

On their third day of drifting and warping amid the thickening ice a school of belugas swam alongside them moving north, vividly white, and visible to a considerable depth in the clear water.

"Not a dry skin among them," Reid said, as he and Fitzjames watched them pass. "As full of oil as they'll ever be."

Amused by this, Fitzjames suggested fetching Reid a harpoon so that he might practice his old skill.

"They were always our sickly fish," Reid said.

"Sickly?"

The sheen of the creatures' skins and the sunlight gilding the sea gave them the appearance of being almost translucent, as though, like jellyfish, they existed without any obvious skeleton, muscle or meat.

"See them pass under you during a moonlit night and you'd be as hard pressed as many before you not to believe that they weren't the ghosts or the souls of drowned men," Reid said.

Fitzjames acknowledged the comparison. He asked why there were so many young and Reid explained that what they were seeing was known among whalers as a nursery troop, this being only the second he himself had ever seen.

"They give birth in secret places well beyond our reach and then when the young are grown enough to travel they begin their migrations. The last time I saw anything like this was on the north shore of Davis. We were ready to turn for home when a big school of

Greenland fish came straight out across our bows on a course for the pack."

"And did you give chase?"

"We were too full. We'd had a good year, already paid for the ship and the crew three times over." He paused for a moment to retrieve and savor the memory.

The whales continued to cruise past them, a group of the younger fish congregating close to their hull.

"We sold the baleen cheap for sheep pens," Reid said. "One year we'd glut the market, the next we'd leave it empty and begging for every foot of bone it could get." He was distracted from his reverie by the sound of distant gunfire, and both of them looked across to the *Terror*, where a number of men, immediately identified by their blue jackets as marines, were hanging from the rigging and firing down into the water.

Fitzjames was more outraged at this than Reid, and he searched the surface of the sea for any sign that the marksmen had found their targets. At first he saw nothing, but then his attention was drawn to a flock of gulls gathering astern of the *Terror*, and to the stain he was then able to make out on the water.

"What in God's name is Crozier thinking of?" he said aloud.

Attracted by the noise, others came to the rail and some cheered at the sight of this first kill.

A man with a pistol climbed their own rigging and fired into the water at the nearest of the small whales. Fitzjames ordered him to stop and a chorus of aggrieved disapproval rose around him.

The whales, apparently unconcerned, or perhaps oblivious to what was happening, made no attempt to leave the ships or dive out of range.

Franklin and Gore arrived to look. The others dispersed, and Franklin asked Fitzjames if he knew why the men on the *Terror* were still shooting at the fish. As he spoke, the whales passing them by decreased in number until they were gone completely. The shooting ceased and the *Terror* sailed on in silence, leaving only her stains and echoes and small dabs of gunsmoke astern.

Fitzjames reported their day's progress and the distance they had made during the previous four hours of drifting and sailing.

Franklin appeared distracted, his eyes still on the distant ice beneath which the whales had finally disappeared.

"What do they tell us, Mr. Reid?" he asked, silencing Fitzjames, who did not immediately understand what was meant by the remark.

Reid considered his answer for a moment before giving it. "I'd be a happier man if they'd passed us going south, Sir John."

"My thoughts precisely. And yet the current still draws us on."

All around them the build-up of grounded and floating ice was narrowing both their choice of channels and the channels themselves. They were, in effect, sailing into a funnel, their course now determined by the most promising-looking of the leads still available ahead of them.

The horizon they referred to as their "western shore" was not in fact land, but old dark ice ruptured and mounded in the semblance of land, stretching from north to south as far as they could see. It offered them a possible refuge, and everyone took comfort in its presence in a seascape whose more immediate features changed from one hour to the next.

Vesconte had taken readings as best he could from their moving platform, estimating that the uppermost peak of this western ridge approached a height of 500 feet. From this he concluded that it was ancient and undisturbed ice, remarking that if they were caught too close among it then they themselves might grow ancient and remain undisturbed for just as long.

The Boothia Peninsula still lay invisible to the east, and they had detected no current to suggest that any inlet or navigable passage lay between themselves and Prince Regent's Inlet on its distant shore.

Franklin left them and returned to his cabin.

The men remaining on deck considered the channel ahead of them. It had narrowed considerably during the past two days, its banks of ice growing ever more solid, and soon the two ships would be forced to sail close together if they were to avoid being separated. When sailing abreast became impossible, they would line up astern and follow a single course.

Vesconte said that his magnetic instruments had become unreliable and that his azimuth compasses and dipping needles were now useless, so close had they come to the shifting Magnetic Pole. They took some consolation from the fact that they were the first men to approach this since James Ross had marched to it from the trapped *Victory* fifteen years earlier.

Their conversation was cut short by Gore, who pointed out to them a new and prominent peak which had just then come into view above their southern horizon, and which they immediately all examined through their glasses.

Realizing that their unhindered drift might be about to come to an end sooner than he had imagined, Fitzjames ordered their winch ropes to be coiled, and then signaled for the *Terror* to take note of what lay ahead. At best the distant peak might be the ice-capped summit of an island; at worst it might represent the highest point of a land mass blocking their way forward.

At first he believed they had once again come within sight of land and that they might make for this through the thickening floe and establish their winter quarters there. But as the afternoon progressed and the sun fell lower in the sky, he saw the way in which this new landmark reflected the light, and knew that like the "land" off their starboard bow, this too was mounded, mountainous ice.

As anticipated, the ice-packed channel continued to narrow during the following days, and on the 4th of October the *Terror* came astern. All around them the smaller pieces of ice began to crash against both ships with increasing frequency and force.

On the 7th of October, after twenty-four hours during which they had sailed less than two miles, they spent their first full day warping themselves into a secure position within the ice field ahead.

They could not allow themselves to be caught on the thickening fringes of the floe where fractures and collisions were more frequent, and where the probability of damage among the large and unstable ice masses was correspondingly greater. Bulk attracted bulk, and the bergs now gathering around them varied from the size of their own boats to islands the size of cathedrals, and all of them shifting and grinding together in a bed of shattering and reforming surface ice already several feet thick.

At noon Fitzjames gave the order for what little remained of their sail to be taken in, and for Reid and his party to go out on the ice. A second party led by Thomas Blanky climbed down from the *Terror*. The two groups congregated for a moment and then dispersed.

Reid and a dozen men returned to within hailing distance of the *Erebus* and the slack of her two hawsers was pulled tight across the fixed ice. A few minutes later their first anchorage point was gouged out and the anchors secured. Winching parties then rewound the ropes, and hauled the *Erebus* into the ice shelf, crushing it beneath her as she went.

The solid-looking ice gave easily beneath the ship's weight, and the men ashore ran ahead of the splintering deltas which spread around them.

After an hour, her winching crews exhausted, the *Erebus* had been warped seventy yards and had reached her anchors.

Aboard the *Terror*, the work was again made easier by following the path already cleared through the ice, and she was pulled by her boats into the gap behind the leading ship.

The ice closed quickly around them, and they moored that night having warped themselves 150 yards into the field. When the temperature fell the displaced water froze all around them and a watch was posted to warn them of any further movement in the ice which might threaten their planned route the following day.

For the first time since leaving Beechey, they felt as well as heard the movement of the ice, felt as it squeezed their timbers, and as it knocked against them with a drumming sound where fresh ice, unable to rise to the covered surface, rolled along their hulls in its attempt to float clear.

That night a powerful collision woke everyone and they gathered on deck to see that a slab of ice twelve feet thick and rising to a height equal to their own had been suddenly and violently pushed up fifty feet off their port bow. Their lanterns were reflected in the lustrous surface of this slab, and in the darkness its upper edge could not be discerned. They heard and felt the more distant collisions where the larger masses ran together or broke up, and heard too the unsettling groan of trapped air skimming beneath the thickening surface. Those who watched were deafened by the noise of all this, and shaken by the vibrations which gripped both ships and spilled the mounds of stores on their decks.

The upended slab continued to rise as though it were being squeezed up from some vast underwater machinery. Though some returned to their bunks and the warmth of the stoves, most remained on deck to watch what might happen next, ready to take to the boats until the danger had passed.

With the first light of day they saw that the risen slab was wedged and held fast by a series of lesser blocks which had appeared around its base, and which now supported it upright where it stood. To some it rose in silhouette like the prow of a sinking ship.

The sun was fully risen by ten, and at eleven Reid and Blanky met on the ice to plan their route past this disturbance.

The warping crews were on the ice at noon, and by three the jagged eruption had been reduced to a small mount three hundred yards astern.

For a further hour they forced their way across a broad and level plain using only their engines. Their progress by this means was comparatively effortless, but they were frequently forced to reverse where the ice would not give to their gentle shoving. There was no longer any possibility of turning back into the rapidly freezing channels they left behind them.

They steamed until darkness, driving themselves into the ice until it became impossible to go any farther.

They were further hindered by a storm which lasted for two days, and when this finally abated on the morning of the 14th, they emerged to find themselves sitting on a vast plain barely distinguishable, or so Franklin remarked, from the snow-covered Lincolnshire landscape of his home. In support of this comparison, he pointed out to them the low rounded mounds of the Wolds, the level horizon of the frozen North Sea, and here and there the jagged spire of an otherwise concealed village church.

It being Sunday, a service was held and hymns sung, and afterward their bells were tolled, pealing hour after hour to celebrate their arrival, and as though in determined summons of some other, more stubborn congregation in that so-far Godless place.

Following a stocktake of their provisions, Fitzjames reported to Franklin that they still possessed enough fuel to keep their stoves burning for the next thirty-six months. Alternatively, he suggested, they had sufficient for twelve months' heat and 200 miles' steady steaming at six knots. Franklin told him to overhaul their boiler and engine in readiness for further use. He still anticipated a drift to the south in the coming winter and was determined to be ready to move with it when it came.

They finally abandoned all hope of winching themselves any farther on the 21st of October, after six hours during which they were able to make no progress whatsoever.

That evening both ice-masters reported that they were now deeply embedded in a field of ice which extended for at least ten miles behind them and possibly ten times that distance ahead.

Over the previous days, parties had explored in all directions, returning with the news that there were no major fissures or recent upheavals for at least five miles on either side of them. They brought back samples, from which Goodsir deduced the age and density of the ice, and this too reassured them, convincing Franklin that they had reached a secure position on the plain, and one from which they might continue south with the breakup the following summer.

When asked to calculate the depth of the thickening ice beneath them, both Reid and Blanky were confident that it extended to at least forty feet. Vesconte silently added a further ten to that, disappointed that he did not possess sufficient bits and drilling rods to find out for certain. All three men were united in their belief that there was moving water far beneath this, and that these submerged currents would remain flowing through the winter, exerting their pull, however slight, on the ice above.

On that final day of warping there was an accident when one of the *Erebus'* winching ropes parted, frayed by the strain imposed upon it during the previous two weeks.

The six men hauling on the rope were thrown to the ice, and one of them, seaman William Orren, hit his head on the claw and knocked himself out. He also gashed his cheek and forehead and bled badly until Stanley and Goodsir were able to reach him and stem the flow. Reid inspected the broken rope and found it to be useless, angry with himself that he had not spotted the wear on it sooner.

Sawing parties worked for a week after the *Erebus* had stopped moving, chopping out the ice in ton blocks, until it was sufficiently weakened and opened up for the *Terror* to continue pushing forward behind her. So rapidly was the water refreezing now, that the men on the ice had also to cut it free of the *Terror*'s stern, where it clung to her timbers and worked against them as they pulled her forward.

The blocks they sawed free were dragged away over the lubricated surface and positioned around both ships to act as supports when they rose in the ice. A lift of six to eight feet would prove sufficient, and to assist in this the bulk of their stores were unloaded and stacked out on the stable ice.

The *Terror* began to rise only four days after coming to rest, slowly at first, and controllably, but then with a succession of tremors which shook her along her full length and damaged both her fore- and main-royals. This damage was not serious, but the show of destructive strength acted as a warning to everyone who congregated out on the ice to watch. She was lifted six feet clear of her unloaded waterline, her stern at first staying down until it too eased itself up and she came level. When she had finally settled into this new position her supporting blocks were wedged more firmly against her until she was sitting as tight as a hen on a nest.

The *Erebus* was lifted where she sat two days later, and to assist in this she was pumped dry of all the water she had shipped. In a single day they cleared thirty-six tons from her bilges, pumping this overboard, where it froze in an icy talus over their own supporting blocks, sealing her tight.

Having been heavily sedated, William Orren did not regain consciousness until the next day after his accident. He studied his bandaged face in a mirror and asked Goodsir about his chances of making a full recovery. Goodsir expressed his surprise at the man's cultivated accent, and by the informed nature of the questions he asked. Taking him into his confidence, Orren confessed that he was an Oxford graduate and that he held a degree in Law. He had practiced for two years and had failed, after which he had enlisted as a seaman. His father was an acquaintance of George Back's and he himself had sailed with Back on the *Terror* as a boy ten years earlier before entering university. Of all the others, only Graham Gore, Back's mate, was aware of his background and he too had been sworn to secrecy.

A week after both ships had settled in their cradles and been tented, Franklin outlined his plans for the winter ahead.

There was little alternative now than to remain anchored to the ice and take their chances with it. He estimated their present position to be somewhat less than a hundred miles north-northeast of Point Victory, James Ross' Farthest West on King William Land, and with any luck they would come within sight of that same place early the following summer. Prior to that, when spring signaled its approach, he intended to dispatch a number of expeditions to explore to the south and the southwest of where they were now beset. They were all encouraged by this plan, by its simplicity and the momentum it sustained, and they toasted it and themselves before communicating it to the lower ranks, leavened as it passed from man to man by their enthusiasm and determination, and by the knowledge that they had already achieved so much where many before them had failed, that they had come farther along the true course of the Passage in a single season than anyone before them. They were convinced they had not driven themselves into the blind alleys of Frobisher and Hudson and Parry and Ross, forced only to endure and then retreat in the new season. And nor did the unknown stretch so far ahead of them as it had during their previous wintering. It was even possible, Crozier suggested, that next year they might meet men coming toward them from Bering, unhindered by the open coastal waters they themselves had yet to enjoy in completing their dash to the west.

FIFTEEN

Following a month of calm, their days were again disturbed by upheavals in the surrounding ice.

"The Day of Creation," Goodsir said absently, watching a particularly violent eruption far to the north of them.

They felt nothing of this, but heard the noise it made, like that
of an avalanche. They saw too the flashes of light as pieces of shattered ice were thrown up into the low and concentrated rays of the
sun, rising like disembodied flames against the dull horizon all
around them.

An hour earlier, Franklin had led them in their first church service
out on the ice, officers and men congregating between the two ships
to take advantage of the protection they offered, and where an altar
of ice had been built, upon which was fixed a wooden cross. "The
Day of Creation indeed, Mr. Goodsir," Franklin said aloud, walking
ahead of the small party of officers as they came out from the
shadow of the ships and stretched their legs on the ice.

Goodsir's instinct was to apologize in case Franklin had misinterpreted his remark as blasphemous. He waited to see what Franklin might say next, expecting him to turn and confront him.

Franklin, however, continued walking. It had been a week since
he had left the *Erebus*, having complained of feeling unwell, a pain
in his chest and a cold in his head, which Stanley had diagnosed as
a recurrence of his previous year's influenza. It was against his sur-

geon's advice that Franklin had left his cabin that morning to conduct his service.

"Or perhaps not the Day of Creation; perhaps we are now looking out upon the landscape of the Day of Judgment," he called back, pausing for those following to gather around him. His sermon earlier had concerned the duties of Man to God and the acceptance of God's trials. "What do you say, Mr. Crozier?"

Crozier, who had been walking at a tangent from the main party called out that he believed Franklin was right.

"I once spoke to a missionary," he said, coming forward. "An American in Reykjavik, who warned me never to communicate the true nature of Hell to any Eskimo."

"And why was that?" Fitzjames asked him, entering into the discussion with some enthusiasm, invigorated by the cold air after five days of overheated confinement.

"Because, Mr. Fitzjames, sir, Hell to an Eskimo might appear less than totally repulsive, consisting as it does, as we are all agreed, of eternal fire and damnation. These people care nothing for damnation, and eternal fire cannot appear so repellent to them, debased as they already undoubtedly are by the animal nature of their existence." Crozier spoke as though he were answering the naive and unwelcome questioning of a child.

Goodsir prevented Fitzjames from responding to this, and Fitzjames remembered the similar remark made by Reid as they had waited to row ashore at Whalefish.

"So you believe that all this, all we see around us, that this is Hell on earth?" Goodsir asked Crozier.

"I believe it is the closest we shall come to that condition without the fire," Crozier said seriously.

"But surely, each man's Hell is a different thing entirely. How can you suggest that this is Hell to the people who live here? To many of them it must surely be a paradise."

Crozier was reluctant to be drawn any further into the argument, and felt undermined by Franklin, who called, "Mr. Crozier?" to him in the hope of encouraging an answer.

"Sir John," Crozier began, pausing before he went on. "You and

I have both sailed to other so-called paradises. We were both young men then, and so that might have had some bearing on our thoughts. We are older now. I cannot change my mind upon the matter and must be given leave to disagree with Mr. Goodsir, who is clearly so much better educated than I am. I bow to his superior knowledge of these things."

A moment of silence followed, and Franklin regretted having encouraged the discussion to this tense and inconclusive impasse.

Sensing this, Goodsir ran across the ice to Crozier and declared loudly that, on the contrary, *he* bowed to his superior experience. He held out his hand and Crozier took it. Harmony was restored and the party resumed their walking.

To the east was a vast area of rippled, barely broken surface where it looked as though the sea had frozen in an instant, the peak and trough of each wave solidifying as it rolled toward some distant shore.

To the north lay the sea of ice through which they had already come. This was no longer flat. Bergs formed the centers of frozen tors, upon which new ice had formed, and against which boulders and slabs had built up and spilled outward in exact replicas of those other land-locked features.

To the west the high, peaked ridge had continued to rise and to build ever since they had come to their anchorage. In the early sun it caught the light and looked sharp and clean, but when the sun went from it, it became dark and forbidding, looking more like rock and earth than ice and snow. Lately it had acquired the sheen of tarnished silver. It cut off their wider view in that direction and cast its own long shadows like loose scree toward them.

It was from this mountainous range, which they were all agreed might persist for fifty years after their departure, that the loudest and most vigorous disturbances reached them. Even fixed as solidly as they were to the ice beneath them, both vessels were occasionally shaken by the upheavals in this direction. Some of those aboard were even tempted to believe that what they were witnessing was not merely the gathering together of the ice, but the upheaval of submerged land, the birthing of another volcano perhaps, pushing into existence and ready to declare its arrival with a fountain of flame and pillar of smoke. Even those whose imaginations did not stretch this far believed that with the onset of the thaw they would see dark rock showing through the surface as the ice fell from it in patches like the winter coat of a moulting fox.

It was to the southwest, however, that their greatest attention was directed. Here there lay an endless mass of fractured ice so confused and disjointed that all who looked out upon it doubted if it could ever be penetrated to discover what lay beyond. In places this was broken by long straight avenues along which a coach might be driven, but elsewhere a man would exhaust himself in a day's journey of 200 yards.

"How does it suit you, Mr. Fitzjames?" Crozier asked unexpectedly, indicating the view ahead of them.

Caught unaware, and unwilling to voice his true thoughts on the overland expedition he was to lead the following spring, Fitzjames could only gesture dismissively, hoping to suggest that he was little concerned by the terrain he might be forced to cross.

"Mr. Fitzjames?" Franklin said, having overheard Crozier's remark, and wanting to hear Fitzjames' answer for himself.

"Your own Farthest East," Fitzjames said, turning to acknowledge his captain. "I'll do Back's work for him. It can surely be no more than two hundred miles to the mainland coast." Franklin was gratified and encouraged by the remark.

Crozier left them to return to the *Terror* in the company of his own lieutenants.

Franklin and Fitzjames walked back together, Franklin pausing frequently to cough and then to regain his breath. Stanley and Goodsir walked ahead of them, and Franklin pointed the two men out to Fitzjames, conscious of why they were remaining so close to him. At one point the spasm of coughing which racked Franklin was so violent that he stumbled and almost fell, afterward standing for five minutes until he felt sufficiently composed to continue.

They reached the *Erebus* half an hour later. There were fifty men still out on the ice, singly and in small parties. Gunshots indicated where some were hunting, outbreaks of cheering and applause where others were engaged in some sport. Their two dogs barked incessantly and ran from one man to the next. Gore had set up his camera, and earlier, while the brighter light had lasted, he had taken a picture of both ships' marines in full dress uniform against a backdrop of freshly cut ice, carved and stacked to look like distant mountains, and fooling no one but the camera.

At three in the afternoon a maroon was fired to call everyone back to the ships. It rose weakly and exploded prematurely low, leaving the imprint of its small black moon floating above the converging men.

The first dark day of their second Arctic night came with the unexpected death of Edward Little on Christmas Eve.

He was discovered by Thomas Jopson, Crozier's steward, who arrived to wake him at seven in the morning, and found him, as he at first believed, unconscious. Securing Little's cabin, Jopson went immediately to fetch Crozier, speaking to no one he encountered on his short journey.

The two men returned fifteen minutes later. Peddie and Macdonald were sent for, and Little's cabin remained locked until they arrived. Macbean was told to clear the corridor and secure the door at its far end, allowing entry to no one except George Hodgson, who had also been sent for.

There was barely room in the confined space of the cabin for Crozier and his two surgeons, and Crozier reluctantly stepped back outside to join Irving while the two medical men examined Little. It was still not apparent to Crozier that Little was in fact dead.

The young lieutenant had not been out of his cabin for the previous four days, confessing to his fellow officers and the stewards who attended to him that the problem was not only the continuing cramps in his leg, but also the violent cold he had contracted. Only Peddie was not deceived, but this had not prevented him from prescribing solutions of laudanum in increasingly potent doses.

Little's cabin was spartan. His clothes lay packed in his chest, his instruments in their cases, his books on their shelf. A tin and a box on his bedside cabinet were opened to reveal his more personal belongings and a collection of letters awaiting their eventual delivery.

Dropping his stethoscope, Peddie stooped to retrieve it, and saw in the darkness beneath Little's narrow bunk the glint of glass, knowing what he would find before he slid his hand across the polished boards. He collected nine empty vials and held them in the dim glow of the lantern for Macdonald to see. Both men understood immediately what had happened. The revelation shocked them, and for a moment neither could speak. Peddie moved to stand against the door, preventing anyone from entering. The voices of Crozier, Irving and Hodgson could be heard outside.

"His leg," Peddie said, indicating the soiled sheet covering Little. Macdonald lifted this to reveal that beneath it Little was naked, his bandages loosely coiled around his feet. The bruising on his thigh was more prominent than ever, infected and yellow and swollen with pus. They also saw that Little had emptied both his bowels and bladder into his mattress.

Both men started at a sudden rapping on the door, and as Crozier called to be let in, Macdonald looked to Peddie, who rubbed a hand across his face and nodded once. He gathered up the empty vials and pulled the sheet back over Little's legs.

Crozier knew the instant he saw the look on Macdonald's face that Little was dead, and he came into the cabin as though in a trance, standing beside the thin pale body and looking hard into the corpse's closed eyes. For several minutes no one spoke.

"Do you know how?" Crozier asked.

Peddie and Macdonald exchanged a glance. Crozier saw this and grabbed Peddie's bag from him, pulling it open and tipping its contents on to the bed, where they fell and settled around Little's sheeted legs.

"He took his own life," Macdonald said quietly, indicating the closed door. "His pain became too great for him to bear and he took his own life." He spoke mechanically.

"He would not have wanted to become a burden," Peddie added.

Crozier shouted, "No!" This response shocked the two surgeons. "But how great can his pain have been? He was in bed with a cold.

His leg was healing every day. Was he lying to us?"

Macdonald nodded, and then stood aside as both Irving and Hodgson appeared in the doorway anxious to learn what had happened. A glance at the bed told them everything they had feared.

Little's mouth was open, his jaw pulled tight and jutting slightly, pushing his bottom lip away from his teeth, as though he were straining for a drink he could not quite reach.

"My God," Hodgson said. He had visited Little shortly before eleven the previous night. He pushed closer to the bed and saw the empty vials.

Peddie drew back the sheet so that they might all look at Little's wound, and so they might all smell the faint but distinct aroma of his tainted urine. Crozier, being the closest, took out a handkerchief and held it to his mouth.

At the sound of footsteps in the corridor outside, Irving called for the door to be shut and barred.

"What do we do?" Hodgson said after they had all silently given the matter some thought.

It was Irving who reached down and for the first time pulled up the sheet to cover Little's face.

"First we have a duty to inform Sir John," Crozier said.

The real question, they knew, was what the crew of the *Terror* would be told regarding the death.

Crozier sent Irving and Peddie to inform Franklin of their discovery, warning them to keep nothing from him.

They returned fifteen minutes later with both Franklin and Fitzjames. Fitzjames too had seen Little the previous day, having come from the *Erebus* to tell him of a fox-hunt he was organizing. Little, a keen huntsman, had faked enthusiasm for the project, and although Fitzjames had guessed immediately that the painful effort was being made for his sake alone, he had encouraged the deception until Little became too tired to continue with it.

He drew back the sheet and looked down, his gaze drawn to Little's open mouth.

"If you let me have his personal effects, I'll write to his family."

"Not your responsibility, Mr. Fitzjames," Crozier said.

"I know them. I visited them a few months before we sailed."

"And what will you tell them?"

"That he—"

"That he chose to absolve himself of every responsibility for the men under his command? That he chose to die like a—"

"Francis," Franklin warned.

"My apologies. But the responsibility for communicating the news of Mr. Little's death remains with me alone, and I shall do it as I see fit. I would appreciate it if Mr. Fitzjames would not interfere, and if he would take more care in future not to allow so-called friendship to become confused with prescribed duty and professional obligation." He turned sharply and left them.

Fitzjames drew the sheet back over his friend's face. He would write privately, reassured by the knowledge that it might be two or even three years before any letter was received, and before Edward Little finally died where death was at its most complete—in the hearts of those who loved him.

It was ten in the morning by the time they left, and the clouded darkness showed no signs of brightening, however briefly, in the glare of the hidden moon. Even without the sun they were accustomed to speaking of their bright days and their dull ones.

Fitzjames crossed the ice with Graham Gore.

"Did you have any idea, James? I mean even a suspicion?"

"I knew his suffering was greater than he revealed to us."

"But this great?"

Fitzjames nodded. Of all their senior officers, Little's promotion had been the most recent, and he had the least experience of both the ice and the handling of men. They were both aware of this, and their judgments on his death remained unspoken.

"I believe the wisest course would be not to reveal the exact nature of his death," Fitzjames said. "Allow the gossip-mongers to do their work, and let the others believe or disbelieve entirely upon their own dislike or affection for the man."

"Dislike?" Gore said loudly, surprised by the bluntness of the suggestion.

Fitzjames walked ahead, regretting how sanctimonious and judg-mental the honest remark had sounded.

Little was buried on the second day of the new year, having first been laid out in a roughly built mausoleum on the ice. The presence of the corpse tolled a mournful note over their festive celebrations, particularly aboard the *Terror*, where the morale of the crew had been low since the discovery of the body.

The funeral took place mid-morning, a party having left several hours earlier to saw through the ice of the grave-site two hundred yards west of the ships. Here the surface had long since folded and overlapped and lay now in a succession of slabs, each with several feet of level surface. It was one of these near-horizontal pieces that had been chosen to accommodate Little's grave.

As with their earlier burials, Franklin read the service and related something of Little's previous history, most of which he had learned from Fitzjames earlier that same day. Men threw in handfuls of crushed ice just as they might, in other circumstances, have thrown in soil. An artificial wreath had been made and this too was thrown down upon the coffin.

The temperature that morning had been measured by Vesconte at 49 degrees below freezing, their coldest yet, and despite the bra-ziers they had brought with them, no one was able to stand for more than a few seconds without flapping his arms or stamping his feet.

A headboard had been carved, to which a printed tin shield was attached. This disclosed nothing other than the name of the man buried there, his dates of birth and death, and the expedition upon which he had been embarked. Crozier had suggested to Franklin that an appropriate line from the Scriptures might be added, but having considered this in the light of the nature of Little's death, Franklin rejected the idea, unwilling to make this everlasting and damning judgment on the man.

Graham Gore speculated on the creation of the first wholly photo-graphic panorama of the Arctic, similar to those he had visited in

London prior to their departure. He had taken his wife and three children to the Haymarket Gallery, queueing for two hours to see Brownlow's Polar Panorama, part photographed, part painted, the detail and beauty of which had impressed him beyond all expectation.

He had sailed in Arctic waters before and knew how great the difference was between the reality and what Brownlow had skillfully created using photographs taken in the Alps and the Norwegian fjords, and it was only now that he felt he had mastered the equipment in his charge that he seriously considered the possibility of attempting such a project.

His thoughts on this as he gazed out into the surrounding darkness were interrupted by the arrival of Goodsir and Vesconte. They were accompanied by the boy Robert Golding, who had been more distressed than most by the death of Edward Little, having been seconded to him by Crozier on Peddie's recommendation to assist Little with all the routine activities and duties he found too tiring or painful to carry out. The boy had responded well to this new responsibility and was frequently Little's only companion during the hours of his confinement. In the month before his death, Little had taught the thirteen-year-old Golding the elementary moves in chess-playing and was teaching him to read and write.

The first Gore heard were the whispering voices behind him; he turned and saw the two men and the boy all holding up their gloved hands and framing him in the squares made by their fingers and thumbs. It was something he himself had been advised to do by Adamson, and something he now did almost without thinking whenever a particular composition of men or natural features presented itself to him. Eventually it had become a substitute, particularly now that the light had gone, for making the picture itself.

Participating in the joke, Gore drew himself upright, pulled straight his jacket and stood with his arms by his side. Goodsir started the slow count to twenty and Gore spoke to them through his clenched teeth.

After inquiring about Golding's reading lessons, which others had volunteered to continue, he told them about his idea concerning the panorama he intended to make when the opportunity next arose during the following spring or summer.

"A circle encompassing the full three hundred and sixty degrees, myself as its pivot. Fifty, or perhaps even a hundred individual plates, each one overlapping in a broad sweep. Here the ships, there an imposing mountain of ice; here a boat of rowing men, there a distant horizon blanketed with fog; here, perhaps, a blowing whale or colony of seals, and there a party hauling a sledge of stores." Gore raised both hands, as though holding up invisible balls. "To the left the returning sun, its rays solid and fanning out upon the scene, and to the right the waning moon, spectral in the brightening sky."

The others were amused and then intrigued by his enthusiastic speculations.

"Can there be a bear with the dogs setting about it?" Robert Golding asked, the first of them to speak.

"Two bears, a dozen bears," Gore told him.

"And men with their rifles fighting them off?"

"And men with their rifles," Gore conceded, aware that he was allowing too much, but unwilling to put a brake on the youngster's imagination.

"And all this would be present on the day you made the pictures?" Vesconte asked skeptically.

The remark pleased Gore, allowing him to draw in the reins of their speculations. "That's the great beauty of the camera," he told them authoritatively. "None of it need be happening in conjunction with any other part of the design at the same time. I might expose the plates over several days, weeks even, and then piece them all together to suggest a single moment."

Vesconte was disappointed by this. "So, in effect, you would be doing no more and no less than the painters attempt to do when they profess to be portraying these regions without ever leaving their Hampstead studios?"

"Except that the photographic record would be indisputable truth that it had been made amid everything it showed."

Goodsir interrupted: "And might we *all* be present upon the ice so that anyone who looked at this panorama would recognize us and be able to point us out?"

"Naturally," Gore said, sensing the return of their own interest in the project.

"So we might stand bravely alongside one of the bears and not have it anywhere near us in reality?" Vesconte said.

"Not right next to the creature, not so as he could reach out and swipe you with his paw?" Robert Golding said, confused and then alarmed by what he believed Gore was suggesting.

"I could place *you* the closest of all. This far from the monster's claws," Gore told him, opening his arms to suggest the distance and succeeding only in adding fear to the youngster's alarm.

SIXTEEN

Fitzjames, Reid and Des Voeux were inspecting the recent buildup of ice around the *Erebus'* stern when Des Voeux grabbed Reid's arm, spun him around and pointed him in the direction of the higher land to the west. At first Reid saw nothing, but then, guided by Des Voeux, he made out the form of a large animal crossing the skyline.

"What is it?" Des Voeux asked, instinctively crouching, and ready to call for one of the marine marksmen at this unexpected prospect of fresh meat.

Reid pulled down his hood and called softly to Fitzjames, who had moved ahead of them and was sounding the surface ice.

"Bear," Reid said, crouching beside Des Voeux and indicating for Fitzjames to do the same. He felt the breeze on his face. "He won't scent us. He might not even see us against the ships."

"What's it doing?" Des Voeux asked nervously. Even from that distance they could see that the bear was fully grown, and seemingly unconcerned by the presence of the ships.

"Just come to look us over." Reid rose slowly and watched as the animal patrolled along the ridge of high ice, now more clearly silhouetted against the sky beyond.

"Will it come down to us?" Des Voeux asked.

"I doubt it," Reid told him.

Fitzjames raised his iron bar in readiness, conscious of how useless a weapon it would prove to be if the bear did decide to come down and investigate them more closely.

"He sees us and we see him," Reid said.

"How can you be so sure it's a male?" Des Voeux asked.

"Look at his size, at how his weight's distributed." He stopped and watched without speaking as the animal finally dropped below the skyline and was lost to view. "The farmer," he said suddenly. "That's what we used to call him. The farmer. Look at him—a well-fed squire pacing up and down his spring corn, smug and self-satisfied."

They were joined a few minutes later by the *Erebus'* two other mates, Robert Sargent and Edward Couch, and upon being told of what they had just missed, both men became excited about the prospect of a hunt. Fitzjames, too, acknowledged the appeal of this, particularly since they had been so unsuccessful against the scavenging foxes, the killing of which hardly repaid their efforts and seemed only to encourage the countless others which arrived to take the place of the dead.

It was by then the beginning of March. The sun had returned a month earlier, but it was still too late in the day for them to pursue the animal immediately. Sargent and Couch left them with the intention of getting Franklin's permission to set out in pursuit at first light the following morning.

Conscious of their need for diversion after their months of confinement and idleness, Franklin agreed. Two parties would be dispatched, one from each ship, and a prize would be awarded to the crew who succeeded in killing the bear.

That night, in an attempt to keep the animal in the vicinity of the ships, rotten meat and other waste was left at intervals along the ridge on which it had been spotted.

The hunting party from the *Terror* was to be led by George Hodgson, and was to include Tozer and three of his marines. That of the *Erebus* chose Fitzjames as its leader, and comprised, in addition to Bryant and their own marines, Goodsir, Vesconte and Gore, the mates, their warrant officers, and two dozen other petty officers and seamen. Reid, at first reluctant to become involved, was finally persuaded by Fitzjames.

In all there would be almost sixty men out on the ice, half armed with rifles and pistols, the others with clubs and boat-hooks. These latter would serve as beaters and then drivers, ensuring that if the animal was still in the vicinity then it would be found, surrounded and driven upon the guns.

A great many preparations were made for the hunt. Weapons were cleaned and ammunition made, and stories of earlier hunts were repeated long into the night.

At eleven Fitzjames left his cabin in search of Reid. It was only during dinner, as he had speculated about the following day's sport, that he had become aware of Reid's lack of enthusiasm for the adventure. Gore, renowned as a marksman with a pistol, had requested permission to deliver the coup de grâce to the animal should it first be wounded. Goodsir was more interested in acquiring samples of its fur, and in the retrieval of its liver so that he might distil and examine its poisons. Everything about the hunt was discussed, and in this way the pleasure of it was infinitely extended, infecting even those who had chosen not to participate. So encouraging was the air of fervid expectation aboard the ships that both Franklin and Crozier acquiesced to purser Osmer's request to open a book on the outcome of the chase.

Reid's reluctance had also been noted by others, and this tipped the balance in favor of the *Terror*'s huntsmen. Thomas Blanky was optimistic about their chances in pursuit over good ice, and even the aggressive nature of Solomon Tozer counted in their favor as wagers were laid and covered.

The two parties drew up their plans for the following day and then guarded these as jealously as plans of battle.

Finding Reid in his bunk, Fitzjames asked him if he wished to be excluded from their party, quickly adding that he personally would feel much happier if he were present considering the distance to be covered and the numbers involved.

Reid acknowledged both the apology and the concern. He closed the book he had been reading and rubbed his eyes. It was late and he hadn't slept for thirty-six hours.

"With any luck he'll see he has no chance of escape and charge us the minute the first of us gets within his reach. As long as we don't try and fill him full of number four shot he should fall fast enough."

This suggestion worried Fitzjames. "Is that likely? I always imagined they would run away from any trouble rather than confront it."

"And that's precisely why the hunt's going ahead. I'll come along, if only to make sure that the creature isn't forced into a position where he has to turn and defend himself. Prepare and organize all you like, but once you take that many men out on the ice you'll have little control over their comings and goings. Shout at them as much as you please, but one sight of the creature and they'll all be after him like schoolboys after a ball. Plan for the kill, listen to Mr. Gore's fancy words for a bullet in the head, but once they see him they'll let loose with everything they've got, shooting wild as savages and as fast as they can suck and blow."

Fitzjames guessed that he was speaking from experience, and reassured him that both he and Hodgson would exercise as much control over the hunt as possible. But he spoke with little real conviction and neither of them was convinced by what he said.

He left after only a few minutes, knowing that he had achieved nothing other than make his own uncertainties public.

The two hunting parties left the ships the following day and crossed the ice in opposite directions, intending to move in a wide pincer and drive the bear back toward where it had first been sighted.

The party from the *Erebus* set out at a steady pace, each man partnered with at least one other, and those with firearms divided among those armed only with clubs. Bryant and his marines made a separate party in advance of the officers, spreading in a line abreast as they left the ships behind.

In contrast to this, the party from the *Terror* disembarked and ran in a crowd in the same general direction. Unrestrained, several men fired their rifles into the air and those around them cheered and yelled.

"They're more likely to shoot each other than anything else," Goodsir remarked, as he, Fitzjames and the others climbed to the summit of a low rise and looked down on the confusion below. Reid scanned the plain ahead of them, but saw nothing.

"In which case old whitey is ours for certain." Gore cocked the hammer of his pistol, held it rigidly at arm's length and swung it in a wide, steady sweep.

"Perhaps if we come across the unfortunate creature asleep in its lair," Goodsir said, winking at Fitzjames and the others, "then you could deliver your card and invite it to come out and duel with you."

"In which case it certainly would be an unfortunate creature," Gore said, suddenly jerking back his arm in the prescribed manner until his pistol was held vertically against his shoulder.

They all laughed at him, knowing that he had participated in no duel, and that his shooting experience was restricted to the Marlborough and District Target Shooting Club, of which he had been voted Captain for the seventh year in succession prior to his departure, a position he would hold for the duration of his absence.

In his cabin, Gore kept a case of the medals and trophies he had won, and these, apart from the letters written to him by his wife—thirty-six in all, and which he read, as promised, one a month—were among his proudest possessions.

"Mr. Reid," he said loudly, silencing them all. "All I require of you is that you point out to me that part of the creature where my ball might do the most good. I believe you and I understand each other perfectly in this matter. You yourself are unarmed, so might I suggest that you stay close by my side. Together we are certain to make a winning team." He said all this with mock seriousness, as though he were reciting to a theater audience who already knew what the day held in store for them. He beckoned for Reid to join him and then led them all forward to where Bryant and his marines waited.

The ice ahead of them was tilted and mounded, and pushed up into steep ridges in places, over which they were forced to scramble on all fours. It was old ice, revealing the striations and coloring of many years' accumulation.

Inspecting the contours as they went, it became clear to Reid that they were walking over floes that had drifted, built upon each other and been compacted for the past seventy-five years, ice which had been laying down its frozen foundations since before any of them had even been born.

"We ought to have brought the dogs," Des Voeux said, arriving breathless alongside them with his fellow mates, both of whom carried blunderbusses.

Gore considered the inadvisability of this. "Or perhaps we could have brought the ape, and the bear could have used it as a plaything before I stepped in to do the honors."

Des Voeux felt uncomfortable at the rebuff, and shouldering their arms the three mates left to join the main party.

Many, disappointed that there had so far been no sign of the bear, wandered over the ice singly and in pairs, their course now determined by whatever caught their attention.

Philip Reddington suggested that they might already have passed the animal and that it might now be lying up behind them. Those who agreed with him turned to look in the direction they had come, but there was nothing to see, not even the distant ships, hidden behind the ridges they had climbed.

It was after they had eaten and as they prepared to resume the hunt that one of the marines called down to them from the low peak upon which he and the others had been resting. The bear had been sighted to the north, he shouted, but instead of moving away from them it was now crossing their path directly ahead of them.

Running round a large ridge of jagged ice, they finally saw the animal. It too was running, at some speed, but not away from them; instead it appeared to be making for an area of broken ground away to their left in which to seek refuge.

At the first sight of the bear, the staggered line of them broke up and everyone raced toward it in a noisy group.

As they ran, Reid grabbed Fitzjames' arm and shouted, "It's not the same animal."

"Does it matter?" Fitzjames said, catching his breath.

"This one's a female. She's carrying some winter fat, but she's still much smaller."

Fitzjames resumed running, and Reid joined him.

Ahead of them, the first shots were fired. The leaders of the group were now less than a hundred yards from the bear. Others were running along the same path as the creature. Further shots were fired and several of the chasing men stopped to reload. A louder explosion indicated that one of the blunderbusses had been fired.

Pausing again to see if any of these shots had had any effect on the bear, Fitzjames watched as the animal continued running ahead of them, apparently unhurt.

A further volley rang out, this time from the marines, who had formed themselves into a firing box. The bear responded by pulling sharply to the left, stumbling for several paces, and then running on at the same rapid pace as before.

By now the men running along parallel courses to the animal had climbed among the first ridges of the crumpled ice, and as it approached them they fired down on it from above.

The bear stumbled again, but again it didn't fall. Instead it turned and ran for a short distance in another direction, then turned again and ran directly toward the main body of men now closing on it.

Still at a distance from all this, Fitzjames called for them to clear away from its path, but was uncertain if he could be heard amid the confusion. He stopped beside a slab of upright ice, upon which Goodsir had positioned himself. Gore knelt beside him, his pistol held at arm's length. A dozen others gathered around them, concerned by this turn of events and by their sudden proximity to the bear.

The wounded animal continued toward them. The men it passed gathered behind and came after it. The air was filled with the smell of gunsmoke and with the cries and cheers of the men close enough to see that the hunt was about to draw to a successful conclusion. Some paused to look down at the splashes of blood on the ice.

A second blunderbuss was fired, and those still gathered beside the slab of ice saw Robert Sargent raise his weapon in the air and wave with his free arm. Twenty feet ahead of him the bear had finally fallen, its front legs buckling beneath it as it tried to continue running, its hind legs kicking uselessly behind it. Men gathered around it and discharged their weapons into its white flanks. The air above the body grew dense with smoke.

Graham Gore shouldered his pistol and then returned it to the holster strapped across his chest.

Fitzjames ran forward and called for the hunters to stop firing. Men were already dancing around the corpse, and at his arrival they cleared a path for him and each man made claims for his own part in the killing.

The bear was dead, and despite the number of wounds it had received, there was surprisingly little blood on its coat, only a long dark smear on the ice where it had finally gone down.

He was joined by Reid, Goodsir and Gore.

Gore took out his pistol, held it to the dead creature's skull and fired into it. He did this dispassionately, making the act appear almost a gesture of apology. At the recoil of the shot he stepped back, a look of surprise on his face, as though he were shocked by what he had done.

Around him the hunters fell silent. There was no wind and the gunsmoke hung in a pall above them.

They were all distracted from the corpse a moment later by the appearance of the party from the *Terror*, the leaders of which ran out from behind the mounded ice in which the bear had sought shelter. They ran to where the men from the *Erebus* were gathered. Two of them pulled something on ropes, which Fitzjames at first assumed to be the body of a seal they had shot. When the men came closer, however, he saw that what they were dragging was the small and bloody corpse of a cub, their ropes fastened to its hind paws.

"*That's* where she was headed," Reid said to him.

Solomon Tozer pushed through the men around the body of the larger bear, and without warning, he too discharged his rifle into it, followed by the marines who accompanied him. Satisfied, they stepped back from the corpse and began to argue with the marines from the *Erebus* about which party had been the first to kill their own bear.

Reid went alone to inspect the body of the cub, and saw that it had been shot just as many times as its mother. He untied the ropes from its paws, and picking it up he carried it to the adult bear and threw it down beside her.

Philip Reddington approached Fitzjames and asked for permission to take one of the larger bear's paws as a trophy. A few minutes later both it and the cub had been virtually dismembered in the quest for souvenirs. One man took the eyes and others the tongues. Yet another smashed loose several teeth and immediately offered them for sale as mementoes of the hunt.

Goodsir took his examples of fur, but could not bring himself to open up the body and take out part of the liver.

One of their burners was lit, and the men who had cut out the tongues cooked and ate them.

Shortly afterward they left the scene of the kill and returned to the ships in a broken line stretching for almost a mile over the darkening ice.

A number of foxes appeared out of the shadows to take advantage of the abandoned carcasss. Men fired at these, but none was hit. Fitzjames himself shot at one as it raced across the path immediately ahead of him. He missed, watching as the small animal darted left and right in a practiced maneuver of evasion which seemed to mock him before it finally bolted into a fissure and was lost.

THE UNKNOWN GRIEFS
OF FUTURE YEARS

May—July 1847

SEVENTEEN

Fitzjames set out to explore in the southwest accompanied by eleven men and provisioned for sixty days. He left the *Erebus* on the 4th of May, allowing for outward and homeward journeys of a month each, with orders to turn back on the 3rd of June whatever progress he might have made.

The midday temperature throughout February and March had fluctuated between minus 45 and minus 30, but during April this rose steadily to stand around 20 degrees. He hoped to make contact with any Eskimos he encountered, seek information from them regarding the land to the west, and barter with them for food and assistance. A sack of gifts, largely needles and other small tools, was included in his stores.

He took with him Reid, James Fairholme, Goodsir, Philip Reddington, five seamen and two marines, including David Bryant.

On the *Erebus*, Graham Gore was temporarily promoted to second in command, and he read out a speech of farewell as the expedition assembled itself on the ice and finally left the ships at noon on the 4th.

Fitzjames and Reid walked in front. Then came the seamen hauling their sledges, two men to each and the fifth walking between them and rocking them free whenever they became stuck. Others walked alongside them to their boundary posts, where they stood waving and shouting until the expedition was out of sight.

Despite their eventual destination, it was Fitzjames' intention to depart due west, to where the distant ice ridge broke the horizon, and then to follow this south until it became low enough for them to cross, or until, as Reid suspected, it eventually sank down into the surrounding plain.

They walked out of sight of the ships at three in the afternoon.

By sunset they had covered three-quarters of the distance over easy solid ice, Fairholme fixing and plotting their progress each hour against the tallest of the peaks ahead.

At seven Franklin had arranged to fire a signal rocket by which the expedition might more accurately fix its position in the falling darkness, and at that hour all twelve men stopped walking and scanned the eastern horizon. Reddington was the first to see it, directing them all to where the single spark rose wavering into the night sky. This brief sighting was sufficient for Fairholme to align his instruments and confirm their position.

After this, their hands and faces numbed by the rapidly cooling air, they pitched their tents, each man unrolling his Mackintosh floor cloth and down sleeping-bag and sliding into this as best he could fully clothed.

The following day they reached the ice ridge and turned south, soon exhausted as they began traveling over more difficult terrain.

Fairholme and Reddington climbed a low crest in the hope of seeing the distant ships, but were foiled by the glare of the sun on the ice. They all wore black crêpe and gauze shields to protect them from snow blindness, and some had on gutta-percha nose-guards lined with soft flannel to shield against burning.

They traveled south for a further four days before arriving at a breach in the ice barrier, by which they were able to make progress to the west. They walked between cliffs two hundred feet high, sheer for most of their height, and with an overhang the full length of their surface rim. It was darker and much cooler in this chasm and they kept their voices low for fear of causing any unstable ice above them to come loose. They walked less widely spaced, and the men pulling the sledges changed places hourly.

They did not emerge from the gorge at the end of the first day, and so they camped inside it, pitching their tents and stowing their supplies close against its concave north wall in case of an ice-fall during the night.

They were woken at three the following morning by the noise of such a fall and, fearful that it might have blocked their way ahead, Fitzjames and Reid went to investigate. Fairholme and Reddington explored in the direction they had already come, and they were the first to return with the news that the collapse had taken place behind them and that any retreat back through the chasm was now out of the question.

"So the trap is sprung," Goodsir said with a smile.

Several of the less experienced men asked him to explain. Fitzjames, too, regretted the flippant remark.

"What Mr. Goodsir means," Reid said, "is that we need no longer harbor distracting notions about turning back and seeking out another path."

"Precisely," Goodsir said, unrepentant. He was the first to turn his back on the ice-fall and return to his sleeping bag.

The next day the path narrowed as the ice walls closed in on them, and they moved more slowly, forced to negotiate other recent falls. After midday the sun shone in on the upper edge of the north wall, penetrating no more than ten or fifteen feet below its rim. At the bottom of the canyon they traveled in a perpetual gloom.

It was only as they were about to pitch their tents for a second night in the gorge that Reid returned from scouting ahead with the news that they were close to emerging from it and into the open ice beyond.

"It's hard to see clearly," he told Fitzjames. "The cliffs are low and the light more vivid."

"What do you suggest?" Fitzjames asked him, conscious of the need for them to halt for the day before it became too cold, but also of the desirability of escaping from the restricted path while the opportunity still existed.

"Go on," Reid advised him. "Double up the men in the harnesses and march for as long as it takes. Get out and then rest until noon tomorrow."

Fitzjames agreed with this and gave word to the others that they were going on.

They walked blindly in the pitch darkness, a guide with a lamp twenty feet ahead of them. They could see nothing of the ground over which they walked, not even the walls on either side of them. High above them they were able to make out the pinpoint of light of a solitary star, and by this means alone were they able to distinguish between the night sky and the dark walls rising beside them.

They emerged from the chasm at two in the morning, and as soon as they were back out in the open they pitched their tents and retired on cold rations, all of them frequently waking during the night, cold and stiff after their exertions.

At dawn they disturbed a pair of foxes tugging at the covering of one of the sledges. They shot and butchered these and cooked them in a fire using empty cases for fuel, and the roast meat, eaten with sweet porridge and molasses, invigorated them all.

Those complaining of numbness in their faces, toes and fingers were examined by Goodsir, but no one was found to be suffering from anything other than the most superficial frostbite, which he was able to treat.

They stayed at the camp until one in the afternoon, whereupon they resumed their journey to the west, all relieved to be back out in the open where they could again see and feel the sun.

A march of four hours took them beyond the contours of the ridge and revealed ahead of them a vast, low plain of ice, considerably larger than the one they had left behind. Their first sight of this pleased and disappointed Fitzjames in equal measure. It pleased him because it offered them the prospect of easy travel across its broad open surface, but disappointed him by its featurelessness. He had hoped to scan the horizon and see there the darker smudges of distant land, buried or emergent. He had even hoped that he might also have seen the frozen course of some hitherto undiscovered channel, soon to rupture and reveal itself as navigable, and it was only when Reid pointed out to him that the scene ahead of them was not so featureless as it first appeared that his hopes began to rise.

"Mark the line of that braided curve," Reid told him, calling for Fairholme to join them and plot this barely visible mark on their charts. They studied the feature through their glasses, turning to examine it along its full length.

"A pressure ridge," Fairholme suggested.

Fitzjames agreed with him.

Reid shook his head. "The last of the nip to freeze over. Those irregularities are the last of its floating blocks to be caught and frozen as it closed in on them."

"You mean there's flowing water beneath?"

"Was," Reid said. "When we get closer I can find out if they were frozen into place last year or the one before."

"Or perhaps even the one before that," Fitzjames said, feeling some of his initial disappointment return.

Reid then pointed out to them that the ice farther north was more heavily folded than elsewhere along the ridge.

"That's what caused our explosions," he said matter of factly. "And the reason we didn't feel the tremors is because they were absorbed by what we've just come through."

"Perhaps they forced the ice to split and create our gulley," Goodsir suggested, to which Reid nodded his agreement.

Fitzjames examined this distant upheaval, searching south and west for an indication that open water had already appeared in conjunction with it. Even at that distance—he judged the near-vertical slabs to be five miles away—the disturbance had clearly taken place on a large scale.

"How high do you think they're standing?" he asked Reid.

Reid guessed at a hundred feet, adding that he was more concerned with discovering *why* they had been so violently raised.

They continued walking south until the shadows of the ridge ran downhill and swept over them, chilling them as fully and as suddenly as the first surge of cold water over a bather's feet.

By the end of the first week they had traveled sixty miles, ten less than Fitzjames had hoped for.

David Bryant and his marine private began to suffer from blindness, and Goodsir treated them, substituting goggles for their gauze and then thickening and darkening the lenses of these by the addition of spare pieces he carried.

On their fourteenth day, Reid, who had advanced ahead of them over a broad sweep of more broken ice, returned with the news that he had spotted something to the south.

"Land?" Fitzjames asked hopefully.

Reid shook his head. "Something on the ice."

He led them back to where he had made the sighting, and they examined the dark shape through their glasses, its outline lost in the liquid glimmer all around them.

"A morse," Reddington suggested, meaning a walrus.

"Too far south, surely," Fitzjames said.

"If it is, then it means open water near by," Reid said, unconvinced, but silencing them all and causing them to search around the object for any sign of this. They saw none.

"Wreckage," Fairholme said as he moved ahead of them and was the first to approach the shattered prow of a small boat firmly embedded in the ice. They speculated on how it had come to be there, deciding finally that it was old flotsam, ten or fifteen years old perhaps, and that it had been lost or abandoned by a whaler far to the north, afterward becoming trapped in the drift and being carried farther and farther south each year.

They searched the area around it but found nothing more. Goodsir attempted to chip away the ice into which the prow was frozen to determine how much more of the boat existed beneath the surface, but the old ice defeated his efforts and broke beneath his blows in only the smallest of chips.

Going on, they began to stumble over rougher ground, frequently falling and tipping their sledges. Climbing a piece of ice which rose to shoulder height, Fairholme indicated the flow lines all around them stretching in unbroken furrows from north to south, and fanning there like a horse's tail. He also pointed out that the terrain in the direction they were traveling was more faulted and uneven than that over which they had already come.

Later, a second low range, flat-topped and less spectacular than the first, rose and stretched across their western horizon.

They made no further progress that day, and for the following four days continued to travel toward this new landmark.

On the fifth day one of their sledges was damaged, its runner breaking loose of its brass fittings. This caught against a block of ice and then snapped as easily as an old bone.

"New ice," Reid called to them as a repair was attempted, having released himself from the harness and climbed the low cliff which now faced them. This stretched unbroken for as far as they could see and was covered over most of its length by an old fall of snow.

The others climbed up after him, manhandling the sledges and stores up the steep slope. They were encouraged by the new terrain ahead of them, smooth again, and less angular than the faulted sea ice over which they had come.

"Permanent land ice," Reid told them, indicating the full extent of the channel beneath them. "We've crossed what might or might not be open water in the summer, but this stays as it is."

"So are we near land?" Goodsir asked him.

"Perhaps even on it."

"We surely haven't reached some promontory of the continental coast," Fitzjames said, scarcely daring to believe that this was what they had achieved.

Reid doubted this. It was his guess that they had crossed a channel which remained frozen most summers and that they were now on the edge of a permanent ice shelf which had grown outward from a large land mass even farther to the west, an island rather than any part of the mainland, and that to reach the channel between it and the mainland they would now need to turn due south again. It was too early to see if the water in the frozen channel resumed flowing, but they might at least be able to determine the course of this waterway and find out whether or not the ice was likely to break up of its own accord, or if it became shallow enough and sufficiently loose for them to forge a passage through it once the ships had come several degrees farther south and into contact with it.

They were twenty days out from the ships, had covered 170 miles, and could afford to continue for ten or twelve days more before turning back. For three days they crossed flat open ground with nothing to break the monotony of the receding horizon all around them—three days at the center of a white and disorientating disc, with only the rise and fall of the sun to keep them on course.

Then, on the fourth day of crossing this empty space they finally sighted land ahead of them, an undifferentiated smear at first, a charcoal line upon the whiteness, which slowly became clearer, revealing distinct peaks and dips the closer they approached.

One of the seamen had been the first to spot this, and upon confirming the discovery, Fitzjames promised the man, Thomas Tadman, that if it was previously undiscovered land then they would name its most prominent feature after him.

The day was warm, and walking unburdened by their thicker clothing they made good progress.

They stopped at dusk, the land to the west now only two or three miles away. They were all confident that they would reach it the following morning, after which it was Fitzjames' intention to continue exploring south until the time came to turn back. He had already discussed with Reid and Fairholme the possibility of finding a different route back to the ships, turning due east and then north and thereby avoiding the range of faulted ice which had slowed them on their outward journey.

The following morning they were woken an hour before dawn by Thomas Tadman, and emerging from their tent they saw that Reddington and several others were already out on the ice, some of them carrying lanterns and burning brands.

"We saw a light," Bryant shouted to Fitzjames. The men around him nodded in emphatic confirmation.

Fitzjames' first instinct was to say that this was impossible, to suggest that what they had seen was a low star, or a freak of reflected light. The first dim glow of the unrisen sun was already behind them, staining rather than illuminating the sky. Making no comment, however, he asked to be shown where the light had appeared, and half a dozen arms swung to point in the direction of the land toward which they were moving.

"It must be a fire," Reid said.

The light reappeared, remained in view for several minutes and then vanished again.

They dismantled their tents, awaited the first appearance of the sun so that Fairholme might establish their position for his journal, then resumed their journey.

It was Reid who called them to a halt half an hour later, having once again spotted the light, which had been hidden from them by a fold in the land.

For the first time since leaving Beechey they began to walk on frozen ground, shingle and then limestone, rather than on ice. Goodsir collected samples, the noise of his hammer ringing in echo all around them and unsettling several of the seamen by announcing their presence in such an exposed place.

They were stopped less than a hundred yards farther on by a sudden call which, under any other circumstances, they might have identified as the cry of a disturbed bird or the bark of a fox, but which they were all now convinced had been human. The marines loaded their rifles, and Fitzjames and Fairholme drew out their pistols. They gathered together around the sledges. The fire which had burned ahead of them for the past quarter of an hour was suddenly obscured.

"There *is* someone there," Fairholme whispered.

There was a further call, after which they waited in silence. Other, less distinct and equally unintelligible voices could be heard, and in response to these Reid cupped his hands to his mouth and called out a single word three times. It was a word few of them understood—"Temya"—but by which they all immediately realized that they had at last encountered their first Eskimos.

The sun had risen fully by then, casting their elongated shadows ahead of them as they advanced, Reid still calling out for the figures around the fire to reveal themselves.

At a gesture from the ice-master those around him stopped and waited. The rest gathered in a group several yards behind.

- Reid then called out something different, a full sentence.

Ahead of them a man appeared, short and barely distinguishable against the dark land behind him. A second figure rose beside him, and after this several others, until they were eventually confronted by a group similar in size to their own.

Reid went forward alone, speaking loudly, his empty hands held above his head.

The others watched as he walked within reach of the men beside the fire, some of whom held short spears, and who began to speak among themselves as Reid approached. He communicated with them, the same few words repeated over and over, and then turned to indicate the direction from which he had come. He beckoned for Fitzjames to join him, and Fitzjames went forward until he too was face to face with the natives.

"I told them you are our leader and that you bring with you a greeting and promise of peace and gifts from our Queen. Apparently they've heard of the Queen. One of them has traded with whalers." Reid pointed the man out to Fitzjames, and thus prompted, Fitzjames made a short speech, emphasizing everything he said with exaggerated gestures. He too motioned back in the direction they had come, and when he at last fell silent, uncertain whether or not his display had served its purpose, the two men closest to him came forward to embrace him, causing him to stoop to accommodate them, and coming away from them with soot and grease on his cheeks. Then they embraced Reid, who returned the gesture with equal enthusiasm.

The others came forward and the introductions were repeated until each man of both parties had embraced with everyone else. Then they were led back to the fire, where they saw beside it the skinned carcasss of a dozen large seals. Alongside them lay their bloodless pelts, looking as though they had been sloughed off naturally rather than stripped by force from the dead creatures.

Wedged into the fire were two iron pots full of rendered oil, and all around the blaze lay the scattered debris of at least another dozen skeletons, most of these reduced to only a skull and a spine, and looking like giant white serpents crawling over the ground, the illusion of movement completed by the flickering shadows of the fire.

The novelty and delight of the encounter was as great for the Eskimos as for the members of the expedition, and the meeting was celebrated long after their introductions had been concluded.

Later, Reid explained to Fitzjames that they had come across a hunting party, that the Eskimos lived far to the southeast, and were operating now from temporary shelters a short distance to the south, at the junction of the land and the ice. Encouraged by this, Fitzjames sought information concerning the presence of either land or open water in the direction of their home. Reid attempted to convey the question, and the man who had traded with the whalers drew a simple map on the thawed ground with a stick. It was difficult to decipher, consisting of only a few confusing lines, which the man attempted to explain by pointing to the corresponding land and ice around them. Reid confessed that he could understand little, but believed that the man had suggested there was both land and water to the south and southeast of them. He also thought that this was presently covered by ice, and that the man had signified this by blowing upon his ungloved hand and sweeping it over everything he had drawn. As before, Fitzjames felt encouraged and disappointed in equal measure by the revelation.

It had been his intention to continue south, but he was persuaded by the others to delay until the following day so that they might spend some time in the company of the Eskimos.

Later in the evening, the sun only moments from touching the horizon, the Eskimos indicated that they were about to withdraw to their shelters. Fitzjames, Goodsir and several of the seamen walked the short distance with them, surprised both by the weight of meat and oil the natives' frail-looking sledges were able to bear, and the ease with which they slid over the difficult ground. They were built of bone and held together with knotted thongs. When empty they collapsed into a bundle and could be easily carried strapped across a man's back. Fully loaded, Fitzjames estimated them to be capable of carrying 120 pounds, while themselves weighing less than ten.

The shelters were crude constructions also made of bone, over which hides had been stretched, and around which low ice walls had then been built. A single broad antler rocked in the breeze, and a short distance away a rack of drying meat stood like a giant abacus.

An hour after their arrival Fitzjames gathered his party together and indicated to the Eskimos that it was time for them to leave, which they eventually did after a ceremony as long and as involved as their introductions.

The following morning they rose early and set off in the direction of the camp on their own journey south.

Arriving there, they were surprised to discover that the Eskimos had already departed, and that little remained to indicate they had ever been there. Searching for a souvenir, one of the seamen found the antler they had seen the previous evening. He was about to take this when Reid told him not to, explaining that it had been left by the Eskimos as a marker for others coming after them.

Reid then searched the ground where the shelters had been and indicated that the hunting party had set off toward the north. They all turned to look, but saw nothing against the low outline of the land in that direction.

Reluctant to delay any longer, Fitzjames gave the order for them to resume their march south. Only four days of their allotted outward journey time remained to them.

By midday they had covered six miles, walking wherever possible on the smooth shallow ice where it abutted the land, and then returning to the rock and loose stone where the ice was fractured, or where it showed signs of thawing, making it unpredictable and likely to give beneath their weight.

An hour later Reid called for them to halt while he climbed a low rise to examine something on the horizon ahead of them. A few minutes earlier they had heard a distant crack, and then the long drawn-out scratching of moving ice. Reid called for Fitzjames to join him and pointed out the strip of cloud which lay across both the land and the ice ahead of them. At first Fitzjames had difficulty in making this out, and then in accepting that it was a cloud and not a finger of land running across their path out into the frozen channel. As the two men stood and examined this they heard again the distant noise of breaking ice.

"Is it ice in *this* channel, do you think?" Fitzjames asked, indicating the broad expanse beneath them, across which lay their return journey to the ships.

"For our sakes I hope not," Reid said calmly. "If it's starting to move now, this early, then there's no saying what it'll be up to when we turn to cross it on our way back." He examined the furrowed mass as he spoke.

"I think the cloud is moving toward us," Fitzjames said, now accepting that this was what Reid had spotted."

Reid watched for several minutes before confirming this.

"Perhaps that's why the Eskimos turned north."

"Possibly." Reid was more concerned with their own need for evasive action. He called down for the men on the ice to pull the sledges up on to the land. "If we turn inland we might avoid the worst of it, and we'll at least be safe from any sudden movement in the ice."

Fitzjames agreed with him, and a moment later, seeing that their sledges had not yet been hauled clear, he himself shouted for the men below to hurry, a note of undisguised urgency in his voice. Looking back to the advancing cloud, he saw with some surprise, shock almost, that far from drifting slowly north, this was now coming toward them with considerable speed, and seconds later a blast of cold air caught him in the face. He turned to Reid, but saw that he was already running down the slope to help with the sledges. He followed him. The others too felt the chill of the oncoming cloud and were shocked into action by it.

Those in harness started to run; others helped to push the sledges, and all of them crossed from the ice to the land. Fitzjames stood apart from them, calling down his orders and motioning for the casks and cases they spilled to be gathered up. He felt the unexpected sting of ice in the wind and then watched helplessly as a shower of pellets drove into them like shot. Several men called out in pain as they raced for shelter, uncertain of where they might find this.

Fairholme and Goodsir ran together, buffeted by the wind which caused them to run leaning into it, and which repeatedly sucked off their hoods until they were forced to fold their arms over their heads to protect themselves. They eventually arrived at a small depression in the ground and directed those following them into it. One of the sledges was pulled safely into this hollow, but the second, the one that was already damaged, overhung the rim and broke in half, scattering its load on the men below. Fairholme was struck by a sack containing a cone of sugar, was badly cut and briefly concussed. Men leapt and fell into the scalloped depression, scrambling over one another and the spilled provisions in an effort to pull themselves out of the wind, until eventually they were all together, crouching on their hands and knees with the worst of the wind whipping immediately above them.

Loose ice was driven into the hollow and this collected all around them. Bryant and his marine pulled out their tents, and although there was no possibility of erecting these while the wind still battered them, the two men were at least able to stretch the cane hoops and canvas over their bodies and legs. Beneath this outer covering they packed their furs and traveling-rugs, padding out the spaces between themselves until they were tightly cocooned. The wind and the ice still penetrated, but they were at least safe from the worst of it. Fairholme regained consciousness between Goodsir and Fitzjames. Molasses from a damaged cask had congealed in the fur of his hood, in his hair and in the stubble of his unshaven cheeks, and pressing closer to him, Goodsir began to lick at this before it froze against his skin.

They endured in this uncomfortable fashion for six hours, and then, as suddenly and violently as it had arrived, the wind fell, by which time the depression was filled with ice.

Reid was the first to pull himself free and to scramble back up to the rim. He saw blue sky all around them, darkening in places, but still clear, and already streaked yellow where the sun shone diffused and wavering through the airborne ice.

He climbed out of the hollow and walked a short distance, searching for the telescope he had dropped while running for shelter. The once-dark ground was now uniformly white, and the thin covering of fresh ice crunched beneath his boots. He followed a trail of broken cases and spilled food until the polished brass tube glinted in the sun and was revealed to him.

He was joined by Fitzjames and Reddington, and all three looked to the north and saw the tail of the storm still driving over the land and sheeting it white as it went.

"Should we stay where we are?" Reddington asked, but before anyone could answer him the sudden crack of moving ice distracted them all, and looking back to where they had come ashore they saw that the once-smooth and shallow ice had ruptured in a series of curving blocks, and was being driven upon the land for a distance of twenty or thirty yards, plowing up the loose stone ahead of it as it went. The noise had come from the distant edge of this ice, and hearing it again they all watched as more of the frozen surface rippled and burst and then thrust itself along the shore.

"It felt so solid and stable when we were crossing it," Reddington said, dismay and disbelief rising almost to panic in his unavoidable observation.

"She'll settle and refreeze," Reid told him. "Too early to be breaking open to stay open. Farther north, perhaps, but not this far in."

Despite this blunt reassurance, Reid too could not completely disguise his surprise at the swiftness and extent of this early breakup.

"Are you sure?" Fitzjames asked him. "Look over there." He pointed to the center of the channel. A dark lead had opened up, narrow and straight, and stretching for as far as they could see in both directions, as though it were a thin film on a shallow sea, suddenly pierced and then riven by the fin of a cruising shark come unexpectedly to the surface.

Looking out over this, and seeing ahead of them the remnants of the distant cloud, Fitzjames realized that the time had come to turn back to the ships before they were cut off. He looked along the path to the hollow and saw the line of their spilled provisions, many of these now irretrievable.

The ice continued to grind against the land as they turned their backs on it and began to salvage what had not already been lost to them.

Two of their remaining three casks of lemon juice had been smashed. Their canned provisions lay all around them, shining like giant coins in the returning sun, and these were gathered up and stacked beneath the rim of the hollow.

The seamen excavated a hole in the side of their inadequate shelter and lit a fire on which they cooked a meal, after which they awaited the onset of darkness.

A watch was posted, and at two in the morning Fitzjames was woken by Goodsir with the news that a dense fog was forming around them. He left his sleeping-bag and climbed out into total darkness. The two men sat together and discussed the events of the day, both conscious of the impenetrable void which surrounded them, but reassured by the few noises—the sound of men snoring or turning in their sleep—coming from below. Goodsir said he thought that Fairholme had suffered more than a mild concussion during their scramble for shelter. He was presently asleep, having had his wound dressed, but earlier he had woken shouting in a near-delirious manner, stopping immediately upon being grabbed and held. For several minutes he had not known where he was and nor could he remember what had happened to him.

If there had been any doubt in Fitzjames' mind earlier, then he knew as he listened to Goodsir that there was now no alternative but to turn back at the first opportunity.

The fog blanketed them for the whole of the following day and night, during which they were unable to move. Anyone walking ten feet beyond the rim of the shelter was completely lost to sight, his loudest shout muffled at only twice that distance.

An inventory was made of everything they had salvaged, leading to the alarming discovery that they only had enough food to last them a further ten days on full rations. Fitzjames immediately reduced this to two-thirds, which, allowing for the generosity of their traveling-rations, would not prove too great a hardship. Their greatest loss was that of their lemon, and three-quarters of the vinegar in which their pickled foods had been preserved.

Eventually the fog lifted, and they left the hollow two days later.

Reddington supervised the loading of the remaining sledge, but the weight proved too great for it, and having removed the excess this was distributed among the men to carry.

Fairholme was not fully recovered from the blow to his head, and after a few minutes' exertion in the harness alongside Reid, he collapsed unconscious and could not be revived for several hours, during which time he too was carried so as not to delay them any further. Coming round later in the afternoon, he called to be put down, insisting that he could walk unaided, but after only a few steps he stumbled and fell again, and from then on he required help in walking. His head wound reopened in the fall and bled heavily into his eyes and mouth.

On their first day of traveling north along the shifting border of ice and land they made only two miles, reaching the site of the Eskimo camp, by then wholly obliterated, as dusk fell.

"We stumble," wrote Fitzjames in his journal, the uneven hand betraying the conditions under which the words were written, the word itself broken in half, as though he had paused, undecided about what he truly wanted to say. "We marched out with every hope and expectation of success, and of fulfilling our goal of discovery, but we stumble home." He wrote no more.

They had been marching north, retracing their steps along the edge of the frozen strait for three days. They pulled and carried their provisions, grateful when the heavy cases and cans could finally be emptied and discarded.

Fairholme continued to lose consciousness, and they constructed a stretcher to carry him rather than waste time repeatedly tending to him where he fell.

Frustrated by their first two attempts to cross the ice, they were finally able to make headway several miles north of where they had previously crossed the frozen channel marching west.

Reid and Reddington went ahead of the main party, taking with them the two marines in the hope of encountering game.

They had all lost weight, and some were starting to feel the ache of scurvy in their joints, made worse by their exhaustion and the blight of despair which already infected the weakest among them.

Fairholme could not eat for five days, despite Goodsir's attempts to liquefy his food and help him to take it through a straw.

On the second day of their crossing, the ice beneath them started to judder and shift, only inches, but sufficient to let them know that they had exposed themselves upon dangerous ground and that they might all now become sudden victims of its capricious nature. Each time this happened they stopped walking and waited for the movement to pass, as though the ice were some stalking creature and their movement betrayed them to it.

With Fairholme unable to fulfil his duties as surveyor, it fell to Fitzjames and Goodsir to continue plotting and calculating their progress. Their compasses spun uselessly, repulsed and attracted in equal measure by the contradictory forces of the buried Pole to the east. The two men calculated independently the speed they were traveling and thus the distance they covered each day, but in the absence of any reliable landmarks their calculations varied greatly, and they were forced to the realization that their estimates were in truth little more than poorly informed guesses.

On the fourth day of crossing the ice, the horizon ahead of them rose in a succession of low ridges, and they convinced themselves that this was an extension of the range through which they had come on their outward journey.

They were possibly twelve days distant from the ships, and after a week of two-thirds, and then five days of half-rations they had all continued to weaken, and were now resting for as long as they walked. Where previously they had made ten, twelve or even fifteen miles a day on their outward march, they were now achieving as little as four or five, and this only through the greatest of efforts.

Camping in the shelter of a ridge they lit a fire and cooked on this the two geese the marines had brought down during their crossing. Their spirits were sufficiently raised by the meal for them to discuss what the coming season held in store once they were back on board the ships. This forced optimism did not last long, however, for upon opening a case marked canned vegetables they discovered instead only rolled strips of lead sheathing, intended for making repairs to their boats. The case weighed sixty pounds and they had been hauling and carrying it for fifty-one days. At the sight of this, one of the seamen threw himself down beside the lead and started trying to tear it apart as though it were card, weeping and beating on the ground, and then throwing each piece of sheathing as far as his strength allowed, until finally he knelt exhausted and silent, the dark lumps strewn around him in an almost perfect circle like the numbers on a clock face. No one approached the man. The frustration and anger he was releasing was the frustration and anger of them all.

Fitzjames and Goodsir left the others and walked to where they were able to mount a block of ice and look out over the darkness below.

"Even on these reduced rations we have less than half of what we need," Goodsir said, his voice low.

Fitzjames knew this, and felt angry at the useless reminder.

"What do you suggest?"

Goodsir paused before answering. "That the strongest of us continue due east until we find the ships and then return with help."

Fitzjames shook his head before he had finished speaking. He had considered a similar plan the previous sleepless night.

Goodsir pressed him, listing those of them he believed were still capable of making the journey, and those who had long since become weak and a hindrance.

"And what if those who set out to reach the ships don't find them?" Fitzjames said, knowing that this was unlikely to happen, but being something else he had considered as they covered shorter and shorter distances each day and with no exact idea of either their true course or position.

Goodsir abandoned his plea. The two men continued walking away from the others, pausing occasionally to turn and look at one another, silently sharing their fears.

They finally agreed that if they left the easy ground and turned directly over the low ridges then they might at least come within sight of the parallel channel upon which the ships sat, that they might even see the ships themselves, no more than specks in the distance perhaps, but nevertheless within sight and reach and a boost to their failing spirits. Then, Fitzjames conceded, they might split into two parties, the strongest of them going on ahead to send back help.

They returned to the others and told Reid and Reddington of their decision.

Not until three days later did the uneven land begin to level out and then stretch ahead of them in a long downhill slope to the eastern horizon.

They drank the last of their lemon juice and vinegar, all of them by then showing signs of scurvy, all of them enervated and sore, and some bleeding and bruised and vomiting and wanting only to stay where they were in the hope of being rescued without any further effort being wrung from them. But this too was out of the question: their return to the ships was not yet overdue, and even when this point was reached a further week or more might be allowed to pass before any attempt was made to find and assist them. Fitzjames pointed this out, but only to those who would not be alarmed by the news.

The next day they traveled three miles over easy ground, and at the end of it they were all too exhausted to pitch their tents or stake out their groundsheets. They slept where they sat or fell, some pressed face to face in twos and threes, and others wherever they could find any shelter.

There was a light fall of snow during the night, and Fitzjames woke to see that the wind had blown it in among them, icing their faces and hoods, and already frozen hard where it collected in their exposed hair and beards.

He tried to climb free of his sleeping-bag and push himself up, but the numbness and then the pain in his legs caused him to fall back down. He rubbed his thighs and calves and slowly felt his circulation return. Brushing the ice from his own face he saw on his gloves the slivers of frozen blood from his lips and from where new sores had opened on his cheeks and neck. He felt too where his callused knuckles had finally ruptured, and he dare not uncover his hands for fear of what might be exposed.

Beside him, Reid stirred, and he too forced himself upright. He began to cough, shaking violently at each exertion. He had difficulty opening his eyes and turned to Fitzjames for help. Reid's face was by then gaunt, the skin of his cheeks tight with hunger, his own eyes and mouth blemished with liquid sores.

Eventually the two men rose together and woke the others, scraping away the snow and ice from among the stiff and swaddled bodies.

An hour later they had all assembled and were ready to resume their downhill march. They had with them now only flour, beans, four pounds of cocoa powder and nine pounds of boiled sweets, which they crushed and dissolved in hot water before starting out. A final package of pemmican was opened and found to be rotten, but they warmed and ate this too, all of them complaining at the way even the softened pieces of pounded meat hurt their weakened gums and loose teeth.

Fairholme at last showed some signs of recovery. He was still unable to walk unaided, but he no longer needed to be carried.

They left their miserable camp and walked due east in two single-file parties a hundred yards apart. At noon it was warm enough for them to take off their jackets, and the sun warmed their arms and faces and thawed the ground ahead of them.

During the afternoon they killed a hare, and the small strips of meat and warm internal organs were divided up and eaten raw.

That night they camped in a sheltered cleft beneath a tent of ice formed by two plates which had been forced together and then lifted aslant before freezing in place.

For the first time since his injury, Fairholme was able accurately to fix their position, and he returned from his observation point with the news that they were possibly only twenty miles from where they had two months ago left the *Erebus* and *Terror*. Upon hearing this they all began to speculate on their chances of reaching the ships some time in the next few days.

At three the following morning they were woken by the sound of a distant explosion, not unlike the first thunderclap of an approaching storm, and then by the trembling which passed through the ice upon which they slept, and which continued to reverberate for several minutes afterward, going on as they woke in alarm, and as each man realized what was happening and struggled to get himself clear of their precarious shelter, the roof of which had already been shaken loose by the tremor. They were all out and gathered together in the darkness before this finally collapsed, dropping in two heavy blades upon the ground where minutes earlier they had all been asleep, the last of their meager provisions lost to them beneath the fallen slabs.

They waited, uncertain of what had caused this destruction, and bracing themselves against any further movement, but which did not come.

Fitzjames led them back to the rubble of their buried camp and found a new sleeping space for them clear of any other stacked ice which might yet be shaken loose. Those who had lost their bags wrapped themselves in whatever they were able to retrieve and sat pressed together for warmth.

They slept uneasily for three more hours, waking frequently and then gathering in the pre-dawn light, all of them eager to complete their journey, spurred on by the alarming prospect of further nights like the one they had just endured.

They walked for two more days, during which they ate only flour mixed into a cold unleavened dough, and made hardly any more palatable by the addition of their last few ounces of cocoa and sugar.

"The last of everything," Fitzjames wrote in his journal after a gap of nine days.

During those two days they covered seven miles, and on the third morning, the 3rd of July, Fitzjames announced that the time had finally come for them to split into two parties, and for the strongest of them to go on ahead and seek help. No one argued with this decision, but as the two groups were being decided upon, a distant noise was heard, which many in their desperation were convinced was a pistol shot and not merely some further echo of the cracking ice.

David Bryant fired his rifle in reply, and a moment later a second shot was heard, followed by others fired at random. The men on the ground rose to their feet and searched around them. Those who could not rise cheered and shouted where they lay, and some prayed.

There was now no thought of separating, and those who could not walk unaided were propped between two others or carried on the backs of those few who still had the strength to bear them.

They went forward as fast as they could manage, firing their weapons and pausing only to listen for answering shots. There was still no sign of the ships, or the men signaling to them from the broad sweep of folded ice ahead.

Moments later Philip Reddington called out that he could see something below. He fired his pistol and ran to a low rise. Scrambling up this on his hands and knees he shouted back to them that he could see the ships, and hearing this the others called upon the last of their strength and ran forward to join him.

Reid and Goodsir supported Fairholme between them, and Fitzjames walked alongside. Sitting Fairholme at the base of the small rise, the three others climbed it and stood beside the men already gathered there, where they too saw the tiny dark outlines of the distant ships, and then the men beneath them, running up the slope to meet them and firing their weapons as they came.

Rockets were fired, and looking up from where he was giving thanks for their safe deliverance, Fitzjames saw that the ice around the two ships was littered with shelters and stores and offloaded boats, and that broad circles of gray had been trodden out of the surrounding whiteness, which at that distance and from that height gave the vessels the appearance of being the burned-out hearts of two dead fires surrounded by their scattered, paler ashes.

He closed his eyes and resumed praying as the men approaching them came closer. Then he rose, brushed the ice from his legs, and watched as those around him left their vantage point and continued down the slope, falling and sliding as often as they remained upright and running on their weakened legs.

It was only a moment later, as he watched these two parties of men converge, that it struck Fitzjames that something was wrong.

He could not explain this, but nor could he dismiss the idea, and he watched the distant figures more closely in an effort to understand why he felt this way.

The men crossing the ice below were slowing in their approach, being restrained and then called back by those who came behind them.

Goodsir too noticed that the excitement of this imminent reunion appeared to have been suddenly and inexplicably defused, and he asked Fitzjames if he had seen anything to account for this. Fitzjames shook his head, intent on examining the men below through his telescope.

"Crozier," he said eventually, pointing out the figure walking to the rear of the others, and who now passed through them as they stopped running and congregated ahead of his own descending party, most of whom were still shouting and firing their weapons long after those ahead of them had fallen silent.

Reid and Fairholme approached.

"You've seen it too," Reid said.

They watched Crozier approach the first man to arrive at the bottom of the slope and then hold him by the shoulders for a moment after which the man fell to his knees, as though the last of his failing energy had been suddenly and completely drained from him by the brief encounter.

Fitzjames searched among the other figures, the running and the still, for Franklin, but he was nowhere to be seen.

Reid suggested that they ought to continue down to the frozen plain, and supporting Fairholme between them they went on.

When they next looked, the ice around the ships grew dark as a cloud passed slowly across the face of the sun.

They reached the man who had fallen to his knees at Crozier's touch, and saw that it was Philip Reddington, one of the strongest of them all. Fitzjames spoke to him, and was surprised to be answered only by tears. He felt Reid's grip tighten on his arm as Fairholme sagged between them.

"Let him down," Reid said, and they lowered Fairholme until he too was kneeling on the level ice, barely conscious of the sobbing man beside him. Reddington reached out and held the confused Fairholme, and his tremors shook them both.

Fitzjames approached Crozier, taking off his gloves as the two men came close. John Irving and George Hodgson stood beside their captain, both waiting for Crozier to speak first.

"What's wrong?" Fitzjames asked, confused by the nature of this greeting.

All around them the two parties came together and the strong helped the weak. Some men went on cheering and loudly praying; others met and immediately fell silent, and a few began crying as convulsively and uncontrollably as Philip Reddington.

Hodgson was the first to come forward, his hand out, but Crozier stepped quickly between the two men.

"Sir John," he said, bowing his head and then raising it and breathing deeply.

Fitzjames looked to Hodgson, and Hodgson nodded once in confirmation and bowed his own head, followed by Irving. For the first time, Fitzjames saw the black bands on their arms, and seeing these he looked all around him and saw them too on the arms of the men moving among them with food and drink, already picking up the sick and the weak and the injured and carrying them back across the ice.

Weak and in pain himself, and with his mouth full of blood from his bleeding gums, Fitzjames was barely able to comprehend the enormity of what he believed he had just been told, and when Crozier spoke again, coming back toward him with both arms held out, he felt the words like a physical blow and his legs buckled beneath him and he fell unresisting to the hard ground, striking it full on his face.

THE RIVER OF DREAMS

July 1847—January 1848

EIGHTEEN

He came round forty-eight hours later to a warbling, near-hysterical scream—whether his own, or from close by, or from elsewhere in the otherwise silent ship, he could not tell. Nor could he even be certain that the sound had actually been made, conscious that it was just as likely to have been some unreal fragment or receding echo of one of his own nightmares carried with him into an abrupt and anxious waking.

His body felt heavy, pressed down, and he could scarcely open his eyes to peer at the unfamiliar objects in the dimly lit room around him, aware only that he was in Stanley's sick-bay, surrounded by pungent and reassuring odors, and that there was an empty bunk alongside his own. The effort of raising his arm or sitting upright was too much for him, and so he lay perfectly still, dulled by whatever medicines he had been given, stupefied almost, and waiting only to fall back into his drugged sleep and come round again when he was better able to attempt his recovery.

It was then, as he felt himself falling, that he heard a scraping sound beneath him, as though a small creature, a rat most likely, were scratching at the timbers as it scrambled blind along one of the ship's numberless buried passages and ducts. He tried to ignore the noise, but it continued and distracted him, at times penetratingly clear, and then as insubstantial as the scream which might or might not have waken him. He wanted to call out, to scare whatever it was away, but could find neither his voice to form the words nor his mouth to issue them.

He was about to try again when the same shrill cry sounded immediately beside him, and he turned in panic to see the outline of a small, near-demonic creature sitting on the empty mattress and watching him closely. At first he believed his suspicions had been confirmed, and that it was a large and bedraggled rat, but as he watched it more closely he saw its long thick tail curl upright and then stiffen, after which it looped from side to side. It was the monkey, and realizing this, he felt himself relax. He mumbled to it and continued watching it. The animal rose on its hind legs, stood regarding him for a moment longer, and then collapsed, after which it had difficulty pushing itself back into a sitting position, scrambling and making the noise that had first alerted him to its presence. Its limbs, he saw, were stick thin, the knots of its elbows and knees bulging with edema. It continued to flail around, swinging its arms and legs as though it had no control over them, as though they were moved only by the dying momentum created by the shaking and twisting of its wasted body. Its eyes were yellow and enlarged, and a string of glistening mucus hung from its chin to the matted fur of its chest.

He watched it for several minutes longer, until he at last understood more fully what he was seeing, and until the small creature had exhausted itself and lay on its back with its head turned to him, breathing hoarsely through chattering teeth, and staring vacantly toward him through the darkness, as though he too were not real, merely the illusory residue of some dream.

He slept for twelve more hours, and this time was woken by the voices of men in the room around him. One of these sounded like Franklin, and the instant he heard it, still on the boundary of sleep and arousal, he called out to let whoever it was know that he was awake. For a moment he could not square what he believed he had just heard with what he had learned three days previously, and for the few seconds it took him to come round more fully, he was convinced that the news of Franklin's death during his absence was all part of that same forgotten nightmare.

Stanley leaned over him, a vial of blood in his hand, which he shook and then held to the light of a lamp.

"Not yours, James," he said without looking down. "Another fatality during the night."

Fitzjames asked who, but the words came out as little more than a dry croak.

"Not who, what." Returning the vial to a rack on the wall, Stanley lifted the corpse of the monkey by its tail. It hung barely weighted, an outline of bone in a bag of loose skin, spinning as its limbs untangled. "A great pity. Killed by its own gluttony and yet reduced to this. Three pounds two ounces. At Greenhithe it weighed eight pounds six." He carried the small corpse to a case beside his chair and let it drop.

"Franklin," Fitzjames said suddenly, the thought, realization and word arriving simultaneously, and together being strong enough finally to pierce the cloud of his leaden senses. He felt a sharp pain in his mouth and tasted fresh blood. Seeing this upon his lips, Stanley wiped them with a soft cloth.

Using his tongue, Fitzjames felt teeth loose in their sockets. He also felt the flaps of skin which hung from his cheeks and from the roof of his mouth; his tongue too felt sore, raw, as though its sensitive surface had been peeled away at the tip. He looked down and saw the blood slowly soaking into Stanley's cloth.

"You yourself have also lost a great deal of weight," Stanley said.

"Franklin," Fitzjames repeated, allowing himself to sink back into his pillow as Stanley drew away, and as the strain of leaning forward became too great for him.

"Sir John died on the eleventh of June," Stanley said with his back to him. "Captain Crozier has assumed command of the expedition. He asked me to let you know that he would call on you when you felt up to receiving him."

"How?" Fitzjames asked, some innermost part of his mind still not fully convinced of what he had been told once upon his return and was being told again now in his struggle to recover.

"A sudden brain fever. Cerebral hemorrhage. He was struck down shortly after dinner on the ninth, lingered beyond his senses or rational thought for a further thirty-six hours, suffered a second, more powerful attack on the morning of the eleventh and passed away only minutes later. At first we believed it might have been Caesar's disease, but my examination . . ." Here Stanley paused, turning further away from him. "His body is out upon the ice, in our mausoleum, awaiting your return so that everyone might be present at his interment. Mr. Gore and his party had returned from the south only a week earlier. We expected you back sooner." He paused again. "When you were spotted on the slope we thought at first you were Eskimos. Mr. Gore returned marching in formation, barely half his supplies used up and every one of his party in better health than when they departed."

Fitzjames was sufficiently recovered by then to recognize the veiled criticism in this remark.

Stanley went on, becoming uncharacteristically emotive as he strayed further from the immediate facts of Franklin's death.

"Sir John spoke of Lady Jane in his delirium. He spoke with great affection and respect. I stayed with him, as did Peddie and Macdonald, throughout his entire confinement. We hoped at first that he might retain his spirit and gradually regain his senses, but after the second, more violent seizure it became clear to all who saw him that there was nothing more to be done. Each day the men pay their respects to the body out on the ice." He stopped speaking and regained his composure.

They were interrupted a moment later by the appearance of Goodsir. He came into the room and stood behind Stanley. He moved awkwardly, and it was not until he leaned against the wall that Fitzjames saw he was walking with the help of crutches.

Stanley criticized him for having left his own bed in the adjoining cabin. Unlike Fitzjames, Goodsir appeared to be suffering none of the after-effects of any medication. It was the first time Fitzjames had seen him out of his thick outdoor clothing in a month, and he was shocked to see how thin he had grown, how discolored his skin was. A large patch of hair above Goodsir's temple had fallen out completely and there were dark circles around his eyes. The skin of his chin and cheeks was bruised, and his lips were pulled to one side, as though an invisible finger were jabbed into his jaw.

Looking at him, Fitzjames realized that in all likelihood he too must have looked much the same.

"Hair loss," Goodsir said, as though pronouncing a verdict on someone else entirely, his spirits apparently undiminished by his symptoms now that he was in charge of his own recovery. "To be expected. Rest assured that I am saving every single strand to send to all those heartbroken young women I scatter behind me wherever I go. Say the word and I shall bring you a small casket in which to save your own."

Angered by this outwardly cavalier disregard for his own health, Stanley said again that it was too soon for Goodsir to be out of his bed and warned him to stay no more than a few minutes, pointedly remarking that Fitzjames was not yet even partially recovered and that any exertion would quickly tire him. He left the two men, retrieving the corpse of the monkey as he went.

"Bryant's marine died in the night," Goodsir said solemnly when they were alone, and when Stanley's receding footsteps no longer sounded like the tapping finger of someone watching over them. "The man had been walking for a week on two feet frostbitten beyond salvation as far as the ankle. Stanley operated last night and he died a few minutes later. Joseph Healey, twenty-three."

Fitzjames pushed himself up into a sitting position.

"Bryant himself lost two toes," Goodsir went on, and before Fitzjames could respond, added, "And Fairholme is once again unconscious, but appears to have a gangrenous calf; Mr. Reid is strapped up for ice-lung, and eight more small toes, two ears, and one nose have been slight-cut. In fact I myself—" here he faltered. "I myself appear to be incomplete by half a thumb." He held up his hand, and Fitzjames saw for the first time that it was heavily bandaged. His feet too had been reduced to balls of white padding, making them look ridiculous and pathetic in equal measure.

Fitzjames tried to pull his arms from beneath the blankets, but was unable to until assisted by Goodsir.

"You, too," Goodsir said the instant Fitzjames' own bandaged hands were revealed, and before Fitzjames could remark on them. The dressings were tight, and he could feel little beneath them.

Goodsir reassured him that every one of his fingers and thumbs was intact, and that Stanley had only bandaged them as a precaution. He looked at his own dressing as he spoke. It was the joint of his right hand which had been removed, and a small stain showed through the bandage, looking as though it had been dabbed on the surface rather than bled through from deep within.

After a brief silence between them, during which Goodsir inspected the contents of the room, picking up and coiling the collar and lead of the monkey, Fitzjames said that Stanley had told him about Franklin.

"We'll pay our respects together when you're well enough to walk," Goodsir said. "There's no urgency. I believe Crozier intends to make a fitting occasion of the funeral. There are those who believe the body should be preserved and taken home with us."

"What about Reid?" Fitzjames managed to say.

"He'll recover. His chest is strapped and he has a warm mask."

A steward arrived with tea for the two men, and he shared their feeble laughter when both held up their bandaged hands to him. The man sat with them for several minutes, holding the cup to Fitzjames' lips and catching in the saucer what he spilled.

When he had finished drinking, and when the steward had wiped the fresh blood from his lips, Fitzjames felt revived and better able to speak. He asked the steward to find out how well or sick the other members of the expedition were and to report back to him.

Waiting until they were once again alone, he asked if Goodsir believed that what they had found on their march would be of any benefit to them when the breakup came and they continued to the south or southwest.

Goodsir became evasive. "I visited Reid this morning," he said. "Blanky was with him."

Guessing what he was about to be told, Fitzjames said, "Are we going to be late in freeing ourselves?"

"Blanky says he can see no sign whatsoever of the breakup, nor even of cracking or fissures."

Momentarily stunned by this, Fitzjames could think of nothing to say in reply.

Goodsir went on. "Gore and Des Voeux put us only twelve to fifteen miles north of King William Land, and Crozier is convinced that if we don't get open water by the first week in August then we ought to continue overland to Back's River, and from there west and south in the hope of contacting an outpost of the Hudson Bay Company. By his reckoning we are less than a hundred miles from Franklin's own Farthest East of twenty-five years ago. Imagine—the gap remaining to be bridged is suddenly that small, James, and so easily attainable."

"But the Passage—the Passage—needs to be completed by sea," Fitzjames almost shouted, flecking his sheets with blood.

Goodsir only shrugged. "A week ago the Terror was squeezed in a pressure ridge. Nothing too savage, but her starboard prow was crushed. If the ice around her thaws or disperses before repairs can be made then she'll take on water faster than she can be pumped clear."

"Is there any sign of that?"

Goodsir shook his head. "Blanky calculates at least fifteen feet of ice beneath her."

"Surely not," Fitzjames said. "Not this late."

"By his estimation—and Reid agrees with him—it's been building up beneath us all winter, freezing downward and stacking in slabs. When our release comes—if it comes—it is unlikely to be in the form of a gradual thaw and disintegration as it was at Beechey. According to Blanky, the ice in this strait has been accumulating for at least thirty years. It seems we entered it during a good year and that we were altogether too keen to haul and cut our way into a good harbor. I went on deck before coming to see you. There's a range of peaks, some up to a hundred feet high, which wasn't there when we departed. Solid ice, dark ice. There might very well be open leads toward the southwest, but there's little chance that we can make our way toward them in the ships as we now stand."

Each piece, each aspect of this scarcely believable news dismayed Fitzjames further, and he could not accept that the outlook had become suddenly so dark after all they had achieved during the previous year.

The two men were distracted by several gunshots fired in rapid succession.

"Hunting?" Fitzjames said.

"Possibly."

Fitzjames knew from Goodsir's continued evasiveness that something else was being kept from him, and he demanded to be told.

"Tozer and his marines have already abandoned their damaged quarters on the *Terror* and built themselves a shelter on the ice. They were asleep aboard when the ice started to squeeze. One man was nearly killed, several others injured by sprung planking. The chain store was crushed and half her cables lost."

"And Crozier hasn't yet commanded them to return to the ship?"

"I think he fears the confrontation. Their sleeping-quarters were damaged beyond repair. Where would they go?"

"Six men?"

"I believe a dozen others followed them. They took the two waist boats. In view of the damage to the *Terror*, it might—"

"And they take their orders from whom?"

Again Goodsir shrugged, unwilling to answer.

"And they provision themselves from the stores already out on the ice?"

Goodsir nodded. "A great deal more has been taken out since the *Terror* was damaged. All her coals are offloaded and her engine dismantled."

It occurred to Fitzjames that Crozier might transfer his command to the *Erebus*, supplanting his own, and that if the *Terror* was found to be damaged beyond repair then she might eventually be abandoned to the ice when the time came.

"What others are with Tozer?" he asked.

"Seamen, mostly. Two stokers, hold captain Goddard and foretop captain Peglar." Having become the bearer of so much bad news, Goodsir was beginning to feel uncomfortable.

"And Joseph Healey?" Fitzjames said absently as their conversation lulled and he felt himself suddenly weaken.

"To be buried alongside Edward Little tomorrow or the day after." Goodsir pushed himself upright on his crutches and then left before anything further could be asked of him.

Stanley woke Fitzjames with the news that Crozier would shortly be paying him a visit.

"Is he already aboard?"

"For the past few hours." Stanley glanced at the door as he spoke.

"Is there something else?"

"He's in Sir John's cabin, going through his papers. It is my opinion that certain proprieties ought to be observed."

"Respect for the dead," Fitzjames said.

At the sound of footsteps outside, Stanley said, "Mr. Reid shows considerable improvement, and Lieutenant Fairholme regained consciousness less than an hour ago."

Crozier entered as he finished speaking and stood in the doorway watching the two men.

"I was passing on to Mr. Fitzjames the news of his party," Stanley said.

"Is that so?"

Stanley rose and Crozier immediately took his seat.

"And no doubt of my ransacking of Sir John's cabin. Your loyalty does you credit."

Unwilling to tolerate this provocation, Fitzjames said, "I hear you have some damage and a small mutiny on your hands, Mr. Crozier."

Crozier looked at him hard and considered his reply before he spoke. "Tozer and his band?" he said with disdain. "I keep a close enough watch on them. Everything they do has my sanction and they are no drain on our stores other than those to which they are entitled. Please, don't concern yourself. It is a problem easily enough solved should the need arise. From what I hear, you put your own sergeant through some pretty severe paces. A man can ill afford to lose two toes."

For the first time Fitzjames felt the absence of Franklin's mediating presence.

Dismissing Stanley, Crozier took a sheaf of papers from the satchel he held. Fitzjames recognized them immediately by their ribbons. "I want to talk to you about my own proposals for the expedition's advancement in the event of the ice not releasing us this season."

As he spoke Fitzjames guessed that the damage to the *Terror* was greater than Goodsir had suspected, and became aware too that Tozer and the men on the ice posed a far greater threat to Crozier's authority than he was prepared to admit.

"Your own loyalty, of course, is not in doubt. But Sir John is dead."

"And dead men's wishes spear no fishes," Fitzjames said, remembering the whalers' rhyme.

Crozier hesitated, uncertain if the remark was intended to mock him. He would make no allowance for Fitzjames' weakened condition, and the tone of his voice as he went on indicated that he would tolerate neither challenge nor interruption.

"If the ice shows no sign of freeing us, then overland is our only way."

"Over thawing ice and into uncharted terrain?"

"If necessary, yes. This may be *your* first experience of any such adventure, but I personally am no stranger to uncrossed boundaries."

Disregarding this, Fitzjames said, "And if the ice does free us?"

"Then a crew will remain aboard one of the ships to take advantage of the opportunities offered."

"You intend dividing us?"

"I intend obeying the dictates of the ice and the season. Any man who cannot see the importance of communicating our position to someone on the mainland who might in turn get word to the Admiralty, is a fool."

The ease and speed with which Crozier clearly believed this might now be accomplished put Fitzjames on his guard, and despite his own misgivings he was careful not to contradict him.

"I am as saddened as any of us by Sir John's death," Crozier said, recovering his papers before Fitzjames asked to see them. "He and I were old comrades. What I do now, I do for him. As far as I am concerned, it is still his expedition."

"And one you consider close to success," Fitzjames said.

Crozier rose and walked to the door. "Recover, rest, wait until you are stronger, and we'll talk again."

He left before Fitzjames could ask him if there would be any point, slamming the door to emphasize the anger he felt at not receiving the full support of his second in command.

Fitzjames next went back out on the ice ten days later. He was accompanied by Graham Gore and Henry Vesconte, these two walking on either side of him ready to help him if he stumbled or fell, and both watchful for the first sign that he was over-exerting himself. He went out against the advice of Stanley and Goodsir, the former absolving himself of all responsibility for his recovery, and then afterward ensuring that his two companions would remain close to him, ready to help him back to the *Erebus* if the need arose. Goodsir, on the other hand, wished him luck, Fitzjames having confided in him his intention of visiting Tozer and the others in their separate encampment. Neither man considered there to be any real danger in the confrontation.

Since the operation on his thumb, Goodsir had continued to run a high temperature, and for the past two nights had been feverish, calling out in his sleep about the movement of the ice beneath him, as though he were still camped out on the frozen sea, and then shouting to warn of an attack by some as yet unidentified foe. Fitzjames had heard this in the adjoining room, and was careful not to remark on it during their time together.

"I've vowed to make myself ambidextrous," Goodsir had said the previous evening, raising his bandaged hand.

Fitzjames could not avoid the forced nonchalance in his friend's voice.

"How long will it take—a week, two?"

Anything other than this shared deception would have been unthinkable.

"Perhaps even a month," Goodsir said. He paused before going on. "In fact it's been in my mind to ask Stanley to remove the remaining joint to be certain of containing the infection. One bone or three, it will make little difference."

Fitzjames looked at his own hand. When he was next alone, he experimented to determine for himself precisely how much of the use of his hand Goodsir had already lost.

Out on the ice, Fitzjames walked with two sticks, having chosen these from the dozen offered. The one in his left hand was a gift from Thomas Blanky; that in his right from Crozier, having been presented to him by the governor of Cape Town upon his arrival there with James Ross after their withdrawal from the Antarctic four years ago. It was made of horn, polished and light, and slightly curved with a handle carved of ebony.

Having climbed down from the *Erebus*, Fitzjames stood for a minute, breathing in the intoxicating air as deeply as he dared. He was conscious of the fact that Reid had not yet fully recovered from his own injuries, that his breathing was still painful, and that he was still forbidden to speak. During their enforced convalescence the two of them had frequently sat together, holding long, one-sided conversations composed of reminiscence and speculation. A flannel cloth and swabs of soft wool were packed into Reid's mouth to soak up the blood from his injured gums. His hands were still bandaged, but other than the loss of four complete fingernails and the skin from one palm, he had suffered no other injury. In addition to soaking up the blood, the cloth in his mouth was also intended to encourage him to breathe through his nose, this being considered preferable by Stanley until the full extent of the damage to his lungs became clear, but which made his breathing sound labored and more of an effort than it actually was.

To begin with, Fitzjames, Gore and Vesconte avoided the upturned boats, the ice-houses and Franklin's bleak mausoleum and walked instead among the piles of stores and coals, all neatly stacked and marked, and each with a well-trodden track running to the main path leading back to the ships.

"What's that?" Fitzjames asked, pointing one of his sticks at a sheeted mound close to the *Terror*.

Neither Gore nor Vesconte could be certain and so they went to investigate.

The tarpaulin was frozen stiff, coming up from whatever lay beneath it like a disused trapdoor.

"Their engine," Fitzjames said, as the pieces of dismantled machinery were revealed to them. Giant levers and stripped cogs shone silver and black in the bright sun. Elsewhere the dismantled drive-shaft and casing lay coated in sculpted grease, solid and lava-like where it had bled and then cooled from the abandoned works.

Gore prised loose, a small piece of this, inspected it and then threw it with a grunt into the open space beyond them.

Sensing Fitzjames' anger at seeing the engine so completely discarded, and knowing that there was little possibility of it ever being reassembled, Vesconte lowered the tarpaulin.

"Their orders were to take out as much of the useless weight as possible," he said. "The smiths and stokers did most of the work. The boiler was sealed to go on producing hot water for them." He hesitated before going on. "I believe he was right to do it. It was a dead weight and the *Terror* was suffering under the burden. There were men on board who were with Ross in the *Victory* when—"

"Then damn Ross for his example," Fitzjames shouted, striking the ice with his stick and almost falling at the sudden exertion.

Neither Gore nor Vesconte spoke, both watching him closely.

Fitzjames composed himself. "No—praise Ross for his four winters to our two." He lowered the scarf from his mouth, took several more deep breaths and then replaced it.

"Franklin was insistent that our own engine should remain," Gore said to appease and reassure him. "Goodsir proposes that at the first sign of a break in the ice ahead of us, however distant or however late it comes, we should detonate a line of explosives along our path, fracture the ice more deeply and then use our screw to cannon back and forth until we are once again back out in open water." He seemed genuinely excited at the prospect, as though the simplicity of the plan, and the confidence of the man who had proposed it, would in some way ensure its success. Vesconte shared his enthusiasm, but not Fitzjames.

They left the dismantled engine and, avoiding Tozer's camp, made their way toward the new ice-range which had appeared during the expedition's absence.

The previous day, just as dusk was settling, the watches on both ships had reported a disturbance in the direction of these new peaks, and out on the ice the spreading tremor of this disturbance had been powerful enough to topple carefully balanced stacks of crates and knock men off their feet. Alerted by the commotion, they had watched as a slab of ice almost a mile distant rose vertically out of the lower slopes of the new range and then stood there aglow in the last of the sun.

This uplifted slab was calculated to be forty feet thick and twice the height of their own mainmasts. They watched it in silence, waiting to see what it might do next—whether it would continue to rise as it was forced up by further movement beneath, or whether it would become unstable and collapse, sending a further fast-moving tremor rushing toward them.

Neither of these things happened; instead the monumental block began to sink, silently at first, and then with a grinding noise louder than any they had heard so far, and as it sank geysers of spray were forced up all around it and these too ignited in the last of the sun.

The dying moments of the sinking block were as spectacular as its beginnings: it appeared to slow for a moment, as though it had encountered some buried obstacle, after which it shook vigorously for a few seconds and then dropped with a sudden roar and rush of spume, slamming into the ice at its base. By that time the sun was almost gone, and as always when this final crescent of light sank beneath the horizon, complete darkness descended in minutes.

The three men walked toward where all this had taken place. They attracted the attention of a small group of men who followed them at a distance, several of them armed with rifles.

"Watch the ground," Gore warned suddenly, stepping back from a piece of ice which had unexpectedly rocked beneath him.

"Recent fissures," Fitzjames pointed out, noting the cracks and barely visible ridges, little more than inches high in most places, which now criss-crossed the ice-field all around them.

"Where was it?" Vesconte asked them both, searching for signs of the previous evening's upheaval.

Gore believed it was to their left, indicating a higher ridge and a series of crevasses which extended from the plain into the lower slopes beyond.

Fitzjames confirmed this by pointing out a mound of ice whose edges were clean and sharp. Gore went ahead alone, moving from side to side on the sound ice and testing the uncertain ground before he committed himself to it. He stopped suddenly, crouched down and then called for them to join him.

The raised slab had been part of the surface layer, and where it had been tilted and raised there was now a depression in the ice so geometrical and sharply defined that it might have been cut out by men using saws. More interesting than this was what lay at the level base of this depression, for there, entombed in ice as clear as glass, were the corpses of at least three hundred narwhals, most fully submerged in their tomb, but some with their tusks and tails and backs breaking the surface, all of them giving the appearance of having died instantaneously as they were long ago coralled together and then trapped by the encircling ice.

The three men stood and looked down in silence. They had all seen small whales frozen in blocked leads before, but never in such great numbers or in such packed confusion, and they could only wonder at the frenzied panic of the creatures as they realized that every route of escape into open water had been cut off to them, and as they were forced to circle closer and closer, crammed side by side and one above the other as the water all around them began to solidify.

The bodies stretched from side to side and end to end of the great depression, suggesting that even more might lie buried beyond those they could already see.

"A fortune in ivory for the man stupid enough to sling over a ladder and take down a saw," Gore said, his words interrupted by a creaking beneath them which caused them to back away from the edge. At the far end of the depression a slab of ice several feet thick came loose and fell in on the whales, shattering as it struck their frozen bodies and then skittering over them.

Gore and Vesconte helped Fitzjames away from the lip of the excavation, pointing out where cracks in the ice which had been closed on their outward journey were now several inches apart.

Turning back, they encountered the men who had earlier followed them, and who had stopped short at the first distant rumble of the ice.

Fitzjames recognized several of them as marines under Tozer's command. He greeted them and they said they were pleased to see him so well recovered. One of them pulled a recently killed hare from his jacket and offered it to him.

"Fresh meat," he said simply. The gift was not made grudgingly, but the man's manner suggested to Fitzjames that he wished he could have given it without the others looking on.

Fitzjames took the hare and pressed its still-warm body to his face for a moment. He thanked the man and then warned them all against proceeding any farther in that direction. He made no mention of the whales for fear of encouraging the dangerous plunder of their horns.

"Are you with Tozer?" he asked, trying to appear more concerned with tying the hare to his belt than with their answer.

The marines exchanged glances before admitting that they were.

"We thought of paying him a visit and looking over your new quarters," Fitzjames said, again attempting to make light of the matter, but noting the alarm on the men's faces at the suggestion.

He felt Gore's hand on his arm and turned to him.

"I don't think you're ready for this," Gore said quietly.

Already exhausted by their morning's walk, Fitzjames agreed with him, to the obvious relief of the watching marines.

"We are expected back aboard," he told them, and the men turned and walked away from him without speaking.

Halfway back to the *Erebus,* just as they had once again entered the stained and trampled ice surrounding their stores, Fitzjames felt faint, dropped one of his sticks and then fell. Neither Gore nor Vesconte was fast enough to catch him, able only to pull him up and brush the moisture from his face.

NINETEEN

Sailing north in his search for tin and amber, the Greek navigator Pytheas imagined that a sea unicorn had pointed the way for him upon leaving the cold island of Thule, and that another had emerged from an impenetrable barrier of ice and fog and pointed in the direction he had come, warning him to turn back into those warmer waters with which he was already familiar. None of his masters or oarsmen had argued with these interpretations.

Twenty years later Pytheas suggested that the original home of these strange creatures might once have been the moon, and that they had possessed the wings which enabled them to make the journey from there to their new home in the icy northern sea. Speculating further on this, he was led to the conclusion that the surface of the moon was also composed of ice, which had once been liquid, but which had gradually hardened, forcing the unicorns to seek out their new home.

Goodsir recounted all this with obvious relish, his common-book open on the sheets beside him. Fitzjames took down his intermittent dictation for him.

"And write this, James. Write that on his second voyage into the Arctic, Frobisher himself came upon a narwhal frozen into the ice at the mouth of the strait afterward to bear his name, and that he too identified this strange creature as a unicorn, dug it from its tomb, sawed off its horn, and took it home with him as a gift for Elizabeth, who—" here Goodsir took the book from Fitzjames and searched back through its pages. "Who received it 'graciously and full of awe, as though it were the most precious of jewels.' Her own words, James. The most precious of jewels. Afterward to be kept guarded, admired and untouched in her wardrobe of robes until her death." He handed the book back to Fitzjames so that he might finish taking his notes. "And forever afterward regarded as 'a creature of mythical proportions, born in unfathomable depths or otherwise escaped from some strange bestiary'."

As Goodsir spoke he frequently wiped the sweat from his brow. On occasion, he spoke quickly, hardly separating his words, and at other times he became distracted, behaving as though he were alone and unobserved, as though he had forgotten what he wanted to say and was having to make a great and silent effort to retrieve some elusive word or lost meaning.

All this Fitzjames attributed to his fever. He finished writing and waited.

"Of course, it is unlikely that Frobisher's specimen was anything like as well preserved as any of your own fish," Goodsir said suddenly, staring at his bandaged hand. "More likely that he came upon a beached and rotting corpse, from which he pulled out the horn with no more effort than he might pull a carrot from its bed of sand."

He laughed at this and then drew up his sheets to wipe his face. There remained a mark on his bandaged hand where old blood and the darker stain of cauterization still showed through. When he lowered the sheets, he had stopped laughing, and was staring directly ahead of him, trembling slightly.

"You felt us rocking in our cradle earlier?" he said.

"Distant tremors. We may yet be released."

"Ah, yes, release." This time he spoke almost mockingly, making a flourish with his good hand.

"Whatever," Fitzjames said, reluctant to continue.

"You used the word corpses," Goodsir said, stopping him.

"They were all surely dead, even those deeper down."

"No—'corpse'—that is where they are supposed to take their name. Old Norse. 'Nar' and 'Hvalr'. Corpse and whale. It was later believed that their flesh was poisonous, and that this was also how they had come to be named." Goodsir was now speaking loudly and quickly, as though he were addressing a larger audience. "Scoresby refutes this, of course, and I trust his rigor. According to him, the cooked flesh is a powerful antiscorbutic, better than any of our ordinary meats, that it is greasy and pungent, but that it tastes of chestnuts. Imagine that—chestnuts—as though it were a wild pig rooting for mast all day in a submerged forest."

"Have you eaten it yourself?" Fitzjames asked.

"Once."

"And?"

"Scoresby was right."

It occurred to Fitzjames that a party of men might be sent to excavate a number of the frozen bodies and add these to their stores, but in view of what Goodsir had just told him, and the sinister connection made, he did not suggest this.

Goodsir went on, his excitement growing. "Buffon believed that the whale would attack without warning, that it reveled in carnage and would eat human flesh wherever it could find it. There is a marsh on the coast of Iceland, Pytheas' Thule, known as the Pool of Corpses. In the twelfth century, Anhald, the first bishop of that island, was shipwrecked there, and among the washed-up bodies of his sailors and the flotsam of his ship he discovered a large number of horns, upon each of which was carved runic symbols colored in red."

"Signifying?" Fitzjames said, believing he had missed Goodsir's point.

"Who knows? Signifying perhaps that each man had been given some warning of his own inescapable and terrifying end."

"Ridiculous," Fitzjames said, unhappy at the morbid turn their conversation had taken, at the divide they had crossed.

"Perhaps. But such associations take hold in men's minds. And as both you and I are well aware, there is no mind more open to such prophetic suggestion than the mind of a sailor." Goodsir laughed at this, and seeing that the laughter was genuine, and that he was being made fun of, Fitzjames laughed with him.

Goodsir retrieved his journal, read closely what Fitzjames had written and then slapped it shut.

Prior to embarking on his own expedition six weeks earlier, Graham Gore had arranged for John Irving to make a photographic record of his preparations and of the members of his party.

Gore himself set up the equipment, explaining to the reluctant Irving how to expose the sensitive plates and how long to keep them uncovered, afterward going to great lengths to arrange his men and their stores in a variety of compositions, running back and forth to examine them through the eyepiece before handing over to Irving. Of the nine plates exposed, only three were successfully developed.

The first showed a broad sweep of ice with broken ground and peaks in the distance, the foreground composed of various piles of stores and four unrecognizable men looking directly at the photographer. One of the dogs was also present, but only as a blur, the animal refusing to sit still for the necessary length of time.

The second plate was more successful, showing the entire party standing side by side with their arms folded across their chests. They had been arranged by Gore in order of height, declining from left to right, a slope reversed on the finished plate.

The final exposure showed only Gore and Des Voeux standing against the *Erebus*, their elongated shadows stretched across the ice and then curved against the hull. Both men held their right arms rigidly upright as though waving to the photographer, this being Gore's first attempt to include any suggestion of action into the otherwise artificial immobility of the plates.

On his journey south, he took with him mates Des Voeux and Edward Couch, and five others, including James Rigden, captain's cox, and a single marine private, Robert Hopcraft.

They left on Monday the 24th of May, Gore's orders being to march until he reached King William Land and establish the true distance and the nature of the terrain between their present position and that part of the known coastline. Current estimates of this varied between twenty and a hundred miles.

They took with them a single sledge on which to haul their tents, and each man carried his own marching rations in his pack.

During the first day's march they covered seven miles, delayed by a field of pressure ridges intersected by narrow fissures.

The following day they were held up when Edward Couch fell and injured his ankle. Having strapped his foot, Couch felt able to continue, but rather than add to the four miles they had already covered, Gore chose to make camp.

At sunset, James Rigden, who had gone ahead of the main party, returned with the news that there was land to the southeast of them, and encouraged by this, and convinced that what Rigden had seen was not the distant shore of Boothia, Gore agreed that they would turn in that direction at first light the following day.

They reached this exposed shore an hour before noon, having come a distance of only sixteen miles, and dividing into two parties, they searched in both directions along the low, ice-filled shore.

By Des Voeux's calculations they were on King William Land at the base of the Boothia Peninsula, but were still to the north and east of James Ross' Point Victory, reached seventeen years earlier and unvisited ever since. It was difficult to make precise calculations, being so close to the Magnetic Pole, but Des Voeux estimated that they were still fifty miles from Ross' Farthest West.

It was Gore's intention to visit neither the Pole nor Point Victory, but to remain for several days longer and explore inland and to the south of where they had come ashore, this being the most valuable area of exploration should a later evacuation to the south become necessary.

They searched for the cairns Ross had built during his journey west, but found only the stakes of an abandoned Eskimo dwelling and the nearby scattered bones of a large animal, whether butchered and stripped or dead of natural causes they could not tell.

Gore set the men to work constructing their own cairns, six in all, at half-mile intervals both north and south of their landing-point, and tall and solid enough for one to be seen from any other. Using a chisel, he numbered these, so that anyone coming after them might know immediately where on the coast they had come ashore, and in each he placed a canister containing the details of the route of their expedition to date. He also wrote that Sir John Franklin was still in command and that all was well, choosing not to mention the deaths they had already suffered.

He buried the last of these canisters on the 28th of May and then recalled his men to their base, from which they set out back across the ice to the ships.

The sea was still frozen for as far as they could see, but ashore the confused stacks of broken ice suggested to Gore that some recent movement had taken place. Inland, large areas of rock and shingle were exposed, and a succession of low smooth ridges tempted them to the east.

On a short hunting trip immediately prior to their departure, Robert Hopcraft found a discarded cartridge case, and upon inspecting this, Gore was convinced that their path had at last crossed with James Ross.' He organized a further search along the line taken by Hopcraft, but nothing more was found, with the exception of a large patch of sorrel, which they collected and boiled.

They turned back across the frozen sea on the 31st of May, and following their own tracks they reached the ships two days later.

Franklin congratulated them on their discoveries, pleased that their current position had been so swiftly and easily fixed. Privately, however, he expressed his regret that Gore had not pushed farther south until he came upon more positive proof of Ross' presence, or perhaps east, crossing the full width of King William Land to determine once and for all whether it truly was a part of the Boothia Peninsula, or if it was in fact a separate island linked only by an ice-bound sea to that larger land mass.

Following his first excursion away from the *Erebus*, Fitzjames did not visit Tozer and the others until ten days later. Since that first trip he had not exerted himself and had continued to recover his health. His one true disappointment during this time was the loss of four of his back teeth, which had come loose from his injured gums, and detached themselves completely during dinner one evening. He had gained half a stone in weight since his return, but his face still bore the signs of his illness. His hair continued to fall out, and despite Goodsir's assurances that it would grow again, he regretted the change in his appearance. That he should feel genuinely saddened by this loss surprised him. He knew he was not a vain man, but since his return he frequently found himself comparing what he saw in the mirror with a photograph of himself taken a month before their departure from home. Only a little over two years separated the faces, but the one he now considered daily in the mirror looked at least ten years older. He knew that a man's years between his mid-thirties and mid-forties represented a dangerous passage, and one for which he now realized he had not yet properly prepared himself.

Also of continuing concern to him was the worsening condition of James Fairholme who, following his rapid recovery, had since suffered some form of relapse and was again feverish and delirious. On one occasion he had left his sick-bed and pulled out all the drawers of the chests around him, spilling their contents and then sitting among these and tearing to shreds any books or papers which came within his reach. Afterward he shouted and screamed until he was discovered by Stanley, who immediately sedated him.

He slept for the next thirty-six hours, and when he woke he had no recollection of anything that had happened. When he saw the results of his destructive rage, he collapsed and wept. He continued to sweat heavily and at the same time to complain of a bone-chilling cold; he cried out in his shallow sleep and became incoherent and distracted when anyone tried to hold a conversation with him. He demanded to see Franklin long after he had been told of Franklin's death, and on the few occasions when Fitzjames was called upon to help subdue and reassure him, Fairholme did not recognize him, cursing and lashing out with his feeble arms without warning. He was fed regularly, but was seldom able to keep down even the lightest of foods.

Fitzjames visited him on the morning of his second attempt to meet Tozer, and was alarmed to see how much more weight he had lost during the previous few days. Before he left, Stanley drew back the blanket to reveal Fairholme's near-skeletal body, with its swollen joints and the bruising which covered his stomach and groin. He had become incontinent, and the smell filled the small room. According to Stanley, his condition was stable, but the progress of scurvy once it had taken hold was unpredictable, only its symptoms following the same irreversible and terrifying pattern.

Disheartened by what he had seen, Fitzjames left the room and then the ship, and walked the quarter of a mile from the *Erebus* to Tozer's shelter. With him again went Gore and Vesconte, accompanied this time by Hodgson and Irving from the *Terror*. Crozier had urged him to take a party of "loyal" marines from the *Erebus*, but Fitzjames had rejected this, knowing that the approach of any armed men in his company might provoke the confrontation he was hoping to avoid. He was convinced that the situation concerning the men on the ice was not so serious as Crozier believed, and that, in his mind at least, matters of loyalty and self-preservation had become deliberately confused.

The five men passed through the mounds of stores and came to the first of the two upturned boats, to which tarpaulin canopies had been attached, and within which small fires burned. The men gathered around these fires did not notice their approach, and Fitzjames stepped beneath the canopy of the nearest boat before those inside were aware of his arrival.

"Gentlemen," he said, drawing back his hood and stamping the wet from his boots. He moved closer to feel the warmth of the fire. Empty cans and bottles lay scattered around him, and a mound of bones showed powder white in the embers of the fire.

"James Daly, isn't it?" he said. "And William Heather," recognizing the two marines sitting by the entrance, and having already checked with one of the *Terror*'s warrant officers the names of all the men who had so far chosen to follow Tozer.

Both men nodded and Daly took off his cap, followed by Heather.

"You've made yourselves very comfortable," Fitzjames went on, hoping neither man misinterpreted the tone of his remark. He saw them look over his shoulder to see who had accompanied him.

There were three others in the upturned boat, all seamen, only one of whom—George Kinnaird—Fitzjames recognized. He greeted him too, and then asked if it was possible to see Tozer.

The five men agreed to this, and offered to accompany him to the larger ice-shelter where Tozer now slept. It was clear that his presence made them uneasy, causing some of them to behave as though a trap were about to be sprung on them.

"We had no choice," Kinnaird said to him before Fitzjames could ask anything further.

Gore and Vesconte appeared in the doorway and called in to identify themselves.

James Daly invited both men in. He smoked a pipe, which filled the low space with smoke and collected in a cloud above them.

"Choice?" Fitzjames asked Kinnaird.

"Go and look at her. Her forecastle head's all stoved in. The first sign of a sea under her and she's going to say her prayers. I know they're trying to repair her, but I doubt they'll stop her tipping in a fast thaw or if the ice drops her. I wouldn't never have left her otherwise. We haven't abandoned her, Mr. Fitzjames, but we couldn't go on living in her as she was, not forward of that smashed hold."

Fitzjames acknowledged both the sincerity and the despair in the man's voice and assured him that he had not come seeking to punish anyone or to persuade them to return with him.

"Then what?" William Heather asked contemptuously, drawing nods and anxious glances from the men around him.

"Simply to find out how you are situated and to see what might now be the best way forward," Fitzjames said, afterward addressing his remarks to the more sympathetic Kinnaird.

At the appearance of Irving and Hodgson, the two marines took up their rifles and looked as though they were about to run.

It was Kinnaird who defused the situation. "Tell Captain Crozier that most of us will be happy to return to his command if he will only berth us farther astern so that we might at least stand a chance of orderly abandonment if she does suffer any more damage and go down in a crush."

George Hodgson took out a pad and read from it a list of two dozen names, asking those present to confirm if the men on his list had now joined them. He did this under orders from Crozier, and all five officers regretted the ominously formal tone it cast upon the proceedings. The number of those living out on the ice had doubled in the past five days, several men from the *Erebus* also having joined them. Fitzjames realized that with one or two possible exceptions, these were not men who would panic easily, many of them, Tozer and Kinnaird included, having wintered in the Arctic several times before.

"There is one thing," Kinnaird said hesitantly, as Fitzjames and the others prepared to leave and go in search of Tozer.

"What's that?"

"The two boys have come out to join us. Scared as rabbits at harvest, they were. They're around somewhere. Take them back with you. They have no part in this or its consequences."

The others nodded their agreement at this request, and Fitzjames promised to find the boys and take them back to the *Erebus* with him, where they might share the bunks of their own two apprentices.

Leaving the boat, the five men, now accompanied by half a dozen of those living on the ice, made their way toward the more substantially constructed shelter beyond.

Tozer appeared in the doorway at their approach, shielding his eyes against the sun to make them out.

"Mr. Fitzjames," he called out. There was neither surprise nor suspicion in his voice; Fitzjames had anticipated a more hostile reception. "And Mr. Gore, Mr. Vesconte, Mr. Hodgson, Mr. Irving," Tozer added, identifying each of them as they came forward out of the glare.

Fitzjames went ahead alone and asked Tozer if the two of them might talk in private. Tozer considered this and then agreed, calling into the dwelling behind him for those inside to vacate it. Nine men came out, and behind them came the two boys, whom Fitzjames greeted, but who remained nervously silent in his presence. He signaled to Gore to approach them and persuade them to return with him to the *Erebus*.

"Come in," Tozer said brusquely, holding open the door for Fitzjames to precede him into the hut. Light entered by a solitary small window in its south wall. Cases and clothing filled most of the space, along with scattered furs and groundsheets. A smoking lamp burned on the table at the center of the room. Tozer drew up chairs and the two men sat down. Here, too, lay scattered the debris of empty cans and bottles, and Fitzjames caught the smell of alcohol, mixed with that of grease, gun oil and the warm, rank smell of men.

"Kinnaird told me what happened," Fitzjames began.

"Go and see for yourself. Go and see the so-called repairs Captain Crozier thinks he's making. She'll dip as soon as she's afloat. That is if she isn't caught and crushed first. You've only got to look at all the precious stores they've offloaded. We fulfill our duties and obligations as posted. We stand ice watch through the nights, but we aren't going to be tempted to return until we see some chance of salvation if the need arises."

"There are many still aboard who have no intention of joining you," Fitzjames said.

"Then more fool them." Tozer smiled. "But we do worry them an awful lot, don't we, Mr. Fitzjames? They're there and we're here, and they can't help but have that nagging doubt at the back of their minds, can they?"

Fitzjames conceded that this was an accurate assessment of the situation. "Did you think Crozier might send armed men to bring you back?"

The suggestion silenced Tozer for a moment, but he had clearly given this alternative course of action some thought. "Then he'd have had a fight on his hands. Besides which, for all his faults, he isn't stupid enough to let any such action leave a stain on his career. Especially not now—not now that he's in command. Surely you'd guessed that much, Mr. Fitzjames, surely you'd realized that that was why he let *you* come out here and held back himself?"

Fitzjames had considered this, but had willingly accepted his own role in the negotiations. A balance had been struck, an understanding reached, and neither man spoke for a moment. Then Tozer lifted a hot kettle to the table and made them a drink.

"We'll take back the boys," Fitzjames said eventually.

"I'd be grateful. And in turn I shall do nothing to encourage the others to join us."

"You do that simply by being here," Fitzjames said.

"No more nor less than they are encouraged by the lack of concern with which Captain Crozier treats his damage and his repairs. If I were you, I'd watch my own berth on the *Erebus*."

Fitzjames agreed to make his own inspection of the repair work and return with his views of it.

"She was a bad berth to begin with," Tozer said.

"In what way?"

"The story goes she shivered her timbers in the shipyard and that they double-banded her instead of stripping her back to her keel ready for her shakedown."

"Are you certain?"

Tozer shrugged.

Fitzjames had only ever heard of one other ship with which he was acquainted having shivered her timbers during her construction, and that was the *Rosemary*, supply and sister ship to the *Clio* in which he had sailed the South China Sea for four years. She was built in 1829, and days after having had her keel laid and her spars fixed, the insufficiently seasoned timber of her inner hull had responded to the new strain imposed upon it by shaking itself loose, requiring it to be stripped off and replaced.

"I was with Back in her ten years ago," Tozer went on. "She got caught, lifted and squeezed and all but shook herself to pieces then. When we got back we thought she'd be dismantled or sent for a hulk, but instead they doubled her, refitted her and sent her back for ice-service."

Fitzjames rose to leave.

Back outside they were approached by Gore and Vesconte, Hodgson and Irving having already departed to report to Crozier. Fitzjames regretted not having had the opportunity to speak with them before they conveyed their own impressions of the camp to Crozier. The two boys stood with Gore and did not appear unduly concerned at the prospect of returning to the *Erebus*. Kinnaird approached with a pot of freshly rendered grease for Fitzjames to take for Fairholme and any others suffering from swollen joints.

TWENTY

Franklin was finally buried on the 15th of July, St. Swithun's Day, five weeks after his death. Following the delay caused by the return of Fitzjames' party, the ceremony was further postponed by the arrival of a summer storm which lasted three nights and two days, and which covered everything with six inches of powdered ice, including Franklin's coffin and recently excavated grave.

It had been Crozier's original intention to bury Franklin away from the graves of the others, but the ice in the direction of his chosen site had recently shown signs of faulting, its elastic surface folding in long strips like crimped ribbons. In other places, equally distant, leads of dark water had temporarily appeared, only to be frustratingly sealed as lids of thick ice were then drawn and shunted over them.

The nearest of these leads had appeared a mile distant from the ships, but so far none had been broad enough or long enough to suggest any prospect of release.

On one occasion a broad channel of broken ice and water had appeared to the southwest, and because this was the direction in which they waited to sail, a larger party than usual, led by Hodgson and Irving, had been sent out to investigate. The surface ice had shattered during the night, and it was not until five the following morning that this distant but promising-looking channel was spotted. Irving's initial estimate of a mile proved optimistic, and after traveling almost two they were little closer to the distant water than when they had set out. After a few more minutes of their wasted journey, Hodgson called a halt.

The twelve men rested and shared their disappointment. Eager to confirm that their release was imminent, many had run the whole way and were now exhausted, their cheeks dripping with sweat in the heat. An inch of molten surface water skimmed the plain around them and they scooped this up and splashed it on their faces.

From where they now stood at the center of an unbroken basin, nothing of the lead could be seen, and in every direction they were dazzled by the sun on the ice. Those who had brought their veils and goggles put them on; those without shielded their eyes and walked back to the ships with their faces down.

On their return journey, Hodgson made notes on the condition of the ice through which they might yet have to forge a path, remarking with dismay upon its thickness and solidity, and upon the fact that much of it was old ice which had neither moved nor ruptured for some years past.

Crozier was critical of their failure to locate the distant lead. He took his two lieutenants on the deck of the *Erebus* and pointed it out to them, his anger barely suppressed in the presence of the others working all around them. He pointed to where the root of dark water still appeared to snake toward them, and to both Hodgson and Irving it seemed impossible that they could have traveled so far and not come upon it; it looked now to be little more than a mile distant from them, the intervening space lost in the confusion of the glare.

"An illusion, I'm afraid," Irving ventured, immediately regretting having spoken, realizing how provocative this excuse might be to someone whose hopes had been so high.

"An illusion? You dare to speak of illusions to men for whom—" Crozier fell silent. "Rest assured that I intend making a full report of your failure for the log. Of your failure, and your lack of commitment and concern."

Neither Hodgson nor Irving responded to this, aware of all the men around them who had paused in their work to watch.

Fitzjames arrived, knowing only that the party of men had returned.

"Good news?" he called to them, aware only as he spoke of all
the silent men around him.

Crozier stood with his back to him. "The matter has been dealt
with, Mr. Fitzjames. What passes between myself and the *Terror*'s
officers is no longer a matter for public consumption, and I'll thank
you not to interrupt."

Surprised by the vehemence in his voice, Fitzjames said, "Surely
an explanation is not too much to ask for."

"Explanation, Mr. Fitzjames?" Crozier shouted at him, surprising
him even further. "I think not. Look for yourself. You see what I
see. You see, in all probability, our salvation. You see an avenue
leading us toward an open sea and the completion of our task."
Crozier strode away from the four men, speaking as he went. "*You*
see it, *I* see it, everyone upon this deck sees it, and yet neither Mr.
Hodgson nor Mr. Irving are able, having been out upon the ice, to
confirm that what we can all see is actually *out* there." He stopped
abruptly, as though only then aware of the violence of his outburst.
He pushed through the men ahead of him and left the *Erebus* by
her rail ladder. A murmur rose from the nervous silence.

Down on the ice, Crozier shouted orders at the men collecting
supplies, calling for a group who sat around a fire to extinguish it
and get back to work. Midway between the two ships he turned and
called for Hodgson and Irving to report to him immediately, and
seeing that they did not instantly respond to his command, he
shouted again, making himself hoarse in the process.

"Go," Fitzjames said to them. "It serves no purpose to aggravate
him any further."

The men on the ice put out their fire and climbed back aboard
the *Erebus*, where the angry confrontation remained the topic of
discussion throughout the day.

All this happened four days before Franklin's funeral, and only
six hours before the onset of the storm, which came swiftly and
caught them unprepared. The men living out on the ice secured their

doorways and awnings and sat out the freezing winds as best they could. The upturned boats were buried completely and then abandoned after the first few hours of the storm. The ice-house was hidden by steep drifts which collected against two of its sides, and by loose ice which mounded on its roof.

Those who suffered worst during the two days of the storm were those aboard the *Terror* close to her damaged bow, where the ice blew inside and built up around them, barely thawing in the warmth of their heaters and ovens. The tented roof of the *Terror*'s deck collapsed and was blown away, scattering the supplies and coals stacked beneath it. The men working there when this happened were unable to retrieve either the canvas or the stores and were quickly forced below. Noon temperatures of 30 degrees over the previous week fell to 10 below freezing in the storm, the ferocity of which surprised them all.

It had long since occurred to Crozier and others that Franklin could not be committed to the ice in the same way as their other fatalities, and that a more ceremonious and dignified service was called for. Franklin deserved to be entombed rather than buried, and his grave needed to be carefully and solidly constructed. It also needed to be prominently marked in case the possibility later arose of retrieving his body and returning it home for the more civilized and acclaimed reburial it merited.

To this end Crozier ordered that a hole be excavated in the old and stable ice off their starboard bow, and that this should be at least nine feet deep, by nine long, by five wide. At first these dimensions surprised those who were charged with the task, but he would consider no reduction.

It took nine men three days using picks and axes to excavate a hole to these specifications, and only when Crozier was satisfied that this had been done did he explain to his officers that he intended constructing a tomb, using the sand and Portland cement the ships carried as ballast.

The base of the vault would be laid down to a depth of four feet, thus providing a solid slab upon which the coffin might rest. The walls would be built up from this foundation, and Franklin's coffin slotted between them. A concrete lid would await the lowering of the coffin and be slid into place above it. The whole tomb would then be sealed with fresh concrete, in which a marker might later be fixed. In this way the coffin would be sealed but not cemented into its base and walls, easily capable, once the grave had been located, of being lifted free. The empty tomb might afterward remain as a monument to Franklin and the expedition as a whole.

On the day of the funeral, Crozier read the service and then each of the senior officers said a few words of their own. This took place close by the ships, and when a prayer had been said ropes were attached to the trestles of the makeshift bier upon which the coffin had been laid, and forty men pulled Franklin the level, frozen mile to his grave. It was Crozier's intention that every one of them should play some physical part in the ceremony, and only those who were injured or still recovering from scurvy were excused their turn at the ropes. The giant sledge moved easily over the new powdering of ice.

Tozer led his men from their camp and they too took their turn at hauling.

The gravesite was reached and further prayers said. Throughout the proceedings a mixed flock of gulls and ravens hovered above, attracted by the prolonged disturbance below, and it was not until a salute was fired over the grave that the birds were finally dispersed, rising higher and then separating as clearly as grain from chaff, black in one direction, white in another.

The lid of the tomb was manhandled into position, and following Crozier's speech of thanks to everyone involved, the officers and men drifted slowly away. The concrete to seal the grave was mixed on the ice, and Fitzjames remained behind to supervise this, and then to attach the beaten copper plaque upon which Franklin's name and honors had been engraved. No epitaph was added. Jane Franklin might add this later upon her husband's possible reburial in London; or she might choose one and despatch it with some later expedition, having decided that her husband's present resting-place was the most fitting.

TWENTY-ONE

Reid and Blanky walked the frozen sea for as far as Reid's strength would allow. His feet were still bandaged, but the earlier padded dressing had been replaced by a much lighter one and he was able to pull on a pair of thin overboots. The bandages on his hands and his mouth pads had also been removed, and his healing wounds benefited from exposure to the clean air.

The two men carried staves to sound the ice, which they did at regular intervals, or whenever some feature along their course caught their eye.

They walked toward the southwest, all attention now being focused on this quarter, searching the ice for any indication of its breakup, and probing it for faults and any other weaknesses by which they might soon release themselves from its grip.

It was obvious to them both that the ice beneath them was neither thinning nor weakening in the usual manner. It was already the 2nd of August, and if dispersal was not already under way, then there ought at least to have been some indication that this was imminent.

"She's here and there, up and down," Blanky said, frustrated by the ever-changing pattern of the contorted ice beneath them, by its age and its clouded impenetrability.

"New has come in on top of old and then held," Reid said, unscrewing the augered tip of his stave and studying the ice caught in its thread. "Nothing we didn't already know before we set out." He banged the iron rod to clear it.

Blanky inquired after his feet, and Reid lifted one and massaged it through the soft leather. As usual, he did not answer the inquiry and Blanky did not persist.

The chief problem in assessing the nature of the ice through which they might eventually have to cut a passage was that it was uniform in neither depth, density nor configuration. Layer upon layer of fractured and faulted accumulations had been folded one upon the other and then flattened over many years, creating a stratification which had more in common with rock than with ice. In places they could detect the movement of deep water where a slipped plane had allowed the buried sea to rise into an empty space, but elsewhere it would not have been difficult for them to believe that they were walking on ice which extended right down to the sea bed, and that it was keel-ground and anchored there for all time to come. It was this, the fact that a great deal of the ice all around them appeared to have neither thawed nor moved during recent years, perhaps not since the time of Parry, which caused the two men the greatest concern.

"Nine summers out of ten we wouldn't have come halfway from Barrow Strait to here," Blanky remarked. "She's seen us coming, opened a door for us and then slammed it tight shut behind us."

Reid nodded slowly in agreement.

The following day they intended making a similar search to the north in the hope of discovering how far they might have to retreat to come into open water in that direction if the necessity arose. Neither man was hopeful of this.

"And she's not only slammed the door on us, but she's piling up the furniture on the other side," Blanky said.

They rested on a low mound and lit their pipes.

"He's growing impatient," Blanky said after several minutes of silence, distracting Reid from his thoughts.

"Crozier?"

Blanky drew up a ball of phlegm and spat it heavily to the ground.

"What does he suggest we do? Stamp our feet like Rumpelstiltskin and wait for the ice to open up beneath us?"

"I might suggest it to him."

Reid examined the horizon to the southwest and then scored an arrow on the ice at his feet pointing in the direction they hoped to continue. "Safe harbors," he said disparagingly. "We try too hard with these heavy boats to drive them into secure winter berths instead of letting them ride up and drift on the surface of the ice where it remains at its most vigorous. We need ships of shallow beam and less displacement to sit clear and to take full advantage of every new nip and lead."

"It's a risky business with so many men," Blanky said.

"We push too hard," Reid went on. "Weight and strength, weight and strength." He rose suddenly and continued walking in the direction of the arrow he had drawn. Blanky followed him.

They stopped again an hour later. They were several hundred yards apart, and at the call to halt, Blanky saw Reid drop to his knees and then fall forward. Fearing that he had finally exhausted himself, he ran to him. At his approach, however, he saw Reid rise back to his knees and then stand upright. Reid apologized for having alarmed him and then pointed out to him what he had found.

Twelve or fifteen feet directly beneath them was a submerged stream of dark water, barely visible through the intervening ice. This was little more than a yard wide where they looked down at it, but following Reid's arm, Blanky saw that this narrow channel quickly widened, and that within only a short distance of them it broadened to five or six times this width.

Blanky ran along the line of this buried flow, dropping to the ground himself and then calling out upon reaching a point where he believed he could see some indication of its movement, of its scouring along the underside of the surface ice.

Reid estimated their distance as a mile and a half from the ships.

"What do you think?" Blanky asked.

"If she's moving, then she's at least moving in the right direction." Reid positioned himself at the center of the dark channel and pointed along its upstream course. In the distance, the *Erebus* and *Terror* rested on his palm.

Any other two men might have cheered this unexpected and heartening discovery, but Reid and Blanky were content to reassure themselves that they were not exaggerating the significance of their find. They followed the line of the ice-capped fissure, one man upon each "bank," until they were certain that it did not suddenly end against a dam of tilted ice, or that it did not drain deeper into the solid unfathomable mass beneath and become lost and useless to them.

At one point the underside of the ice-roof was raised above the water by a height of three feet, this empty vault having been gouged clear when the flow of water beneath was more vigorous.

The ice separating them from the moving water was still as hard as rock, but satisfied by the dark band stretching ahead of them that the channel might later prove to be navigable, they returned to the ships.

They parted, and having warned Blanky against appearing too optimistic in front of Crozier, Reid went in search of Fitzjames.

He found him with Des Voeux and the *Erebus'* quartermasters.

"Can we blast and haul our way toward it?" Fitzjames asked, having listened to all Reid had to say, and disappointed that the probing edge of the submerged fissure was still such a great distance from them.

To Crozier, however, who was now undecided between forging their release and abandoning at least one of the ships and continuing overland, the discovery of the lead came as little short of a godsend, and he was unable to conceal his enthusiasm at the prospect of making headway toward it.

Later he sought out Fitzjames and informed him that in view of the short amount of time still remaining to them, he would take over the command of the *Erebus* and she alone would attempt to push her way through into open water. He admitted that the *Terror* was not up to the task, but added quickly that the repair work on her hull would continue until she was capable of following in the *Erebus'* wake. No one who heard him was convinced that this would now happen.

Fitzjames woke Gore and Goodsir early and they went to join Crozier's party at the *Terror's* bow. With the exception of the recent storm, nighttime temperatures had not dropped below 10 degrees for two months, but the dawn air still felt sharp as they took advantage of the early light to inspect the *Terror*.

Crozier was waiting for them, along with Hodgson and Irving and an assortment of petty officers and seamen, most of whom were already engaged on the repair work.

A sail had been fixed over the ruptured hull, and this was drawn back to reveal the full extent of the damage. Twenty feet of broken planking had been cut away, at least half of this below the *Terror's* waterline. Her bow rose proud of the ice and the damage was exposed in its entirety. Two of her forward spars had been loosened, and it was these structural supports which caused the carpenters and blacksmiths the most concern. Any repair to the bolted timbers could only be temporary and imperfect, and they would remain a dangerous weakness, with the likelihood of giving completely the next time any real pressure was placed on them.

The carpenters explained all this to Crozier and Fitzjames, and pointed out where they had so far repaired the internal damage, including the replacement of the forecastle wall. A wedge of ice still protruded into the forward hold and could not be removed without causing the *Terror* to tilt and fall lower in her frozen cradle, which now served as scaffolding while the outside work progressed. This intrusive ice had been of some assistance while the internal repairs had been carried out, but later it had become a hindrance, forcing the carpenters to work around it, ever conscious of the fact that it might suddenly slip back beneath the surface as quickly and as destructively as it had first appeared.

Crozier became impatient with all these explanations, making it even more evident that his real interest now lay elsewhere, and he drew Goodsir to one side to discuss the use of explosives to speed up the approach of the advancing fissure.

Fitzjames, Gore and Irving remained with the blacksmiths, warming themselves on their braziers, the ground around them studded with fallen coals.

Samuel Honey, the *Terror's* smith, stood with them, explaining in greater detail some of the more intricate repairs they were attempting. They were joined by Thomas Watson from the *Erebus*.

"We can seal her," Honey pointed out, drawing imaginary planking over the hole. "But we can't make her strong."

"Can you strengthen her sufficiently so that she might sit on the ice if she were to be left here to await rescue?" Fitzjames asked him.

"You mean abandoned?" Watson said anxiously.

"Could she be supported from outside so that she might at least be free of the ice?" Fitzjames said, his words still directed at Honey, who himself became suddenly concerned at the prospect of abandonment. "Answer me."

"She might."

In addition to the coals at their feet, shattered timbers also rose from the ice, upon which the workmen hung their tools and lanterns.

The damage had occurred on the *Terror's* starboard bow, shaded from the sun for most of the day, and it was not difficult for Fitzjames to understand why the men once berthed inside had preferred to abandon their quarters and take their chances out on the ice, nor why others, less threatened or discomfited by the damage, had later chosen to go with them.

"Mr. Goodsir is fully agreed with my plan," Crozier said loudly, returning to join them, ushering Goodsir ahead of him, one glance at whom indicated that he was considerably less enthusiastic about his role in the proceedings than Crozier suggested.

"We'll start blasting," Goodsir said, silencing them all.

Pausing only long enough to take note of their response to this, Crozier left.

When he had gone, Goodsir said they might broaden the submerged lead and bring it more quickly toward them by the detonation of explosions along its projected course. He believed that this was preferable to trying to free the *Erebus* from her cradle before the ice was ready to slacken its grip naturally.

"Where will you start?" Fitzjames asked him, aware of the risks involved in disturbing the ice around the ships.

"Midway between where we now stand and the head of the approaching stream."

"Will it work?" Irving asked.

"Captain Crozier certainly believes so," Fitzjames said quietly.

"I know," Goodsir said. "But it is a perfectly feasible strategy, and if it goes well we should at least get the *Erebus* free."

"And the *Terror*?" Hodgson asked, conscious of the stares of the men all around him.

Goodsir did not answer; instead he dug his heels into the ice beneath the braziers, looked hard at the impression he made, and then left them.

Over the next few days the sick and injured on the *Erebus* were transferred to the *Terror*, where there was now more space for them. In total, these numbered thirty-six. As a consequence of this, both Stanley and Goodsir spent more time there, largely ministering to the growing number who were bedridden, but also performing further small amputations.

Only Fairholme remained on the *Erebus*, his days of unconsciousness and delirium now outnumbering those when he was rational and calm, like an exhausted swimmer surfacing less and less frequently in a heavy sea. He had lost three stone and his skin had acquired the sheen and color of tallow. His swollen joints bruised every time he moved them, suppurating with pus in places and bleeding in others. He could still keep nothing down and was by then completely bald.

It was Stanley's opinion that there was a point along the course of an attack of scurvy from which it was impossible ever fully to recover. In this respect, he considered the disease to be similar to malaria—straightforward in the treatment of its outward manifestations, but essentially untouchable in that part of it which took firm root in the man, and which he carried with him to his grave regardless of the ultimate cause of death.

Both David Bryant and Philip Reddington had recovered only slowly, Reddington in particular continuing to suffer from bleeding gums and patches of raw skin on his cheeks and neck which took a long time to heal, and which scabbed over only to peel and become raw again. New irritations appeared on his stomach and in his groin, and it was these which caused him the greatest pain.

Some of those who had suffered hair loss were already seeing it grow back. Fitzjames himself had watched the bald patch above his temple slowly refill with new growth, and in only one small patch, above his left ear, did the hair come back white instead of its usual dark brown.

TWENTY-TWO

Back's River, gentlemen." Crozier traced his finger down the map. "Or if you prefer not to honor our Mr. Back, the Great Fish." He smiled at this distinction, lifted his finger slightly and then jabbed it back.

A murmur of expectation spread around Franklin's cabin.

"And we are somewhere approximately here." He searched for the mark on the large empty space. Their position had been fixed to within only a few miles, but it seemed to many of them that to mark something so precisely on a map which already took so many obvious liberties in marrying the known to the unknown, was more an act of faith than a reassuring certainty. Pausing only briefly, he drew his finger west along the mainland rim, easing it through the known coastal straits in that direction.

It was across this unknown space, in a neat and direct line drawn between Barrow Strait and the mainland coast running east of Bering, that the route of the expedition had been drawn by the Arctic Council. They could all see it, and they all now saw how misleading and fatal a conceit it had become.

Crozier turned away from them, following more closely the line of the coast until he allowed his finger to be drawn as though by some quickening current out through narrow Bering and into the warm and golden Pacific.

He turned back to them, a look of satisfaction on his face, as though, having mapped their yet to be achieved escape, it was now somehow more firmly within their grasp. The others indulged him, aware that the history of all exploration was a history of men drawing their fingers across empty spaces.

They had been digging in the ice and blowing open its capricious fractures for over a fortnight.

Seeing that he was losing their attention, Crozier said, "Any suggestions, gentlemen?" making it clear to them that this was little more than a courtesy, a polite call for silence. He went on. "The only obstacle, the only *possible* obstacle to us might now be a difficult passage through the ice toward the sea off Ross' Farthest West, a point near enough reached by Mr. Gore and his party." He indicated Graham Gore. "Perhaps Mr. Gore himself might care to enlighten us upon the nature of the ocean at that point and the likelihood of our passage through it into the open sea beyond. Mr. Gore."

Gore rose to his feet, uncertain of what his report was intended to achieve in view of their current situation.

"For as far as I could see, the ocean running to the west of King William Land was frozen solid and showed signs of considerable jamming and disfigurement. The ice was neither level nor stable. For how far this extended I could not say."

"But in all likelihood already beginning to break up and disperse, wouldn't you agree?" Crozier said impatiently. "And, moreover, moving away to the west in the predominant current."

Gore could not agree entirely with this and said so. Like James Ross before him, he had been surprised by the extent of the ice thrown up on that western shore, and at the violence with which this had been done. He had seen blocks of ice a quarter of a mile inland, and in many places the shore itself had been unrecognizable, torn and crushed and buried beneath an impenetrable thickness of sea ice, all of which suggested to him that the prevailing current in that region was *from*, rather than toward the west, as Crozier had hoped to suggest.

"But a fair prospect of open water all the same, wouldn't you say, Mr. Fitzjames?" Crozier said as soon as Gore had finished speaking.

Fitzjames agreed with this. From everything he knew about the waters off the mainland coast, he expected them to remain navigable for longer than elsewhere. He was less optimistic than Crozier about the possibility of their journey into this open sea, but he could not disagree with him on their improved chances once they reached it.

Having spoken, Fitzjames looked at the men around him, several of whom lowered their eyes rather than confront him with their own contradictory estimations.

Crozier held these meetings daily, calling for reports on each aspect of their release work, for which individual officers had been given separate responsibility, and only rarely—as on that particular morning—extending their gaze to the wider landscape and its more distant prospects. The meetings served their purpose in keeping everyone informed, but no one was blind to the fact that they were also Crozier's way of impressing his new authority upon them. Those who had sailed with him before were surprised to see him changed in this way, particularly those who had been with him in the Antarctic, where he had gained a reputation of being one of the most cautious of all ice-captains, drawing back whenever the odds against him even slightly outweighed those in his favor.

The meeting ended with the arrival of one of the men who had been working outside, who went directly to Crozier and spoke to him in a whisper.

"Another fissure, gentlemen," Crozier announced, as though this vindicated everything he had just said. "Running . . ." He prompted the man beside him.

"Running clear across our stern from one side to the other."

"As a result of our own work?" Fitzjames asked him.

The man shook his head. "It appeared first off in the ice twenty yards to starboard and then dashed right under us the same distance out to port." His voice was a mix of awe and surprise.

"Any open water?"

Again the man shook his head.

A similar fissure had appeared off their starboard bow two days earlier, it too having come into being independently of all their efforts. They left the cabin to examine this new rupture for themselves.

Fitzjames and Goodsir were the first to descend and inspect it more closely. There was no sign of any water, but it was undoubtedly a natural weakness in the ice which had opened up in response to pressure from elsewhere, either far below in more volatile waters, or from farther out toward the weakening ice in the south, where explosions were now being detonated almost daily.

"It appears to be open to some considerable depth," Goodsir observed, measuring the width of the gap and then throwing down pieces of ice and listening to them drop. He could gauge little from this, except that the fissure was a deep one, suggesting that it might continue to spread and to open up beneath them in the days to come.

A ladder was brought, and Crozier descended to join them, briefly examining the opening in the ice and then stepping back and forth across it several times. He walked to the stern, where the *Erebus'* screw had been refitted in readiness for when she settled back in the water, and despite his earlier misgivings about leaving the engine intact, he now felt encouraged by seeing the highly polished metal amid so much apparent confusion.

Later the new fissure was staked, and the stores and shelters along its line of advance were moved beyond its reach.

Goodsir detonated his next sequence of explosions three days later. He was accompanied by Gore and Reid and two dozen others, most of them with saws and grapnels ready to take advantage of any weakness the blasts might create in the ice.

In the time since Reid and Blanky's discovery, the widening lead had approached several hundred yards closer to the ships, and they were all encouraged by this.

Goodsir directed the men carrying the gunpowder to lay it down in several caches, and he walked on alone to the tip of the submerged channel and examined it for signs of recent or imminent activity.

Except for the daily thaw, there was still no water on the surface, but where he knelt, Goodsir could feel it moving distantly beneath him, and he could see its shadow. In places he could even feel the ice upon which he prostrated himself ripple slightly. He was not alarmed by this, and included it in his calculations when deciding where best to detonate his charges. He estimated that at least ten feet lay between him and the water below.

Reid joined him and the two men calculated the natural line of weakness the approaching water was preparing to exploit. Choosing a point twenty feet ahead of this, Goodsir told one of the men to hollow out a depression sufficient for a six-pound charge. In calculating this point he also took into consideration the likelihood of any smaller deposits of trapped air, knowing that any charge which exploded into an empty crevasse or ice-vaulted cavern would be largely wasted, and might work against them by creating undesirable weaknesses elsewhere.

From where they waited for the man to finish his digging, Goodsir, Reid and Gore could see the two ships on the near horizon. They had made an early start and the sun was not yet high enough or bright enough to confuse them with its broad reflections and illusory distances.

Of the three, only Reid remained unconvinced that they might yet succeed in driving the open water right up to the *Erebus*, but he knew too that there was now no alternative but to make the attempt. It was already mid-August, and whatever else happened to them, whatever else they might achieve, no effort could be spared during that one precious summer month remaining to them.

The man cutting the ice signaled that he had finished, and Goodsir primed his first charge, pressing it with his good hand into the cold mush, leaving only sufficient space for the short fuse to protrude.

He waved for them all to crouch down—there was no way they might take any more effective cover from the blast—and then he lit the fuse and stood over it to ensure it was burning properly before running back to kneel beside them. Around him, some of the men had thrown themselves flat, their arms folded over their heads. Others had retreated a farther hundred yards and now sat hunched with their backs to the smoking mound.

Goodsir began to count, and upon reaching only eight, the powder exploded, punching up a small bush of black smoke and scattering a shower of ice high into the air.

One by one they all rose and watched as the smoke cleared and as the watery debris fell in a wide and harmless circle all around them.

Goodsir called for silence, and stood with his head cocked toward where the explosion had taken place, its reverberating echo still audible.

"What is it?" Gore asked him.

"Listen." Goodsir pointed, first toward the rising smoke and then toward the ships.

At first all Gore could hear was a ringing sound, but then, as the explosion faded, he too picked up the brittle creaking which suggested that the ice had been split.

"Well done" he said, slapping Goodsir on the shoulder. "But where's she going? Our way?"

Goodsir called again for silence, but this time he went unheeded by the cheering men.

He walked back to where he had laid the charge, searching the ground ahead of him before each step. Then he stopped suddenly, turned to his right, and shouted, "There!"

They all looked to where he pointed, and although little was at first apparent, the few men who were closest also began to shout and point, causing the others to run and join them.

Ahead, and running in almost a straight line from the charge, a clean new crack appeared in the surface ice.

"Do you think we could barge that open if we got this far to try, Mr. Gore?" Goodsir asked, and Gore, still surprised by how much that single small explosion had achieved, nodded, cautiously at first, but then with growing conviction. He ran closer than any of them to the broken unstable ice. A ball of sooty smoke hung in the air, rising from the small crater as though a fire had been lit there.

Goodsir, Gore and Reid conferred. There was little to be gained by attempting to grapple or cut the crack any wider; it might be weeks yet before the *Erebus* was able to reach it. Instead they decided to fire two more charges, and then to spend the rest of the morning searching more widely along either side of the channel.

The second explosion, though larger, was awaited with less awe than its predecessor, most of the men gathering into a single group around Goodsir to observe its effects. The charge was detonated a hundred yards from the first, sixty beyond the leading edge of the new opening, and was exploded in ice beneath which there was no water visible. Warning them all that the results were likely to be less spectacular than the first, Goodsir laid the powder and ignited it using a longer fuse.

This time the blast passed beneath them and men held out their arms like acrobats to steady themselves. There was more smoke and more scattered ice than before, but the after-effects were shorter lived. A new crack appeared on the surface, but this was only superficial and would in all likelihood reseal itself when the temperature fell. Goodsir went alone to inspect the results. He knew that it was not necessary to cut a continuous line through the ice, that a series of perforations would serve their purpose equally well.

This time the two lips of ice had remained level, but along half its length the new crack had come apart, revealing a gap of several inches in places. Cheered by this, Goodsir knelt and held his ear to the opening.

"Water," he called out, drawing Gore, Reid and several others toward him. They knelt beside him and they too heard the sound of moving water far beneath them.

"Is it rising?" Gore asked.

"Not here," Reid told him, listening intently. "Old ice has melted, but the upper, newer stuff is still intact."

Around them, others approached the crack, and some began to prod at it cautiously with their staves. Reid warned them to hold off for fear of unsettling the ice upon which they stood.

Before planting his final charge, Goodsir called them all together and listened to their reports.

A quarter of a mile to the west, one man said, there were holes in the surface of the ice through which a fountain of fine spray occasionally rose.

Elsewhere, further submerged channels had been located, none so obvious, so broad or so deep as the one upon which they were presently working, but all of them running in the same general direction toward the ships.

"A balloon," Goodsir said unexpectedly. "Just imagine what we might learn if we possessed a balloon for purposes of observation." He looked up into the pale sky as he spoke, and many around him did the same.

Knowing that little would be achieved by firing his final charge to extend the openings of the first two, he led them all back to a point midway between the first explosion and the ships.

"I intend to conduct an experiment," he told Gore and Reid. "A considerably larger explosion in much deeper, immovable ice."

"To what purpose?" Gore asked him.

Goodsir considered his answer. "So that we might not be fooled by our successes so far, and so that we might not be deceived by the apparent ease with which we are about to make our escape." He spoke in a low voice so that none of the others might hear him.

"Is that wise?" Gore said.

"I believe it is. What have we achieved this morning other than to blast useless cracks into already weakened ice? Cracks which will in all likelihood disappear before we get within a mile of them in the *Erebus*."

Choosing a point on the ice beneath which nothing was visible, Goodsir called for several men to dig out a much deeper hole, and as they did this he explained to the others what he was doing. Some of them responded as Gore had done, complaining that the powder was being used to no practical effect, and Goodsir repeated what he had told Gore, convincing some, but leaving many unhappy at such a wasted and pessimistic conclusion to an otherwise encouraging morning's work. He reassured them by pointing out that for another month at least the natural dissolution of the ice from the south would continue at a faster rate than they themselves might be able to blast a path through it.

The men digging the hole called to him that they were finished.

This time he packed twenty-four pounds of powder into the space, leaving most of it in its waxed packets, and tipping it loose from one of their small kegs to ensure that every gap was filled. Others helped him pack the shattered ice over this, only leaving him as he took an augur and drilled a clear passage for the fuse, which he inserted and then withdrew several times until he was satisfied it was properly placed. Having lit it, he warned them about the likely extent of the blast and the weight of ice it would throw up, and they waited with their arms ready to cover their faces.

He counted confidently to thirty, and then more slowly and quietly to forty. When this was passed he added a further ten silent seconds before slapping his hands together and cursing. Around him men rose to their feet. He silenced their inquiries and told those who had started to move forward to stay where they were. Each second which now passed seemed to reaffirm an ill-judged decision, proof that he should not have attempted this last wasted effort.

It was as he was about to address them again that the explosion eventually came, catching them all unawares, throwing some off their feet, buckling the ice upon which they stood, and stinging their exposed faces with its force and with the needles of ice it blasted through them.

Pushing himself up from where he had fallen, Goodsir turned to see the pall of rising smoke, solid and dark as a graveyard yew, rise high into the air above them. This time men ran clear of the cascade of falling ice, abandoning their tools and sledges.

Gore called for them to remain where they were, but few heard him and he did not repeat the command.

They waited for a response from the ice. None came. All the explosion had achieved was to blow a crater twelve feet wide by six feet deep, and leave this half-filled with steaming black water.

Goodsir, Gore and Reid remained standing over this, but the others, having looked briefly into the dirty hole, muttered derogatory comments upon it, and some upon the man who had caused it, and resumed their journey back to the ships.

TWENTY-THREE

The *Erebus* floated free on the 25th of August. Streaks and patches of open water had appeared throughout the previous week, and during the past few days the surface ice had fractured and broken loose, lubricated by the hidden surges all around them. Most of these new fissures were as narrow and as short as the one which had appeared beneath the *Erebus'* stern, but some, particularly those in the direction of the plain beyond the encampment, were considerably larger, and in places too wide for a man to leap with any certainty.

Due east of the camp, the ice ruptured in massive blocks and created tremors which shook both ships. It ground together in a confusion of angles and shapes, swallowing new and exposing old ice. Pieces ran in opposing directions, collided and continued to press over one another until they rose in islands of rubble which looked as though they had been cast down from above. Depressions appeared like the one in which the frozen narwhals had been exposed, and in the distance, visible to them only when the sun was low, a succession of pillars and slabs rose into being which looked to them all like the giant standing stones of some ancient circle, abandoned by its heathen priests and worshipers, but confident now in its rebirth of their return.

"The temple of Asgard?" Goodsir remarked, as he, Fitzjames and Reid walked in the direction of this recent creation, not intending to reach it, but to find out for Gore if the conditions were favorable for him to take a photograph of the unusual features before it collapsed or was shaken down.

"Who was Asgard?" Fitzjames asked.

"I'm not entirely certain if it was a who," Goodsir said. "Asgard was—is, perhaps—the Norse citadel of warm zephyrs and brilliant light."

"On the other hand," Reid said, "it might just as easily be Niflheim." His back was to them, but Fitzjames could imagine the grin on his face.

"And Niflheim," Goodsir explained with a flourish of his good hand, "was the name given to the howling wasteland of unending darkness and ice hung over with the stench of death."

This caused them all to pause for a moment and look toward their distant goal.

"And they believed that both these places existed?" Fitzjames said.

"There are still nonexistent islands on the Admiralty charts less than two hundred miles off our own shore, James. What do *we* believe?"

The dock around the *Erebus* had been fully excavated a week earlier, and work now concentrated on exploring weaknesses in the ice at her prow. She would try to move forward like a mole through the earth, forcing her own path, and keeping around her only as much open water as she needed to remain afloat. It no longer mattered if the water behind her refroze, as long as she was able to continue pressing forward into the weakening pack ahead. Using her engine she made six runs into the ice, the last two of which finally caused the frozen surface to buckle ahead of her.

By the 8th of September they had pushed themselves a hundred yards and were a quarter of a mile distant from the *Terror*. Patchy floes sealed the gap between them and their crippled sister ship, and already she looked abandoned, awaiting only the retribution of the patient ice.

To those watching from the *Terror*, there could be no hope whatsoever of following along that same path.

The next day they made little progress, the ice ahead of them refusing to give way at their assault.

They retreated from this and turned several degrees to port. This proved more successful, and during the evening and night they were able to zig-zag a farther sixty yards toward the southwest, where they finally came within sight of Goodsir's crater.

On the seventh morning of bulling the ice the *Erebus'* prow was damaged, and shortly afterward a small explosion finally put her over-taxed engine out of service.

They were all aware that soon the divide between summer and autumn would be crossed, and that the ice would then start to consolidate faster than they could dislodge it and pull it clear. Some argued that they had waited too long and should have started their escape attempt earlier in the summer, and some now believed that they ought to abandon it completely and start making preparations for a third winter. Some even proposed a partial disembarkation and a fast march to King William Land and beyond in the hope of making contact with someone who might then be able to return with them and rescue those left behind.

The ice ahead of them was explored on foot, but offered little encouragement. The leads Goodsir had earlier tried to exploit were still tantalizingly out of reach, and the intervening distance remained as solid and as little disturbed as any part of the frozen plain through which they had already come. Their boats might be hauled and eventually launched, but in the face of the approaching winter, the distance yet to travel, and the large number of men left behind, this too was unthinkable.

In the company of several others, Fitzjames returned across the ice to the *Terror*. They walked largely in silence, and were joined by others, small parties and individuals, all of whom had left the scene of their labors to pass on the news of what had happened to those left behind. Signal flares were exchanged and men used firearms to communicate with each other.

With Fitzjames went Goodsir, returning to see Stanley about his thumb, the pain from which had grown steadily worse over the previous few days, and who was now convinced that there was no alternative but for the remaining infected joints to be amputated.

Midway between the two ships they encountered the walking sick and wounded from the *Terror*, these few men stumbling and crawling toward them like the exhausted survivors of some other, more distant catastrophe, and as the two parties met in the fading light the strong helped the weak and they exchanged their news and then speculated upon this until it was difficult to decide who had suffered the worse—those left behind to watch as they were deserted and committed to their own failing resources, or those who had bloodied and exhausted themselves in trying to get away.

Fitzjames and Goodsir helped up a man who had fallen at their feet and half-carried, half-dragged him until others came forward to share the burden. Relieved of their load, the two men paused to recover their own strength and to look around them at the ships and the camp, and to watch as countless lanterns and torches were one by one extinguished and the darkness became complete.

TWENTY-FOUR

Only Philip Reddington, about to stand down from his dawn-watch duty, was on deck when the ice which abutted the *Terror*'s hull, and which had so far held her firm, began to quake. Even as he ran to give warning, the ice came free in increasingly larger slabs and these then ground against the ship and shifted along her keel. She was rocked and shaken, and everyone still aboard her was either thrown from their beds or knocked off their feet. Before anyone could leave her she tilted forward along her full length, sending everything loose upon the deck spilling forward into a mound; her fore-top and yard were shattered, bringing down her topsail and rigging and leaving this hanging in a tangle of loose rope and canvas. For several minutes all that could be heard was the ship's groaning at some unseen pressure, and then one by one her scupper pieces were forced up out of their mortices.

All the repair work on her bow was undone in a moment. The block of ice which lay half in and half out of her rose from its foundations and crushed up through her timbers and decking as though they were balsa, taking with it her bowsprit, jib and jib-yard, casting these out on to the ice and then swallowing them completely as a gap appeared beneath the rising block.

Crozier gave the order for her to be abandoned, and for those who had already left her and were running in all directions to go back and help the surgeons take off the sick and the injured. Many were at first reluctant to return, but as the ice gradually subsided a chain was formed along her port bow and the sick-quarters were evacuated.

Those who could walk were wrapped against the cold and then led away along the line of men. Those who could not were man-handled over the side in makeshift slings and stretchers and then carried to the *Erebus*.

This evacuation lasted an hour, during which the *Terror* continued to shake where she sat. Ropes were fastened along her deck to help men move more easily on the tilted and cluttered surface. The last of her boats was released, lowered to the ice and dragged away.

By then it was dusk and several fires were lit using timber from the wreckage. All around them the ice continued to move in the darkness, one minute flowing like the waves of a turning tide, and the next crushing and swallowing its blocks as though an earthquake were taking place directly beneath them.

Once all the men had been rescued an attempt was made to re-cover their stores. Some of these had already been lost when the *Terror*'s stern had risen, spilling several tons of loose coal into the spaces in the ice, followed by the cases of food from which the sick were being fed.

Seeing how little was being achieved by scrabbling around on the sloping deck for the stores which remained lodged there, Fitzjames called for everyone to concentrate their efforts on rescuing the larger stocks mounded below. By some good fortune, few of these had been lost, the ice beneath them having so far remained stable, but barely an hour later, when less than a third of these had been removed and handed along the chain of men toward the *Erebus*, the ice began to buckle and tilt again. The *Terror*'s bow opened up completely and her doubling and the foremost of her spars were torn out.

Standing at a safe distance from the crushed hull, Fitzjames tried to estimate how much they had lost. He regretted that they had been forced to salvage the stores indiscriminately, throwing from hand to hand everything which came within reach.

He held a lantern, and by its dim light he was able to peer into the *Terror*'s open bow. The foremast base had been exposed, sur-rounded by fingers of splintered decking. Clothes and furniture lay spilled all around. A white shirt had caught on a nail and flapped in the darkness like a vigorously waving man.

Another rising groan drew his attention to the *Terror*'s stern, and he watched as she was lifted several feet higher, shaking along her full length as her keel and rudder were exposed. He knew that soon the keel would be weakened and then broken under the pressure of the ice rising beneath it, and that when this happened she would be snapped in half as easily as a toy and lost to them completely.

She hung above the ice for a moment, and then suddenly sagged, coming finally to rest with her deck tilted toward him. He heard her masts and yards straining against their stays and he heard too the distinctive noise made by hemp ropes the thickness of a man's arm parting as cleanly as though someone had taken a blade to them.

He was joined where he stood and watched all this by Gore and Vesconte.

Gore spoke to him, but he could make out little of what he said above the rising wind and the noise of the ice. They motioned for him to leave with them and return to the safety of the *Erebus*. They too held lanterns and lifted them to look into the broken hull, becoming as mesmerized as he had been by the exposed innards and by the realization of how quickly and easily the reinforced structure had been opened up and then squeezed into a useless mass of timber, good now only for fuel, and the greatest part of that beyond retrieval.

The three men stood together several minutes longer before leaving.

Debris lay in a broad sweep between the two ships, and they followed this back to the *Erebus*, passing the few stragglers who remained out in the open.

On November the 3rd James Fairholme, delirious and suffering as acutely as ever, fell from his bed and was racked by his most severe fit yet.

Stanley called for help to restrain him and then diagnosed the violent spasm as an attack of *grand mal*. Goodsir agreed with this, and together they lifted the sedated Fairholme back onto his bed, where they fastened leather straps across his arms, chest and shins, careful not to bruise any further the skin which already barely covered his bones.

He came round several hours later, rational and calm after his convulsions, and calling for Stanley he told him that he had gone blind as a result of his seizure.

Stanley examined his eyes, and said that he believed the injury was only temporary and that his vision would return.

Fairholme made no objection to the straps which restrained him, but complained that his chest ached where the broadest of them held him down. Stanley adjusted this, noticing as he did so that new weals had appeared along the line of Fairholme's ribs, suggesting that some had been fractured as a result of his fall. He bathed and dressed these before bandaging his eyes. He knew that Fairholme was aware of his uncertainty regarding his lost sight, and hoped that he did not misinterpret his remarks as a deliberate deceit. To Goodsir, Stanley confided his surprise that Fairholme had endured his injuries and suffering for so long while other men who had suffered for only a fraction of that time had continually complained of their pain and demanded to have it alleviated at every opportunity and by any means available.

Neither man could be certain if Fairholme's blindness was a direct consequence of his fit, or simply a further stage in the grisly progress of the disease from which he was suffering. He now weighed less than five stone, could not stand unaided, and on some days could barely raise his head to acknowledge whoever had gone in to sit with him and keep him company. Every joint in his body was swollen, and all his hair and most of his teeth had fallen out. It was not uncommon for both Stanley and Goodsir to pause each morning before entering to treat him in the expectation of finding him dead.

He became delirious again two days later, demanding to know why he had been taken out on the ice and why this had been laid in slabs upon him. He demanded to speak to Franklin, and then to know why his eyes had been bound, what it was they were trying to prevent him from seeing.

There was nothing they could do for him except wait for the

rigors of his delirium to subside and protect him from inflicting any further physical harm upon himself.

A week later even his short periods of rationality ceased, and he recognized no one who visited him, railing viciously against them for what was happening to him. He began to bleed uncontrollably from almost every orifice—his ears, nose, mouth and rectum—and the next day, after a further violent seizure during which he called repeatedly for his wife and children, he died, falling suddenly silent, his entire body straining in a painful curve before collapsing and finally settling in a succession of gentle waves which caused his bloody wasted corpse to tremble in its straps.

Goodsir was with him when this happened, and realizing what he was witnessing, he called for Stanley and Fitzjames. Others arrived with them, and upon silently acknowledging that Fairholme was beyond their help, they all assisted in unfastening his body, covering it with a clean sheet and then lifting it from the bed, all of them shocked by the looseness of his bones and the way in which it felt as though they were holding these in their hands without the intervening comfort of flesh or skin or sheet.

"James Walter Fairholme," Fitzjames said over the shrouded corpse, the rhythm and solidity of the names a solemn litany, enlivened only by the affection with which they were spoken.

They left as Stanley prepared the body for removal onto the ice, knowing that its eventual interment would prove difficult, if not impossible, while the ice remained so unpredictable and uneven all around them.

Goodsir suggested that it should be taken and placed in one of the cabins of the abandoned *Terror* until those final arrangements could be made. They were all agreed upon this, and afterward all their corpses were disposed of in this manner.

For six weeks following the loss of the *Terror*, the surrounding plain shook only to the reverberations of distant and largely unseen disturbances, and despite their surprise at this movement so late in the year, they were well prepared for these smaller shocks and able to protect themselves from them.

This peaceful interlude ended on the 14th of December with a sudden tremor which caught them all by surprise, especially the men in Tozer's camp, where it struck most violently, and particularly those who were out on the ice when it came.

Four men were returning to the shelters from their store when a crevasse opened up directly ahead of them, tilting the ice and knocking them off their feet. Others emerged to see what was happening. The crevasse stopped opening, and the block of ice upon which the men had fallen came to rest at a gentle slope. They rose and continued back to the shelters, jumping over the low steps and ridges which had appeared on the surrounding surface.

As they approached the shelters the ice moved again, this time opening directly beneath them and forcing them back to the ground.

At the first indication of the tremors, men had also come out of the *Erebus*, and all eyes were on the distant figures. Some ran to where the four men had fallen and could no longer be seen.

A second fissure had opened up, its two lips drawing apart as it extended in length. One of its edges had tilted upward, and it was this which hid the men from view. They had fallen into the space created beneath them, but rather than find themselves dropping helplessly into the depths of a widening chasm, their fall was broken only four feet down by a broad ledge, beneath which the fissure was no more than a foot wide. Only the surface layer of ice had been disturbed by the tremors, and that beneath was holding fast.

The first of the men pulled himself free, signaled to those running toward him that he was unhurt, and then knelt to help the second man out of the trench.

The remaining two stood where the buried shelf was at its deepest, ready to edge their way along the platform and await their own turn to be pulled clear. Both were aware that the fissure was still opening up away from them and that it might suddenly become much wider beneath their feet.

By then the first two men had climbed clear and a small group had gathered around them, some with ropes, which they threw across the sloping ice to the others.

As the two men in the ice fastened the ropes around their chests the opening began to move in on them, and everyone urged them to hurry, directing them along the shelf to where the drop beneath them was less sheer. The men edged sideways, panicked by this resumption of the tremors. As they did so, the ice upon which their rescuers stood fractured into several large pieces. Men ran in all directions, abandoning the ropes as they stumbled clear.

The pieces of broken ice settled back into place, and one of the two trapped men let out a scream. He slipped from his foothold, and although the chasm had still not opened up beneath him, he was now on his knees in the narrowest part of the fissure, its sides against both his shoulders. The other tried to help him up, but it was difficult to maneuver in the confined space, and he shouted for those above to retrieve the ropes and begin pulling them out. Then he too stopped shouting and suddenly screamed.

The men above scrambled over the tilted rim of loose ice to see what had happened. Some took up the ropes and hauled on them, but one of these was now trapped between two pieces of ice, and the other flew out of the crevasse and caused the men pulling on it to fall in a line on the unstable surface.

Fitzjames and Reid arrived, ran around the main body of men and approached the broken ice from the opposite direction. It was Reid who first saw what had happened to the two men: the chasm beneath them had not opened up, but the shaking of the ice above had forced a large wedge of it into the narrow space alongside them. This wedge now formed a new and unstable lip to the fissure, reducing the space in which the two men stood to less than half its original width.

Taking charge, Reid called for them to raise themselves slowly upright and then to stand perfectly still.

Speaking behind his hand to Fitzjames, he pointed out that instead of trying to squeeze the two men out through this narrow space, they ought to turn their attention to pulling clear the ice which imprisoned them, and which, if it slid any farther into the fissure, would crush them where they stood.

More rope was brought to the scene, tied into wide loops and thrown over the wedge of ice in an effort to draw it away from the two men, allowing them to be pulled to safety behind it. Reid ordered those who were not directly involved in the rescue attempt to move back so as to cause no further disturbance to the already precarious surface.

He returned to where Fitzjames crouched talking to the two men. A moment later they were joined by Tozer, who offered his own suggestions and encouragement.

The rescue attempt began cautiously.

"What happens if she gets the shakes again?" Tozer asked Fitzjames out of hearing of the two men.

"God forbid it will," Fitzjames said.

"I think *He* might have stopped taking an interest in us long ago," Tozer said.

"Then our own efforts will have to suffice."

Momentarily unsettled by Tozer's suggestion, Fitzjames turned his attention back to the men throwing the ropes, and from his vantage-point at the far side of their target he directed them to throw where the ice protruded the farthest over the fissure, and where it might be more easily caught.

Three more casts were made, each as unsuccessful as the last.

"Tozer does have a point," Reid told Fitzjames, dismayed by their repeated failure. He took Fitzjames to one side and showed him where the surface of the ice was again gently vibrating.

"The dying tremors of the earlier shock?" Fitzjames said.

"Possibly. Or the forerunner of another."

They searched around them for any other indication of this, distracted after only a few seconds by a shout from Tozer, followed an instant later by screams from the trapped men.

The wedge of ice had slipped and now rested close against their chests. It was not crushing them, nor was it even propped against them, but in slipping it had deprived them of the last of their space.

Controlling their screaming, the two men pleaded to be saved.

"Could we not prop the gap open and pull them out farther along?" Fitzjames suggested.

Neither Reid nor Tozer was enthusiastic about the idea. A prop would need to be fetched, and its weight and the vibrations it would cause as it was being manhandled and then driven into place would unsettle the overhang further. In addition, the gentle trembling of the ground upon which the three of them crouched was becoming more distinct. Several others had also noticed this and had moved away from the far edge of the ice.

Tozer continued talking to the trapped men. He told them to turn themselves and then to edge slowly to the left where the ice did not come so close to touching them.

They were more encouraged by this than by the efforts of the men with the ropes and they called out for Tozer to tell them that they were going to be saved.

Unseen by anyone but Reid, the marine sergeant gently eased a pistol from his belt and laid it down beside him. He looked around, and spotting one of his privates, he beckoned the man toward him, indicating for him to bring his rifle.

Unaware of this, Fitzjames rose and left them, withdrawing to where Crozier had arrived with Hodgson and Irving. He reported what had happened and then explained their rescue attempts. Crozier listened without speaking, clearly skeptical, and then asked Fitzjames for his opinion on their chances of saving the men now that the temperature was dropping so quickly. He left, calling Hodgson and Irving after him, pausing only to tell Fitzjames to report to him on the outcome of the rescue.

Fitzjames returned angrily to Reid and Tozer. Reid too remarked on the falling temperature and called for more lanterns to be fetched. The previous day a drop of thirty degrees had been measured between two and three in the afternoon. The marine private was now crouching close beside Tozer, his rifle held over the crook of his arm, primed and ready to fire.

By then the two men had been caught in the ice for over an hour, and having been held immobile for so long they would be suffering from the onset of frostbite in their hands and feet. They were well protected by their clothes against the cold, but were threatened by their immobility.

It was as Fitzjames considered all this that the ice shook again—a sudden violent judder, and this time there was nothing any of them could do to prevent the wedge from slipping farther into the fissure, tilting and dropping as it went and crushing the two men below.

They both screamed louder than ever, and then one of them fell unconscious. The other went on screaming, barely pausing for breath as he beat on the ice with his fists and tried to kick his legs free from beneath it.

Seeing that there was now nothing to be lost by rushing forward, the rescuers abandoned their ropes, ran to the edge of the fissure and tried to push the slab away. But this only caused the man who remained conscious to scream even louder and to call for them to stop. The other remained slumped forward over the ice, his arms spread and his face turned to one side. Blood ran from his nose and mouth and froze upon his cheeks and chin, barely remaining liquid long enough to form in a pool around him. To those with lanterns close enough to see him more clearly, he appeared to be already dead.

Reid lowered himself into the gap beside the unconscious man and felt his neck for a pulse, which he found. He saw the unstanched blood spreading outward from the man's stomach, squeezed along a joint between two planes in the ice. Careful not to let the other man see him, he motioned to Fitzjames and pointed this out to him. He also called to Tozer, who came as close as he dare to the rim and then leaned over until his face was only inches from that of the screaming man. He too saw the blood. He retrieved his pistol and slid it toward Reid.

Fitzjames called out for them to stop, but neither man spared him more than a second's glance.

Then Tozer reached out and held the head of the screaming man, and as he did so the block of ice moved again. The man stopped screaming abruptly and a sudden spray of blood shot from his mouth and colored the surface all around him. More flowed from his nose and from beneath his jacket, and his legs began to kick and then to run, as though of their own accord, thrashing wildly in the confined space until it too was smeared red and they were lost to view. The sound of his splintering bones was unmistakable, but still he did not lose consciousness, his mouth repeatedly filling with blood, which he spat out in his struggle for air. The ice tilted upward, crushing his lower ribs, riding higher over his unconscious companion and driving even farther into his chest.

Amid all this noise and confusion, Tozer rose and ran to the marine waiting behind him. Grabbing the man's rifle he ran back to stand above Reid, and for a moment the two men looked hard at each other. Then Reid picked up the pistol and held it to the unconscious man's forehead. Tozer knelt and leveled the rifle at the bloodstained face of the other. He was the first to fire, followed an instant later by Reid. The screaming stopped immediately. Throwing down the rifle, Tozer called for two more, passed one to Reid and then the two men aimed again and fired together into the corpses.

The fading echo of the four shots drummed into the distance around them, but close to there was only a stunned silence, and then the murmuring voices of the others as they came to see for themselves what had happened. A pall of gray smoke hung around them in the freezing air.

Fitzjames stood stunned by what had taken place, by the brutality of it all, and by the speed with which the last thirty seconds had just passed, thirty seconds between the last of the screams and the arrival of the others to stare down in fear and revulsion at the soaked and flattened corpses.

Reid climbed clear of the fissure and stood beside him. "It had to be done," he said simply.

Fitzjames knew that the prompt action of the ice-master and marine sergeant had absolved him of his own responsibility in the matter. He nodded in acknowledgment, but could not bring himself to speak, his gaze still fixed on the bloody mess below.

There was no possibility now of retrieving the bodies until the following day, and one by one the men moved away.

Fitzjames returned to the *Erebus*, reporting the outcome to Crozier before making his way alone to his cabin. He was tired and dazed and sickened by what had happened, and also shamed by his own indecisive part in the tragedy. He wrote in his journal only that two men had been lost to the ice, that their names were George Cann and William Shanks, that both had been seamen on the *Terror*, more recently resident on the ice, and that their loss brought the number of deaths to date up to twelve. He drew two small crosses in the right-hand margin of the page.

Christmas was a subdued and cheerless occasion that year, a celebration in name only, marked by storms, hymns and prayers. As life out on the ice became harder still, some left the camp and returned to the broken *Terror* to find shelter amid the abandoned cabins and quarters of her mangled innards. Some even tried to return to the relative comfort and safety of the *Erebus*, but Crozier continued to refuse them admission, and an untidy cluster of unauthorized shelters grew up on the ice all around her.

Scurvy spread more rapidly, and by the end of the year its symptoms had appeared in all but a dozen of their number.

There was talk of an expedition leaving the *Erebus* and striking out northeast across the frozen sea and the Boothia Peninsula in the hope of reaching Fury Beach, of rebuilding Ross' shelter and surviving on the stores known to be still cached there.

The idea came from Graham Gore, who was supported in his application by Fitzjames, Vesconte and Irving. Crozier refused them on the grounds that they were 250 miles from Fury Beach, but only half that distance north of Back's River, via which, if all else failed, they were almost certain to find salvation. He also rejected it on the grounds that it represented retreat in the face of adversity. He conceded that continuing north from Fury Beach the following summer was likely to lead to rescue, but that this would come only to those who were strong enough to make the journey in the first place. Their main responsibility, he insisted, remained with the weak and the sick. This did not convince those who wanted to attempt the journey, but they backed down in the face of his angry rebuttals.

The March South was by then firmly established in Crozier's mind as the only feasible alternative to being freed by the ice and continuing to Bering under sail.

Later, as the old year became the new year, prayers were held, and afterward, well protected against the cold, Graham Gore went out on the tented deck and played his flute. A small audience gathered to listen, and in the freezing air of the Arctic night the notes seemed to last forever. To some they sounded like distant birdsong, to others like the receding babble of voices. They reminded Fitzjames of the even more disturbing near-human cries of peacocks heard on a summer dawn. Other than the cries of badly wounded men, it was the most distressing sound he had ever heard, and after a few minutes he excused himself from the muted revels and returned below.

TERRA DAMNATA

January 1848—

TWENTY-FIVE

Fitzjames supervised one of the parties which crossed from the *Erebus* to the rapidly disintegrating *Terror* to collect firewood. As the men worked, they heard the shots and clattering ricochets of bolts and treenails snapping free, fingers of ice quickly poking through the evacuated holes, and they smelled too the distinctive aroma of turpentine as it was squeezed from the newer planking of the *Terror*'s refit.

Fitzjames had been aboard two days earlier when the latest of her spars had been squeezed and then snapped by the ice, as though the yard-square sheathed and bolted timber had been nothing more than a doweling rod. The blossoming ice, almost as though it were spring-loaded, had immediately pushed in to take full advantage of its gain.

The *Terror*'s bow was now completely severed from the rest of her hull. She was tilted forward, her stern raised, and her head-boards frayed and lifted up into the air like the feathers of a lifeless wing.

The ice which had once been mounded outside had collapsed under its own weight and spilled into the cleaved body. From a distance, and in the dim and shifting light of the men's lanterns, it looked as though she had split under pressure from within, and as though a loose cargo of lime or saltpeter had suddenly spilled out, its spread quickly arrested on the freezing surface.

As they left they were replaced by a party of men led by Tozer, come to salvage wood for their own fires.

Following the incident with the men in the crevasse, and seeing how well Tozer had maintained order in the camp, Fitzjames' earlier dislike of the man had turned to respect. He wished he were back aboard the *Erebus* to help strengthen the weakening chain of command there, but knew that neither Crozier nor Tozer himself would countenance this while the other remained aboard. He asked him how they were faring in the camp.

Four men there were already ill, two of them, in Tozer's opinion, close to death. Stanley and Goodsir visited all those living out on the ice as frequently as the weather permitted, but with their medicines now greatly reduced, they could do no more than they were already doing for the sick on board the *Erebus*, where at least six others were not expected to survive long beyond the end of the month.

Vesconte had calculated that the sun would not rise high enough in the sky until the beginning of March for them to gain any benefit from its warming rays. On the 15th of January, minus 52 degrees was recorded, their lowest yet.

The previous day Fitzjames had visited Goodsir, who had shown him a number of bottles of medicine, retrieved from the *Terror* and then inadvertently left beneath the canvas of the *Erebus'* deck. The glass of these had shattered in the intense cold, but their frozen contents had retained their shape and stood uncontained where they had been left, some of them bearing their manufacturer's imprint from the disintegrated glass.

Their first death of the new year came on the 26th of January. His name was William Fowler, purser's clerk to Charles Osmer. His emaciated body had been washed and then dressed in his best clothes. His mouth and eyes had been stitched shut, his feet bound together and his arms strapped to his side.

"I traveled to London with him on the coach from Wiltshire," Goodsir said unexpectedly as he and Fitzjames lowered the shrouded corpse to the ice and then released their hold on it.

"Was he married? A family?"

"I believe so. The names of his wife and children are embroidered on the collar of his shirt."

Fitzjames regretted that he had neither known nor noticed this. "When did he fall sick?" he asked, partly out of indifferent concern for the dead man, whom he had barely known, and to whom he had spoken only once or twice during the whole of the voyage, and partly because he knew that the death of William Fowler was likely to be the first of many in the coming year, and that as each one took place they might all soon become resigned and then indifferent to the losses.

He climbed down and called for the men fastening the corpse on the sledge to wait a moment. Untying the drawstring at the neck of the canvas shroud, he pulled this back to reveal William Fowler's contorted features, his dark, sunken eyes, his hollow cheeks, and the frayed and bloody mess of his mouth. He unfastened the top few buttons of his jacket. On one side of his collar was the single name "Mary," and on the other "William" and "Mary." He smiled at the coincidence and wondered if this royal echo had ever occurred to William Fowler, eventually deciding that he must have known, and that it was patronizing of him to think otherwise. To qualify as assistant purser to the expedition Fowler must have been accomplished at his work, trusted, and his capabilities respected by the Admiralty.

Fitzjames had intended making a note of the names so that he might make his letter of condolence to the man's widow more personal, but there was no need now that he had seen them and knew that he would never forget them. At first he thought that the simple repetition suggested a lack of imagination, but as he refastened the shroud he realized that he had confused repetition with continuity and its more admirable qualities founded in the strength of belief and, in this most obvious of ways, guidance by example. He covered the dead man's face and then tugged on the coarse material so that nothing of its hidden contours, its protruding nose or jutting chin might show through.

He returned to Goodsir, who had watched him throughout.

"When did he fall ill?" he asked him.

"William and Mary, am I right? Goodsir said. "I remembered from the coach. "Just now, as you were looking at him, I remembered. And the same for his children. We, you and I, thank God, do not have that unsupportable burden to bear."

Fitzjames avoided remarking on this. "How long was he ill?"

"A month, no more. He began to ache, then he began to grow tired. And then he began to die. It really is that simple." Goodsir controlled the anger in his voice. "Everything else, all these incidentals of suffering, are merely the awful surface dressing of that simple and straightforward progression. It takes root in our mind, and is then nurtured by what we see happening to others. You tell me— you were the one who went to look closely into his stitched-up eyes. How often do you study your own bruises or rub your own aching joints and limbs with more than the merest suspicion of dread?"

They parted before Fitzjames could think of an answer to the unanswerable question, Goodsir back to the sick below, and Fitzjames to accompany the makeshift hearse.

Midway to the *Terror* he climbed upon a mound of empty cans, frozen into a solid mass and resembling a fallen meteor, and looked back in the direction of the sun, its weak glimmer reddened and diminished during the half hour since it had appeared.

It was four days since anyone had visited the *Terror*, and the usual means of entry to her was no longer available to them, having been blocked by a jag of risen ice. Others in the small group were concerned that the room which held their dead might itself have been penetrated, and Fitzjames climbed aboard to investigate.

Inside he discovered that the corridor leading to the mortuary had been blocked by collapsing timbers, and that the room had indeed been lost to them. He saw too that the corpses already resting there were beyond retrieval, and that when the time came to collect them, either for burial or passage home, then a considerable amount of work would be needed to get them out.

He returned to the men on the ice, informed them of all this, and then helped them to manhandle the body of William Fowler into another passageway, where it might be left until somewhere more suitable was found.

The others were anxious to leave, but Fitzjames insisted on saying a final brief prayer over the body. They stood silently around him, and when he had finished they raced to get out of the faintly trembling hull.

TWENTY-SIX

Toward the end of February, Stanley noted in his register that he was treating two of their four boys for the first symptoms of scurvy, aggravated by nausea and stomach cramps, possibly brought about by eating spoiled food.

George Chambers had attended to Franklin, and Robert Golding had signed on the *Terror*, where he had been instructed and watched over by George Hodgson, the two of them sharing the same home town of Chatham. Neither boy was yet fifteen, George Chambers having celebrated his fourteenth birthday only a week earlier.

In the column alongside their names and the date at which they came to his attention, Stanley kept detailed notes of their deteriorating condition. In part he was concerned because he knew how well fed they had been prior to falling ill. Older men had befriended the apprentices, sharing their own dull meals whenever any of the boys complained of hunger.

Examining George Chambers, Goodsir made light of his swollen joints and nausea. With Golding too he did his best to reassure him, and he put them both to bed in the same cabin, away from the other sick-bays, where the recently ill were now forced to lie alongside those approaching death.

Robert Ferrier, seaman of the *Erebus*, died the day after the boys were admitted. He had been suffering since the late autumn and had eaten nothing for the past ten days, spending a good deal of that time dictating a letter to Fitzjames to be forwarded to his wife. In it he made light of his suffering, and whenever he could think of nothing to say he expressed his devotion to her. He frequently asked Fitzjames to translate his intentions into more precise and expressive language, and this Fitzjames did, reading it back to Ferrier for his approval.

Ferrier died during a pause in his dictation, having exhausted himself by a sustained effort lasting an hour. Fitzjames had known by the way he had spoken that the dying man was aware of how close he had finally come to death, and he finished the letter with words which were entirely his own, but of which he felt certain Ferrier would have approved. He then sealed this in an envelope and put it in the sack of Ferrier's belongings which he delivered to Crozier.

Ferrier's body was taken to the *Terror* the following day, making room for the three others waiting to take his place in the sick-bay.

Stanley expressed his concern over the sick boys, and the apparent weakening of the two others to Fitzjames, convinced that some part of their dwindling supplies had again become tainted. He had recently inspected a barrel of pemmican, reserved in readiness for even darker days, and instead of the rump steak and suet specified in the chandler's docket, he had found cheap meat, possibly horse, embedded in Russian tallow—equally sustaining he conceded, but considerably less appealing to men with no appetite who had difficulty keeping down what little they did eat. He had seen starving men eat candles before and knew how devastating this could prove to their already weakened digestive systems.

Fitzjames shared his concern over the boys and visited them daily, taking with him small luxuries gathered by the other officers—a few glacé cherries or roasted almonds, honey or pieces of sugar.

Robert Golding remained the stronger of the two, and he accepted these gifts with delight, confessing conspiratorially to Fitzjames that Stanley would later confiscate them and then ration them out when they had eaten their less tempting meals. George Chambers, however, said very little. He was the smaller of the two boys physically, and a week of vomiting, bleeding and diarrhea had sapped his strength even further. His listlessness and the look of resignation in his eyes made Fitzjames fear the worst.

"The miners have their canaries, we have our rats and our pampered boys," Goodsir remarked when he and Fitzjames were alone in his cabin. "I sometimes wonder if that isn't the real reason we include them in our crews. They act as a balance and regulator— our indifference and brutality against their innocence and blind desire to become a part of it all."

"Brutality? Surely not."

"I'm afraid so. We pin our hopes on brute strength and ingenuity, and whereas the latter might be the most admirable and readily acknowledged of our qualities, deep down we are convinced that without the former it is all to no avail." He could see that Fitzjames was still not convinced. "Look around you. What have we done but pitted our strength against the ice, barging and blasting our way into this miserable dead-end? Where is the ingenuity in that?" This tirade was born of Goodsir's own suffering and of his concern for the boys, especially Chambers, whom he estimated had only a fortnight or twenty days to live.

"Surely we also *benefit* by their presence," Fitzjames insisted.

"Possibly," Goodsir conceded. "Even if it is only to be constantly reminded of our own regrets, our own losses." He gestured to suggest that his words should be ignored.

Five days after the body of Robert Ferrier had been transferred to the *Terror*, both ships were struck by a series of shocks, resulting in a number of new and superficial fractures in the ice. Crozier called for Reid and Blanky to explain what was happening, but they were as mystified as he was as to the cause of this unexpected disturbance, neither man having anticipated any further movement for another three months.

Later, the *Erebus'* rudder mounts were found to be damaged, and a length of her hull beneath the ice had been fractured and shoved in. The vibrations also shook off the last of her gingerbread work, and jolted her mizzen mast sufficiently for both her cross-jack and topsail yards to come loose. All this was of little consequence to them; no one was injured by the damage, and for as long as they were held firm in their dock there was no danger of shipping any water before repairs could be carried out.

Later, during an inspection of their lower quarters and ice-filled bilge, Graham Gore discovered damage to their spars that could only have been sustained the previous autumn when the basin of water in which the *Erebus* had briefly floated free had refrozen. Two of the timbers had come loose of their iron shoes, their cross-bolts having sheared completely, and the balks now held in place by the frozen bilge alone. Alerted by this, Gore made a more complete inspection, and although he found nothing else of such consequence, he calculated that in addition to the ice which pressed in on them from outside, they were now carrying at least eighty tons within their hull. This was not an unduly excessive weight measured against their ballast capacity, but it unsettled him to realize how completely and surreptitiously they had been breached and then undermined by the ice.

Discussing what he had found with the others, he was reassured by Reid's remark that it had at one time been common practice not to pump deep-hulled whalers clear of water if it became apparent that they were about to be trapped in winter ice. Flat-bottomed and shallow-keeled boats would dry out and rise up on the surface of the thickening pack, but deeper vessels were often secured by allowing themselves to be set into it, the only danger with this method coming during the days of release, when the ice inside needed to be thawed and pumped clear before the surrounding floe broke up and dispersed. Asked if they were capable of doing this themselves, Reid said that he thought they were, but omitted to mention his reservations concerning the repair of their spars when that time came.

On the 1st of March, Thomas Tadman, the seaman who had accompanied Fitzjames on his journey to the west, and who had been the first to sight land after their crossing of the frozen strait, was found hanged from their taffrail, having gone on deck to exercise after being laid up for a week. David Bryant discovered him, and sent for Fitzjames to help cut him down. As they severed the rope and the body fell, Fitzjames remembered the promise he had made to the man to name the land he had discovered after him, but about which, overtaken by the events of the last nine months, he had done nothing. It was he who found the misspelt note of apology in Tadman's mouth, and who sent for one of their smiths to cut the rings from his swollen fingers so he might return these to his mother.

TWENTY-SEVEN

Now without any of her masts, and with her low outline lost beneath the mounds of piled timber and drifts of snow and ice which coated her inside and out, the *Terror* was barely recognizable for what she had once been, resembling instead a small tumulus on a vast plain, weathered by the elements, exfoliated, gutted and crushed, and waiting only to disappear completely beneath the slopes of her own spreading debris. Her back had long since been broken, and it was now only a matter of time before some whim of the ice swallowed her and her cargo of corpses whole.

The men from the camp, desperate for fuel, approached the ship with caution, as though, in addition to being their mortuary, she had become the lair of some hidden dormant beast they dare not arouse for fear of their lives.

She was stripped of her chains and ropes. Doors were lifted from their hinges and carried out on the ice. As much of her glass as remained unbroken was retrieved and taken to the *Erebus*. A dozen sacks of potatoes were discovered, hard as stones but otherwise undamaged. Crockery and cutlery was taken out, and copper pans. Even the oven and the remaining stoves were dismantled and carried out in pieces on to the ice. Dozens of chairs, small tables, chests and cabinets were collected and arranged as though at a country auction. A mound of frozen bedding was removed, along with several dozen mattresses as stiff as boards.

All this lasted four days, after which there was nothing left for them to take, and the *Terror*, apart from her useless detritus and corpses, lay eviscerated.

The more valuable pieces of this bounty were taken directly aboard the *Erebus*, but by far the largest part of it was left out on the ice between the two ships where it had been carried and then discarded. Heavy chests and tables were dragged only yards before being abandoned, and once thawed, most of the bedding was found to be unusable, waterlogged and rotted. The crockery and cutlery, over three thousand pieces in all, was sorted into Navy issue and that which was privately owned, and only the latter was taken aboard the *Erebus*. Most of their silver plate had long since been retrieved, but the few items which had been overlooked were delivered to Crozier for safe-keeping. Some complained that valuable pieces had been stolen by men from Tozer's camp, but Tozer denied this, and without any evidence Crozier was reluctant to pursue the matter.

Later, Tozer and his marines foraged among the spreading circle of abandoned possessions, returning with their spoils only to discard them themselves later upon finding they took up too much valuable space in their overcrowded dwellings, several more of which had been rendered uninhabitable by the recent bad weather.

Some of the shelters surrounding the *Erebus* had also been abandoned, and the more substantial of these empty structures now served as storerooms for the supplies which could no longer be accommodated aboard. Others, those less well constructed, had been flattened and their contents scattered by the wind.

All around them their debris lay spread like that of an army in urgent, unexpected retreat, and it was impossible, thought Fitzjames as he looked out over the countless dark shapes on the ice—the hundreds of buried mounds and the strangely unsettling pieces of furniture, tables and chairs arranged as though men had just vacated them—impossible for anyone coming after them to look out on that same desolate scene and not to believe that the greatest disaster imaginable had already befallen the men who had once been there.

Considering all this, he felt a sudden pain in one of his ungloved hands, and when he lifted it from the rail on which he had been resting, the skin of his palm tore where it had frozen to a bolt. He had been careless in not noticing this and avoiding it. The wound was a perfect circle, an inch in diameter, and he stood watching it for a moment, unable to take his eyes from the button of blood which rose slowly into the hollow. He wrapped a handkerchief round the wound and went in search of Goodsir for a proper dressing.

March was a bad month too for their sick and their dying, and in the space of four days they lost six more of their number, including the boy George Chambers.

For the first time, those physically incapacitated by either injury or scurvy outnumbered those who remained healthy and capable of reduced duties. Word from the camp and the surrounding shelters suggested that the situation there was even worse.

Chambers' death was followed by two more the next day, both long-term sufferers: James Rigden, the captain's coxswain on the *Erebus*, and seaman John Handford of the *Terror*.

The day after that another man died, but this time it was not one of the sick or injured who succumbed, but Henry Wilkes, one of Tozer's marines. He and several others from the camp had been alerted to the presence of a fox amid the debris of the *Terror*, and they had gone to investigate, hoping to shoot the creature.

At first they saw nothing, but were then alerted by a noise coming from within the empty hulk. They were reluctant to wander too far inside in search of their prey, and so two men were sent to the far side of the ship to shout and throw pieces of timber in an attempt to flush the creature out toward the hunters waiting opposite.

The fox appeared several minutes later at a hole in the *Terror*'s side, and in its mouth it held a length of cloth. It stood motionless for a few seconds, assessing the ground ahead of it, and conscious only of the noise of the men behind. It came down a broad sloping spar to the ice, stopped again, sniffing the air, and then left the ship at a steady trot toward where Wilkes and the others were hiding.

It came close to another of the marines who knelt behind an upturned chart table, and as it passed by him he rose, fired and shouted all in a single action. His shot scared the fox, but did not hit it, and the animal turned and ran, this time directly toward Henry

Wilkes and the man beside him. At its approach both men rose and confronted it. Wilkes was the first to fire, but the charge in his pistol failed to detonate, and he called for the man beside him to shoot, which he did, hitting and instantly killing the fox, which fell where it stood. Wilkes cheered and called to the others. The successful marksman picked up the small animal by its brush and swung it above his head.

Wilkes retrieved the piece of cloth it had been carrying and saw that it was a collar. He examined this more closely before suddenly realizing where it might have come from. Then, enraged by what he had deduced, he grabbed the fox and threw it back to the ground, and cocking the hammer of his failed pistol he crouched down, pressed it hard against the animal's head and fired again. This time the charge detonated, but instead of firing the ball, the stock and barrel exploded in Wilkes' hand and the full force of the blast caught him in the face, throwing him backward, his cheeks and forehead glossy with blood. The others ran to help him, but he was dead before they reached him. His face smoked with powder burns and blood seeped onto the ice from the back of his head; all four fingers and the thumb of his right hand had been severed.

His body was carried back to the camp, where the incident was reported to Tozer. Wilkes' pistol was retrieved, its shattered barrel peeled back like the petals of a steely flower, its walnut butt splintered and frayed. Tozer guessed that it hadn't been fired since the last time Wilkes had hunted, and that meantime he had become careless and allowed ice to penetrate either the firing mechanism or the barrel, fatally sabotaging the weapon.

Wilkes' body was covered and left outside, awaiting inspection by Peddie prior to its removal to the *Terror*. The man who had killed the fox showed Tozer the collar the animal had been carrying, and Tozer immediately snatched it from him and threw it into the fire.

They skinned, gutted and cooked the animal whole, each of the ten hunters receiving barely half a pound of edible flesh and gristle for his trouble.

When the time came to wash, dress and remove the small wasted body of George Chambers, Stanley was visited by the carpenters

John Weeks and Thomas Honey, who had built a coffin in which the boy might be carried to the *Terror* with more dignity than their other recent fatalities. Crozier officiated at the ceremony, and two dozen men followed the pall-bearers across the ice. The loss of the boy saddened them all.

Their remaining losses during March came on the 28th and the 30th with the deaths of two of the *Terror*'s petty officers—Luke Smith, engaged originally as a stoker, and Samuel Honey, blacksmith and younger brother of Thomas, who set about making another coffin so soon after the last.

TWENTY-EIGHT

On the morning of Saturday the 2nd of April, Crozier called his lieutenants and other senior officers together and informed them of his intention to abandon the *Erebus* completely and for them all to make the short crossing to the southeast to the shore of King William Land, where a camp would be established. They would take with them as much as they required or could carry, making several return journeys if necessary. He spoke quickly and firmly, allowing no one to interrupt him. Once established on the land they would survey the situation and then the strongest of them would make the hundred-mile journey farther south to the estuary of Back's River, where there was a good chance they would make contact with the natives known to be living in that region, and by that means communicate their situation to someone in a position to come to their assistance.

If necessary, he went on, a second camp would be set up on either the southern shore of King William Land or on the mainland itself. Depots of stores would then be laid down between these two points and communication between them maintained. No one was about to be abandoned, he insisted, but nor would those who had become their greatest liability now be allowed to hold back those others upon whom rested the greatest chance of them all being saved.

He stopped abruptly and, stunned into silence by this announcement, those around him began to consider what he had proposed, and to wonder into which of the two categories they themselves fell.

However drastic and sudden this decision might have seemed to some, it was not entirely unexpected by those more fully apprised of the true extent of the damage to the *Erebus*, and who, along with Crozier, had come to the realization that what had happened to the *Terror* during the previous year would almost certainly be her fate if she did not get free during the coming season. What did surprise some of them, however, was that Crozier had decided upon abandonment so soon, and that it was to involve them all and at the expense of their ship, rather than be undertaken by a smaller party in conjunction with their continued efforts to free the *Erebus*.

Crozier's own experience of Arctic marching had been gained with Franklin on his last overland expedition, and it was this, and the knowledge that they were so close to where he and Franklin had once stood, that convinced him he had made the right decision.

In the discussion which followed he received support both from those who had given up all hope of ever freeing the *Erebus*, and from those who knew that any overland journey must begin before the onset of the heavy summer thaw made marching treacherous. Acknowledging the truth in this, those who argued against the abandonment of the *Erebus* focused their argument on the poor condition of so many of their number and the effort Crozier was about to ask them to make, even those who would only cross the short distance to the northern shore of King William Land and await their rescue there.

Rather than answer these individual points, Crozier called for silence so that he might outline his plans in greater detail.

He proposed that they should aim to make landfall in three weeks' time, preferably by Easter Sunday, which fell that year on the 23rd of April. The date struck them all as propitious. In addition to gaining for themselves as long as possible to make their way farther south, this would also allow them to recover some of their strength before crossing the ice to where Gore and Blanky had already made landfall the previous year, and then to bridge any other ice-locked strait which might lie between King William Land and the mainland before the ice started to break up beneath them.

He intended to dispatch a small party within the next few days to establish that no new barrier had been created between themselves and the land. This expedition would direct itself to Gore's marker cairns, and then plot a route across the ice by which they would later haul their boats. The blacksmiths would build detachable runners upon which these might be dragged, sturdy enough to withstand the roughest terrain, and easily removable in case they encountered open water.

If upon reaching King William Land the going proved harder than anticipated, they would return to the ice-bound sea, and follow this, rather than the land, south. On reaching Back's estuary a party would then be dispatched upstream to make contact with whoever lived on its banks. Another boat might also be sent west along the coast toward the Coppermine until contact was also established in that direction.

Most voiced their doubts at this over-optimistic assessment, but in reply Crozier argued that if anyone had already set out to discover their whereabouts, then they were just as likely to be sailing east from Bering and Icy Cape in the open coastal waters as they were to be seeking a path south or west via Lancaster Sound.

Their biggest problem concerned the small number of men who might be accommodated in their remaining boats should they be forced to take these, and this was compounded by the fact that for much of the time these would be laden not only with their stores but also with the men who were unable to walk. Stanley and Peddie calculated that there were already a dozen of these, and that this number might easily double before they made landfall. Thereafter it would increase with every day's marching and hauling. Crozier countered this by saying that he intended to increase all their rations over the next three weeks, both to assist the recovery of the sick and to reduce the load with which they would be burdened over the first part of their journey.

Gore and Blanky volunteered their services to lead the preliminary route-finding expedition, and while accepting Blanky's application, Crozier turned down Gore in favor of one of the *Terror's*

lieutenants, finally choosing George Hodgson. Fitzjames also volunteered, but was refused on the grounds that Hodgson was the
stronger, fitter man.

Harboring the suspicion that he had been rejected because of the
failure of his own expedition the previous summer, Fitzjames did
not argue his case, but later, upon confiding his feelings to Goodsir,
he was told that Crozier had been right to choose Hodgson, that he
himself probably was too weak to lead the expedition, however short
or straightforward.

Goodsir had been suffering more than usual over the previous
week with his injured hand. The partial amputation of his thumb
had not prevented further infection, and having delayed for as long
as possible, he urged Stanley to amputate the remainder of the rotten
flesh. Because of this delay the extent of the gangrene was worse
than Stanley had feared, and in addition to removing the lower
bones of Goodsir's thumb, he was forced to cut away the diseased
bone and flesh of both his fore-and index-finger. It was his opinion
that the remaining two fingers might also later be lost, and that to
prevent any further suffering Goodsir ought to have his whole hand
amputated as a precaution. Goodsir agreed to this, aware that once
the gangrene entered his arm under those conditions it would be
impossible to stop.

He was in acute pain for five days and nights after the operation,
dosed with laudanum to help him gain brief periods of fitful sleep,
and closely watched by Stanley throughout. He became feverish and
lost more weight, but recovered well enough to start eating again,
and then to sit and talk with his frequent visitors.

He was visited by Hodgson and Blanky on the morning of their
departure for King William Land, and he reminded Blanky to attempt some measurement of the ice close to the shore, and to assess
the depth of the wind-driven blocks on the land. Blanky agreed to
collect this information and, following several awkward handshakes,
he and Hodgson departed.

Leaving mid-morning, the expedition was within sight of land as
the sun set late that same evening. The distinction between the ice-

covered shore and the frozen sea which surrounded it was not so marked as when Gore and Blanky had been there the previous year. The contours of the intervening ice had also changed, having gone from a smooth and unbroken surface to one of ridges and scarps, few of these taller than a man, but forcing them either to scramble over these or to make wide detours in search of a broader passage through which they might later drag their boats to the shore. There were indications that the movement of the ice had been more vigorous where it was forced upon the land, but no sign of any current movement or disturbance.

Blanky discovered one of Gore's cairns and, searching for its marker stone, he calculated that they had come ashore less than a quarter of a mile south of where he had landed the previous year.

They continued to search the shore for several hours, assessing the extent and condition of the ice over which they would later travel *en masse*. Hodgson then traced their own route on the map Gore had compiled the previous year, marking on it the area of more recently contorted ice, and plotting the path by which they might make their least difficult approach to the shore.

It was too late to begin their return journey, so they spent the night on land. A few patches of immature lemon-grass were discovered, more root than actual growth, and this was fastidiously collected and cooked.

The following day they retraced their steps to the *Erebus* in a march lasting seventeen hours, arriving back just as the sun set behind them.

Hodgson joined Crozier for dinner, showed him the revised chart, and told him at great length about everything they had seen. Blanky went to Gore and Reid, and then the three men sought out Fitzjames, who was sitting with Goodsir.

The next morning Crozier announced to the assembled men that they would now leave the *Erebus* as soon as the weakest among them were sufficiently recovered to attempt the first stage of their journey. The lower ranks cheered him, and he felt gratified and vindicated by this, gesturing to them and prolonging their applause.

•   •   •

They had one more shock to endure before the eventual abandon-ment of the *Erebus* on Easter Eve. On the morning of April the 12th, John Irving was found dead, having died in his sleep. Stanley and Peddie agreed that an apoplectic fit resulting in heart seizure was the cause. No post-mortem was carried out to confirm this, and an hour after he was found, Irving was washed and dressed and taken from his cabin. Because the *Terror* was finally so close to complete disintegration, he was taken instead to the *Erebus'* empty forward hold, where he was laid out on trestles, and where the others came to pay their last respects.

Steward Hoar had been the last to see him alive the previous evening, having called on him at nine. He wept upon hearing of the death and related how Irving had told him that earlier in the evening he could have sworn he had heard a nightingale somewhere out in the darkness on the ice. Both men had laughed at the ridiculous notion.

Fitzjames felt the loss more acutely than many, having lost a friend and an ally, and one of the few remaining officers who might have sided with him against the more ill-considered of Crozier's preparations for their overland march.

The following day all the accessible corpses were retrieved from the *Terror* and brought back to the *Erebus*. Careful records had been kept, and only three of the frozen bodies—those deposited first, before the destruction of the *Terror* had seemed so inevitable—were not located.

On the 17th of April they felt the first faint reverberations of that year's breakup. As a precaution, their two heavier boats, which had already been fixed upon their runners, were pulled a short distance from the *Erebus* and loaded with part of their stores. It quickly became evident that hauling the boats over even level ice was going to prove more difficult than they had expected. In addition to the 750-pound weight of the boats themselves, Fitzjames estimated their bolted-on runners to weigh another 650 pounds. The boats were thirty feet in length with a seven-foot beam. A pulling harness for fourteen men had been attached to each, and he wondered if they now had twenty-eight men with strength enough for the task.

It was also clear that they would not be able to cross the ice in a single body as Crozier had hoped, and that this could not be achieved in a single day's march.

They were delayed by strong winds and a further succession of faint shocks passing through the ice all around them, but on the morning of the 22nd, Easter Eve, they doused their boiler and stoves and gathered out on the ice to the boatswain's piping of "abandon ship," followed by the signal to drag ropes.

Crozier supervised all this activity from the vantage-point of the *Erebus'* rail, dividing the two crews into those who would take their turn in the harnesses and those who were too weak and would need assistance from the others. Eight of their number were unable to walk. Six of these were to be carried on stretchers, the remaining two pulled in the boats.

Hodgson, Tozer and his marines went ahead with posts to mark out the route Hodgson had followed three weeks earlier.

An hour after this advance party had left, and while they were still within view, a second party of three dozen men set off dragging supplies on sledges. They had orders to march as far as possible, make a depot of their provisions and then return with their empty sledges to relieve the men hauling the boats of part of their load. When these depots were reached a new hauling party would be formed and the process repeated. In this way Crozier hoped to move as much as possible in the time available to them, and to ensure that not only were the strongest men undertaking the most work, but that supplies were available to anyone falling behind on the march.

Next the men hauling the boats departed, making good progress for the first mile over the smooth ice which had been cleared in that direction, but then slowing as the first of the troughs and ridges were reached.

There was some argument over what they should take with them, and inspecting the line of marchers, Fitzjames saw men dragging two of their heavy cooking stoves and others with their copper lightning conductor, and even the brass curtain rails from the cabins.

Ordering them to leave these and find something more useful to carry, the men argued that the pieces of metal were to be used to barter with the Eskimos. They appealed to Crozier, who decided in their favor. All of these heavier loads quickly sapped the strength of those who carried them.

By noon they had crossed three of their estimated twelve miles.

Those helping the injured began to fall behind, conscious of the pain caused to the suffering by every jolt of the rough terrain. Word was sent back for them to rest and then continue at their own speed.

By mid-afternoon the drawn-out column was almost four miles long, Hodgson and the marines having already come within sight of the distant low shoreline, while the stragglers at the rear were only just out of sight of the *Erebus*. Small depots were laid for those beginning to fall behind, and men coming out of the boat harnesses rested and then waited to take over with the carrying of the sick.

By early evening the boats had been dragged eight miles and a halt was called. Signals were fired and the pathfinding party re-treated from its advance position. Hodgson expressed his surprise at being recalled, having come within striking distance of the shore, and hoping to have reached it and set up camp there within the hour.

A second signal warned those who had fallen farthest behind not to attempt to cover the intervening distance to the main party in the darkness, but to camp where they were and to resume traveling at first light.

They all spent an uncomfortable night on the ice, but even at midnight the temperature did not fall below 5 degrees and they kept their fires burning using case-wood.

Fitzjames began to suffer from a sprained ankle, sustained a week earlier during a fall. Before setting out Stanley had applied a cam-phor poultice and strapped this up for him, but after the day's march the ankle was again swollen and painful. He removed the bandage and applied a new warm poultice. In his already weakened condition every step he now took caused him to wince with the pain which ran up his leg and into his spine. To support the injured foot, Stanley added two splints to the bandage. At Fitzjames' insistence, the injury was not reported to Crozier, who had spent most of the day in one or other of the boat harnesses, leading and encouraging by example, and who had then fallen asleep where he sat, having eaten little of his evening meal.

The following morning they were roused before the sun had risen and they redistributed their loads in preparation for their second day's march. Before their departure, a signal was fired to alert the men following behind, as yet invisible in the poor light. An answering flare rose silently from the horizon.

They resumed marching, this time with Blanky and the marines taking their turn in the harnesses.

Fitzjames hauled alongside Reid, followed by Goodsir and Vesconte, talking at first and then falling silent as they exhausted themselves and as obstacle followed obstacle on the path ahead.

On several occasions the boats tipped over on their runners and the hauling teams knelt or sat on the ice as they waited for those walking behind to pull them upright and reload them.

There were two deaths that second morning. The first less than an hour after their departure, when one of the men being pulled in the boats was found to be dead as he was picked up from a spill. He was wrapped in a blanket, carried thirty feet from their path and laid on the ice with two of their route markers nailed into a cross beside him. A note was left with the body telling those who were following without any load to retrieve it if possible and bring it to the land for proper burial.

Their second fatality took place within sight of the shore. Six men were relieved of their places in one of the harnesses, and seeing the dark outline ahead of them they ran forward. One of these men ran faster and farther than his companions, fell to his knees and started praying. After a minute's rest, during which the others waited alongside him, he slumped gently forward, his head touching the ice, his praying hand still clasped beneath him. Pulling him back up, his companions found him dead. He too was wrapped in a blanket and laid to one side with a marker.

They spent the night of the 23rd on the ice again. The shore lay two miles ahead of them, but because of the contorted nature of the ice over which they were now traveling, it was unlikely that even this short distance would be covered in anything less than another half day's marching.

They stopped on that Easter Sunday at three in the afternoon, most of them again exhausted to the point of collapse, and some asleep within minutes of having released themselves from the boats. A brief service was held and prayers said.

Crozier delayed sending that night's signal to their stragglers until they had covered more ground, thus reducing the growing distance between them. He had anticipated that these slower-moving groups might join the main body of men some time during the early evening, but by sunset there was still no sign of them, and their eventual flare was answered by one disappointingly distant.

Later, during a brief conference with Crozier, Stanley suggested that he and their other medical officers might retrace their tracks in the morning, taking with them several empty sledges upon which to carry those who could no longer walk. Crozier was against this, insisting that the men hauling their boats and the bulk of their stores remained his priority. A compromise was eventually reached: sufficient haulers would stay with the boats to ensure that land was reached the following day, and those already too weak for this task— eighteen men in all—would remain where they were under the command of Stanley and Peddie. The stronger of these would then march back to meet up with those following behind, while the rest would stay at the camp ready to take over upon the arrival of the sick later in the day. After a break, they might all then resume marching and reach the shore by nightfall. The first of the advance party to arrive there would light beacon fires to guide those still crossing the ice in the darkness. Whatever happened, Crozier privately warned Stanley, he was to reach the shore before daybreak on the 25th.

The next morning the weather began to deteriorate. At nine o'clock, the time of their intended departure, the temperature stood at only seven degrees and gave no indication of rising.

Vesconte and Stanley turned back into the wind and went in search of the others, making slow progress against its persistent buffeting. Powdered ice clouded the horizon all around them, restricting their vision to only twenty yards at times.

Anxious not to lose his own advantage now that they were so close to their first goal, Crozier ordered the landward march to continue.

Fitzjames fastened himself into place alongside Philip Reddington. They did their best to encourage each other as they began pulling, but both were quickly exhausted, defeated by the uneven ice which either tipped or trapped the runners every few minutes. Fitzjames stumbled and fell, crying out as his weak ankle folded beneath him. Unstoppable tears mixed with the heavy sweat on his cheeks. Then Reddington collapsed beside him and lay without trying to push himself back up. When Fitzjames asked him if he was injured, he could only groan. He passed out completely a moment later, and releasing them both from their harness, Fitzjames dragged him to one side. Their places were taken by two others and the boat was pulled slowly away from them. Fitzjames called out that he would wait for Reddington to regain consciousness and then help him to continue. Others approached them, but passed by without speaking, men barely lifting their feet from the ground, drained of all their strength after only half an hour's pulling.

The powder-filled wind continued to blow, and Fitzjames wrapped a blanket around Reddington to protect him. He came round a few minutes later and looked at the figures moving silently past them, propped up by the following wind as much as by their own momentum. Helped by Fitzjames, he rose to his feet. Neither man could move any faster than the other and they shared what little strength they still possessed and shuffled forward as though hobbled.

It took them seven more hours to cover the two miles over uneven ice to the shore. They arrived less than an hour after the men with the boats, and found them lying on the frozen ground where they had fallen, most of them still in harness, only a few having managed to release themselves and crawl a few feet before dropping. Most had been covered with blankets and rugs by those who still had the strength to walk among them. Several small fires had been lit. By then the wind had fallen and the smoke from these drifted low over the scene and collected above the covered bodies.

Propping Reddington against one of the boats, Fitzjames called for someone to help him. Graham Gore appeared, himself barely able to walk. He sank to his knees beside Fitzjames and helped him remove his boot and the splints from his bandaged foot. He lit a lantern, and in its dim glow Fitzjames saw that his foot was swollen to twice its normal size, and that the flesh had darkened from toe to shin.

After leaving the main body of men, Vesconte and the others walked for four hours in the face of the wind, covering a mile and a half before coming upon the advance members of those they had gone back to help. Two men were sitting on the ground, and a third lay on his back at their feet.

These three, they discovered, had come ahead of the others in an attempt to catch the advance party and return with some assistance. There were now too many of them unable to walk, and those who were able to stay on their feet had barely the strength to keep moving, let alone assist or carry the others. As far as the three men knew, no one in this second party had yet died, but many had sustained injuries through falling, and at least four of them had lost and not yet regained consciousness. In addition to their other injuries, they were now suffering from hunger and the cold, and were further disheartened by what they saw as their abandonment by the main body of marchers.

The two men sitting with their backs to the wind had finally been defeated by the ice, and the man at their feet had collapsed a few minutes after stopping.

Peddie and Macdonald stayed with Stanley, preparing themselves for further arrivals, while the others set off in the hope of meeting up with the remaining stragglers and helping them back.

They came upon the first of these exhausted men sheltering in a hollow. There were eight in all, only five of whom were able to rise and stumble feebly toward them. Advising them to continue toward Stanley, they went on, retracing a farther two miles of their previous day's journey before coming upon the last of the men, most of whom fell after even the slightest exertion.

By late afternoon this smaller body of stragglers was gathered together closer to the shore, and the knowledge that they were within striking distance of the land helped them find the strength they needed to complete the journey. The rest were carried ashore by nightfall, and found the camp there in just as great a state of exhausted confusion as Fitzjames and Reddington had found it the previous night.

The sight of these sick and weakened additions to their number convinced Crozier even further that for an overland march now to succeed they would have to separate into at least two parties, with the sick and the weak dependent on the speed and success of the stronger members in finding assistance and relaying it back to them.

Listening to him comment on all this, and realizing how quickly the men left behind were likely to succumb to their scurvy and other illnesses, Fitzjames made another suggestion. He had recovered from his journey with Reddington, but could now only walk with the help of a stick. It was Stanley's opinion that he had fractured a bone in his foot or ankle and that this was only likely to heal properly with complete rest. It was upon being told this that Fitzjames realized he would very likely be put in command of the men left behind, and that, ultimately, he would be responsible for their deaths if they failed to recover over the coming weeks.

His suggestion to Crozier was that this second body of men be again divided: those who were willing and strong enough to remain on the shore while they recovered should follow Crozier south after as short a delay as possible, taking advantage of small depots of food, including fresh meat, laid down by the leading party, which would be better able to provide for these others in addition to themselves. Accepting that this suggestion had its merits, and pleased that it would not delay his own expedition, Crozier told him to outline the remainder of his plan.

This second part, Fitzjames knew, was likely to prove more controversial. He proposed that a small number of the able-bodied should return to the *Erebus* and remain with her until she either drifted free of the ice into the sea to the southwest, or toward King William Land, or until she finally broke up, in which case they would have to abandon her again and return to the shore. There was some support for this idea, and upon further consideration Crozier agreed to it.

TWENTY-NINE

Of the 104 officers and men who landed with Crozier on King William Land, only sixty-eight set off with him for Back's River on the 26th of April.

Commanded by Fitzjames, and including Gore, Goodsir, Reid and mate Des Voeux, a party of sixteen prepared to return across the ice to the *Erebus*. With the exception of the *Terror*'s two boys, all had been members of her original crew.

The remaining twenty men, under the command of Vesconte and Stanley, included their most seriously ill, those who could not walk, those who could barely stand, and none of whom would survive either the return journey to the ship or Crozier's overland march. Of these, four had remained unconscious and delirious since their arrival ashore. None had eaten, and it seemed likely to everyone who attended them that they would all soon die. Upon agreeing that the four men were beyond salvation, Stanley and Peddie stopped administering their valuable drugs.

Having prepared the boats and unloaded all their unnecessary supplies, Crozier's party started to leave at six in the morning, with the first liquid glimmer of the rising sun to guide them. Their farewells were prolonged and emotional, and filled with promises to return.

George Hodgson and clerk Edwin Helpman led the first group, harnessing themselves to one of their boats along with a dozen others, including Tozer and the marines who were still capable of pulling. Men walked ahead of them, alongside them and behind them, pacing a path along which the boat was slowly hauled. At first this route was erratic, weaving left and right to take advantage of firm ice and to avoid those patches of exposed ground which already threatened to turn soft.

The mates Robert Thomas and Frederick Hornby harnessed themselves in lead position in the second boat, followed by Macdonald and second master Macbean. The four men were relatively healthy, and had recovered sufficiently from their march across the frozen sea to now have some real hope for their prospects in the days ahead. Thomas Blanky, weakened by the progression of scurvy, and limping from a fall, walked alongside Macdonald. He was to be their guide, following the tracks left by the leading boat and re-routing them whenever he saw fit. He and James Reid said their own brief farewells, each handing over letters to be delivered to their respective wives upon their return home. Others had urged Blanky to remain behind and begin marching when he was more fully re-covered, but Crozier had made a personal appeal to his ice-master, and Blanky had agreed to accompany him.

Those going on foot with Crozier gathered up their supplies and moved among their crewmates and friends offering hope and en-couragement, severing their ties and then separating only slowly, as though they were flotsam pulled apart by some unstoppable drift. Many knelt and prayed together for a final time.

Crozier was one of the last to leave. He said his farewells to Fitzjames and the others, and left written instructions to be opened only in the event of the *Erebus* coming free of the ice and being in a condition to continue sailing later that summer. He knew as well as any of them how unlikely this was considering the damage she had sustained and the massive reduction in her crew, but neither he nor Fitzjames remarked on the fact, the seal on the papers as un-breakable now as the seal of their unbroachable deceptions.

A quantity of medical supplies was left behind with Stanley, both for those remaining on the land and those returning to the *Erebus*, and Crozier warned Fitzjames and the surgeon to be judicious in their use.

Edward Couch and purser Charles Osmer waited until Crozier had finished before saying their own farewells. Osmer dragged behind him a sack stuffed with money, handed it over to Fitzjames and asked for a receipt, confessing that he had no idea of how it might still be of any use to him, but that he could not bring himself to abandon it. Fitzjames said he understood and the two men shook hands. Osmer then turned and followed Crozier, calling for the boy David Young to accompany him. As yet the sixteen-year-old showed no sign of the sickness which had killed George Chambers, and from which the two other apprentices were now suffering.

One by one, individually and in small groups, all those who were leaving rose from the beach, gathered up their belongings and began walking south. Some were delayed, and some returned several times to take again their leave of old friends before finally departing. Some stopped after only a few yards and lightened their loads by throwing down clothing and other unnecessary weights.

Those remaining behind watched them go, the drama of the separation prolonged by the tortuously slow progress of the teams pulling the boats and by the low-lying nature of the land over which they went.

Fitzjames gazed along the line of men and saw that some of them were carrying umbrellas to keep off the sun, looking to him at that distance like the smooth black caps of toadstools marking out the course of some otherwise invisible spoor-line.

At noon even the leading boat was little more than a mile distant from them, the second closing on it. They could see every one of the walking men, now drawn out along a struggling half mile, some following the boats, others finding their own paths over the hummocky ground and across the frozen shallows. A small sail had been rigged up on the second boat, but this had so far proved ineffective in the absence of any wind.

Making a full inspection of the thirty-six men now under their command, Fitzjames and Vesconte ordered those who were able to walk to gather up everything that had been left strewn upon the shore and bring it all back into the center of their camp. The bulk of this detritus consisted of clothing of all descriptions, from dress-

and dinner-jackets to countless sets of woolen underwear, at least three hundred cotton shirts and ninety pairs of boots and overboots. The best of these pieces were sorted through and exchanged for those of poorer quality. Mattresses were built of coats and ground-sheets, and tents were erected to protect the unconscious and those unable to stand.

When this gleaning was done, Fitzjames, Vesconte and Reid walked inland to the first of the ridges, where they turned and in-spected the scene before them: Crozier's two boat crews were still in sight to the south, but some of those walking ahead had already disappeared into the thin sunlit haze which surrounded them in that direction. It was a warm bright day and the gelid glitter of the frozen sea blinded them every time they looked back in the direction of the *Erebus*. There was already some danger of a surface thaw, and be-cause of this, Fitzjames declared his intention of setting out for the ship the following morning.

Vesconte said he would build a more substantial shelter and wait a fortnight or three weeks before making a decision on his own march south. He spoke with little enthusiasm for the task, knowing as well as any of them that a dangerous and unpredictable balance had been struck—a balance between the rate of recovery of those who were sick and exhausted, if they recovered at all, and the speed with which those who had so far suffered the least now began to deteriorate. He said he would wait until those who were already close to death died and thus reduced the burden on the others.

"You could return to the *Erebus*," Fitzjames suggested, knowing that this contravened Crozier's orders.

"And what if some of those who set off with Crozier discover the going too hard and return to take their chances with us?" Vesconte answered, having considered the possibility of his own retreat.

"Either way, they'll stop you from moving," Fitzjames said, im-mediately regretting the observation.

"There's a great deal can do that," Vesconte told him.

They were interrupted by Reid, who had left them to walk a short distance to the east. He told them he had seen fresh caribou tracks, and that he believed the animals had passed them moving north during the night. Several hunters hidden low against the ridge might have some chance of success if other animals followed the same path. The caribou might not be at their best after the winter, but a single carcass would provide them all with several pounds of fresh meat each.

They then turned their attention to the scene below where, despite their earlier efforts, the shoreline was still littered with abandoned stores and possessions as far as they could see, and where, from their vantage-point, the mounds of clothing piled over the men on the beach looked ominously like freshly dug graves.

Later, Fitzjames asked Vesconte if there were any letters or journals he wanted taking back to the *Erebus*. Vesconte declined the offer, and after a pause admitted that he had already handed these over to Crozier. Fitzjames silently considered the implications of this and made no further mention of it.

Afterward, Vesconte spoke of his wife and daughters at some length, creating a succession of small pleasures out of all that was happening around him, and then swallowing the names when he could no longer bear to savor their fond taste.

An hour before sunset they answered a wet-powder signal in the south with one of their own. They built several small fires, divided their remaining stores and tended to the sick. During his tour of inspection, Goodsir discovered that one of the men who had remained unconscious since coming ashore had finally died.

Four hunters led by David Bryant spent a sleepless night on the ridge, but despite a number of shots fired blindly at noises and imagined movement in the pitch dark, nothing was killed.

There was one further fatality during the night: Thomas Armitage, the *Terror*'s gunroom steward, was found in the morning bent double and with his blankets thrown aside. His mouth was open in silent rictal agony and he was clutching his stomach. He had also taken off his boots and his toes were curled and darkened with frostbite. Unable to straighten him out from this grotesque position, Vesconte and Goodsir covered him over with clothing until he was hidden from sight.

．　．　．

Fitzjames and his party set off back across the ice on the morning of the 28th.

The weather remained good for the crossing, with a light following wind, and of the sixteen men in the party, all were able to walk for the first day, making six miles by late afternoon.

The boy Robert Golding spent an uncomfortable, sleepless night, complaining of stomach cramps, pain in his feet and hands and a violent headache. Goodsir tended to him, finally administering a small dose of morphine to help him sleep. The only other man to suffer badly was Thomas Watson, carpenter's mate, who, already weakened by the long tight squeeze of scurvy, now developed severe nausea and could not keep down any of the food he ate. He complained of pain in his knees and thighs which kept him awake, until he too was sedated by Goodsir.

Of the remainder, no one was unaffected by their labors of the previous week, but so far Reid, Goodsir, Edward Couch and the carpenter John Weekes appeared to be suffering from scurvy in only its earliest and mildest manifestations.

The two carpenters had volunteered to return to undertake repairs to the *Erebus* to keep her sound enough for them to remain aboard. The more severe damage to her hull was already beyond them, and any work they were now able to carry out would be only makeshift and temporary.

Des Voeux complained of increasing periods of dizziness, and moments when he felt his strength drain from him, and both Philip Reddington and seaman Thomas McConvey had difficulty walking for more than twenty minutes at a time.

Fitzjames continued to limp from his injured ankle, and this was attended to by Goodsir, who could do nothing more than keep the swelling down until they reached the *Erebus*. Graham Gore walked alongside him, ready to lift him when he fell.

Their number was completed by Joseph Andrews, captain of the hold, steward Hoar, and Robert Hopcraft, one of Bryant's marines.

The second day they moved more slowly, covering only four and a half miles. Thomas Watson and Robert Golding were carried, Watson on a stretcher, and the boy in the arms of whoever was strong enough to hold him, passed from man to man as they all quickly weakened.

Two hours before nightfall, Fitzjames twisted his ankle and fell again, this time heavily, landing on his shoulder and the side of his face, which rose in a bruise from his temple to his chin. Gore and Reid helped him back to his feet and supported him between them as they went on.

He tried to make light of these new injuries, but the pain from his foot grew worse and he was forced to call a halt. Goodsir inspected his ankle, and as he unwound the bandages, Fitzjames passed out.

He came to several hours later. Thomas McConvey lay beside him, asleep, a small pool of vomit by his face. The light was beginning to fade and he saw that most of the others were asleep around a small fire. Goodsir came and knelt beside him. He told Fitzjames that McConvey had collapsed and was bleeding from his bowels and his ears. It was Goodsir's opinion that the man had put on a pretense of being healthier than he actually was to avoid being left behind with the others.

They came within sight of the *Erebus* at two o'clock the following day, having crossed only a mile and a quarter of ice in five hours, frequently stopping to change stretcher bearers, to pass on Robert Golding, and to rest and recover from their increasing exhaustion.

David Bryant approached Fitzjames with the suggestion that he and Hopcraft should strike out ahead of the others and then return with whatever was needed for them to spend another night on the ice before completing their journey the following morning. They might even relight the *Erebus'* boiler and several of her stoves in an attempt to warm up the ship prior to the arrival of the others. Both men were fit enough to make the crossing and carry out this work, but Fitzjames was reluctant to let them go; instead he announced they would abandon their stores and all of them would attempt to reach the ship by that evening.

Unburdened, they walked until dusk, stopped for an hour, and then went on.

Fitzjames suffered with every step he took, and he strapped a jacket around his foot in an attempt to further cushion it from the ground.

Des Voeux collapsed early in the evening, recovered, and then fell again as they continued walking; by dusk he could no longer walk unaided. Reid left Fitzjames to help him, and his place was taken by Joseph Andrews.

Both the boy and Thomas Watson remained unconscious, and it was for their sake that Fitzjames was determined to get back aboard the *Erebus* before nightfall. The other boy continued healthy and cheerful, and Fitzjames began to wonder if it wouldn't have been better for him to have taken his chances with Crozier.

By eight in the evening they started passing through objects on the ice they had cast aside nine days earlier, and an hour after that they found themselves amid the more thickly scattered debris and wreckage of the ships themselves, and of the dismantled dwellings which now stood derelict and open to the night air.

The *Erebus* had lost her outline in the falling darkness, and was soon little more than a presence ahead of them, a large and amorphous shape amid the confusion of other half-noticed outlines all around them.

The two marines were the first to reach her, climbing aboard and firing their rifles to announce their return. They hung ladders over the side and secured these to the ice.

Couch and Weekes were the next to arrive, carrying Thomas Watson, and handing him over to the marines, they ran back into the darkness to help Thomas McConvey, who had half-walked, half-crawled the last few hundred yards.

Next to appear were Goodsir and Andrews, supporting Des Voeux, and behind these came Reid, carrying Robert Golding and with Thomas Evans holding on to his arm.

Fitzjames brought up the rear, hopping more than limping, and helped by Reddington and Hoar.

Weakened by the final climb aboard, and by the weight of those they carried, they all fell on the cold deck and gave thanks for their safe return, men and boys indistinguishable from the clutter of canvas, wood and rope into which they collapsed.

THIRTY

Fitzjames woke from a dream in which he had already woken to the sight of the feeble, scurvy-ridden monkey dragging itself around his cabin like a ghoulish marionette, and he lay disorientated for a moment, waiting for his head to clear, and for this tattered fragment of that earlier nightmare to dissolve as he came slowly to his senses and looked around him.

Beside him lay a low mound of plates, each holding a flattened, uneaten meal, and alongside these, and on the floor beneath him, he saw a number of broken vials and empty syringes. The cabin smelled strongly of surgical spirit, woodsmoke and vomit.

A noise at the bottom of his bunk caused him to sit up and peer through the dim light. Goodsir lay asleep in a chair, his jacket off and his shirt sleeves rolled up. His scarred and tapered forearm lay across his chest. A yellow handkerchief was fastened around his elbow and another syringe lay in his lap. Whether he had drugged himself to sleep or to help him stay awake, Fitzjames could only guess. He called to him, surprised when no voice came, then cleared his throat and called again. This time Goodsir stirred, rubbed his face and opened his eyes. He considered Fitzjames without speaking, took out his pocket watch, read the time and replaced it. He did all this slowly, mechanically, as though he too were not fully aware of his wider surroundings and of the man watching him from the bed.

"Harry," Fitzjames said, raising an arm to him.

Still Goodsir looked at him without speaking. Then he began to tug absently at the cloth on his arm, finally pulling it free and rolling down his sleeve. He rose abruptly, stood unsteadily for a moment and then slumped back down. He laughed aloud, throwing wide his arms and kicking forward both his legs. He lay like this for several minutes before rising again and coming to stand beside Fitzjames. He walked on the vials and crushed them, and pushing himself into the space between Fitzjames' bunk and the cabin wall, he dislodged the mound of plates and sent them clattering to the floor.

"How are you?" he said, pulling open Fitzjames' mouth before he could answer, then turning his head from side to side and prodding his jaw and cheeks. "You ought to eat more." He laughed again at this and then dropped to his knees until his face was only inches from Fitzjames' own.

"How long?" Fitzjames asked.

"The 4th of May. Nearly midday."

"And the others?"

Goodsir pushed himself back in the restricted space, knocking his head on the wall. He breathed deeply before answering. "Thomas Watson died yesterday. He couldn't sleep, couldn't eat. He started raving and then cursing, followed by complete dementia."

"Cursing what?"

"You mostly. Me, Reid, Gore, Des Voeux and everyone else who bound him hand and foot and dragged him back to this doomed wreck instead of letting him take his chances on the glorious march south with the gallant Francis Rawdon Maria Crozier. He seemed to think that Crozier would be living like a lord by now at some Bay Company outpost, gorging himself on good food and drink and making a fortune by telling the story of his heroic struggle to the world." He smiled at this and then sniffed cautiously at the shriveled skin of his arm.

Neither of them spoke for a moment as the death was accorded its dutiful silence.

"And is she a doomed wreck?" Fitzjames said eventually.

Goodsir said nothing for a minute, then shook his head. "Not yet."

"But near enough?"

Even in the darkness it had been clear to all those who had struggled back to reclaim the *Erebus* that she had suffered further ravages during their short absence: her jib had gone, along with her mizzen and fore-top. She had been lifted astern by several more feet, her rudder fittings had been twisted out of alignment, and various points along both sides of her hull had been crushed.

Fitzjames resolved to make a complete inspection for himself. He rose unsteadily, helped by Goodsir, who himself appeared only then to be fully coming round from his own drugged sleep.

Fitzjames asked him again about the condition of the others.

"The boy is still suffering, getting worse. Des Voeux is in his bed, as is McConvey." Goodsir paused, his hand held to his brow.

"And the others?"

"Of those who came back fit, only Reid, the two marines and Couch show signs of any real vigor. The rest you can see for yourself, but probably don't need to. Look in a mirror; you're all the same." His tone was a mix of anger, despair and resignation.

"And you?"

Goodsir glanced back to the chair in which he had been asleep. "Physician heal thyself." He searched in his pockets, took out several full vials, looked closely at these and then replaced them.

They went on deck together, moving slowly amid the jumble of wreckage and stores, as mixed and scattered on the ship as they were on the surrounding ice. Fitzjames' foot had been splinted and rebandaged, but was still too painful to bear any weight. He could no longer fit a soft outer-boot over the dressing, and a padded leather pouch had been adapted for this purpose.

He had expected to see others already out on the ice, but there was no one. He was dismayed by what he saw, unable at first to believe that this scene of dereliction and disarray was the one they had left behind them. Rigging and braces hung loose from the spars, lengths of rail were missing; their remaining small boat stood upright against the mainmast; clothing and books lay scattered everywhere, and along their entire deck, planking squeezed by the ice had sprung loose and lay as curled as shavings on the ribs of its joists.

The scene which greeted them as they looked out over the surrounding ice disappointed them even further.

"We laid Watson in one of the collapsed huts." Goodsir indicated the toppled slabs of ice and lengths of timber directly beneath them. "There seemed little point in carrying him any farther, even if we could have managed it."

Fitzjames shielded his eyes and studied the remains of the *Terror*. With the exception of her main mast and the outline of her bows beneath the wreckage, she looked like little more than the stacked timbers of a massive fire waiting only to be lit.

Above them, the sky, which had for so long been cloudless and blue, was now gray, deepening to charcoal and banded red across their southern horizon.

"Reid thinks she'll go down the moment the ice begins to fracture beneath her," Goodsir said, nodding toward the *Terror*. "Her keel's split in three places and her spars are barely holding as it is. According to him, she's only sitting on top now because of the equal pressure of the ice inside pushing out."

Fitzjames was distracted by movement on the ice below. Two men were coming toward them, laboriously hauling a half-loaded sledge, which they pulled with straps fastened across their chests.

Goodsir identified them as Reid and Edward Couch.

Fitzjames asked him how he could tell at such a distance.

"Because the marines have gone to set traps, and Reid and Couch are the only two capable of doing what they're doing."

They both turned to watch the figures on the ice. The two men appeared to be walking on the spot, their load standing still behind them. They stopped after every few paces to regain their breath, and one or other of them frequently fell to his knees.

When they came within hailing distance, Fitzjames called down to them. Reid and Couch released themselves from the sledge and walked to the *Erebus* supporting each other. Both expressed their pleasure at Fitzjames' recovery, and he asked them what they were pulling, doing his best to mask his surprise at their appearance. Couch in particular had lost more weight. There were open sores around his mouth and eyes, and small patches of dried blood on his cheeks where he had rubbed at these. His hair too was coming loose, and pale patches showed through his beard. Reid appeared the healthier of the two, but the skin around his own eyes was loose and waxy; his greased lips were cracked, and drops of clear liquid appeared each time he spoke. His gums were also bleeding and he had lost the first of his teeth.

"A sack of beans and a dozen eight-pound cans of oxtail soup," Couch said, indicating the sledge below.

"No medical supplies in either Peddie's or Macdonald's cabins?" Goodsir asked.

"Not even a cabin in Macdonald's case," Reid said. "And nothing worth salvaging in Peddie's."

"We brought back his journals and papers," Couch added.

"We thought you'd want everything we could save in that line," Goodsir said.

Fitzjames asked them how much else remained to be salvaged.

"Precious little," Reid said.

"The Eskimos have been in before us," Couch added.

The remark surprised Fitzjames. "Eskimos? Have they come here?" He looked out over the broader expanse of ice beyond the *Terror*, and then in the direction of the abandoned camp.

"They've been in the *Terror*," Reid said. "But it's not likely they'll be after the same things we're wanting. They're stripping her for iron braces and good small timbers."

"How can you be so certain they've been aboard?" Fitzjames asked.

Neither man was willing to answer him.

"They've disturbed the bodies," Goodsir said. "Unwrapped them and then left them with only their faces covered."

"What about here, the *Erebus*? John Irving?"

"Him, too," Goodsir said. "There's been no mutilation. Just the same as on the *Terror*. They undressed him and then left him with only his face covered."

"Perhaps they thought we'd—" Fitzjames stopped himself. He had been about to suggest that the Eskimos might have thought they'd abandoned the corpses for good, but this now felt almost sacrilegious even to suggest.

A week later Fitzjames was woken by Reid with the news that a small party of the Eskimos had been spotted out on the ice half a mile to the north of them, that they appeared to have spent the night there, and that as yet they showed no sign of leaving. It was Reid's opinion that they were awaiting some approach from the ship, possibly too frightened of their reception after their looting to come any closer. He had already woken Des Voeux, with whom he was now sharing a cabin, and who, like himself, was able to speak a few words of the natives' language.

Already fully dressed beneath his blankets and furs, Fitzjames pulled himself from his bed. He rubbed his legs and arms, massaging the cramp in them, and hiding the pain from his foot, which had given him another largely sleepless night. Reid waited in the doorway, watching him and guessing. There was the smell of baking bread in the air as the day's ration was prepared, and the appetizing aroma of freshly roasted coffee being ground.

Fitzjames, however, had been sick the previous evening, and the smell made his stomach turn. He told Reid to inform Goodsir what was happening and then to wait for him on deck. Reid had been gone only a few seconds when Fitzjames began to retch and was then sick, bringing up a thin and bitter bile into his water bowl. He sweated heavily, and his chest, throat and jaw ached with the strain. When he had finished he rinsed his face and combed his hair. He looked at himself in a mirror. He had not shaved since returning to the ship, and the dark growth made his cheeks appear fuller than they had become. He felt unsteady for a moment, and then went out to catch up with Reid and the others.

The sun was not yet fully risen, but there was sufficient light for him to make out the distant shelter, the glow of a shielded fire, and the six or seven figures crouched around it.

Bryant, Hopcraft and Joseph Andrews accompanied Fitzjames, Reid and Des Voeux as far as the edge of the *Terror*'s debris, but would go no farther. Their reaction puzzled Fitzjames, who was eager to make contact with their visitors, and who fell several times as he stumbled toward them, moving with the help of sticks rather than the crutches he had been using.

He hoped the Eskimos might be a smaller group of the party he had encountered the previous year and that they might remember him, but as he called out and they rose to greet him none gave any indication of recognizing him. He spoke and gestured to them, wanting to convey that they were welcome and that he hoped they would accompany him back to the *Erebus*.

They showed little sign of understanding, but when he had finished they indicated their fire and the pot upon it, in which a piece of seal meat sat in its rendered fat. Sickened further by the smell, he nevertheless accepted the offer and crouched down beside them. Reid and Des Voeux did the same.

All around them, the three men saw the crockery and pieces of cloth and wood which the Eskimos had already scavenged from the wasteland surrounding the *Terror*. In addition to the iron bars and various blades they had gathered up, the men also carried spears and clubs, but apart from their unsettling show of indifference to Fitzjames and his party, they exhibited no hostility.

The meal was shared, and with each mouthful he swallowed Fitzjames was convinced that he was again about to be sick. He put down his bowl when it was only half empty, signaling to his hosts that he had eaten enough. They were satisfied by this and one of them took back the bowl.

They were joined by Gore and Reddington, the latter with his forehead and both arms heavily bandaged. This was a source of great interest to the Eskimos, but despite their curiosity they did not approach too close to him, repulsed by his growth of beard.

After an hour, the natives prepared to leave. They extinguished the fire and retrieved the sticks of their shelter, letting the unsupported ice collapse into the shallow depression beneath. When they made it clear that they were not about to accompany Fitzjames back to the *Erebus*, he protested to them and then tried to persuade them with promises of gifts. But his raised voice only alarmed them, and after a short conference one of the men answered by shouting something unintelligible back at him. Fitzjames regretted the misunderstanding he had caused and tried to appease them before they left. He indicated the detritus all around and signaled for the Eskimos to take as much as they liked. The man who had shouted at him took a cup and saucer from beneath his jacket, showed it briefly to Des Voeux and then replaced it. Others followed his lead, proudly displaying what they too had already taken.

Reddington suggested going back to where the others were waiting midway between the two ships and returning to force the natives to accompany them to the *Erebus*.

Reid shook his head and asked him what purpose he thought this would serve.

"We alarm them by more than our disgusting appearance," he said. He gestured for the Eskimos to leave, but they remained motionless, watching him.

Angry at Reid's criticism, Reddington asked him what he meant.

"Our size, our numbers, the ship that might have sailed down from the sun or the moon or the stars with such sorry-looking specimens as ourselves on board. They might even think we want to steal their meat and then butcher and eat *them* from the same pot. Perhaps—" Here, prompted by a glance from Fitzjames, Reid paused. "Perhaps we aren't even human to them. Perhaps they look upon us as they look upon the spirits of the dead, their dead, turned white—" He stopped again, unwilling to continue his alarming speculations and all they implied for their own future.

There followed a minute of silence, during which the two parties stared at each other, the only noise coming from the distant men who were growing impatient with the encounter.

Finally unable to control his stomach, Fitzjames was sick on the ice at his feet, bringing up everything he had eaten. When he had finished and wiped the mess from his mouth and chin, he tried to apologize, but felt too nauseous to persist, finally frustrated and angered by the obdurate and ungiving nature of the men with whom he was trying to communicate.

Rather than allow any further suggestion of ingratitude or hostility to mar the failed negotiations, he turned and left them, his teeth clenched and the mixed taste of oil and blood in his mouth.

Upon his return to the ship, Fitzjames went to inspect John Irving's corpse. It had already been dressed as fully as possible, but this had proved difficult, and whoever had attempted the task had been unable to push Irving's legs back into his trousers or his arms into his sleeves; instead they had pressed rolled blankets around the body and then cut his shirt, jacket and trousers up the back and moulded these over him until he once again looked as though he were properly clothed. Seeing the result, Fitzjames wished something similar could be done for the desecrated corpses aboard the *Terror*.

Afterward, he examined the full extent of the internal damage to the *Erebus*, noting where the blossoming ice had made its dangerous gains since she had been left without heat three weeks earlier.

Upon leaving Irving's body, Fitzjames called for Goodsir, and together they inspected the crates and casks mounded on the *Erebus'* deck. Fitzjames was surprised by how much had already been collected, but Goodsir remained pessimistic, pointing out how little of this was of any value in fighting scurvy, and reminding Fitzjames of how many of their number—himself included—were scarcely able to keep down half of what they ate. Securing fresh meat, he insisted, was vital to their survival.

Almost as though prompted by this discussion, the two men were distracted by a distant gunshot out on the ice.

"Our hunters," Goodsir said in the same unhappy tone. "Shooting at shadows and at skin and bone."

"Have they killed nothing so far?"

"One fox, two gulls and—" Suddenly and without warning, Goodsir began to cough violently and uncontrollably, almost choking at the exertion. He bent double and then fell against the foremast to support himself. Fitzjames moved to help him, but Goodsir pushed him away until the seizure was over. Afterward, gulping to recover his breath, he wiped the sweat from his brow and spat heavily into his handkerchief.

A moment later he returned to their inventory as though nothing had happened, and before Fitzjames could comment on what he had seen.

Later in the day they found a further dozen places where the ice had breached their hull, in some instances pushing through into the quarters within and rendering these uninhabitable. Timbers had warped along her full length, and the *Erebus* was filled with the sound of creaking and scraping where the ice continued to assault her, probing and fingering as it came, searching out her weaknesses as meticulously and as relentlessly as it had sought out and then exploited those of the *Terror*.

The extent of all this and the speed with which it had taken place during their short absence concerned Fitzjames, and it worried him even more when he thought of how this prolonged and strength-sapping war of attrition might one day be so suddenly and easily lost.

The two men parted at Stanley's surgery, where Goodsir had taken up residence. He made it clear as he unlocked the door and then stepped quickly inside that he did not want Fitzjames to follow him.

The pain from Fitzjames' foot had grown worse, and as he negotiated the narrow passageways and stairs back to his own cabin, he frequently found himself having to rest until it subsided.

He came first upon Thomas McConvey, asleep in his bunk. His bedclothes were dirty and strewn across the floor. His pillow was stained with vomit and blood, and both disfigured further his pock-marked face. His breathing came hoarsely and erratically, punctuated by painful grunts, and it was only as Fitzjames stood beside the sick man and looked down at him that he fully understood the burden that had been placed upon Goodsir over the previous week, and to which he had now begun to sacrifice his own failing health.

Leaving McConvey, he went into the adjoining room, in which the two boys had been quartered. Thomas Evans was awake and sitting in a chair which Fitzjames recognized as having come from Franklin's cabin. In answer to his inquiry as to his health, the boy only pointed to the sleeping form of his sick companion.

Fitzjames had not seen Robert Golding buried beneath the blankets of the bed, and moving closer he pulled these back to look at his sleeping face, the features immediately reminding him of the dying monkey. The boy's eyes fluttered as he slept, and a thin brown line ran from his nose to his chin and was dotted upon his pillow.

"Mr. Goodsir has been looking to him, sir," Thomas Evans said.

Fitzjames looked around the bed for any more of the broken vials and then pulled one of the boy's arms out from beneath its mound of blankets, feeling its weight and the rigidity with which it was held by the sleeping child.

"You shouldn't be in here with him," he said to the other, knowing that Golding was close to death.

Thomas Evans couldn't answer him, his only response being to draw his knees closer to his chest, wrap his arms around them and then press his face into his thighs as though he believed he was about to be pulled from his chair and dragged from the room.

Fitzjames left him without saying anything more.

The next half a dozen cabins he inspected were all empty, their contents strewn around them, charts emptied from their cases and torn into fragments, pieces of glassware and crockery smashed in drifts where they had been thrown by men with no further use for them.

Coming repeatedly upon these small scenes of wanton destruction, he wondered if any of it had been caused by the scavenging Eskimos, and how much more they might yet attempt as those who had come back aboard gradually lost the strength and the will to resist them.

At the end of the short passageway he came upon the starved, bald bodies of a dozen rats nailed to the wall, the result of a hunt by the two marines bringing aboard the last of their stores. He wondered if they had been hung in display as trophies, or if they were waiting to be cooked and eaten. Regardless, he swung his stick at them and knocked half of the stiff and elongated corpses to the ground, where they rolled around him like bowling pins.

He entered John Irving's cabin, sought out his chronometer and sextant, and packed the remains of his library into a case which he then dragged into the passageway to collect later when he had the strength.

He came upon the rest of the men gathered together in the galley. The stove was alight and the room and those adjoining it were warm. A thin pall of sulfurous smoke hung across the ceiling, barely disturbed by the few draughts of fresher air which penetrated that far into the raw innards of the ship.

At his approach, those who were able to stand did so, and of them all, only John Weekes and Edward Hoar showed little sign of the sickness which all too clearly burned inside the others.

Greeting them, Fitzjames made the effort to appear optimistic about their chances of recovery during the easier, recuperative summer months ahead, and in return none of the men gave voice to their own individual fears, preferring instead briefly to submerge these in this shared delusion of hope.

A small piece of cooked meat was taken from the oven and laid on the galley table. This was then cut into six smaller pieces, and each man spent longer looking at his share and juggling it from hand to hand than he did eating it, savoring the expectation rather than the taste.

Fitzjames returned to his cabin, surprised to find Goodsir there ahead of him. As he entered, Goodsir was withdrawing the needle of a syringe from his inner arm. He then sucked at the drop of blood which appeared before bending his arm double and acknowledging Fitzjames. A bottle of port and another of rum stood on the table beside him, both uncorked, their mixed scent adding an edge to the more usual fetid muskiness of the room.

Neither man spoke, and when Goodsir finally threw one of the bottles toward him, Fitzjames made no attempt to catch it, watching as its contents spilled onto his bed, whether rum or port he could not tell through the pain which blurred his vision, and a minute later he fell asleep to the sound of Goodsir's laughter, neither knowing nor caring about what he found so amusing.

THIRTY-ONE

Robert Golding died on the 21st of May. He was alone and barely conscious, unable to speak or respond, and with hardly the strength to keep his eyes open for the final few moments during which he came round from his drugged sleep.

Gore and Goodsir stripped and washed the small corpse, and afterward Goodsir inspected it to determine the severity and extent of the disease which had finally closed tight its grip on the boy. He scraped away the dried pus which had leaked from Golding's swollen joints and washed him clean of the blood which had accumulated from the raw skin beneath his finger- and toe-nails. Gore, who had seen such ravages before, could hardly bring himself to look at them on the weightless shrunken body of the child.

Goodsir performed his work silently and clumsily, directing Gore in all the tasks he himself could not perform, and when they had finished the two of them dressed the boy in clean clothes, combed down what little remained of his hair and invited in those waiting to pay their last respects.

The body was taken out an hour later and placed alongside John Irving's in the empty engine room, now ice-caulked and airless.

The boy's death cast its desolate spell over them all, and alerted by the speed with which it had come, Fitzjames established a rota of daily medical inspections from which no one was exempt. Those confined to their bunks were visited twice daily, and last thing each night Goodsir reported to Fitzjames on the condition of them all.

With the few medical supplies at their disposal, treatment was largely confined to the washing and dressing of wounds.

Fitzjames' own injuries were growing worse, and there were now days when he was barely able to stand, and when he too was confined to his bed.

Following his request to be informed by Goodsir on the condition of the others, he also secretly asked Reid to confide in him on the health of Goodsir himself, convinced that he was now taking larger and larger doses of his stimulants to enable him to carry out his duties.

In addition to his injured foot, Fitzjames felt his other limbs stiffening, and the skin of his joints turning ever more tender and sore as the flesh became swollen and hard and then split. Having regained most of his hair after losing it the previous year, it was once again becoming brittle and loose, and skin peeled from his scalp in small circles. He began to sleep for longer and longer each night, twelve and then fourteen or fifteen hours, but after waking from even these long periods he felt as though he had scarcely rested and remained in his bed until something required his attention.

The disappointing inventory of their stores was completed, and upon being told of what remained, Fitzjames cut their ration of lemon juice to an ounce and a half, and six days later to an ounce.

A candle was lit alongside the body of the boy as a mark of respect, but so cold was the engine room that this burned only down its center, leaving intact a tube of translucent wax inside which the flame was quickly extinguished.

A month after the meeting with the first party, a second group of Eskimos arrived alongside the *Erebus*. There were thirty of them this time and they came directly to the ship. They called up to the men on deck, signaling that they wished to trade with them. Des Voeux saw them arrive and went immediately to tell Fitzjames. In his opinion, the Eskimos had not expected to find anyone aboard the ship.

"Or alive," Fitzjames said without thinking. He also considered it unlikely that the natives had approached with the sole intention of trade when so many of their possessions already lay scattered all around them, and from which their earlier visitors had scavenged and stolen with obvious disregard for the men on the ship.

Philip Reddington and the two marines stood at the rail looking down at the men below, and both Bryant and Hopcraft held their rifles ready to fire, targeting individual figures as they moved amid the wreckage of the huts and bunkers and the discarded timber and rigging.

"I think they've come from the others, from Vesconte and Stanley," Reddington told Fitzjames. "They keep pointing back in the direction of the land. And see—" He indicated the lengths of leather harness coiled around the shoulders of several of the men. Others held the small canvas satchels and pouches used to carry personal belongings ashore.

Reid volunteered to go down and communicate with them. He warned the marines not to fire while he was on the ice. Des Voeux and Reddington went with him.

At this approach, the Eskimos drew back, speaking among themselves and laying at their feet what they had already collected.

Fitzjames watched closely as Reid and Des Voeux approached them, and as they raised their arms in peaceful gestures, revealing that they were unarmed. Philip Reddington remained standing behind, his own hand raised as though he were about to signal to the marines. One of the Eskimos pulled back his hood, laid down the bundle of timber he was carrying and copied Reid's gesture. He came forward, holding out the satchel he carried to Des Voeux, and having handed it over he turned and pointed to the east.

It suddenly occurred to Fitzjames, watching as Des Voeux fumbled with the buckles of the satchel, that the men might be acting as messengers, having come with papers from either Stanley or Vesconte, or perhaps even from Crozier himself, sent to inform them of their progress during the six weeks they had been separated. Realizing this, he made a rough calculation: even allowing for daily marches of only two or three miles hauling the boats, Crozier and his advance party might have easily covered the eighty or ninety miles south over King William Land to the mainland. And even

Vesconte, allowing for a stay of two or three weeks on the shore where they had landed, might now be moving more rapidly south with his own less heavily burdened party and closing the distance between them.

So involved was he with all these silent calculations that he did not at first see Des Voeux crouch down and then tip the contents of the satchel onto the ice, and it was only when Reid called up to him, and as he too knelt and then quickly rose, that his attention was drawn back to the men below. He knew immediately from the silence, and from Reid's bowed head as he came back to the ship, that he had been wrong to have allowed his hopes to rise so sharply at the encounter, and he waited in silence as Reid and then Reddington climbed back aboard.

From his jacket, Reid pulled out a handful of the contents of the satchel. Cutlery, buttons, watch cases and cap bands fell to the deck. He took out scissors and shaving gear, the firing mechanism of a broken pistol, a compass, a clothes brush, several horn combs and a letter nip. Fitzjames and the marines looked on in silent disbelief as he let all this booty fall to the deck and scatter at their feet.

Out on the ice other Eskimos approached Des Voeux and handed over to him their own collections. One had brought only empty bottles, another a collection of gaming boards and clay pipes. Others took out pieces of folded clothing with which they were reluctant to part, especially the brightly colored handkerchiefs and scarves and the pieces of starched, brilliantly white table linen.

Des Voeux looked down at all this piling up around his feet, and it was several minutes before he could bring himself to attempt to communicate with the Eskimos. He guessed from the confident, almost beseeching manner in which they displayed their booty that it had not been taken by force from the men on the land, and that if this was the case then it had either been discarded by those men to lighten their unbearable loads, or it had been taken from their bodies and their packs where they had finally fallen and died. Having guessed this much, he searched among the objects at his feet for some indication of their owners, hoping to determine whether they had come from Crozier's party or the men on the shore. He found a backgammon board he knew to belong to George Hodgson, and a shaving kit, each piece of which was engraved with the initials of Alexander Macdonald, and looking beneath a mound of clothing, he came upon a copy of Moore's *Garden Almanac* for 1845 inscribed with Thomas Blanky's name, a gift from his wife given to him only days before their departure. All three men had set off with Crozier on his march to the south. Picking this up, Des Voeux indicated to the man who had brought it that he wished to keep it. He tried to ascertain if the man could remember where it had come from, if it had been found discarded or still in the possession of its owner, and whether that man had been dead or alive, but none of his questions brought forth an answer. He knew that Eskimos seldom spoke of the dead, especially those who had died in unnatural or painful circumstances, preferring instead either to pretend not to know the person in question or to point to the horizon and say that he had gone away on a long journey. He guessed too that they might be unwilling to admit to having plundered corpses, although this was hardly how they themselves would look upon their finds.

Indicating for them to wait where they stood, Des Voeux returned to the *Erebus* and told Fitzjames and Reid what he thought had happened, adding that he believed the Eskimos thought they had something to gain by returning all these objects to the ship. Fitzjames could not accept this, and in his anger he called down, cursing the men below. They did not understand him, and other than pause briefly as they gathered up their loot, they took little notice of him.

Des Voeux gave Reid Blanky's *Almanac*, and seeing its inscription stung him to tears. Fitzjames fell silent. He apologized to Reid and Des Voeux for his outburst and then ordered the marines to put down their weapons.

"Do they intend to stay, do you think?" he asked Reid as the men below dispersed to search further among the spreading waste all around them.

"A short while perhaps. They'll want whatever they can get while it's still there for the taking."

"Give it to them. Barter for whatever else they've brought. And make it clear that if they intend returning to the land I want a message taken for whoever they might come across."

The hour upon the deck and the shock of the revelation had weakened Fitzjames considerably. He spotted several books amid the clothing below and asked Reddington to retrieve these for him, hoping there might be a journal or log among them. But in this too he was disappointed.

At first many could not bring themselves to believe what the encounter suggested, but others received the news philosophically, too weak to argue whether the men on the shore were dead or alive when the Eskimos had come across them and started picking through their loads.

"They only tell us what they think we want to hear," Reid remarked later, sitting beside Fitzjames' bed.

A wind had blown up and it was colder than usual. Out on the ice the Eskimos had erected their shelters amid the derelict dwellings.

Fitzjames had fallen on his way back to the cabin, unable to push himself up until Gore came to help him.

Later, Joseph Andrews arrived with the alarming news that the Eskimos had been heard in their abandoned forward hold and the adjacent quarters. An armed party was sent to evict them, but no one was found. Some said they had never been aboard at all, except as a figment of someone's dream; others believed that the Eskimos had acquired their booty by attacking those on the land and that they were now preparing to do the same to them.

Goodsir arrived, having slept through the whole encounter, and listened without speaking to everything that had happened. He took Alexander Macdonald's shaving kit and examined it for signs of recent use. Then he unbandaged Fitzjames' foot and drained the liquid from his swollen ankle. Afterward, he gave Fitzjames a potion to help him sleep.

He had just come from visiting Thomas McConvey, who was now suffering from bouts of delirium in addition to his physical pains. He complained of being unable to see, and Goodsir had swabbed

the dried blood from his eyelids, both of which were torn. To reassure him that he was not about to go permanently blind, Goodsir
had doused these with a weak solution of spirit and then bound
them. He was concerned that his increasing medication appeared to
be having little effect on the seaman, and when Fitzjames asked him
how long he expected McConvey to live, he thought for a moment
and held up five fingers, then reduced these to four and then three,
before finally abandoning his guessing entirely.

THIRTY-TWO

Thomas McConvey fell unconscious two days later, and the day after that he died.

Six days later a fissure appeared three hundred yards off their port bow, and the surface on either side of it rose and broke and crumbled. The last standing walls of the distant camp were shaken down, and the mound of timber under which the *Terror* lay buried slid from around her to reveal the unsettling skeletal remains beneath, the angle of her broken back and the collapsed hoops of her ribs.

Over the next few days there were further shocks and fractures in the ice. Some hopes were raised higher than others. Joseph Andrews, now bedridden, became convinced that they would soon be sailing in open water, surrounded by clean white bergs, negotiating the edge of the dispersing floe, and nosing into leads as these split and opened ahead of them. He began, like McConvey before him, to suffer from bouts of delirium, during which he called out orders as though they were already sailing in that open sea. He shouted in his drugged sleep, and then when he woke and his hysteria temporarily abated, he became confused about what was actually happening to them and what his feverish mind had so vividly and desperately imagined. Also like McConvey, he started to complain of periods of near-blindness, when he could make out men and objects in only the dimmest outline. Two days after his eyes were bound, he started to bleed from the bowels, and blood dribbled from his mouth each time he spoke.

So that they might not be taken entirely by surprise by any slackening in the grip of the ice, Reid and Couch, along with the few others who were still fit enough to work, set about trimming their rigging. Their mizzen had been rendered useless and Reid ordered this to be removed at the cross-jack, throwing everything above overboard. To compensate for this loss they removed the fore-mast above its top-yard, and the same with the main. The result of all this was to halve the area of their sail and to make the *Erebus* appear unwieldy, but Reid knew that if they could rig their main-and-fore-sails then the few of them still capable of the work might later add to these if the need arose.

The work was hard and slow, and quickly exhausted everyone who participated in it. Everything which they neither needed nor were able to operate was chopped free and abandoned, and the remnants of the shelters below were finally flattened by the weight of timber and rope thrown down on them.

As he worked one morning trimming their main rigging, Reid was surprised to hear Joseph Andrews on the deck below, calling out orders as though to several dozen men working all around him. He stumbled from one side of the deck to the other, his loose bandages a dirty scarf around his neck, frequently falling over the heaps of tangled rope and blocks which had been cut free and fallen loose. Reid hurried down to him, held him by the shoulders and tried to reason with him. Andrews pulled free and saluted, addressing him as though he were Crozier and then commenting on the sight of their full sails and the open water ahead of them. Reid sent Des Voeux to fetch Goodsir, playing along with Andrews until the two men returned. Hearing them approach him from behind, Andrews became suddenly suspicious, pulled away from Reid and then ran for a few feet before becoming entangled in a mound of discarded cable. All three men ran to restrain him. They coiled a rope around his arms to prevent him from striking out and looped another around his ankles. Andrews cursed and struggled for a moment and then he fell silent and began to cry. His sightless eyes lay deep in their sockets, made even more prominent by the red mask where blood vessels had burst, causing him to weep thick bloody tears.

They helped him to his feet and led him, still weeping, back below, where they discovered the contents of his cabin smashed and scattered.

The following day, as work on the rigging neared its completion, the body of Edward Hoar was discovered on the ice. He had gone out with the two marines to check their traps, and had parted from them as they passed the *Terror*, saying that something had caught his eye and he wanted to investigate. Neither Bryant nor Hopcraft had been keen to accompany him into the ruin of the dead ship, and so he had gone alone, arranging to meet them on their return.

Later, there was no sign of Hoar and so they called for him, the only response to this being the appearance of several of the Eskimos close by the ruins of Tozer's camp. The natives watched as the two men went closer to the *Terror*, calling into her open hull for Hoar to come out and join them. When he neither appeared nor answered, the marines assumed he had already left and returned to the *Erebus* ahead of them.

It was as they were picking their way back out through the debris that they saw his arm, the rest of him being hidden beneath a mound of clothing. A quick inspection told them he was dead and they searched his body for any indication of how he had died or been killed. They found nothing.

As they rose from their examination, Hopcraft pointed out the Eskimos, who were moving toward them, each man holding a spear or a club. Bryant told him to leave the body and to walk calmly back to the *Erebus*, but Hopcraft, upon seeing the natives quicken their pace, panicked and fired a shot high above them. This caused them to throw themselves to the ground, where they lay for several minutes as Bryant considered what to do next, and as Hopcraft reloaded and aimed his rifle. Bryant ordered him not to fire, but Hopcraft remained convinced that the Eskimos were about to attack, and that they had earlier killed Hoar, having come upon him picking through what they now considered to be their own. Bryant thought all this unlikely, and was relieved when the Eskimos finally rose and ran back to their shelters.

Reassuring Hopcraft that they were beyond the reach of anything that might be thrown at their backs, the two men returned to the *Erebus*.

Neither Fitzjames nor Goodsir accepted that the Eskimos had killed Edward Hoar, believing that his death had been accidental, that he had fallen, concussed himself and died as a result. They pointed to his physical debilitation and to the absence of any wounds or other marks on his body to support this view. Others were less certain, most notably Hopcraft, Weekes and Reddington, and to placate these, Fitzjames agreed to a daytime watch being kept aboard the *Erebus* to alert them all of any further approach by the Eskimos.

Reid confided his fears to Fitzjames that they were over-reacting to the presence of the natives, making them appear threatening when no threat existed, and depriving themselves of a possible source of assistance. Fitzjames agreed, but knew there was nothing they could do to convince the others of this.

Three days after the death of Hoar, the body of a freshly killed seal was found on the ice alongside the *Erebus*, a single bloodless spear wound in the back of its head. Goodsir responded enthusiastically to this gift and called for help to drag it aboard.

He butchered and cooked the carcass, slicing the greasy flesh into strips and boiling these on the galley stove. The others complained of the stink. Goodsir himself ate the meat raw, the amber oil running down his chin. He disguised his repugnance of the taste and forced himself to swallow each small piece. In an effort to help the others overcome their own distaste, he served it to them with freshly baked unleavened bread, into which much of the dissolving fat drained, and with honey, which he planed from a frozen cask, the shavings of which melted on the meat as the men attempted to swallow it without chewing. He then rendered as much oil as possible from the blubber and internal organs, taking over fourteen pints in all. Afterward he worked on ways of making this too more palatable, mixing small quantities with sugar, then adding nutmeg and ground cloves until the liquid formed into a paste which could be moulded into pastilles and swallowed whole.

Only Reddington and Hopcraft refused to accept any part of the seal, interpreting its appearance as an admission of guilt on the part of the Eskimos.

Regardless of their protests, Fitzjames asked Reid to arrange for a package of gifts to be placed at the spot where the seal had been found. He hoped to encourage the natives to bring more fresh food for them. In this he was thwarted by Hopcraft, who, waiting until a party of Eskimos approached the package, again fired over their heads. The men took fright and fled back across the ice to the safety of their shelters.

Upon hearing the shots, those below were at first alarmed, having lived with rumors of an attack ever since the death of Hoar. Others believed the shots to be a signal, and Reid went to investigate.

Confronting Hopcraft, he understood immediately what had happened, and looked down over the ice at the abandoned gifts and the distant figures. Resisting the urge to strike the marine for what he had done, for the fragile and vital link he had so ignorantly severed, he returned below to report to Fitzjames, advising him against any further reprimand while feelings concerning the Eskimos remained so mixed.

That night, and for several nights following, fires were visible amid the wreckage surrounding the *Terror*, and on at least one occasion figures were seen around a blaze which had been lit upon what little remained of her deck.

On Thursday the 2nd of July an explosion of timber alerted them to the final moments of the *Terror*. This was followed by a succession of tremors across a wide area of ice, alerting everyone aboard the *Erebus*, and sending those who could walk up to the relative safety of her deck. Fitzjames was carried up by Gore and John Weekes, the two men sitting him at the starboard rail before returning below to help the others.

The noise and the violence of the tremors convinced them all that they too were about to be struck and damaged, and their remaining boat was provisioned and manhandled to the rail ready to be lowered.

The sky was clear of cloud, and with the sun high it was warm, 36 degrees at eleven in the morning. Those who had not been on deck for some time were laid out on blankets, and Goodsir moved from man to man exhorting them all to breathe deeply in the invigorating air.

Fitzjames himself tried to come out into the open at least once a day when he felt able to walk, but he had not been down on the ice for over a fortnight. He had long since considered the possibility that his foot might need to be amputated, but had so far avoided suggesting this to Goodsir, knowing that if the need did arise then the surgeon would have to instruct someone else on how to perform the operation. Fitzjames' already irregular routine of sleeping and waking had been disrupted even further by the medication he now took, and he frequently woke in the night sickened by the smell of his own decay.

Beside him on the deck sat Reddington and Thomas Evans, the man holding the boy, who now sat shivering in the sun, cocooned inside his blanket. A short distance away, Edward Couch held Joseph Andrews in the same way, describing to him what was happening out on the ice. Andrews, his eyes still bound, showed little sign of hearing what the mate said to him, let alone understanding any of it.

Coming clear of her debris, the *Terror* exposed her few upright spars against the glare beyond, her remaining timbers bulging with the weight of ice inside her, long since warped out of true and ready to spring loose from their fittings.

"Like a skull split by beans," Goodsir said, inspecting both Reddington and Evans as he spoke.

"Like a what?" Fitzjames asked him.

Goodsir sat beside him, his thin bloodless face and dark eyes mapping out his own exhaustion and weight loss. Shreds of blistered skin hung from his beard and he plucked at these as he spoke.

"Phrenologists and anatomists. To split a skull they boil it in ammonia to first remove the flesh and sinews, and when they are left with only the clean white bone they pack it full of dried beans and then sink it into a pail of water. The beans swell, and gradually—" He cupped his hand to the side of his head and slowly opened his fingers.

Beside him, Thomas Evans began to cough and then to spit up bloody phlegm. Reddington rubbed his back and then wiped the viscous mess from his mouth.

Goodsir tried to light a pipe, but his shaking hand would not allow him to pack it with tobacco. Exasperated, he threw it down and then stamped on it, refusing all offers of help.

The sound of splintering timbers turned them all back to the *Terror*, and they watched as a dozen boards were sprung from her side and sent skidding over the ice, the farthest coming to rest a hundred feet away. All around her the level ice started to fracture and heave, transformed once again into a sea of frozen breakers.

David Bryant shouted that he thought he could see moving water running into a fissure beneath her stern, a dark and spreading patch following her buried contours.

"Then God help her," Gore said.

A moment later the remains of the ship were broken in half by a block of ice which rose suddenly beneath her and snapped her fractured keel.

Even before some on the *Erebus* fully realized what was happening, the *Terror* began to disintegrate, sinking in pieces into the grinding ice as the surface churned all around her, until after less than five minutes nothing remained except a few boards and ropes which had been thrown clear. To Fitzjames it looked as though a whirlpool had formed in the ice, its relentless crushing lubricated by the water rising into it from below.

And even when there was nothing left to see but these few scattered pieces, the men on the *Erebus* sat and stared, some still unable to grasp the speed and ferocity with which their sister ship had been destroyed.

Fitzjames asked Reid why the activity in the ice had been so localized, why they themselves had been shaken only by its dying tremors.

"She dug herself into a bad spot in the first place," Reid suggested. "Perhaps she drifted over a fault that would have been quick to break up in any case. Perhaps she was just ready to go." It frustrated him to have to make such imprecise and useless guesses. Fitzjames saw this and did not pursue the matter.

By his own calculations the drifting ice had taken them twenty miles south since their return. There was now a possibility that they would come within sight of the most westerly part of King William Land, and he asked those who went regularly upon deck to keep a look-out for any indication of this.

Looking to where the *Terror* had finally been lost, he saw a number of the Eskimos approach the remaining few pieces of wreckage. They walked in a wide encircling movement rather than a direct line, conscious of the hidden danger in the ice beneath them.

Beside him, Thomas Evans started to cough again, and Reddington picked him up and carried him back to the hatchway. Fitzjames heard their cries as Reddington fell on the steep ladder and as both man and boy were pitched to the grating below.

THIRTY-THREE

They sighted no land on their slow drift south, but after a week of firing signal flares in an attempt to make contact with anyone still alive and within reach over the low horizon, an answering flame rose directly ahead of them. Only Reid saw this, and he knew immediately that it had been fired too close to them to have come from the shore.

His news of the flare caused great excitement, and within minutes six men were on deck searching the surrounding ice. They fired further rockets, but received no answer. It was early evening, and as the sun began its descent a strong wind blew up. By nine it had become difficult to see and they returned below, some now convinced that Reid had been mistaken about what he had seen.

At first light the next morning, Reid, John Weekes and the two marines left the *Erebus* to search the ice on foot. The wind had fallen during the night and the early sun revealed that nothing other than the broken surface of the ice lay ahead of them.

They blew whistles and waited as the notes died around them. For two hours they heard nothing in reply except the call of a disturbed bird or the choking bark of an unseen fox as it loped away from them.

Approaching noon, and having changed the line of their search, Hopcraft called out that he could see something ahead.

There was a man on the ice, dead, facedown, and several yards beyond him another, also dead, this time in a sitting position, his arms by his sides, his legs splayed. Beyond him lay a broken sledge, a trail of discarded packages stretching behind this in the direction the two men had come.

None of the four could identify the first man. His skin was blackened by exposure and he had lost both his lips to frostbite. David Bryant thought he might have been Alexander Berry, a seaman on the *Terror*. They searched his clothing, but found nothing to confirm this. He carried two target pistols, several watches, and beside him lay a bag of silver plate, which they immediately recognized as part of Crozier's bartering collection.

Reid identified the sitting man as Richard Aylmore, the *Erebus'* gunroom steward. This surprised him. Berry—if that was who the first man was—had left with Crozier, whereas Aylmore had been left in the charge of Stanley and Vesconte on the beach.

He pointed this out to the others and they began to speculate on how the two men had come together, and then why they had left the others and struck out across the ice, presumably in the hope of returning to the *Erebus*. Unwinding the scarves that bound Aylmore's own darkened face, they saw that he too had lost his lips and most of his nose, and that the liquid in his eyes had frozen and forced these from their sockets on to his cheeks. Reid rewound the scarves and tried unsuccessfully to push the sitting man over.

Weekes suggested following the trail of spilled packages in the hope of finding anyone else who might have set out with them. He did not consider it likely that the two men would have attempted the journey alone.

His suggestion proved fruitful, and as they moved from object to object on the ice they saw at some short distance three more corpses.

Of these, only one was identifiable, the others having been visited by scavenging animals. This was Thomas Jopson, Crozier's steward, and seeing him they feared the worst.

Like Berry, Jopson had been strong enough to leave with Crozier, and would have remained with him until being relieved of his duties.

Of the two others, one had suffered a severe wound to his leg, which had been crudely bandaged. Surprisingly, he wore no thick jacket, only a blue calico shirt, stiff with blood. His hands were clasped as though in prayer and half his fingers were missing.

The third man had a bandaged jaw, the dressing strapped tightly under his chin and over his head. Pulling off his hood and cap they saw that he had short blond hair, tightly curled, and this led Bryant to suggest that he was William Strong, a seaman on the *Terror*. He too had lost his eyes, and the skin of both his cheeks was torn and hung in flaps.

Reid confirmed this identification by taking a letter and a paybook from Strong's pocket. He tried to estimate how long the three men had been dead, but in their present condition this was difficult.

They resumed walking in the direction the men had come, continually signaling in an effort to attract the attention of anyone else who might still be alive on the ice.

They passed a small mound of clothing, neatly folded and held down by a can of preserved vegetables. A second sledge was found, both of its runners snapped, its small load scattered around it.

It was a short distance from this that they came upon the body of Charles Osmer, flat on his back in his sleeping-bag. His eyes and mouth were open wide and the skin of his face tightened by the wind, which had already scalped him. A mound of cans stood stacked close by, and alongside these lay a compass, its needle still quivering inside its rosewood case. By Osmer's side lay a number of books and loose papers, Service Certificates mostly. Reid gathered these up and then covered Osmer's face and said a short prayer.

Ahead of them lay a dozen more corpses, and scattered among these the stores and possessions the men had been carrying when they had fallen and died, claimed in equal measure by exhaustion, sickness and the cold.

They saw what at first looked to be a severed hand, but which turned out to be a kid glove with a measure of powder tied into each finger. Nearby was a pair of calf-lined bedroom slippers and a mass of broken Delftware, looking like small blue flowers on the ice. Turning one of the corpses, Bryant found a grass-weave cigar case he knew to belong to second master Macbean, and close to this a frozen packet of unreadable letters.

The two marines were reluctant to continue their grisly attempts at identification, preferring instead to return to the *Erebus*, which was long since out of sight.

It was as Reid persuaded them to go on searching that John Weekes called out that he thought he could see someone moving. He pointed to where several mounds lay together fifty yards ahead of them and, unable to ignore the possibility that someone had survived, they all left Osmer and went to investigate.

At first it looked as though Weekes had been mistaken, that all he had seen was a piece of loose cloth, but as they knelt to examine each of these new corpses, the one in David Bryant's hands groaned and then reached out feebly, the man's stiff hooked fingers clawing the air. Bryant pulled him closer into his lap and brushed the loose ice from his eyes and mouth and spoke to him telling him he was saved.

They had found Abraham Seeley of the *Terror* but, hardly aware that he had been found, Seeley fell from Bryant's arms and lay without moving. Further attempts to revive him were unsuccessful. Part of one side of his face had already been destroyed, whether by illness or other agents, they could only guess. He could not open his eyes and his lips were gone, exposing the swollen root of his tongue and what few loose teeth remained.

Gathering several pieces of discarded clothing, Reid wrapped these around the dying man and then poured water from his flask into the hole of his mouth. But this was like pouring raw spirit into a wound and Seeley gasped and jerked away.

By then it was turned midday, and seing no more bodies on the ice ahead of them, the four men turned back, taking turns to carry Seeley and frequently checking to see that he was still alive.

Reaching the ship, Seely was delivered to Goodsir, while Reid reported the details of what they had encountered to Fitzjames.

During their absence a party of Eskimos had climbed aboard the Erebus and had openly started to search the empty cabins, stealing bedclothes and whatever else they could carry. Only Couch and Graham Gore had been strong enough to confront them and eventually warn them off. It was Fitzjames' belief that the Eskimos had waited for Reid and the others to leave before climbing aboard, convinced that those left behind were in no condition to resist them. He wondered now if the natives didn't also know about the bodies on the ice.

Two days later, Abraham Seeley was sufficiently recovered to tell them something of what had happened.

Members of Crozier's party had returned to the beach only four days after their departure. Dragging the boats overland had proved far more difficult than any of them had imagined, and a large part of the supplies they hauled had been discarded. Men had fallen and died from the very beginning, the weakest of these barely out of sight of the beach where they had landed. Crozier himself had continued marching, allowing his party to become drawn out over several miles, a distance which increased with every day. Peddie and Blanky had gone with him, and Thomas Hodgson had been left in charge of the first abandoned boat. This, and the supplies it contained, had been hauled for only eight days before the men pulling it had dropped and died in their harnesses.

Seeley's small audience sat silenced and stunned by everything they heard.

To help him get through everything he wanted to tell them, Fitzjames recited a list of names to him, and when Seeley knew for certain that those mentioned were already dead, he would close his eyes; otherwise he would do nothing and Fitzjames would go on reading. Every one of the Service Certificates collected by Osmer had come from dead men.

As far as Seeley knew, Stanley and Vesconte were still alive on the King William shore, but there was little chance now of any of those in their charge leaving and following in Crozier's wake. The losses among the sick and exhausted had been great, averaging one a day during the first week, and then twice that number in the days which followed.

Ater two hours of this, Abraham Seeley fell unconscious, and later that night, attended by Goodsir and Des Voeux, he died without coming round.

The next day the boy Thomas Evans died, and three days after that Joseph Andrews was found dead in his bunk.

All three corpses were carried to the engine room and laid alongside those already there.

On the night of the 14th of July, having been confined to his own bed since the questioning of Seeley, Fitzjames remarked in his journal that it would have been better for Reid to have found the man dead than for him to have brought him back alive to pass on his baton of suffering and dread to those few still aboard the *Erebus*.

Fitzjames came upon Goodsir leaning over their stern, a cloth held to his mouth to catch the spray of blood which accompanied his violent coughing. He eased himself down on a balk of fallen timber.

A week had passed since the testament and death of Abraham Seeley had stripped them of the last of their hope and turned them all from men struggling to survive into men waiting to die.

"Alexander the Great," Good sir said unexpectedly, distracting Fitzjames from his thoughts.

"What of him?"

Goodsir swung his bandaged arm at the scene around them. The sky was leaden with cloud and the ice dark.

"When Alexander the Great looked out from a hilltop and saw the width and breadth of his domain stretching before him he wept because there were no worlds left for him to conquer."

He came and sat beside Fitzjames, wrapping a fur over his shoulders. He started coughing again and leaned forward with the cloth pressed to his face. Fitzjames held him, unable to steady him or absorb his shaking.

Reid and Gore found them like this an hour later and helped them both below.

Later that night, Fitzjames unwrapped his bandage to find that the hardened skin of his sole and heel had become completely detached from his foot, leaving the wet flesh beneath exposed. Alarmed by this, but in surprisingly little pain, he called for Goodsir, who came and looked and confessed that there was nothing he could do except keep the wound clean and hope for it to heal. It was a solution in which neither man could believe.

Fitzjames lay awake all night, listening to the comings and goings all around him, as though he were an animal in a shared burrow, picking up every vibration and sound of his fellow creatures.

The next morning Bryant arrived with the news that the Eskimos had once again been aboard, and that a kettle had been found tied to their foremast stuffed to the brim with buttons, cap badges, insignia and other pieces of braid. Couch later delivered this to him, tipping out and sifting through its contents as though it were a hoard of soft gold coins.

They still saw and heard the natives out on the ice, and the threat of an attack still stoked the nightmares of some of them. But a regular watch was no longer kept, and only when the evidence of a small fire was found at the base of their mizzen stump was any real, but again fruitless attempt made to keep the Eskimos from climbing aboard unchallenged.

Des Voeux died in a fit of delirium three days later, and the next day Philip Reddington went out on the ice to check their traps and did not return.

A brief search was made for him, but nothing was found. Saddened by the loss, they could only conclude that he had abandoned them, and that he was attempting against all the odds to return to the shore, driven more by what he was leaving behind than what he expected to find there if he succeeded, guided and perhaps sustained by the trail of abandonment and marker corpses which had already led Reid and the marines to the dying Seeley.

staring eye and the line of dry blood, little thicker than a line of red ink, running from Goodsir's nose to his lips, and from there down his chin to the papers and crushed vials on his desk, that he knew his friend was dead.

A small bottle of ambergris lay spilled under Goodsir's hand and Fitzjames saw that there was also a dab of this on his forehead, as though his final act had been to annoint himself with the precious liquid for want of holy water, seeking forgiveness for the act of sacrilege he was about to commit.

All around him lay the evidence of his labors over the previous months. In addition to his numerous journals, labeled and dated and neatly arranged along his shelves, there were his monographs, illustrated and stitched in cloth, and alongside these were stacked packets of unbound papers, several thousand pages in total.

Opening the drawers of the desk, Fitzjames found hundreds of letters, and a cursory examination of these revealed recipients in over a dozen countries ranging from America to Europe to Australia. A note attached to the largest of these bundles indicated that they were intended for Goodsir's close family and that if the dictates of space or weight meant that not all of them could be carried to their destination, then these alone should be saved. Only the clumsy writing of the later letters betrayed Goodsir's unpracticed left hand.

In addition to these, Fitzjames found a case containing Gore's photographs, entrusted to Goodsir by Gore when his supply of plates was finally exhausted. It was with a succession of small shocks that he looked through these, catching sight of himself on several occasions and barely able to bring himself to do anything more than glance at the man he had once been before turning to the others. He saw himself upon the beach at the Whalefish settlement, and then again in a near-identical pose—the same stiff smile on his lips—on the shore at Beechey. He saw himself in the company of others, men now dead or lost, beside them on the ice, posed in front of the ships, standing in their boats, among their dwellings. He saw himself with his head turned to one side and remembered the distant feature he had been directed toward, but which had failed to materialize on the finished plate. He saw himself and the others shaking hands, as though something had just been achieved, some victory gained. He saw too the pieces of Gore's unfinished panorama, and wondered who now would fit these together and what artifice and wonder they might reveal as the seams were lost and the ribbon of arboreal landscape emerged in its entirety for the first time.

He stopped searching, unable to look beyond the group of men who had accompanied him on his march to the southwest, unwilling to exchange the expectant determination which shone from their faces for the anguish and hopelessness which all too soon replaced it.

He found a letter on the desk addressed to himself, and he took this and pushed it into his pocket, already knowing everything he might later need to be told. A pen and blotter lay beside the envelope, convincing him that this had been the last of his friend's awful preparations.

He took a blanket from Goodsir's bunk and draped it over him, careful not to disturb the papers. He prepared to leave and find Reid and Gore, but looking back from the doorway, he saw that this crude shroud made Goodsir look ridiculous, and so he reached for its corner and pulled it away.

His progress in search of the others was slow.

He passed the galley, in which sat Bryant, Weekes and Hopcraft, and he looked in at them without speaking as they stared equally silently back at him. They were all now ghosts and they resented the intrusion of other ghosts to remind them of this fact.

Eventually defeated by the steps leading up to the deck, he fell for a final time and dragged himself into the square of sunlight and draught of fresh air which penetrated from above. He looked up, waiting for someone to appear, and high above him he saw the sun and was blinded by it and felt it beating down on the dry flesh of his face and then searing direct and magnified into the thin bone of his unprotected skull.

THIRTY-FIVE

Graham Gore became delirious and then fell unconscious. David Bryant sat with him, but other than attend to his more obvious physical needs, he made no attempt to revive him. He undressed him, wiped clean his broken skin and mouth, and occasionally changed one or other of the sheets beneath which he lay until there was little to choose between the clean and the soiled.

He collected together Gore's shooting trophies and medals and arranged them along the shelf close to his bed, each of the tarnished silver cups reflecting the ember of dim light which was the sickroom's only illumination.

The ship had become a mausoleum, but without the dignity conferred by polished granite or Carrara marble; or if not a mausoleum, then a hidden valley of sarcophagi, wherein the occupants were laid to rest like ancient princes or pharaohs surrounded by their prize possessions and the familiar objects of their lives, stacked all around them to ensure their swift and untroubled journeys into other, more certain existences.

Two days after Gore's confinement, the first large body of Eskimos came aboard. They arrived unnoticed and unannounced, twelve or fifteen in all, and wandered freely along the full length and breadth of the ship, moving from the fallen rigging and the deck to its innermost spaces, in which lay silent and unattended the oldest of its mortuary cargo. They wandered without restraint or fear, and with little concern for the few remaining vestiges of life, the living men included, which they encountered on their journey through the disemboweled shell the *Erebus* had become. *Erebus*, the primeval darkness born of chaos, half-brother to night, and reluctant father to air and day, Aether and Hemera, the Lower World of the ancient Greeks, fearsome and forbidding and filled with impenetrable darkness.

Only Weekes and Hopcraft took genuine fright at the appearance of the natives, and because they alone still possessed the strength to walk and to climb, they left the warmth and security of the galley and fled out onto the ice, where they hid themselves fearful and expectant amid the last of their jettisoned waste.

The Eskimos showed no hostility toward the two men, nor surprise at their alarm and extreme actions, and they stood at the rail and looked down at them before resuming their exploration of the ship.

News of the boarders reached Reid and Fitzjames as the two men sat together in the latter's cabin, and where they awaited the intruders calmly and without any thought of expelling them.

The previous day, one of Fitzjames' cheeks had torn, and Reid had attempted to sew the loose flaps back together, knowing the repair was unlikely to last, but acceding to Fitzjames' demands to cover the grotesque hole of his mouth and upper jaw until some more permanent means of concealment could be devised. Reid sought out the needle and surgical thread from Goodsir's cabin, along with the spirit and laudanum to clean and then render insensitive what remained of the eroded flesh. At first the translucent skin tore each time he tried to find a place for the needle, but eventually, by increasing the length of the stitches until he was sewing in sound flesh, he managed to draw the two halves back together. The result was little less unsightly or disfiguring than the original wound, but Fitzjames accepted this and repeatedly studied it in a mirror as the effects of the laudanum wore off and he was better able to assess what Reid had attempted.

Now, as he sat and waited for the Eskimos to appear at his cabin door, the growing pain from the stitches was almost too great for him to bear, and he frequently felt himself drifting into semiconsciousness, hardly aware of what Reid was saying to him about why he thought the natives had finally come aboard in such a large and single body.

They could hear the men in the galley and adjoining rooms, hear them gathering up the tools and cutlery and other objects they so covetously desired; hear them examining the cooking pots and the cold remains of uneaten meals; hear them pulling bedclothes from unoccupied beds and searching among drawers and chests, bottles and books. They could hear too the unintelligible chatter of their conversation, spoken largely in a near whisper, but occasionally high and childlike, which through the distortion of distance and pain sounded like laughter.

Reid reassured Fitzjames that there was nothing to fear in all this, and because he could not speak, Fitzjames responded with nods and with his hand upon the ice-master's arm. Nor could he spit or swallow, and every few minutes he leaned forward so that a gob of bloody saliva might fall in a string from his mouth into the crystal bowl in his lap, and each time he did this, Reid dabbed dry his chin. Even these small exertions now made Fitzjames feel as though he were about to lose consciousness.

The Eskimos finally reached them, two of the short dark men stopping in the doorway to look inside. They wore hide smocks and gray fur trousers, satyr-like in the sepulchral illumination. Their hair was long and untidy and their copper faces glistened with the pungent oils with which they annointed themselves.

Reid spoke a word of greeting to them, but neither responded to this, content simply to stand and stare at what they had encountered.

Fitzjames saw that one of them held a Bible, and that he was studying the embossed gold and silver of its binding, as though this rather than the words inside held some reverential significance for him. There was little point in guessing to whom the Bible had once belonged, or in which of their three separate and devastated parties that man had perished; even less to be gained in trying to take it back so that it might one day in the distant future accompany its owner to his grave. Many other Bibles and hymn books and tracts of Scripture had been found along the trail of corpses out on the ice, retrieved from the dead, if not the dying, and long since wrung dry of their final drops of spiritual succor by the wind which blasted clean the plain upon which not even the shallowest or crudest of graves had been dug.

The two Eskimos moved away and were replaced by others, all equally inquisitive to see what had been discovered.

Eventually only a solitary man stood in the doorway. He appeared older than his companions, shorter and heavier. His hair was trimmed in a line at his ears, and he bore a scar running vertically from his nose to his throat. He looked in at the two men, and then stared with greater interest at the contents of the cabin all around them.

On the point of blacking out completely, Fitzjames raised his hand to him.

The man did not respond, but a moment later he reached into the pouch at his waist and drew out a small live gull, its feet trussed and its wings tied to its side. The bird was vividly white, almost luminescent in the fetid gloom of the passage.

Momentarily distracted by screams and laughter from the others, and then by the sound of crockery being smashed and paper torn, the man held the gull out toward Fitzjames and Reid as though he were making a gift of it to them.

The small bird struggled briefly, incapable of flapping or kicking out, but still able to twist its neck from side to side with sufficient vigor to shake itself free of the man's hand, and from where it then hung suspended on its slender cord. Without looking down at it, the man flicked it back into his palm and with an equally deft and invisible motion released its wings, causing the bird to resume its attempts at escape. This time it flapped blind and unsynchronized, beating against the door-frame until several of its feathers came loose and were carried into the room on the draught of this wild flapping.

Fitzjames watched closely as one of these was blown clear of the struggling bird and drifted to the floor at his feet, mesmerized by it, almost as though it were a solitary and long-awaited light in the darkness through which he had for so long been limping and then shuffling and then crawling, constantly shedding the skins of his own humanity as he went. It landed and became still, and although it was only inches from his feet, he knew that the effort required to bend and pick it up was now beyond him.

In the doorway the bird began to screech, and in response to this the man swung it gently from side to side until, calmed by the motion, it fell silent again, its wings stretched to their full span, loose and yet at the same time tensed, as though the fragile bones to which the feathers were attached might either snap under the unbearable weight of this unnatural position, or might just as likely come suddenly back to life when sufficient lost energy had been regained.

Again the man held the gull forward as though making a gift of it to them, and Reid held out his hand to receive it.

Fitzjames watched him, but without any other indication that he understood what was happening, and as hypnotized now by the perfect black beads of the bird's eyes as he had been by the detached and floating feather.

All around them the cries and the voices of the others had ceased and there was silence, broken only, or so it seemed to Fitzjames, by the hoarse and irregular sound of his own tortured breathing.

He watched as the man took a step toward Reid, pushing the bird closer to him, and in a moment of unexpected clarity he remembered what Reid had once told him many years previously about how the Eskimos, upon trapping a bird and not wishing to damage its plumage, would kill it by pinching tight its beating heart through its chest; and remembering this he looked from the Eskimo to the bird, to its wings and its beak and shining eyes, and finally to its throat, where the man's dark fingers were already probing the plump white cushion of its breast.